BRIAN FLYNN

⊤⌐ ⊓⊓⊓⊓⊓ OF

Brian Flynn was born in 1885 in Leyton, Essex. He won a scholarship to the City Of London School, and from there went into the civil service. In World War I he served as Special Constable on the Home Front, also teaching "Accountancy, Languages, Maths and Elocution to men, women, boys and girls" in the evenings, and acting in his spare time.

It was a seaside family holiday that inspired Brian Flynn to turn his hand to writing in the mid-twenties. Finding most mystery novels of the time "mediocre in the extreme", he decided to compose his own. Edith, the author's wife, encouraged its completion, and after a protracted period finding a publisher, it was eventually released in 1927 by John Hamilton in the UK and Macrae Smith in the U.S. as *The Billiard-Room Mystery*.

The author died in 1958. In all, he wrote and published 57 mysteries, the vast majority featuring the super-sleuth Antony Bathurst.

BRIAN FLYNN

THE RING OF INNOCENT

With an introduction
By Steve Barge

DEAN STREET PRESS

Any work of fiction whose language is entirely cleansed of the idioms and expressions of its time would rightly be condemned—by that fact if by no other—as being an unfaithful witness to the world it seeks to portray. Therefore, no apology can be considered necessary for the occasional term or phrase that reflects the era of this book's original publication, even if some may now view such words with unease.

It is hoped that modern readers will approach these passages with an understanding of the historical context, and with the assurance that no malice was intended then, nor is any endorsed now.

INTRODUCTION

"Having once constructed my main plot, I sit down to write and permit the puppets to do their own dancing."

Thus wrote Brian Flynn in an article for Crime Book Magazine. They had awarded Black Agent (1949) the Society's Selection for that issue and asked Brian to introduce himself. While Brian had, until recently, been long forgotten as a crime writer, it is unclear how unknown he was when he was writing his fifty-seven mystery novels. From the tone of the article, it would seem that he viewed himself as something of a lesser author—when mentioning *"the distinguished authors who now write detective stories"* and *"the brilliant examples they constantly offer"* he refers to his own *"comparative unworthiness for the fire and burden of the competition."* However, he ends that section on a positive note:

"The stars have always been the most desired of all goals, so I allow exultation and determination to take the place of that but temporary dismay".

At this stage of his writing career, Brian was writing exclusively for John Long, a publisher that focussed primarily on the library market. His first book, *The Billiard Room Mystery* (1927), was published by John Hamilton, as were the next four, and then he moved to John Long for the rest of his career. (For the sake of accuracy, I feel that I should note that the first John Long book, *The Five Red Fingers* (1929), was actually published before the last Hamilton book, *Invisible Death* (1929).)

A selection of books was published in the US as well, the last of these being *The Case Of The Purple Calf* as *The Ladder Of Death* in 1935. A few other titles were translated into French (*The Case Of Elymas The Sorcerer* (1945) as Bryan Flynn), German (*The Mystery Of The Peacock's Eye* (1928), *The Horn* (1934) and Swedish (*The Case Of The Black Twenty-Two* (1928)). There is, according to a comment by Brian in an article, also a Danish translation, but I am yet to discover any evidence of this.

In the UK, there were some paperback reprints, all by John Long. A few appeared in their Four-Star Thrillers series, and some later titles such as *Such Bright Disguises* (1941), *Reverse the Charges* (1943) and *The Swinging Death* (1949) in the company's Pocket Editions, alongside such authors as Edgar Wallace, John Creasey and Frances Durbridge. By the time of *Men for Pieces* (1949), Brian's books were solely being printed in hardback, destined primarily for library shelves. Of course, this is one reason why copies of his books are particularly hard to find . . .

For those of you who are new to Brian's work, the majority of his output, fifty-three of his books, featuring the gentleman-detective Anthony Bathurst. One other is a children's book, *Tragedy at Trinket*, which can be recommended if you think most schoolboy murder mysteries don't have enough schoolboy cricket in them or vice versa (and features Bathurst's nephew, despite being published by a different company, Nelson). The final three are the Sebastian Stole mysteries, written under the pseudonym Charles Wogan. Stole is the exiled Crown Prince of Calorania, but his exploits only last three books. While the first book is quite distinctive from the Bathurst mysteries, the third one, *Cyanide For A Chorister* (1950), could have easily been one of Anthony's adventures with only minor alterations, and perhaps that is why this one, published between *Men For Pieces* (1950) and *Black Agent* (1951) was the final case for Stole and thereafter Brian focussed exclusively on Bathurst.

Writing exclusively for one sleuth might be seen as problematic, but it is notable how the style of the books varies as the series goes on, which may well be a reflection of the times as well. The country house settings of some of the early titles has long since gone by the time *Men For Pieces* (1949) is published, and there have been some changes to Brian's writing style. While Bathurst's character remains constant, there are far fewer books that are narrated by a third party—all of the five books from *Men For Pieces* (1949) to *The Ring Of Innocent* (1952) are written in the third person. As the series progresses, there are some books that veer away from the whodunit element as well.

A case could be made for the first such deviation from the norm being the inverted mystery *Such Bright Disguises* (1941), but there is still a whodunnit element at the end of the tale. The first of the out-and-out thrillers, however, was *The Grim Maiden* (1944), swiftly followed by *Conspiracy At Angel* (1947) and *Where There Was Smoke* (1951), all of which being tales of a criminal conspiracy where the story is more about the puzzle of what exactly is going on, rather than the identity of the villain of the piece. There are earlier examples of these conspiracy stories—*The Case Of The Purple Calf* (1934) and *They Never Came Back* (1940) for example, but these also have an unmasking at the end of the tale.

This is a reflection, though, of Brian's overall style at this point. The third person focus on primarily Bathurst and occasionally his co-investigators means that the focus of the book is on the investigation. Once Bathurst arrives on the scene, there are few scenes depicting suspects discussing things—we are exclusively seeing what Bathurst sees. One local newspaper review made comparisons to Freeman Wills Crofts, the creator of Inspector French, and this comparison is a reasonable one. Of course, that may not inspire some readers, as Crofts is one of the authors who has been in the past dismissed as "humdrum", thanks in part to Julian Symons' critique, but the Inspector French books are another until-recently-lost highlights of the Golden Age and I do recommend that readers who have dismissed him give him another go. Once you've read all the available Brian Flynn books, of course. After all, an entire narrative spent in Anthony Bathurst's company is no bad thing.

As there were no reprints of the titles from *Men For Pieces* (1949) onwards, we are lucky to be able to bring these five books to you. We have to thank Brian's estate for *Men For Pieces* as in my eight years collecting his work, I have never seen a copy for sale on the second-hand market. I can see why, as it's a really fun mystery, with Bathurst himself all but dismissing a dead body as suicide (he clearly doesn't realise that he's in a detective novel) until the victim's sister spots that the plug from the bath is in the wrong place! That's enough for our hero to dive into a mystery involving stolen and returned money, a plethora of suspects and a genuine surprise at the end. The original cover billed it as "Tense and Exciting" and they are not far from being wrong.

Black Agent (1950)—at this point Brian was clearly using his Big Book Of Quotations to find his titles—has a typically odd set-up for a Bathurst mystery. Barbara Marsden disappeared without trace from a New Year's party in her village. The only trace is spotted a month later when the distinctive yellow dress she was wearing is spotted being used as a costume in a play, only for the woman wearing it to also disappear . . . It's an original (if odd) concept and once the inevitable bodies appear, Brian does a great job of ratchetting up the tension. We also get another appearance of Bathurst's sort-of love interest and one of the earliest examples of a female Scotland Yard officer, Helen Repton.

The aforementioned *Where There Was Smoke* (1951) goes even further with the odd set-up. Donald Finney, a chemist, is offered work by the mysterious Mr Rehoboam, only for Donald's body to be discovered with no obvious cause of death. Questions abound however. Why was his skin discoloured? How did he have a printed note with the local Inspector Stire's name on it? And why was a piece of cooked bacon rind hidden in his belly button? A thriller following Bathurst's investigations—and there are some impressive Sherlockian deductions that Bathurst makes just from the crime scene—and a really fun adventure. Oh, and there's the only creative use of Alphabetti Spaghetti that I've aware of in a mystery novel . . .

Another Macbeth quote provides the title for *And Cauldron Bubble* (1951) although a reader hoping for a witch related mystery may be disappointed. Back to the whodunnits, and this time Bathurst is investigating a disappearance and a murder. Lady Blanchflower and her companion Mrs Whitburn left *The Red Deer* together after dinner, only for Lady Blanchflower to be found strangled and of Mrs Whitburn, there is no trace. And under Lady Blanchflower's body is, for some reason, a man's wig. This is one of the books where we see Bathurst being more fallible. With mostly just his intuition to go on, he follows several dead ends until the truth is revealed. This is similar to the later serial-killer title, *The Seventh Sign*, although we don't see Bathurst sinking to the same levels of frustration and despair here.

The final book in this set of re-releases is *The Ring Of Innocent* (1952) and we kick off with that old chestnut, the overheard conversation. Martin Scudamore overhears a mention of four rings and that if a certain Mr Lovelace interferes, "I'll slit his throat—without the slightest compunction or hesitation". Scudamore mentions it to Helen Repton, who promptly tells Bathurst, they arrive in time to hear Lovelace's dying message—the two words "*innocent*" and "*teaspoon*". It's a good mystery and moves along at a rapid pace, and, most importantly, is probably the title where we get the most insight into the Bathurst-Repton "relationship".

It brings me great delight that we are able to continue to bring the adventures of Brian Flynn back to the masses. I need to thank the many people who have helped along the way to revive Anthony Bathurst, but most importantly the late Rupert Heath, without whom Brian Flynn—and many other authors—would still be naught but a memory.

Steve Barge

CHAPTER 1

1

The car came away from Scotland Yard, bumped, jolted and then settled down to a steady pace. The man at the wheel spoke to his companion from the side of his mouth.

"All I hope, my dear, is that I'm doing the right thing. Quite frankly, I had no intention of doing this in the first place. It all comes of listening to your persuasive tongue."

Helen Repton smiled at the statement. "You seem—shall we say—just a little critical of my judgement. Do you know, I find that vaguely disturbing. It's not flattering, Martin, I assure you." Martin Scudamore, one gloved hand on the driving-wheel, ignored the implication.

"Where exactly did you say we were going? I've forgotten that already."

"I told you. Quite distinctly. Fenwick Square. Make for Kensington High Street. Then, if necessary, I'll do the directing. In other words, my dear Martin, place yourself unreservedly in my hands."

Martin Scudamore swung the car round a corner and then braked hard as the traffic light began to change a few yards ahead. "Well," he said, "as I hinted just now, I sincerely hope it's all right. But when I came along to see you at the 'Yard' I had no idea you'd bung me in front of the 'big shots'. I didn't bargain for anything like this. What did you say this wallah's name was?"

"Bathurst. Anthony Bathurst. Or—if you'd like it absolutely in full—Anthony Lotherington Bathurst."

The car moved forward at the amber. Scudamore frowned at what he had just heard.

"You seem pretty thick with him. No bon! Subversive to discipline."

Helen Repton smiled for the second time that afternoon. "We've worked together in the past. Usually at his special request. Several times. The honour was mine. Very much mine. I wouldn't have missed it on any of the occasions for—well, for anything in the world."

Her companion's frown developed at the receipt of this additional information. "You seem to think a rare lot of this fellow. What's the attraction?"

Helen Repton leant back and laughed. The laugh was both soft and musical. "My dear Martin, that's putting it mildly, believe me."

"How come?"

"Well, I think he's marvellous. In fact, I strongly suspect I worship the very ground he walks on. What you'd probably describe as the blindest of infatuations."

Scudamore, under a feeling of sharp annoyance, shot her a shrewd glance.

"Must be the eighth wonder of the world at least."

"I thought that was the palace of the Escurial," replied Miss Repton provocatively; "they taught me that at school, anyway, but you can call Anthony Bathurst the ninth, and I'd never argue with you."

"What's so sickeningly marvellous about him?"

"Almost everything," said Miss Repton demurely. "Amazing memory, unlimited personal charm, physique just right, complete and utter reliability, personality to the nth degree—"

"Skip it," said Scudamore. "I've heard enough. How old is it?"

"Oh—forty-ish. Uppingham and Oxford—if that helps at all."

"Does he know that you're his devoted slave? Or does he hold his head aloof in blissful ignorance?"

For the first time since the conversation started a soft spot of colour tinged the lady's cheeks and her mood and tone changed. "Oh . . . forget it," she said, rather sharply.

Scudamore chuckled at the change of mood. "Like that, eh? Really—I had no idea! How far now?"

Helen Repton shrugged her shoulders. "Three minutes—no more." There was curtness in the tone.

"You're sure he'll be at home when we arrive?"

"Yes. Perfectly sure. I 'phoned before we left the 'Yard'—to make certain. I explained how you'd come up to see me and he said I was to bring you along, by all means."

Martin Scudamore gave a quick exclamation. "Even now— and having gone as far as we have—I may as well be open about it I don't like it."

"You don't like what?"

Scudamore hedged a trifle. "I don't like barging into a man's place to tell him a yarn which may give him the impression that I'm a fit case for a loony bin. After all, I've nothing really tangible to go on."

"My dear Martin," said Helen Repton coldly, "the fact that I'm bringing you will be enough. I hate saying it, but you compel me to."

Scudamore grinned at the thrust. "Modest as ever, eh? Well, well, well!"

Helen Repton coloured again. "Turn to the left," she said frigidly, "and we've almost arrived."

Scudamore turned the wheel of the car and began to slow down. About to make a further remark, he caught sight of the expression on Helen's face, and changed his mind. For more than one reason he found himself wishing he had stopped at home.

"Park down here," said Helen. Scudamore obeyed the instruction.

2

Anthony Bathurst opened the door for them. "Emily's out shopping," he explained; "Harrod's, I fancy. But come in, do."

Scudamore's spirits rose at once. Emily? Out shopping! Must be the fellow's wife! Not so bad, that. Why hadn't Helen told him there was a Mrs. Bathurst? Funny how girls keep that sort of thing under their hats. Part of the age-old feminine tactics, he supposed. They were all the same. The Colonel's lady! But Helen was introducing him.

"This is Martin Scudamore. Martin, meet Anthony Bathurst." Anthony murmured a conventional greeting as he looked at the young man whom Helen Repton had brought to him. Scudamore—obviously in the late twenties—was tall, dark-haired and dark-eyed. A slight toothbrush moustache darkened his upper lip. His manner was quick, his movements alert, and altogether he conveyed a strong suggestion of restless efficiency. "Nevertheless," thought Anthony, "there's something about you—don't know quite what it is . . . perhaps I'm wrong, though; let's hope I am."

"Come upstairs," he said, "to my room. We can talk better there. Then when Emily returns from her shopping expedition she can make the tea. How does that sound as a proposition?"

"Couldn't be better," replied Miss Repton; "especially the last suggestion."

3

Martin Scudamore fanned away cigarette smoke with his left hand. "All I hope is," he said, almost defensively, "that you won't think I've a giant bee buzzing monotonously round my bonnet. Because I've little doubt that thousands would. But I take it—as a starting-off point—that you're a firm believer in the prevention of crime? What I mean's this! Besides punishing crime, you should do your best to prevent it, shouldn't you? There's that side to it as well, isn't there?"

"I'm with you wholeheartedly, Scudamore. As far as I'm concerned, the theory's as sound as a bell."

"Good. I feel better already."

"In fact," went on Anthony, "I'd go even further than you have gone. I'd actually be inclined to put prevention as even more important than punishment. So with that in mind, spin your yarn."

Scudamore nodded. He nodded to himself twice—as though he were assessing certain conditions, circumstances and values. Then he turned towards Helen Repton.

"Where shall I begin?"

"Where you began when you told me. In other words, tell Mr. Bathurst exactly the same story as you told me. And in just the same way."

Scudamore lit another cigarette. "That means, then, going right back to the beginning again. Is that it? I shall be sick of the sound of my own voice before I'm through. Still, if that's the way it goes, here it is."

Scudamore settled back in his chair and began his story. He spoke quietly and with an entire absence of fuss. Anthony was impressed. He felt that Scudamore knew what he was talking about.

4

"I live at Loveridge, in Essex. With my people. I'm still a bachelor. I work in my father's business. The office is at Street. Street's just about halfway between Loveridge and town. But I expect you know that. Anyhow, that's just a spot of background. Last evening I was up in these parts. Business had brought me up to town earlier in the day—I'd negotiated a licensed house transfer in Kennington—and I stayed up. Had a bird and a bottle at 'Murillo's', and then—all of a sudden as it were—I fancied a 'flick'. In the end, after considering two or three 'possibles', I went to the 'Galaxy' in the Haymarket. The cinema was pretty full at the time I went in, and I found myself shoved right at the end of a row in the circle. Slap up against the wall. Before the big picture came on there was one of those Fashion Display 'shorts' and I'm afraid my attention wandered a good deal.

"Suddenly—from behind me it came—I became conscious of a whispered sort of conversation. I didn't pay much attention to it at first, except to record the impression, perhaps, that it seemed to be of some serious importance, judging by the tense tones of the speakers. And then, very suddenly, I overheard the word 'Loveridge', which, as you may well guess, only caused me to listen all the more, and also all the more eagerly."

Martin Scudamore leant forward in his chair and said, with a dramatic change of tone, "Mr. Bathurst, I little thought as I sat there in that cinema what absolutely astounding things I was about to hear."

Anthony nodded with understanding. "I am all attention, my dear chap. Please go on."

"Well, as you may imagine, I dared not turn round. That would have given away the fact that I *was* listening and everything probably would have closed up. That's almost a certainty. So I wedged my back well into the upholstery of the seat and eavesdropped for all I was worth. I'm quite unashamed about it and I think you'll soon understand why I feel about it as I do. I quickly discovered that one of the speakers was of better class than the other. Don't get me wrong about that. I'll try to explain. I mean he was in a sort of 'authority' position. The other speaker seemed to me to be making some sort of report to him. As though he'd been employed to do it. The voice of the 'boss' chap was low and vibrant, and . . . er. . . well, 'authoritative'. The other voice had definitely the tone of the underling and was on the servile side. Now I'll tell you what I heard. I'll call one speaker 'the big fellow', that's the 'boss' chap, and the other 'the little bloke'.

"The big fellow said, 'you're absolutely certain you heard four rings?' He stressed the number."

"The reply came 'yes, sir—certain.' "

"Then the big fellow went on again. 'That's vital. It's the real point. Four rings are *essential*. Never forget that all the time you're on this business with me. Three or two, or five even, would mean that it was all wrong. So be on your guard.' "

" 'I heard that there were four all right. Don't worry over that, sir.' Then the little bloke went on again with something else. 'The colours were confirmed, too, sir. By your Mr. Charles Linklater Delevigne or whatever his perishin' name is. Green, blue, red and yellow. He named them in that order. Just as you said, sir.' "

"Then the big fellow gave a sort of hiss of pleasure and said something which I wasn't quite able to catch. It sounded like 'proving somebody's innocence', but I can't be anything like certain whether they were the precise words. Anyhow, you wait to hear the rest. The most extraordinary part's still to come. The little bloke said 'what will you do?' "

"The big fellow said 'go after it, of course. That's my way, and it's always been my way. I go for the things I want—and get 'em. I thought you knew that. You should! Why else do you think I bought that business when I did? Because I loved you?' "

"The little chap said 'when?' "

"The answer came as soon as possible, of course. 'To-morrow, very likely. Why should I wait? Perhaps even before that.' "

"Then the little chap said 'supposing there's nothing doing? And you get the brush-off, how will you play it then?' "

" 'How shall I play it?' echoed the big fellow. 'Why, remove all the obstacles, of course. I meant doing that right from the start. And when I say all of 'em, I mean all of 'em. Haven't I told you that's always been my way? What's the use of my doing business with gloves on?' "

"But supposing,' said the little bloke, 'the chief obstacle was human?' "

" 'No difference,' came the reply; 'if Lovelace stands in my way I'll slit his throat . . . or something equivalent—without the slightest compunction or hesitation.' "

"Then the little bloke wheezed and chuckled. 'That'll suit me all right,' he said. 'I certainly can't complain.' "

"And then," concluded Martin Scudamore, "the big picture came on and I heard them getting up to go out. They'd evidently seen the programme round. I tried to see what they were like, but they moved away from me too quickly in the dark, and I lost them in a matter of a few seconds. They left me to my thoughts. And were they thoughts? I'll say they were!"

Scudamore sat back in his chair and felt for his cigarette-case.

"You see," he said, "there's rather more in it for me than the mere story—I happen to know a bloke named Lovelace. And when I tell you in the same breath that he lives in Loveridge and is by way of being pal of mine"—Scudamore spread out his hands— "well, you see what I mean."

5

There was a silence which lasted a few seconds. Helen Repton then looked over towards Anthony.

"Well," she asked, "did I do right?"

Anthony smiled back at her. "Have I ever questioned your judgement? I, a born questioner?"

Helen smiled too. The reply had satisfied her. Anthony said, "I must ask Scudamore a few questions, though, in justification of what I've just said."

"Please do," said Martin Scudamore; "I'd welcome them. There's nothing I'd like better."

"Good. You've no idea whatever as to what these two men in the cinema looked like?"

Scudamore shook his head. "None at all."

"Which side of the cinema were you sitting?"

"Right by the wall on the right-hand side facing the proscenium. That was the trouble. When the men got up to go out they moved away to the left—that is to say *away from me*. The result is I haven't the slightest idea what either of them looks like. I'm sorry."

"Can't be helped. That's the way it goes sometimes. What age would you say they were? Any idea?"

"It would be no more than a guess," replied Scudamore.

"That's all right. In the circumstances. Have a shot."

"I should say," answered Scudamore, speaking slowly, "that the 'boss', as I'll continue to call him, would be in the middle sixties, and the other fellow somewhere about ten years his junior. I don't think that would be very far out. In either case."

"Well dressed?"

Scudamore shook his head dubiously. "Couldn't see enough of them."

"H'm—pity. Now with regard to the other end of the stick and the story. Your friend Lovelace of Loveridge? What can you tell me about him? Much?"

Scudamore nodded with some eagerness. "Quite a lot. Dick Lovelace is one of the best. In every way. Served with distinction in the last scrap, M.C., D.S.O. and all that. And somewhere about 1947, I fancy, came in for a comfortable little fortune. From an aunt, I believe, on his mother's side. Comes of an old Lincolnshire family who've more or less died out. But Dick found the Fen District rather on the cold side for him—he's a rheumatic subject, so he's told me, and he moved to Loveridge very soon after he came into the money I mentioned. He's a thoroughly good chap—good fellow and a good sportsman. I can vouch for that. I've played cricket and golf with him down at Loveridge and I meet him pretty regularly for all kinds of social occasions. You can see from that why I got in touch with Helen after I'd slept on my problem. She listened to my yarn and eventually whisked me round here to you. Hence these tears."

Anthony had listened attentively to the various details of Martin Scudamore's story.

"Tell me," he said, directly Scudamore stopped speaking, "what establishment does Lovelace keep at Loveridge?"

The reply came without hesitation. "He's a bachelor. Confirmed, I should say. Dyed in the wool. An elderly married couple look after him. Treasures of their kind, I should imagine, from one or two remarks which Dick Lovelace has dropped to me from time to time. A Mr. and Mrs. Toplady."

"Have they been with him long . . . do you know?"

"I couldn't say how long. But they came to Loveridge with him when he packed up the house in Lincolnshire. I do happen to know that. So it's a few years at the least."

"What's the address? Lovelace's?"

" 'Cherry Fair'. That's the name of the house. The full address is 'Cherry Fair, Oriel Lane, Loveridge'."

Anthony repeated the details of the address. He glanced at the time by his wrist-watch.

"Got a car with you—or did you—"

Scudamore sensed the question and replied before Anthony could finish. "My car's parked in that little—"

"Good," said Anthony.

"What did you mean exactly by that question?" demanded Martin Scudamore.

"What did I mean?" repeated Anthony after him. "Why . . . that I'm coming along to Loveridge with you—to have a word with your friend Lovelace."

"At once—do you mean?"

"My dear Scudamore, I'm sorely afraid there's no time to waste. Judging by the terms of the story you've just recounted to me you'll be the first to agree with that, surely?"

Scudamore nodded his acquiescence. "Undoubtedly. But I hardly like dragging a bloke I scarcely know into what may be an absolute 'frost' at a few moments' notice."

Anthony laughed. "Forget it, my dear chap. It's no bother at all—I assure you. In fact, I'm only too pleased there's something turned up for me to get my teeth into. Come along, I've been idle too long. And if Miss Repton here finds herself able to accompany us into the county of Essex, I for one shall be delighted."

Anthony turned to Helen Repton. "Is that at all likely?" he enquired.

Helen smiled back at him and nodded. "Yes. I can manage that all right. Between our two selves I had a word with Chief Detective-Inspector MacMorran before I came along here. He knows where I am and what I'm doing. He actually worked the oracle for me."

"Good," said Anthony. "That's all settled, then. Are you fit, Scudamore? In the circumstances we won't bother about Emily and those cups of tea that were in the offing. A man's life is considerably more important."

Scudamore showed signs of dissent. "But don't you think you ought to explain to Mrs. Bathurst? You make me feel so responsible—carting you away like this." Scudamore coughed awkwardly.

Anthony winked at Helen on Scudamore's blind side. "If I did," he said, "she wouldn't listen to me. She never does. One of nature's hard-hearted wenches. Now where exactly is this car of yours?"

CHAPTER 2

1

The car driven by Martin Scudamore shot down the hill at Matfield Heath, splashed through a tiny ford at the bottom and took the awkward road bend which suddenly presented itself, clear and clean.

"Road's a bit of a you-know-what just here," called back Scudamore to his two passengers, "but I know it, thank goodness."

Anthony looked at the white road that ribboned ahead in the Summer heat. Uphill now for some miles, smooth and dust coated, and between high hedgerows. The sun beat down on the car as Summer looked out from her brazen tower through the flashing bars of July. After some miles the road began to narrow considerably.

"How far now?" called Anthony to Scudamore.

"Twenty minutes," called back the latter. "Not more. Through Priest's Hatch and Grimthorpe. Better road for us in a couple of miles or so."

The car twisted on and up another hill which opened out to a straight road which ran smoothly along to Priest's Hatch and then . . . Grimthorpe. After Grimthorpe came crossroads. The car turned to the left and began to drop down a narrow, winding, high-hedged road which very soon became less of a road and very much more of a cart-track. The car jolted and bumped, but Scudamore drove well and the physical discomforts to his two passengers were minimised.

Anthony looked at his watch. Those twenty minutes of Scudamore's assessment were nearly up. Suddenly he caught sight of the black sign at the side of the road—"Loveridge". Within two minutes the car was running down a village street which might well have been, to all appearances, transplanted from the Sussex downland country. Again the car swung away to the left. Into a rural sort of lane. It ran past a farmhouse with straggling outbuildings and then a hundred yards or so farther on stopped before an old-fashioned house with a low roof. The house seemed to snuggle in a tiny haven of its own at a little distance from the lane itself.

Scudamore turned and spoke. "This is Oriel Lane . . . and the house you're looking at is 'Cherry Fair'. In other words—we're here."

"Good man," returned Anthony.

2

When Anthony found time to look at the house properly he saw that it was a rambling affair and that the pathway to the front door from the road sloped steeply. There was a well-tended hedge of shrub laurel and a large stretch of grass between the hedge and the windows. The grass had been yellowed by the hot sun, but Anthony was able to see that in early Spring, when it had been emerald green, it must have presented a most charming and agreeable picture.

As the thought formed, he saw something else. Something which caused him to catch his breath and sent his heart to his mouth. A blue uniform had passed—just inside the front door. Anthony looked at Scudamore to see if he had noticed it as well. But Scudamore's face was impassive and registered nothing.

"Just a minute," said Anthony to the others, "before we go any farther."

Scudamore stopped. "Why? What's the trouble?"

"I fancy," returned Anthony gravely, "that although we moved quickly we didn't move quickly enough."

Scudamore changed colour at the words. "Why? What on earth do you—"

Before he could complete the question Anthony pointed ahead. His suspicion had been confirmed. Two helmetless, but otherwise uniformed, police officers were approaching them. The elder, in appearance, came up to them and addressed them.

"I'm sorry . . . but what is your business, please?"

Scudamore was quick to answer. "We wished to see Mr. Lovelace. I'm a friend of his—and this lady and gentleman are friends of mine. We've come down from town. Is there anything wrong, may I ask?"

"What's your name, sir?"

"Scudamore. Martin Scudamore. I live here in Loveridge. Mr. Lovelace and I are friends. As I said just now. But would you mind telling me—"

"I'm afraid, Mr. Scudamore, that I've got bad news for you. Mr. Lovelace died this morning from injuries which he received last night."

"Injuries? Received last night? Where?"

"Here, Mr. Scudamore. In this house. Mr. Lovelace was set upon last night very savagely. He died about eleven o'clock this morning in Loveridge Cottage Hospital as the result of a fractured skull."

"But who set upon him?" said Scudamore. "Do you mean that the house was entered by burglars?"

"It would seem, sir, that something of that nature occurred. But, of course, our enquiries are only . . . "

Anthony patted Helen on the arm and stepped forward to the Sergeant of Police.

"In that case, then, officer, perhaps I may be of some little assistance to you."

He passed his official card to the official hand. Official eyes saw the card's official inscription.

"Good afternoon, sir. I'm Sergeant Dixon. That's Constable Marriage just at the back there. Perhaps you'd come in, sir."

"Are you in charge of the case, Sergeant, may I ask?"

"At the moment, sir, I suppose I am. You see, it came along in the first instance as housebreaking with assault and battery. But now that Mr. Lovelace has passed away, sir, it means, I'm afraid, that I must get in touch with the Chief Constable."

Anthony nodded. "When you do, Sergeant, tell him I'm here—do you mind—and ask him, too, to contact Chief Detective-Inspector MacMorran at Scotland Yard. I've a special reason for asking that. Believe me, your Chief Constable will thank you for doing it."

"Very good, Mr. Bathurst," replied Sergeant Dixon. "I'll see to that."

3

Anthony walked with Constable Marriage across smooth, yellowed grass towards the house. Helen walked with Scudamore just behind. The roses gave massed colour and a sweet fragrance. Anthony saw peach and cherry trees heavy with fruit and caught a sudden glimpse of the trim lawns at the back. They were greener there than their fellow at the front of the house, but their corners, too, had begun to yellow under the generous benison of the sun.

"Tell me, Constable," said Anthony, "what exactly happened—as far as you know, of course."

Marriage was young, tall and open faced. His eyes were frank and pleasing. His forehead glistened with running sweat.

"Well, sir," he said, "from what we've been able to piece together since we came along—the Sergeant and I—Mr. Lovelace must have been disturbed in the night at some time. That's evident because he was in his dressing-gown. Entry to the premises had been effected through the morning-room—that's at the back of the place. Glass had been cut from one of the french doors. Mr. Lovelace seems to have come down to see what was going on, and whoever it was that had got in gave him a terrific bash on the head. Inflicted from behind. And that was that."

The constable stopped and wiped his perspiring forehead with a handkerchief. Anthony nodded.

"But what about the people who, as I understand, live here with Lovelace? Didn't they do anything?"

"That's one of the queer parts of it. You mean Mr. and Mrs. Toplady? The old couple that looked after him? According to what they tell Sergeant Dixon they never heard a sound all night. Slept all through it. It seems they sleep at the back, too. It's a bigger place, though, than you'd give credit for seein' it for the first time. Mrs. Toplady says she found Mr. Lovelace lying in the library when she came downstairs this morning to start the day. Would you like to have a word with her, sir? I expect that you'd be able to—"

Anthony smiled at Marriage and shook his head. "I can't very well—yet awhile. I've no business here, really. When it's been sorted out a bit by your people and the 'Yard', it may become another story. We'll see about it then."

Marriage looked at him doubtfully. "Yes, sir," he said, "I see what you mean."

They passed into the house—Anthony, Constable Marriage, Scudamore and Helen Repton. Anthony took stock of his surroundings. The hall in which they stood was not large by ordinary standards, but its general furnishings were tasteful in the extreme. The hearth was long and low. In the corner by the door there was a small table upon which lay a gleaming brass salver. On the floor was a large prayer rug of undoubted antiquity, and on the walls were two pictures. That on the left showed a matador advancing into the arena towards an incredibly live bull, and that on the right was an authentic Birket Foster. The walls were biscuit colour, and against them, at pleasing intervals of space, were two comfortable-looking low chairs and a really magnificent settle, older if anything, Anthony thought, than the rug.

"Very nice," said Helen Repton, "all of it. Particularly that bull." She gestured towards the left-hand picture "I think he's absolutely marvellous. And, talking of fillet steaks—"

Before Anthony could reply to her he was conscious of another man standing but a few yards away from him. This man was tall and thin, and had seen many years. His face was old and cadaverous. His head and hair had said a firm good-bye to each other. But the feature about him which struck Anthony most was the abnormal length of his arms. They stretched, so it seemed, almost to his knee-caps and gave a clear and lasting impression that he had grown out of his clothes years since. Anthony's guess that this was Toplady was confirmed by Constable Marriage.

"Hallo there, Mr. Toplady. Here's some friends of your late master's. Come down from London. The Sergeant knows all about it."

Toplady stepped forward a pace or so and peered uncertainly at Anthony before shaking his head.

"I don't know this gentleman . . . "

Martin Scudamore spoke, however. "I'm the culprit, Toplady. You know me—this lady and gentleman are friends of mine. I brought them along to see Mr. Lovelace. Knowing nothing, of course, of this terrible trouble you're in."

Toplady's face cleared instantly. "Oh—it's you, Mr. Scudamore. Good afternoon, sir. This is a terrible business, sir, as you say, and no mistake. Neither me nor my old lady'll ever get over it. No matter how long we're spared. To think that we were layin' there asleep. . . and that dreadful business was going on down below us! No man could ever have had a better master. And that goes for my missus, too."

Toplady shook his head dolefully. "Did they get away with much?" asked Scudamore.

"Well, Mr. Scudamore, that's the funny part about it. It doesn't seem as though anything much 'as been taken. So far as we can see. Of course, you can't rightly tell—yet awhile—but that's what it looks like."

Anthony, who was listening intently, heard the sound of a footstep behind him. He turned to see Sergeant Dixon at his elbow.

"That's all in order," said the latter, "and our people are already in touch with Inspector MacMorran. They can straighten things out between themselves. That's in accordance with what you said, sir."

"Good work, Sergeant. You told them that I was actually on the premises?"

Dixon nodded. "Just as you said, sir."

As the Sergeant finished speaking there came the ring of the telephone. It rang four times—clearly and distinctly. Anthony counted the rings.

"Where's the 'phone?" asked Anthony.

"In the library," replied the Sergeant. "I'll take it—shall I?" Dixon moved off. Within a few moments he returned. Anthony thought he looked puzzled.

"Couldn't get any reply," said Dixon.

"Why—what happened?"

"Somebody seemed to say something when I said 'Loveridge 222' . . . and after that there was complete silence. Maybe it's a case of the lines crossed. That often happens in these parts." Anthony nodded. "Quite likely."

Dixon said, "I shouldn't be surprised, sir, from what transpired when I 'phoned just now, if you don't get—"

The telephone rang again, sharply and insistently. "Ah," said the Sergeant, "there it goes again—they've got through again, whoever they are."

He made his way to the library for the second time. As Dixon went, Helen Repton came to Anthony's side. "Did I hear something about the 'Yard'? Or did these ears deceive me?"

"You did, lady. How much did you tell MacMorran before you brought Scudamore to me?"

"Quite a lot. Most of what Martin had told me. But I didn't let Martin know."

Anthony heard Dixon's voice calling from the library. "This call's for you, Mr. Bathurst, after all. Will you come along, please, and take it?"

"O.K., Sergeant." Anthony ran towards the library. Or rather, from his point of view, in the direction from which Dixon's voice was coming.

4

Anthony found the library, saw where Sergeant Dixon was standing, and picked up the telephone receiver. The voice he heard coming to him was both welcome and familiar. It was the voice of no less a person than Andrew MacMorran.

"I've heard all the news and I'm coming down," it said. "Can you wait for me?"

"Yes, of course. You haven't wasted any time, I'll say."

"No. Things went pretty smoothly. The Chief Constable came through—had a word with the A.C. and it was agreed between them I should have a look round generally. Get all the dope for me that you can and I'll be with you as quickly as I can make it. That Sergeant that's with you doesn't seem too bad a bloke as things go. Certainly brighter than some. Well, that's about all for now. I'll be seeing you. Oh, I've just thought of something. Is the girl still with you?"

"Yes. She's here."

MacMorran's chuckle came through distinctly. "Tell her to stay put, I've arranged all that for her with the people that count. Tell her it's all O.K. until I release her. G'-bye."

The Inspector rang off and Anthony replaced the receiver thoughtfully. He looked at the time by his wrist-watch. He must get ready for the coming of MacMorran. Then he heard Sergeant Dixon cough at his side.

5

Anthony turned to the Sergeant. "That was Chief Detective-Inspector MacMorran," he said, "speaking from the 'Yard'. He's taking over. Your message has already borne fruit. Your people have co-operated, so it seems."

"When will he be here, sir?"

"He's on his way now. Shouldn't be too long." Anthony looked round the library. "This is the room, I take it, where Loveridge was found by Mrs. Toplady?"

"Yes, sir. This is the room. Just here by the door. Lying on the edge of the carpet."

"Here—by the telephone—eh?"

"Yes, sir; but I don't think that means anything. He was struck down from behind, I should say."

Anthony persisted. "All the same, he *might* have been going to use the 'phone. Or even . . . might have just finished using it. I think we should bear that in mind."

"As a possibility, perhaps," replied Dixon; "but no more than that."

Anthony took another look round the library. It was delightfully furnished from every point of view. Anthony, although far from an expert, considered that the pictures and prints on the walls were choice and almost certainly valuable. The carpet was thick—Chinese, Anthony thought. His feet sank into it noiselessly.

As he looked round a single, low-noted clock on the mantelpiece chimed the hour. The ceiling and the walls were panelled in dark-polished oak. The windows were narrow, small-paned and leaded—and each was set in a kind of embrasure. Thin slants of golden July sunshine filtered through them and brightened the carpet in golden-pooled light. The Sergeant's eyes followed Anthony's as they assessed the artistic merits of the room.

"Nice little place," said Dixon, almost echoing Anthony's thoughts; "they don't build 'em like it these days. Lost the pattern."

"I'm afraid they don't, Sergeant." Anthony walked round the room. Suddenly he turned and spoke to Dixon again.

"By the way, Sergeant, I'd like a word with Mrs. Toplady if she's about. Get her and bring her in here, will you?"

"Very good, sir."

Without demur Dixon made for the door. Before he closed it Anthony called to him. "Oh, ask Miss Repton to come in here, too—do you mind? Tell her I'm in here."

"Very good, sir," said Sergeant Dixon, for the second time. The library door closed behind him.

6

Helen came to Anthony within a matter of minutes. "Miss Repton at your service," she said smilingly, upon entrance, and then "what can I do for you?"

Anthony smiled back at her. "I'm going to interrogate the housekeeper—Mrs. Toplady. For one thing, I thought it would save time. It's all right—the 'Yard' are in. I'd like you to be in here while she serves it up."

Helen's eyebrows were elevated at Anthony's statement. "Not on to anything, are you?"

"Oh no. Nothing like that. Early days. But she found Lovelace in here this morning. She *might* be in a position to tell me something I can't see for myself. And, by the way, Andrew MacMorran's on his way here and you're to stay put until he tells you to the contrary. He's arranged that for you with the particular power that is. That O.K.?"

"Quite—and thanks a lot. That's something of a relief. Clears the mind."

"Where's Scudamore at the present moment?"

"I left him talking to Toplady and the constable. Marriage, his name is, I think. Quite a good type."

Anthony grinned at her. "Perhaps it's the name that Scudamore finds attractive. Shouldn't be surprised."

To Anthony's surprise Miss Repton blushed most becomingly. "I shouldn't be surprised, either," she asserted dryly.

Before Anthony could reply he heard footsteps outside the library door. As he looked up, Sergeant Dixon ushered in Mrs. Toplady. The Sergeant announced the lady by name. As Mrs. Toplady entered the library, the sun, through the window, caught her face and lit it. Anthony saw a big, heavy-faced woman with an impassive, flat-looking face. Her mouth was austere and unyielding, and her lips set. Anthony assessed her as a solid person, of definitely limited qualities, probably devoid of anything in the nature of emotion or imagination, but withal a rigid truckler to what she herself would consider respectability.

"Good afternoon, Mrs. Toplady," he said brightly, "did Sergeant Dixon tell you what I wanted?"

"Yes, sir," she answered sturdily, "he did tell me but I can only tell you what I told him earlier on. When you've told the truth there's nothing more beyond that you can tell. And I was always brought up to tell the truth right from infancy."

"I expect you're more or less right," returned Anthony, "but all the same, there are one or two questions I'd like to ask you. My name's Bathurst, and this is Miss Repton—we're both from Scotland Yard. There'll be an inspector along a little later. Actually he's already on his way here."

Mrs. Toplady nodded as though she understood the position perfectly. Anthony found two chairs—one for Helen Repton and the other to which he invited the housekeeper. Mrs. Toplady seated herself not without dignity and folded her hands in her lap. Anthony sat on a corner of the library table.

"Now tell me, Mrs. Toplady, please—what happened early this morning? That is to say when you came downstairs?"

"There isn't much to tell, sir. You know the ordinary things one does when one first comes down in the morning. Put the kettle on for the first cup of tea, draw the curtains, open some of the windows and doors, and generally start the day, as you might say. When I came into the library—when I came in here, that is—I saw that Mr. Lovelace was lying on the carpet. Just there by the door. Gave me a rare shock, I can tell you."

Mrs. Toplady gestured quietly towards where Sergeant Dixon was standing. Anthony nodded.

"I see. You found your master unconscious on the carpet. What did you do then?"

"I at once called to Toplady, who was upstairs dressing himself. He came downstairs double quick, took a look at Mr. Lovelace and straightway telephoned for the Police and for Doctor Forbes. That's Mr. Lovelace's medical man and a great personal friend."

"Yes I see. Did you realise at once, do you think, Mrs. Toplady—what had actually happened to your master and how he had come to be struck down?"

Mrs. Toplady's face was completely impassive as she replied to the questions.

"No, sir. Perhaps I didn't. At first."

"When did you begin to realise what had really happened?" Mrs. Toplady batted no eyelid.

"Shortly afterwards when Toplady found the pane of glass cut from the french doors of the morning-room. Then we knew we'd had the burglars in."

"Was that before the Police came? When your husband discovered that?"

Mrs. Toplady answered briskly. "Oh yes. Toplady went round the place soon after I called him. Directly he went into the morning-room he saw what had been done."

"Up to that time you yourself hadn't gone in there?"

"No, sir. I came in here first."

"Was that usual?"

A spot of colour tinged the Toplady cheeks. Helen Repton thought that she seemed a trifle annoyed.

"Yes. I always come in here before I go into the morning-room. To open the windows, chiefly."

For the third time Anthony nodded. "I follow. Now tell me this, Mrs. Toplady. I'm just attempting to get the full picture. Why did your husband send for the Police before he discovered the broken glass of the french doors? Couldn't it have been just a possibility that Mr. Lovelace was no more than ill?"

All the Toplady impassivity returned to her. "No. You could see all the blood on the master's head. All matted in his hair. It was easy to tell that he'd been attacked by somebody. But not necessarily by thieves—because there was no sign anywhere of anything having been disturbed. Not half a sign. Seein' the general state of the room, thieves was almost the very last thing you'd ha' dreamed of."

Mrs. Toplady sank back in her chair and cupped her elbows in her hands; her mouth austere, her lips prim. She fired another shot.

"Why don't you ask Toplady? He'll confirm all I've said."

"I hope to have a word with him later," replied Anthony, "but just at present. . . one at a time."

Sergeant Dixon came across to him from the door. "I think I ought to say, Mr. Bathurst, that Mrs. Toplady has told you just the story she told me. In every detail."

"It's the truth," contributed Mrs. Toplady in a stony voice that betokened finality. "That's why."

"Thank you, Sergeant," said Anthony, "I appreciate that, but I'd like to hark back a little." He turned again to the housekeeper. "I understood you to say, Mrs. Toplady, a little while ago, that nothing whatever in the house has been disturbed. Is that an absolute fact?"

Mrs. Toplady sat upright in her chair and once again cupped elbows in hands. "As far as I can see, sir—and that goes for Toplady as well—nothing has been stolen and nothing in any way disturbed. But one must remember, of course, that the thieves never got as far as upstairs. If they 'ad . . . there might ha' been a different story."

Anthony probed the statement. "I suppose you are absolutely certain of what you say, Mrs. Toplady?"

The housekeeper nodded sagely. "Absolutely, sir. And I've already said the same to the Sergeant. As he'll tell you." "How long have you and your husband been in the employ of Mr. Lovelace?"

"Since the Autumn of 1947. Mr. Lovelace engaged us just before he left Orme. That's the name of the little village in Lincolnshire where he used to live. We were there with him for about a fortnight before he moved down here. I think it was about a fortnight."

"What caused him to move? Any idea, Mrs. Toplady?"

The reply came readily. "He always said Lincolnshire was too bleak for him. I've heard him call his old home 'Bleak House' many a time."

"Did he have a housekeeper or anybody of that kind before he engaged you and your husband? Do you happen to know?"

Mrs. Toplady shook her head. "I don't think so. Leastways I never heard him mention it. He hadn't been out of the Army, though, so very long before he went to live at Orme. Perhaps that would account for it."

Anthony slid easily from the corner of the table. "Well, thank you very much, Mrs. Toplady, for the way you've answered my questions. Your replies have been of great help to me."

"Does that mean you won't be wanting me any more, sir?" Mrs. Toplady rose expectantly and hopefully as she spoke.

"That's it," said Anthony, "and as I said before, thank you very much for what you've told me."

At that moment, as Mrs. Toplady stood in the middle of the room, about to leave it, a puzzled expression came over her face. Sergeant Dixon was so placed that he wasn't able to see it, but Anthony and Helen Repton noticed it immediately. Anthony watched the housekeeper's gaze go steadily and deliberately round the walls of the library. It was a puzzled, almost bewildered gaze.

For a moment or so Anthony curbed his impatience and waited for Mrs. Toplady to speak. But the lady failed to oblige him. She stood there in silence. He felt on that account compelled to force the issue.

"What's the trouble, Mrs. Toplady? Something you've just seen that you hadn't spotted before? Or is it something missing?"

"No, sir," answered Mrs. Toplady, drawing her hand across her forehead, "nothing missing—but something else. It gave me quite a turn it did. Those two pictures over there on the wall have been reversed. Can't understand why I never noticed it before. It's not like me. As a rule I'm very observant."

"Which two pictures do you mean?" asked Anthony.

"Those two." The housekeeper pointed to two pictures, one each side of a beautiful hanging mirror. "Those two," she repeated, "the one on the right has always been on the left, and the left-hand one always on the right. Somebody's been tampering with them and turned them round. Now I wonder who on earth could have done that?"

Anthony rose and looked carefully at the two pictures which had excited Mrs. Toplady's interest. From what he saw of them he couldn't be positive that they weren't genuine Constables. If they weren't he considered they were remarkably fine imitations.

"Come and look at them more closely, Mrs. Toplady," he turned and said. "Make sure that nothing else has happened to them, beyond being merely turned round."

Mrs. Toplady did as requested. She crossed over and peered closely at the two pictures.

"No," she announced eventually, "they look all right and seem all right to me. As far as I can tell. What bothers me is that I didn't notice it this morning. They've just been put up in the wrong places—that's all."

Anthony nodded. "Take another look all round the library before you go, Mrs. Toplady. Is there anything else about it that isn't as it should be? On the same reckoning as the two pictures. In any way?"

Mrs. Toplady took a long look round the library. "No, sir," she said, with all her old impassiveness returned, "I can't see anything else that's different—in any way whatever."

"Thank you, Mrs. Toplady," said Anthony again; "if we should need you again we'll let you know."

The housekeeper walked, with much dignity, out of the room.

7

"What do you make of that," said Anthony to his two companions, as the door of the library closed upon the housekeeper. "Not a lot, Mr. Bathurst," replied Sergeant Dixon promptly, "and I'll tell you why."

Anthony looked at him with curiosity.

"Tell me why, then. I'll be interested."

"Well . . . for this reason. The pictures may have been shifted by Mr. Lovelace himself. I think that's very likely. They were his property, and he could do what he liked with 'em. Hang 'em how he liked and where he wanted. People often like a change round in their houses. With regard to furniture, pictures and so on. My old woman's always at it. Can't let things be. Always movin' things. A chair here, a table there. So, personally, I wouldn't attach too much importance to it."

"You mean, of course," contributed Helen, "that assuming that Mr. Lovelace changed the pictures round himself, he did it before he was disturbed in the night? Just as it were, in the ordinary course of things? That there was nothing special about it?"

"Exactly, miss," said Sergeant Dixon, "he moved 'em, I should say, just because he felt like it. Looked at 'em, and then decided he'd like 'em round the other way. No more in it than that."

"Rather strange, Sergeant, if he did," said Anthony quietly.

"Strange, sir? How do you mean?"

"Why . . . from the angle of sheer coincidence. I know the length of the arm as well as the next man, but it would be an extraordinary thing if Lovelace were suddenly seized with the impulse to reverse his pictures on the very day of the night he was destined to receive evildoers in his house, and die at their hands. I'm ready to admit that all sorts of coincidences are continuously happening, but I can't accept this one. Don't you see my point, Sergeant?"

The Sergeant rubbed his top lip. After some little hesitation he said, "Looking at it the way you've just put it, sir. . . I suppose I do. Still . . . "

Whatever it was that Sergeant Dixon had been about to say cannot be accurately assessed for the reason that he was suddenly interrupted by a tap on the library door. When he heard it the Sergeant looked at Anthony questioningly. Anthony nodded.

"Come in," called Dixon.

Constable Marriage entered the library. "Doctor Forbes has called, Sergeant. He's in the hall outside. Shall I show him in here? Is it convenient for you?"

Again Dixon looked inquiringly at Anthony. "Show the doctor in by all means, Constable," said Anthony. "Very good, sir," replied Marriage.

CHAPTER 3

1

Doctor Robert Forbes looked enquiringly at Anthony and Helen Repton as he entered. But Sergeant Dixon suddenly realised that the necessary introductions were up to him and he obliged immediately.

"Miss Repton and Mr. Bathurst, representing Scotland Yard. Doctor Forbes. The late Mr. Lovelace's medical attendant."

Anthony formed the opinion at once that Forbes was by no means pleased to find them there in possession. But the suspicion of a frown that had showed on the doctor's face was quickly obliterated and he said, quite pleasantly, "good afternoon."

Anthony began to take stock of him. He was tallish, with a thin, rather austerely lined face and in age somewhere round the forty mark. His hair was dark, flecked with grey, his nose thin and rather sharp and his eyes alert behind glasses and intelligent.

"A sad and bad business for you, Doctor," said Anthony. "I understand from what I've been told that the dead man was a personal friend of yours. In addition, of course, to being a patient."

"Quite so," said Forbes, lightly and easily, as he seated himself. "Lovelace and I have been close friends pretty well ever since he came to live here. That's really, in a way, what I came to see Sergeant Dixon about. Why I'm here. I certainly didn't expect to launch myself straight into the official arms of Scotland Yard."

Anthony smiled. "It is somewhat surprising, I suppose, but there you are you never know."

Forbes looked round. "Did I see young Scudamore as I came in?"

"Yes. He wanted Miss Repton and me to meet Lovelace. Brought us down from town. Little dreaming, of course, of what he was actually bringing us to."

Forbes nodded. "Like that—was it? Bad show! But my position's this. I'll try to explain. Lovelace was the last of his line. I've no idea how the property's disposed of. That'll be Ilsley's job—sorting all that out. Ilsley's Lovelace's legal chap. Lovelace, Ilsley and I—with the Vicar, Philip Sheridan—were a band of brothers. Bridge almost every week—usually here. And more recently Canasta. What I wanted to tell Dixon was this. So that he can pass it on to the Topladys for their information. There was no proper accommodation for the body at the hospital so I've arranged for it to be brought here. It'll probably be along this evening sometime. I've also been to the undertakers' and explained matters to them. They suggest Saturday morning for the funeral. I've told them to contact Ilsley. Now, is that O.K., Sergeant?"

"I should think so, sir. Don't see that you could have done much else. Which undertakers' did you go to?"

"Gray and Russell's—the local people in the High Street. They're about the only people I know near at hand." Sergeant Dixon made an appropriate note.

"Fractured skull, wasn't it, Doctor?" said Anthony.

Forbes nodded. "Yes. A bad bash. No earthly chance for him from the moment he got it. The upper part of the occipital bone was crushed—almost like an egg-shell. Heavy weapon used. Something like a sandbag I should imagine."

"When did he die?"

"About twenty past eleven this morning. I had him removed to hospital as soon as I could. But there was no earthly chance for him from the start—as I said."

"Was he conscious at all?"

"Well . . . " Forbes fell to consideration, "hardly, I should say. You couldn't really call it that."

Anthony came again. "How . . . do you mean . . . exactly, Doctor?"

"Well, he had a few conscious moments, once or twice. You could scarcely call it—any of them—a period of real consciousness."

"Did he speak at all? Was he lucid during any of those conscious moments?"

Again the doctor considered the questions before he replied. "I don't know," he said slowly, "whether I should have used the term 'conscious moments'. Who can say whether they were lucid or otherwise? Certainly I, as a doctor, can't. You see, I feel that I must be as careful in what I say as I possibly can. It's true that there were occasions—three or four, I should say from memory—when Lovelace tried to speak." Forbes paused.

Anthony cut in. "Were you able to distinguish anything? Of what he attempted to say?"

The doctor rubbed his upper lip. "Yes," he said eventually, "perhaps I was. But it would be two words and two words only. And it might even in the case of one of those words be one of two things."

Forbes finished his statement speaking very slowly indeed. But Anthony was in again immediately.

"What were the words he tried to say?"

Forbes rubbed at his lip again. "The only words that I ever distinguished with anything approaching clarity were either 'innocent' or 'innocence', and the word 'tea-spoon'."

The doctor crossed his legs and sat back. Anthony felt a tingle of excitement, and when he caught sight of Helen's expression away to his left he knew that a similar bell had rung in two brains. He followed up, therefore, his interrogation of Forbes.

"Did you endeavour to make any interpretation of that, Doctor?"

Forbes seemed puzzled. "How do you mean?"

"Well, let me put it like this. Did you consider at all any fuller meaning of what the dying man was trying to say?"

Forbes shrugged his shoulders. "My—er—interpretation was, I think, the eminently natural one. The one that would occur to nine out of every ten people. That Lovelace was trying to tell somebody in authority that somebody else—an entirely unnamed somebody—was innocent of the crime. Amplifying that idea, if I may be permitted to, that somebody was innocent, who in the ordinary way would be strongly suspected of being guilty. But that, of course, may be merely my own idea. The other word—'tea-spoon'—meant nothing to me."

Forbes changed his tone. "But ask the Sergeant here what he thought about it. He spent some time at Lovelace's bedside. He may have formed an entirely different impression."

Anthony turned to Sergeant Dixon. "What do you think yourself, Sergeant? Are your impressions the same as those of the doctor's?"

"Well, sir," said Dixon, "you've asked me frankly and I'll endeavour to answer you in the same way. In my opinion, for what it's worth, Mr. Lovelace didn't know what he was saying. He was just ramblin'. As I see it, his mind might have been anywhere—not even on the crime at all. You know what I mean, sir—might have gone back years. You often get that sort of reaction with person when there's serious damage to the head."

"I see. You don't feel inclined, then, to attach as much importance to what Lovelace said as Doctor Forbes does?"

Dixon was emphatic. "No, sir. I certainly do not. Although I heard the words."

Anthony again caught Helen's glance, but she made no obvious sign. Forbes rose from his seat.

"Well, if you'll excuse me, I don't think I need stay any longer. Now that I've had that word with Sergeant Dixon that I wanted. You know what to expect, Sergeant, and I'll thank you to pass the news to the Topladys. I expect those people I mentioned will probably be coming along some time this evening. That was the arrangement. Good-bye, everybody."

Forbes waved a comprehensive hand to the company and made his exit.

2

The sound of a car in Oriel Lane heralded the coming of Andrew MacMorran. Anthony escorted him from the lane into the house called 'Cherry Fair'. After being introduced to Sergeant Dixon, MacMorran got to work and called for an immediate conference. The result was that while Constable Marriage remained on duty on the outside of the house and Helen helped Mrs. Toplady prepare tea, MacMorran, Dixon, Scudamore and Anthony repaired once again to the library. Again MacMorran wasted no time in getting to work.

"I'll ask you, Sergeant Dixon," he said, "to give me the full facts once again. If you don't mind. Just refresh this memory of mine, will you?"

Dixon duly obliged. MacMorran punctuated the recital from time to time with a series of quick nods. When Dixon had finished, MacMorran said briskly "Now Sergeant—I'll be perfectly frank with you from the start. Get it into your head at once that the 'Yard' isn't interested in this case for nothing and we aren't in on it by accident. Otherwise . . . you know better than I do that I shouldn't be here. But I'll say right away, there's more in the affair than meets the eye—and the 'Yard' knows it. I've told you that because I don't want you adding two and two together and making it twenty-two."

Sergeant Dixon coughed into his hand. "I—er—surmised something of the sort, sir. Indeed I guessed as much when Mr. Bathurst turned up so unexpectedly this afternoon."

"Good. That's all right, then. We know where we are. Well, now I've got all that off my chest, tell me. Have you picked up anything?"

Dixon coughed for a second time and looked at Anthony. "I think perhaps, sir, that Mr. Bathurst could answer that question better than I can."

MacMorran persisted. "I'm asking you—I'm not asking Mr. Bathurst."

Dixon flushed. "In that case, then, the answer, sir, is in the negative."

MacMorran growled. "I see."

He turned to Martin Scudamore. "No blame to you, of course—but pity you left it too late, Mr. Scudamore. You slept on your little problem and sometimes that isn't the wisest plan. That's how it's gone this time. Still, it's easy to be wise after the event. Easiest thing in the world. I don't want you to tell me that."

As the Inspector made this admission, Helen Repton tapped on the door of the library and then put her head round it.

"Pardon my interrupting . . . I don't know whether any of you gentlemen would like a cup of tea . . . "

3

Anthony sat alone with MacMorran. In the library of 'Cherry Fair'. The time was 7.30 p.m. Scudamore had gone home tired and anxious, and Helen Repton had set out to walk to the village "to have a look round" and "get her bearings".

"Now let's have it," said MacMorran, "whatever it is you've managed to get on to. The coast is clear."

Anthony lit a cigarette. "There isn't a lot, Andrew, but two half-clues have peeped out from under the blanket. One may mean less than nothing. The second, I fancy, is a horse of another colour."

"Let's have the second first, then," said MacMorran, "if you know what I mean."

Anthony grinned. "Skip it. That sort of thing's catching. You'll have me at it next. Tell me, Andrew, how much did Miss Repton tell you of Scudamore's story? That is to say before you sanctioned her bringing him to me?"

"More or less what he'd overheard in the cinema. I was extremely busy at the time, and when the girl suggested you might like a nibble at it as a kick-off, I tell you I jumped at the notion and passed the buck. But go on."

"Well—according to Scudamore's story—when he heard last night's conversation in the cinema, one of the things he heard said was this. In Scudamore's idea it was spoken by the man whom he continually called and referred to as the 'big fellow'. Scudamore thought that this big chap said something about 'proving a man's innocent' or 'proving his innocence'. Do you happen to remember any of that? From what was said to you?"

MacMorran nodded. "Yes. Now you mention it I certainly do. Go on, though."

Anthony waited, however. MacMorran looked up and at him. It appeared to MacMorran as he watched that Anthony had paused to find precise words. The wait ended. Anthony spoke.

"Well, Andrew . . . it seems that Richard Lovelace, in his dying moments at the Cottage Hospital, Loveridge in the county of Essex, spoke in much the same way. As a coincidence I find that fact distinctly interesting. How do you react to it yourself?"

4

MacMorran stared at Anthony. "Say that again," he said quietly. "Do you mind?"

Anthony obliged. MacMorran whistled softly. "No doubt about it, I suppose?"

"My information comes from no less a person than Doctor Forbes. He was Lovelace's medical man, he was 'phoned for by Toplady after Mrs. T. had found Lovelace knocked out in here, and he was with Lovelace for some time at his bedside in Loveridge Cottage Hospital. Should be good enough, shouldn't it? Also—if confirmation be needed of such a statement—the word was heard as well by the worthy Sergeant Dixon."

"Was Lovelace lucid, do you know?"

"I asked Forbes the same question. He hedged. I think that's a fair statement. Wasn't by any means certain. But—and this, I feel, Andrew, is the important point—he says he heard the word distinctly. If Forbes is telling the truth there's no doubt that Lovelace said it. Lovelace also said something else before he died."

"Tell me," said MacMorran simply.

"He said 'tea-spoon'."

MacMorran stared as he had stared before. "Tea-spoon?"

"Tea-spoon—also according to Forbes."

MacMorran began to shake his head. "Sounds to me as though the man was incoherent. Now that I've heard that. Delirium of some kind. Certainly not himself."

"May be. Possibility, of course. We might have another word with Forbes about it. All the same, Andrew, that 'proving innocence' suggestion is mighty interesting. It certainly looks, on the face of it, that Scudamore in the cinema stumbled on to something absolutely authentic. I should say that the two men whom he overheard talking are the two gentlemen we have to find."

"And I should say they'll take some finding. They're almost certainly Londoners—and London's one hell of a big place."

Anthony nodded his agreement. "That's true." He sat there for a few moments, thinking quietly. At length he said "we've one huge clue, though, Andrew. Don't forget that."

"I haven't—not for a moment. You mean that name which Scudamore said came into the conversation. I do remember the girl mentioning that. We must get it again from Scudamore. It was an unusual sort of . . . "

"No need. I've remembered it. It was Delevigne. Christian name attachments—Charles Linklater. Shouldn't be too difficult to trace a man saddled with a name like that. Can't be many of 'em. The telephone directory should oblige almost at once and settle any doubts. Because he should hang out somewhere near London. Let's have a shot now. No time like the present."

Anthony walked to the table which held the telephone. He looked round but there were no directories to be seen.

"Nothing here," said Anthony, after a careful inspection. "I wonder why that is. I should have expected to find the directories somewhere near at hand. Mine always are. I have four parts. Volumes if you like . . . I keep them on top of one another.

The one I happen to want at any given time is invariably at the bottom."

"Ask Toplady," said MacMorran.

"That's an idea," returned Anthony. He pressed the bell. "Dignified old bird," he said.

"Who?" said MacMorran. "Me?"

"No. Toplady."

5

Toplady was prompt in answering the summons. "You rang the bell, sir?"

"Yes, Toplady," said Anthony, "I rang the bell—the various parts of the telephone directory—local or otherwise? I don't see any of them here. Do you happen to know where they are? Or where Mr. Lovelace was accustomed to keep them?"

Toplady's glance wandered to the table on which the telephone stood.

"As far as I know they should be over there, sir. That was their usual place."

"Well—they aren't there now, Toplady. You can see that for yourself. Somebody must have moved them. See if you can find them for Chief Detective-Inspector MacMorran, will you? Don't be too long, there's a good chap."

"I will make enquiries of my wife, sir," replied Toplady. "She may have information which hasn't reached me." He turned gravely and made his exit.

"What do you make of that, Andrew?" said Anthony, as the door of the library closed.

"Don't altogether know. They may have been moved for some reason or other. And the reason may well be a perfectly ordinary one and not worth bothering about. Let's see how it turns out. Before we start theorizing."

The words had scarcely left MacMorran's lips when Toplady returned. He carried several differently coloured telephone directories.

"Here they are, sir. The directories that were missing. They had been removed from their usual place by my wife. For the reason, I understand, that one of them—this blue one on the top, sir—actually was a trifle bloodstained. The explanation is that Mr. Lovelace, poor man, was struck down very near to that table, sir."

"Is that so?" returned MacMorran. "Well then—er—put them down there, will you? And thank you."

"Is that all you will be requiring for the time being, sir?"

"I think so. If not we'll ring through to you again."

The library door closed behind Toplady for the second time. "Quaint old bird," commented MacMorran, "as well as dignified— got arms like a gorilla. Must have been a pretty powerful chap in his prime, I should say. Now have a look through for that Delevigne fellow."

Anthony took the appropriate volume and found the relevant page. MacMorran watched him with interest. After a short interval Anthony shook his head.

"Nothing doing here, Andrew. Our man's a non-runner. Nothing like it anywhere here."

MacMorran grunted. "Positive?"

"Certain. Nothing like it."

Anthony closed the appropriate directory. MacMorran grunted again.

"It's quite likely, of course, when you come to think it over. May live anywhere. North, south, east or west. Lancs, Lincs, Leicester or Lanark. Still, leave that to me. In the morning I'll have a word with the P.M.G. If the chap's got a 'phone installed, they'll run him to earth for me. There won't be any difficulty in getting that fixed up."

"O.K. Well, I've already mentioned the second of the half-clues I spoke about just now. You said you'd have it first because I assessed it as having the greater importance. I'll now tell you about the other one. Are you fit?"

"I'm listening," said Andrew MacMorran.

6

"Lovelace," said Anthony, "was found lying in here, by Mrs. Toplady. First thing this morning. Or, precisely, just after she came downstairs. You know that."

"Yes. I know that."

"There was no sign, so she stated to the Sergeant, when he first questioned her, and since to me, of anything in the nature of a disturbance. You've heard that."

MacMorran nodded. "Yes. Go on."

"Continuing, then, with Mrs. Toplady—and I may say there's confirmation of this from Toplady himself—nothing of any value seems to have been stolen. Each of them is fairly certain as to that. You know that?"

"Yes, but as you said, that's only as far as you know. I think one would be fully entitled to say that neither Toplady nor his missus would be cognisant of all that Lovelace possessed. After all, they're but employees— and certainly not of the kind that you could reasonably expect a man of Lovelace's standing to confide in. Don't you agree?"

Anthony nodded. "Yes, Andrew. I agree entirely."

"Go on," said MacMorran. "I know you've got something up your sleeve and that all this is leading up to it. What is it?"

Anthony smiled at MacMorran's words. "You do, do you? Well, listen to this. When I knew for certain that the 'Yard' had taken over the case and that you were on your way down here this evening, I decided to have a word or two with the aforementioned Mrs. Toplady. I thought for one thing that it would save time."

"Good idea. I was hoping you'd get cracking as soon as you were able. What spilled?"

"Not a lot. Sergeant Dixon was in here with me when I questioned her and the story she told was absolutely in accordance with her previous statements. Dixon confirms that. Then, Andrew, a rather peculiar thing happened. Just as she got up to go I notice, that as she rose a look of surprise seemed to come over her face. Perhaps surprise isn't the best word to describe it. She looked puzzled—I might say almost bewildered. I was positive that something about the room—*this* room, Andrew— had popped up suddenly and caught her on the wrong foot as it were. Naturally, I wasn't letting anything like that go by, so I questioned her about it at once. What do you think she told us? Dixon and me?"

MacMorran shook his head.

"Haven't the foggiest. Tell me."

"She looked at the walls of the room, Andrew, and then said that the pictures weren't hanging in their customary places. When I probed for details she said that she was referring particularly to those two pictures that flank that mirror there." Anthony gestured towards the hanging mirror. "They're the two, Andrew. I'm nothing like an expert, but if they aren't Constables they're marvellously fine 'afters'."

MacMorran rose from his chair and crossed the room to examine the two pictures to which Anthony had called attention. "What's wrong with 'em?" he demanded.

"According to what Mrs. Toplady tells me they've been changed round. Reversed—that which was right is now left—and *vice versa*."

MacMorran's frown stayed. "Nothing beyond that?"

Anthony shook his head. "According to the lady—no."

"There's been no other tampering with them?"

"No. Nothing. So says Toplady's lady."

MacMorran considered certain implications. "Lovelace may have altered them himself. They were his. People do, you know. That sort of thing. For more than one kind of reason. I knew a racing man once who did things like that to change his luck. When his fancies were continually running second, for instance. Or, Lovelace may have suddenly come to the simple conclusion that the pictures would look better if he shifted them round. That's another possibility."

"That's more or less what Sergeant Dixon thinks."

"He does, does he? Well, there you are—that's two of us in agreement."

Anthony was silent. MacMorran noticed the silence and was quick to interpret it.

"You *don't* think so? You *don't* agree?"

It was a second or so before Anthony answered. "No, Andrew. Not altogether. And I'll tell you why I don't. It seems an incredibly strange thing to me that Lovelace should have done such a thing to his pictures just before he's assaulted to death in the same room. That's the part of it which strikes me as being so significant."

MacMorran rubbed his lip. "H'm. There is something in that, I suppose, when you come to consider it. Still, you can't get away from the fact that the pictures are still there. On the wall there. If the pictures were extremely valuable, for example, surely the thieves would have finished the job off and taken them? Why be content with turning the darned things round? Or shovin' them up in the wrong places? That's just plain crazy. You see what I mean, don't you?"

Anthony nodded and smiled. "I see what you mean all right. But I boggle at your word 'content'. How do we know that the gentlemen who broke in *were* contented? Seems to me that's highly problematical."

MacMorran waxed critical at Anthony's rejoinder. "But damn it all— why turn pictures round? As I said before, why go to the trouble of takin' 'em down . . . and then a short time afterwards puttin' 'em up again, in the wrong places? Seems daft to me. I just don't get it."

MacMorran shook his head decisively as he finished speaking.

"No, Andrew, I'm afraid I don't, either. Yet. But I may."

Anthony got up from his seat again and walked to the wall of the library. He looked with careful scrutiny at the two pictures of the discussion. As far as he could see from a superficial inspection, there were no signs of having been tampered with on either of them. In other words, he agreed with the judgement of Mrs. Toplady.

"Anything?" queried MacMorran.

"Nothing, Andrew. Nothing at all. That I can see." He came away from the pictures on the wall to the middle of the room. "Lovelace," MacMorran heard him say, "the answer to it all must be with Lovelace.

With Lovelace himself. What was there about him? What did he have in his possession that these others coveted? How far does it go back? To the Fens? To his life in the Army? Before that even? Or has it merely begun here in Loveridge? We must dig and delve, Andrew. As usual. And when the mental shovels get to work I wonder what we shall turn up? Ah well—time will tell."

He stopped speaking to listen to something he had just heard. "There's Helen Repton, Andrew, back from her evening stroll. Coming up the drive. What do you say to driving us back to town? Are you fit?"

MacMorran nodded. "Ay. And we'll be back here early in the morning."

"No option, Andrew," answered Anthony.

7

Anthony and MacMorran came back to 'Cherry Fair' early on the following morning as the latter had promised. To their surprise somewhat, Toplady came to them immediately after his better-half had admitted them to the house. Both Anthony and the 'Yard' inspector could see that the man was labouring under the strain of a severe agitation.

"Good morning, gentlemen," he said. "I'm right glad you've come here early. I am that."

"Why—what's the trouble?" demanded MacMorran.

"If you've nothing better to do to start with, I'd like you to come into the morning-room," replied Toplady, "I've something to show you. Something simple—yet—er—sinister."

Toplady gestured dramatically. "Come this way, gentlemen—will you?"

Anthony and MacMorran followed Toplady into the morning-room. As Anthony entered the room he found himself wondering as to the cause of Toplady's mental disturbance. As far as he could see upon entrance, the room looked entirely ordinary and in what he himself would describe as normal and everyday condition.

Before, however, either he or MacMorran could speak, Toplady declared in a high-pitched voice "this room, gentlemen, has been entered during the night. By somebody who 'ad no legitimate business to be in it."

MacMorran looked round the room and said quietly "what makes you say that, Toplady?"

With another of his dramatic gestures Toplady pointed to the floor. "Look down there, Inspector. And tell me what you see."

MacMorran glanced down to where Toplady was pointing. On the carpet, close to the wall, lay a cigarette-end. Toplady anticipated him.

"That cigarette-end, Inspector, was not on that carpet when Mrs. Toplady and I locked up for the night. I'll swear to that. And Mrs. Toplady will swear to it likewise."

"You're positive of that?"

"Absolutely, Inspector. Somebody 'as been in this room since we closed up last night. Which was just after the undertakers left the house."

MacMorran considered the implications of Toplady's various statements.

"Do you always lock the doors of the rooms when you retire for the night?"

"Always, sir. It's our invariable habit. 'As been so since we entered Mr. Lovelace's service. That's one of the reasons that makes me so sure of what I'm saying."

Anthony stooped to the carpet and picked up the burnt stub. "What brand is it?" asked MacMorran.

Anthony shook his head. "Can't say. Burnt too far down."

"H'm. Pity."

"There's something about it, though," continued Anthony, "apart from its brand, which I find of considerable interest."

"What's that?"

"It's position on the carpet there."

MacMorran looked down and took Anthony's meaning. "Near the wall, you mean?"

"Near the wall," replied Anthony gravely.

"And just below those pictures?"

"And just below those pictures. Somewhat significant, don't you think, Andrew? Bearing in mind what we already know? In other words, pictures again."

"I think you're right." MacMorran turned to Toplady. "Pictures," he said decisively, "your late employer's pictures, Toplady? Did he possess anything in that line that were known to be extremely valuable?"

Toplady's reply came, grave and studied. "I wouldn't know anything about that, Inspector. I'm rather surprised that you should ask me the question."

MacMorran scrutinised him carefully. "You've never even heard such an idea mentioned—or mooted?"

Toplady didn't turn a hair. "Never, sir. Neither from Mr. Lovelace himself nor from any of 'is friends and acquaintances."

"I see. I suppose you heard no disturbance last night? Everything was quiet in the house?"

"Entirely, Inspector. I can truthfully say that neither Mrs. Toplady nor myself heard anything."

"In other words, conditions were no different from those of the previous night? Is that it? You heard nothing, then, I understand?"

"That is so. I have come to the conclusion that my wife and I must be unusually 'eavy sleepers. Thinking things over, I've remembered that my father was. It may run in families. As with other personal 'abits."

Toplady's long arms twitched nervously as he made the statement.

"Very good, Toplady," said MacMorran, "you may leave us for the time being. And thank you for calling our attention to what's happened. We shall have to find the explanation. There must be one."

"Thank you, Inspector," replied Toplady. "Please let me know at once if you should be requiring anything." He turned and closed the door quietly behind him.

CHAPTER 4

1

Anthony sat at ease and confided to Chief Detective-Inspector MacMorran his personal views with regard to attendance at the Lovelace funeral. MacMorran listened to him punctiliously.

"All right," he said at length, "if that's how you feel about it, you go by all means. I don't mind in the least. In fact, now that I've thought it over, it might be a better idea for you to go than for me."

"Good man," returned Anthony, "then it's me for the last rites, as Chowles himself might have said to Judith Malmayns."

"Who?" queried MacMorran.

"A little before your time, Andrew," replied Anthony.

It was on the following morning, therefore, that he dressed himself with excessive carefulness and an unusually studied deference to the sartorial. Clad in the conventional garments of modern civilization when it mourns the dead, Anthony drove again to Loveridge in order to attend the funeral of the late Richard Lovelace. Eventually, but in good time, the car came to the turning and the ascending lane at the top of which stood the ancient parish church of Loveridge, a handsome structure in Early Perpendicular.

As the car ascended the rise to the church the bell began to toll, and when the car reached the crest where the church had been built and Anthony alighted, he turned to see the funeral *cortège* beginning to climb the rise in the car's wake. There were two Daimler limousines that followed behind the hearse.

Anthony, for reasons of his own, kept in the background. He looked across at the people as they got out from the two Daimlers. From the first stepped Martin Scudamore, Doctor Forbes and two other men, one of whom was dressed in clerical garb—cassock and stole. Anthony remembered what Forbes had told him and judged the man in the clerical clothes to be the Rev. Philip Sheridan, Vicar of Loveridge. And if he were right in this judgement, the other man, in all probability, was Ilsley, Lovelace's solicitor. Also via information Forbes.

As Anthony watched this group of men a burst of glorious sunshine blazed into the country churchyard and gilded the white gravestones with its handsome and prodigal touch. The coffin was taken from the hearse and carried reverently into the church, followed by the priest, Forbes, Scudamore and the man whom Anthony took to be Ilsley. Behind them came two men in military uniform whom Anthony hadn't seen before— one a lieutenant-colonel and the other a major. They, so Anthony thought, must have been the occupants of the second limousine. He evidently had failed to notice them getting out. Funny, that. On his blind side, in all probability. As the black-gowned verger was on the point of shooting the last bolt of the church door to its closure, Anthony slipped into a pew just a yard in front of the font. The interior of the church took his attention— piscina, hourglass, frame on the pulpit, brasses and many monuments. The priest walked to the altar, turned and faced the mourners.

The service started . . . they came to the Pauline epic to the people of Corinth . . . and then to a hymn. Anthony, listening carefully, heard the words of the hymn almost mechanically . . .

> "No longer must the mourners weep,
> Nor call departed Christians dead,
> For death is hallowed into sleep,
> And every grave becomes a bed."

The hymn, with its note of eternal triumph, came to its finish. The verger began to open the door. The sounds of the drawn bolts came to Anthony almost as a shock. The company of mourners, led by the borne coffin, filed slowly from the front pews down the middle aisle, into the churchyard and on towards the grave.

Anthony fell in at the extreme rear of the procession. When the coffin reached the grave Anthony stopped in his stride and went no nearer. The voice of the officiating priest came to him distinctly through the sun-drenched air. Anthony saw him close his book and heard the words of the last offices. Earth, dropped from a man's hand, rattled on the coffin after it had been gently lowered into the grave. The priest's voice was quiet now and the words he was speaking failed to reach Anthony's ears.

But suddenly the voice regained its strength and clarity and Anthony was able to hear clearly the last warm words of consolation and comfort . . . "The Grace of our Lord Jesus Christ . . . "

Other words rioted in Anthony's mind . . . "deeds all done, songs all sung, sing it out in sun and rain . . . " Scudamore, Forbes, and the man Anthony supposed to be Ilsley, moved quietly to the brink of the grave and looked down into it. The two soldiers went round to the opposite side. Anthony saw them salute the coffined dead. The priest went across to them and spoke to them quietly. The six men clustered round the grave. Anthony turned his back on them and walked slowly to the crest of the hill where he had left his car. But he waited for the mourners to start off again on their homeward journey before he himself drove off.

Slowly the three cars descended the slope until they came to the end of the lane. At that point the pace of the leaders increased. Anthony followed the example that had been thus given to him.

2

At the risk of a sharp challenge to his manners and his courtesy, Anthony turned his car in the direction of Oriel Lane and the house known as 'Cherry Fair'. After all . . . as he argued to himself in a spate of justification . . . there was no weeping widow to encounter . . . there were no grief-chilled children clinging and crestfallen to stare at him round-eyed. In addition to the mourners there might be present only the two Topladys! Anthony could visualise nobody else. There was also another possibility. Because the funeral had started from 'Cherry Fair', there was no absolutely cast-iron necessity that the returning vehicles should go back there. The chances *were* that way. . . perhaps . . . but as he looked at it . . . there was no cold certainty about it. However, why worry? He would soon be at the house and know.

As the car reached the little streets of Loveridge itself Anthony slowed down considerably—almost to loitering rate. He then ran the car up and down various lanes and by-ways before he glanced at the watch on his wrist. What he saw pleased him rather. Not too bad. He wouldn't arrive, at any rate, hot on anybody's heels. The interval he had created had been solid and sedate. Anthony accelerated again, swept on to Oriel Lane, and alighted almost in front of the Lovelace house—'Cherry Fair'. He parked the car carefully against the grass verge and after giving it and its position a quick glance of approval, he walked up to the front door. The occasion, he considered, was certainly not one to be missed. Seeing things were how they were!

3

Mrs. Toplady admitted him without question and Anthony could find no justified fault in the manner of his reception. Scudamore's presence, however, may have accounted for this in the main. In fact, Scudamore's geniality and general courtesy to him could scarcely have been exceeded. Scudamore introduced Anthony to Sheridan and Ilsley and then to the two Army men who had attended the funeral—Lieutenant-Colonel Mapperley and Major Hargreaves.

After he had spoken to Forbes, Anthony took immediate stock of these four men whom he had not previously met. Firstly he dealt with Sheridan. Words from a schoolroom at Uppingham came back to him. Words down the years from the lips of a wise old classical scholar who had taught him much that he would never forget. That troublous times bred four kinds of men who were much to be compassionated. Fanatics, for one of two sides, who were blind to all else in the burning intensity of their personal faith; men who sought with desperation for something beautiful to believe—and found it not; and lastly, irreverent scoffers who, believing intensely in nothing at all, looked on most things with rare cynicism and on a religious belief in particular as a mere mockery.

Sheridan, Anthony decided, belonged to the third of these categories. He was tall and thin, and his dark, deep-socketed eyes burnt fiercely in a pale, eager, almost care-worn face. At Scudamore's introduction, he held out a thin, nervous hand to Anthony.

"Mr. Bathurst—I've heard of you. Of course I have. Who hasn't? And indeed more than once. I never thought it would be my pleasure to meet you in the flesh."

Robin Ilsley, on the other hand, was very much the solicitor. To that effect he might have worn an invisible label. His manner was professional, peremptory and pompous. He was in the early forties, Anthony judged, clean-shaven and inclined to corpulence, which had already manifested itself in more than one physical symptom. His neck, for instance, was short and thick.

"You won't make old bones," commented Anthony mentally, at their introduction by Martin Scudamore.

Ilsley spoke. "Bathurst! How do you do? Rather a pity you've turned up here at this time. Considering! Just a trifle awkward, perhaps. Still, can't be helped, I suppose."

Mapperley was as tall as Sheridan. Thin, spare, rather dried up. His face, like Sheridan's, was pale, with a prominent chin, a jutting nose and large, staring, light blue eyes—more like a sailor's eyes, Anthony thought, than a soldier's. He stood easily and comfortably at Scudamore's introduction.

"Delighted to meet you, sir. Lovelace served under me in France. That's why I'm here to-day. He was a good fellow. No man could have wished for a better. A damned good fellow and a damned good officer."

Sheridan overheard and smiled. "I do hope not, Colonel. I do indeed."

Mapperley made no reply to the quip. Anthony doubted whether he had taken the Vicar's point. Major Hargreaves was short and stout. Some years younger, evidently, than his Service colleague. Anthony judged him fat, florid and easy-going. He had a big, round, clean-shaven face and a head that had been on such bad terms with its hair that they had mutually decided to part company. His smile, however, seemed as honest as the day. Almost too honest, Anthony thought—it almost advertised the quality rather than betokened it. Hargreaves spoke jerkily.

"Bathurst? Pleased to meet you. Sad occasion for all of us—what?"

And then, as Anthony turned from Major Hargreaves, after the utterance of a returned conventionality, he saw for the first time a woman in the room. For some obscure reason it surprised him to see her there. She was sitting in a seat in an alcove by the window and appeared to Anthony to be bending over something which occupied all her attention. Her head was lowered as she sat and the expression on her face intent. Suddenly she looked up and saw him gazing at her. As she raised her head Anthony realised the manner of her occupation. She had bent over several lines of playing-cards—she had been playing patience. To his further surprise somewhat she put the cards away from her, rose, advanced towards him and extended her hand.

"From what I have just heard," she said, "I presume that I am addressing Anthony Bathurst. I'm worried to think that I wasn't actually expecting you."

4

Anthony smiled as he took the extended hand. "I must plead guilty to both charges," he said quietly, "and it would be superfluous to say that you have the advantage of me."

"I'm Evelyn Forbes," she answered; "you've already met my husband, I understand."

Anthony saw that he was encountering a woman who was beautiful—with a beauty such as is given to few women. There was something almost virginal about her. Whatever she said or whatever she did always seemed to be absolutely spontaneous—almost inevitable. She was a trifle taller than the average height of woman, and at first glance looked even a little taller than that. But for all her height she had a quality of fragility and daintiness that was, in its way, exquisite. Her eyes were dark and quiet—she nearly always seemed to be pondering and pensive. Her head, though, was on the small side, poised on a beautiful slender throat, and looked to Anthony as though it were almost overweighted by her glorious dark hair. And yet her features were her best point. Finely chiselled from nose to chin and to the red bow of her lips. And in addition to this embarrassment of charm her voice was sweet and pleasing. She inclined her head to the alcove where she had just been sitting and to the playing-cards she had relinquished.

"I just had to do something," she continued in explanation, "while the others were at the church. And my husband wished me to be here, otherwise there would have been no hostess. So don't think me callous . . . or . . . er . . . irreverent. Besides, Dick himself wouldn't mind a little bit. He would have approved, I think. He was a generous-hearted soul and he wouldn't have a single person unhappy at any time on his account. I'm perfectly convinced about that."

"You knew him well, I take it?" queried Anthony. Was it imagination on his part or had there been the suspicion of a tremor in her voice? Before Evelyn Forbes was able to reply, her husband came bustling up to them.

"Hallo! So you two have met—eh? I was just going to introduce you. I owe you both an apology. I forgot just now that you hadn't met Bathurst, Evelyn."

His wife took a quick step forward as Robert Forbes spoke. "You shouldn't forget," she said quietly, "you forget too much and too often. I've been going to say that to you for a long time."

Forbes smiled, but his eyes showed displeasure. "Now . . . now, Lyn. Don't hit a fellow below the belt. You know how busy I always am. And with this business on top of it all . . . "

Anthony looked at her face intently. Although she had recovered her composure, her face had definitely changed. He wondered what the exact implication was. Had there been grief, or annoyance, surprise, resentment, fear? One of these feelings, he thought, almost certainly. Or possibly a *soupçon* of each merged together? Anthony felt far from sure.

Evelyn Forbes, however, was speaking to her husband again. "Actually, my dear Robert," she said, with ice in her voice, "if you must know, I introduced myself to Mr. Bathurst. I became for once a forward hussy. The fact that I did so is both a tribute and a compliment to your powers of description. From what you had told me I was able to recognise him immediately. It was gratifying to me to do so."

"May I ask why?" enquired Anthony. "Would such a question on my part be regarded as in order?"

Evelyn Forbes smiled back at him. It was a lazy, sulky, sultry sort of smile—one that her husband seldom saw these days.

"Well," she answered, "perhaps that might be a little difficult for me to explain. Anything like adequately. I think it must have been primarily because I was feeling a little lonely when I first caught sight of you. Isolated, perhaps, would be a better word. Cut off from the company. You see, with the exception of the estimable Mrs. Toplady, I was, and am, the only woman in the house. Being the only member of my sex anywhere invariably gives me that feeling of cut-off isolation. Neither the Vicar nor Mr. Ilsley happens to be married, you see. Each is a confirmed bachelor. But Robert wanted me to come, and out of the regard and respect we both have always felt for Dick Lovelace, I consented to do as my husband desired."

Anthony rubbed the ridge of his jaw. His grey eyes showed a gleam of something like amiable mischief.

"I'm not sure, Mrs. Forbes, whether I regard what you've just told me as a compliment or otherwise. Seems to me it's distinctly complicated. Because you were still the only representative of your sex after you saw me."

Forbes himself cut in before Evelyn could reply. "Trust Lyn to dish out something like that. My dear chap, if you'd had half my experience of Lyn philosophy and Lyn psychology you'd never be quite—"

The rest of his sentence was obliterated by the voice of Robin Ilsley. It seemed that it was raised above the ordinary, and that he was addressing the company in general.

"If you good people would be quiet for just a few moments I'd like to read you the will which Richard Lovelace asked me to prepare comparatively recently and to execute, if it ever became necessary, in the appropriate manner."

Anthony pricked up his ears. The knots of conversation ceased suddenly. The quick, staccato silence which ensued was a little unnerving, Anthony thought. Away to his right he heard the clearing of the professional Ilsley throat. And then came something which was distinctly in the nature of an anti-climax. Timed to a split second, as it were, there came a quiet but firm tap on the door. Everybody in the room waited for Robin Ilsley to act. But Ilsley, very quietly, but at the same time very audibly, said "come in".

It was Toplady who entered. He carried sherry and small, daintily cut sandwiches on a large silver salver.

"Thank you, Toplady," said Evelyn Forbes, with complete poise and dignity, "put them down over there, do you mind? That's it." She indicated the place of her reference.

5

The butler moved with a kind of synchronous inevitability towards the side-table which Evelyn Forbes had indicated. Deftly and almost silently he placed the various articles which he carried on the table, and then arranged them there to his liking. While this was taking place the company in the room was strangely hushed and seemingly expectant. On mental tiptoe, as it were, waiting for the curtain to rise on an uncertain something which not one of them was quite sure about or properly prepared to meet. Toplady finished at the table, turned and bowed gravely to the company in general, and silently took his departure. The men and the one woman whom he left behind seemed relieved at his passing. The tenseness of the atmosphere subsided. Anthony found himself waiting for a massed and audible sigh.

Ilsley, however, had recovered his poise and was on his way to centre stage by this time. Anthony saw the beginning of this activity. He observed that the solicitor held several papers in his hand. Everybody watched Robin Ilsley. Ilsley stopped, looked at the people round him and rather ostentatiously cleared his throat for the second time that afternoon. He began to speak again.

"This is Dick Lovelace's will. As I said a few moments ago. I won't weary or worry you with all the legal preamble that's attached to it. I don't propose to do that because I don't suppose any of you would want it and I know it's not really important. In other words, I'll be as brief as I possibly can. But as things go—with the exception of a legacy of £250 to each of the Topladys for services rendered—everything that Dick Lovelace died possessed of he's left to Evelyn here. Evelyn Forbes—that is. Whom I should like to congratulate most heartily and most sincerely upon her good fortune. There were good reasons, of course, for Lovelace acting as he did. He had no near relatives that he knew anything about, so we are readily enabled to visualise an occasion when a deep friendship has been honoured and rewarded, rather than the normal ties of blood and . . . er . . . kinship. The estate is by no means inconsiderable, as most of you who knew Dick probably guess, so once again, all my very best congratulations and good wishes to Evelyn—Mrs. Forbes."

Ilsley paused. Anthony looked deliberately in the direction of Evelyn Forbes. A pink spot of colour flaunted itself in each of her cheeks. There was no flush—nothing like that—just two bright spots. He noticed, however, that she was careful to avoid the eyes of her husband. She kept her gaze steadily in another direction. Ilsley began to speak again.

"I don't propose to invite the Topladys in to tell them of their legacies just at this moment. That can wait. I'll communicate with them in due course by post from my office. So that's that and I've said what I had to say. In fact, there's nothing else for me to say." He broke away from the middle of the room and advanced towards Evelyn Forbes with his right hand extended.

"My dear Mrs. Forbes—once again my most sincere congratulations and my very best wishes."

He smiled at her happily and his voice was clear, cordial and sincere. By this time Evelyn was completely herself again. Gone were the two pink cheek-spots and the suggestion of disdain.

"Thank you, Robin," she said simply and entirely without affectation, "that's nice of you. But all the same it's a terrific surprise for me. And I really don't know what to think about it all. I had no idea that Dick thought so highly of me. It was rather sweet of him."

She stopped—a trifle abruptly. There was just the beginning of a distinctly embarrassing pause. Everybody felt it—and everybody knew that the feeling was present. Sheridan made gallant haste to cover it. He advanced to Evelyn as Ilsley had.

"My dear Mrs. Forbes," he said, "allow me to add my congratulations to those of Ilsley. From the very bottom of my heart. I am sure that Lovelace felt that he must repay in some way the many hours of companionship and social entertainment that you and Robert gave him and were always ready to give him—who was by way of being a lonely man. I know something of the very great regard he had for both of you. Believe me, you have my very best wishes."

Evelyn made no reply beyond a quick, spontaneous smile. On the other hand, she turned with icy coolness to the table whereon Toplady, to her instructions, had placed the sandwiches and the sherry.

"Bob," she said, rather imperiously to her husband, "you aren't doing anything . . . come and help me hand round these refreshments, will you?"

Forbes looked up and then moved somewhat ungraciously to her side at the table. Anthony watched him closely. As it happened, Forbes came from the table and made straight for him.

"Sherry, Bathurst, and help yourself to the sandwiches."

Anthony thanked him and took the glass of wine and a sandwich. Forbes by now had thrown off his annoyance or whatever it was that had disturbed him. He moved adroitly and with the utmost aplomb amongst the other people in the room. Anthony still watched the general set-up and all the time he was watching he was thinking hard. Scudamore was talking to Mapperley and Hargreaves. Evelyn was looking after them as though the duty had become a special assignment. Ilsley and Sheridan stood together alone, talking seriously and, if gestures counted for anything, evidently intimately. Sheridan began to interest Anthony beyond the ordinary.

A calmness and a severity appeared to have settled on him since he had spoken his congratulations to Evelyn Forbes. It occurred to Anthony that Sheridan dominated Ilsley in the conversation in which they were indulging. It was almost as though the priest in holy were giving unholy orders. He was talking quite calmly but his serenity was akin to that of the commander who, on the eve of battle, reviews the issues of the morrow with complete tranquillity. Habituated to the chances and mischances of war, he nevertheless makes his tactical dispositions, folds his cloak about him and lies down calmly to sleep, knowing full well that the morrow may bring him disaster and defeat. And yet, under this mask which Anthony whimsically placed on Sheridan as he smiled and talked, he felt that he could see the real man all the time.

Suddenly Anthony perceived that Robin Ilsley was looking across the room and beckoning to him. Anthony carefully placed his empty sherry glass on the side-table and went over to the solicitor.

"Mr. Bathurst," said Ilsley, "the Vicar here harbours what I think are purely fanciful notions. I've told him as much—pretty straight, too. I'd like to hear your opinion. I was always one to go to the fountain-head when I was in any sort of doubt. Never believe in roundabout methods."

Anthony smiled and waved away the compliment. "Not as high up as that, I'm afraid, Mr. Ilsley. You flatter me, you do indeed. But what was it you felt you'd like to ask me?"

Ilsley went straight to the point. "Concerning Lovelace's death. That's what the Vicar and I have been discussing. Sheridan here hints to me most strongly that your people suspect foul play. Is that so?"

Anthony deliberately showed surprise for the two men to see and undoubtedly recognise.

"Foul play? Is there any doubt about it, then?"

Ilsley was quick to take the point. "Oh, I see. I spoke carelessly, I suppose. But don't stall. You know what I mean. I allude to 'foul play' from some agency other than that of the Bill Sikes brand. Now you know perfectly well what I mean. I've spoken plainly."

Ilsley cocked his head to one side to see the effect of his words on Anthony. Sheridan, also, was watching intently.

"If I tell the truth," replied Anthony, with a flicker of humour in his grey eyes, "as I suppose I must—you've told me straight out not to stall—I shall be forced to admit that the authorities are in somewhat of a quandary. For this reason. The murder of Lovelace—or rather, shall we say the killing of Lovelace by direct assault— appears to have been entirely motiveless."

Anthony did as Ilsley had. He watched to see the effect of his words. The solicitor, however, came back at him quickly.

"Motiveless? I don't quite see how you arrive there, Bathurst. I'm hanged if I do. Motiveless! Surely the motive was burglary? What other motive could there have been?"

Anthony smiled. "It may well have been burglary, as you say."

A puzzled look came over Ilsley's face. "Do you mean then that you aren't certain?"

Anthony watched Sheridan from the corner of his eye. There was a glint of satisfaction, if not triumph, on the Vicar's face as he listened to these conversational exchanges. He was on the point of scoring off Ilsley.

"I'm afraid," replied Anthony, "that with regard to that I must leave you to draw your own conclusions. After all, in justice to your opinion, the late Mr. Lovelace *may* have been robbed of the hanging gardens of Babylon, or of a vial containing the elixir of life. Who knows? Who amongst us can be certain? You see my point, I'm positive."

Ilsley whistled under his breath. "Like that—is it? I certainly begin to see! In that case, Bathurst, I won't embarrass you with any more of my questions. It wouldn't be fair of me—I flatter myself I can see as far through a blank wall as most men. Sheridan, the honours are yours—I apologise for pouring scorn on those theories of yours. You must have had inside information from somewhere. Horse's mouth business. I had no idea of your strength—you wise old bird."

The Vicar's face changed. Anthony thought that he looked a trifle discomfited. He had certainly not taken Ilsley's remarks as in any way complimentary.

"My dear Ilsley," he returned quietly, "you misjudge me very badly. I had no 'inside' story as you term it. And horses' mouths never open in front of me. My remarks to you, before you called Bathurst over to us, were simply based upon my own conclusions. I assure you that any information I may have had to work on has been drawn exclusively from the same source as your own—the daily Press."

Ilsley remained good-humoured. "Come, come! Nothing from local gossip eh? Nothing at all?"

Sheridan shrugged his shoulders. "Neither from inclination, nor calling, do I ever listen to local gossip, Ilsley. You should know that. I am rather shocked that you should suggest such a thing." He turned to Anthony. "You will have observed by now, Bathurst, that I, at least, have asked you *no* questions. Neither embarrassing nor awkward. Please place that fact to my credit."

Anthony smiled, nodded benevolently and managed to disengage himself. He began to think that the day would bring him no more benefits. There were too many people in the house for one thing and it seemed that some time must elapse before the coast became anything like clear. In addition he had much to think over. What had been very like confusion before was now worse confounded. The heritage of the Lovelace estate to Evelyn Forbes had been a bolt from the blue to almost everybody who had listened to Ilsley. Had it been so to the lady herself? Anthony felt far from certain.

It was with these thoughts uppermost in his mind that Anthony made his *adieux*. More than one person, however, to whom he made them suspected that as far as he or she was concerned it was much more a case of *au 'voir*. Possibly they knew their Bathurst even better than he supposed.

CHAPTER 5

1

W hen Anthony called at 'Cherry Fair' on the following Monday morning he found Sergeant Dixon already in possession. At the precise moment of Anthony's entrance the Sergeant was in earnest conversation with the butler, Toplady. Dixon smiled when he saw Anthony come towards the house and wished him "good morning."

"It is indeed, Sergeant," returned Anthony, "a sunny July morning at its brilliant best."

Toplady looked across at him. Anthony returned Dixon's smile to Toplady.

"No hurry, but when the Sergeant's done with you, Toplady," said Anthony, "I'd like half a dozen words with you, if it's convenient."

Toplady looked askance at the Sergeant. "That'll be quite O.K., Mr. Bathurst," said the last-named with a nod. "I'm nearly through—I'll pass him over to you in less than five minutes."

Anthony strolled away from the two men and then, a few moments later, strolled back to Toplady. Dixon had evidently said all that he had to say. For the time being, at least. Toplady looked up at Anthony expectantly—almost perhaps anxiously. Anthony was quick to see it.

"You were wantin' me, sir?"

Anthony nodded. "Yes, in a way, Toplady. Nothing much. Just a question or two. Any more scares in the night?"

"Scares, sir?"

"Yes. You know what I mean. Come, come! Cigarette-ends and such-like lying in the wrong places. Any more alarms or excursions since yesterday? Since the funeral, shall we say . . . and what followed the funeral?"

"No, sir," replied Toplady, with an element of what sounded like stubbornness, "nothing more of that sort, sir. I'm pleased to say. Although it's not sayin' there won't be. You can't tell—because you never know."

Toplady shook his head with dark and sinister suggestion. Anthony smiled encouragingly.

"Perhaps not. Still, no signs are good signs. Or at any rate, we'll say they are, and comfort ourselves in that fashion. Now for the one or two questions I told you I wanted to ask you. They are not with regard to the happenings on the night Mr. Lovelace was set upon. You've already told us all about that—clearly and frankly. Just general questions, as you might say, Toplady. And I'm sure you'll answer them for me to the best of your ability as you did the others."

"I'll try to, sir," asserted Toplady with sturdy independence, "and no man can do more."

"Did Mr. Lovelace have many people call here? From a social point of view? As a general rule?"

"A fair number, sir. Allowing for the fact that the village is small. Doctor Forbes and Mrs. Forbes. The Vicar of the parish, Mr. Ilsley, Mr. Scudamore. You've met them all, sir, I fancy. They were the usual callers, sir. And fairly regular, at that."

"Anybody else—besides them?"

"Nobody, sir, who called 'ere with anything like regularity, sir. Anybody else would come on the rare occasion. You can take that from me, sir."

Anthony struck at once. "You mentioned Doctor and Mrs. Forbes. Did Doctor and Mrs. Forbes always come here together?"

Toplady batted neither eyelid. "As a rule, sir. I think it may be said that they would visit 'ere together."

"That isn't what I asked you, Toplady. I said did they *always* come together?"

The butler shrugged his shoulders. "Always is so . . . er . . . expansive, sir. So . . . er. . . comprehensive. There may possibly have been an odd occasion or so—when Doctor Forbes 'as come 'ere alone."

The Toplady eyelids were still under strict control. Anthony smiled inwardly at the butler's persistence and adroitness.

"I see. That disposes of Doctor Forbes then. And were there any other odd occasions or so when Mrs. Forbes came here unaccompanied?"

Toplady stiffened himself in ramrod fashion. "There may 'ave been, sir—but they would have occurred so infrequently they would 'ave left no mark on my memory whatever."

Anthony accepted the inevitable. "Thank you, Toplady. Now let me ask you another question. Had Mr. Lovelace had any recent visitor or any recent correspondence which in your opinion had tended to disturb him?"

Toplady remained true to form and played it back plumb on the middle.

"Nothing to my knowledge, sir, but I should like to point out that it was not Mr. Lovelace's custom to discuss with me matters which affected 'is own personal interests."

Again Anthony took what had been handed to him. He tried once more, however.

"You saw no obvious sign, I take it, of any such disturbance as I mentioned having affected Mr. Lovelace? Which, to all intents and purposes, and as far as he was able he had kept to himself?"

"I saw nothing of that kind whatever, sir. No suggestion of such a thing." Toplady was still imperturbable.

"In your opinion, then, Mr. Lovelace was entirely normal during the week or two before he was assaulted? You would assert that without any hesitation?"

Toplady bowed gravely in confirmation of Anthony's question. "I would assert that, sir, without the slightest 'esitation. And if you would care to put the same question to my good lady, I am confident that she would answer you exactly as I 'ave, sir. Is there anything else you would be requiring of me, sir? Because I 'ave many—"

Toplady's face was bland and his manner suave. Anthony changed his tactics.

"In which room of this house did Mr. Lovelace spend the greater part of his time? Would it be the library?"

Toplady considered the question for some time before he answered. "No, sir," he said at length, "I don't think it would be the library. I should say the answer would be in 'is own room upstairs. My good lady, whenever she referred to it, called it 'is den. He did most of 'is writing and conducted most of 'is correspondence up there, at any rate. But perhaps that's not saying very much—because 'e didn't go in for a lot of correspondence—comparatively speaking. I've often heard 'im say that 'e fair 'ated writing letters. In fact, scarcely a day passed without 'im saying it—or something similar."

"Take me up to this room, Toplady," returned Anthony; "I'd like to have a look round it. Few people can have known Mr. Lovelace as well as you did."

"With pleasure, sir," replied the butler; "come this way, will you?"

Toplady turned and Anthony followed him up the staircase.

Toplady, ahead of Anthony, crossed a landing and opened a door. He then stood back a trifle and waited quietly for Anthony to reach him.

"This is the room, sir—where my late master used to spend a great deal of 'is time when he was at home. You can see for yourself the kind of room it is."

Anthony nodded. "Thank you, Toplady. I may have a look round it as I said just now. For the time being—I won't detain you any longer."

Toplady favoured Anthony with one of his best bows. "Very good, sir. If you should require anything further, you will doubtless communicate with me—or with Mrs. Toplady. You know where to find us."

2

Toplady withdrew. Anthony walked round and closed the door behind the butler. The room in which he found himself was bright and interesting. Anthony took quick stock of it. It was obvious that, for Lovelace, it had held more than one interest. It was light and airy—the walls cream-washed. On the right were wall shelves, which held many volumes of light fiction. At the eye-level Anthony caught a quick sight of a complete set of Raymond Chandler. In the right-hand corner of the room was a beautifully made and superbly polished knee-hole writing-table, with an extremely comfortable leathern arm-chair close to it. Anthony guessed that Dick Lovelace had spent much of his time in that chair.

What Anthony described to himself as a single french door, with a window on each side, opened on to a charmingly constructed balcony which commanded the garden of 'Cherry Fair', and away on the farther side of the room were other wall shelves complete with books, and close to them a billiards-table with the necessary accessories in near touch. The position of the table, however, gave ample cue-room. Anthony walked across the room and saw a box of snooker balls and a triangle wedged primly on a rather cunningly contrived stone mantelpiece.

Then he looked at the names of the books on the farther wall shelves. He saw that they were devoted to sport—almost entirely. The Turf, the Ring, Cricket, Football, Golf, Lacrosse were all well represented along the shelves. Anthony had no difficulty in understanding why Mrs. Toplady had referred to the room as Lovelace's 'den.' He glanced along the line of books again and then wandered back to the writing-table. It had nine drawers—four small drawers on each side and an altogether longer and larger drawer in the middle. That is to say—above the knee-hole.

Anthony tried the top drawer on the left-hand side. It answered smoothly to his pull. Upon examination, however, it contained nothing but Lovelace's personal stationery. And the ordinary and commonplace nature of this drawer's contents applied, without exception, to the contents of all the other drawers. In different places, Anthony found various files—"Income Tax", "Army Service", "Sincil Hall—Arabella Braund deceased", "Investments", and the documentary remains of much entirely normal correspondence and of many accounts and receipts.

Anthony sat in Dick Lovelace's leathern arm-chair, cupped his chin in his hands and wondered. The surface of the desk that he looked at in front of him was orderly and generally tidy. Blotting- pad (large), pencil-tray, travelling clock in a case emerald green in colour, telephone in the left-hand corner and table-lamp. Anthony sat and thought of the conventional correspondence at which he had so recently been looking. It had *all* been entirely ordinary, with nothing whatever anywhere to excite the slightest suspicion or aggravate the tiniest anxiety. Yes—all of it!

Anthony sat there, in the chair, as has already been recorded, with his eyes almost vacantly addressing the late Richard Lovelace's neat and tidy area of pale blue blotting-pad. And then, as he looked, the vacancy of his stare vanished . . . the stare became hard and ardent . . . And he looked again . . . quickly and deliberately at what he had seen on the blue expanse of blotting-pad.

3

Towards the left-hand corner of the blotting-pad was a pencilled "doodle". But it was rather more than a merely ordinary "doodle". For this reason! It was clear that there had been a definite endeavour on the part of the pencil wielder to sketch something. And if this fact were clear it was abundantly clear also that the object which had been roughly sketched or "doodled" was a tea-spoon. Not an egg-spoon or a dessert-spoon, or a tablespoon, or a mustard-spoon—but a tea-spoon.

Anthony felt absolutely certain with regard to this. The size of the drawing left no room for doubt. A tea-spoon! For the second time his thoughts reverted to the statement of Doctor Forbes. A statement, moreover, which to a certain extent had been supported by Sergeant Dixon. That, as Dick Lovelace lay dying in the hospital at Loveridge, he had muttered but two words—"innocent" and "tea-spoon"!

Anthony rubbed the ridge of his jaw—according to his habit. Damn' funny business, say what you like about it! A tea-spoon drawn on Lovelace's blotter and a tea-spoon on his lips as he lay a-dying! Anthony looked even more carefully at the blotter in front of him. It consisted of a large pad of blotting-paper folded and fitted into four leather corner-edges. And then, as he looked, he saw something else! Or rather two more things. Two more rough, "doodled" sketches. The first was a very creditable attempt in pencil to reproduce the head of the renowned "Laughing Cavalier", and the second showed quite plainly a ring-master with whip in hand, and also the figure of a clown. These further pencilled sketches were not actually adjacent to the drawing of the tea-spoon but had been made right away from it on the far right-hand side of the blotter area. Which, of course, was the principal reason why Anthony had not noticed them before. What on earth did any one, or all of them, signify? Or were they entirely meaningless?

Anthony sat in the arm-chair at the writing-table and made an initial attempt to puzzle things out. But he quickly realised that he must hold his horses. It might well be that it was Lovelace's normal habit to "doodle" as he sat there at the writing-table where Anthony was sitting, and that the ring-master, clown and cavalier were things in themselves apart and had no connexion whatever with the humble and commonplace—but sinister—tea-spoon.

Anthony began to consider the ordinary urges and incitements that lay behind the popular exercise of "doodling". It was occasioned as a rule, in his opinion, during periods of intensive thought, and was often parented by an unusually potent obsession of the mind in dominant operation at that particular time. He knew beyond any doubt that "tea-spoon" had been on Lovelace's mind at the time of his death—because he had Forbes's professional authority to that effect. "Tea-spoon" and "innocent". Could the latter word be read in any way into the head of the "Laughing Cavalier", or alternatively into the sketch of the clown and the ring-master?

Anthony racked his brains for a possible solution. Was there anything else to be picked up from the blotting-pad? Anything that up to the moment he'd missed?

Anthony looked at the blotter again—even more carefully than before. To no avail, however. There was nothing else there. Beyond these sketches he had noticed and a local telephone number, the surface was clear. Which fact made Anthony feel tolerably certain with regard to another point. This! The condition of the blotting-paper showed that the pad was comparatively new—of but recent initiation. Which meant logically that the tea-spoon should be no antique, either!

Anthony shrugged his shoulders, rose from the arm-chair and made his way downstairs. He went straight into the kitchen to find Mrs. Toplady. When he entered he saw that she was standing at one end of the table. The heavy face turned towards him and regarded him in exactly the same fashion as it always did.

"Mrs. Toplady," said Anthony, "I want you to do something for me, if you don't mind. And if you can—to do it now." Mrs. Toplady nodded and spoke. The tones were flat and flaccid. "What is that, sir?"

"Come upstairs with me, will you—I'd like to have your advice on something in Mr. Lovelace's room."

Mrs. Toplady wiped her hands on her apron, which she then removed, and followed Anthony to the room which he had just vacated.

"This was Mr. Lovelace's 'den', I understand?"

Mrs. Toplady nodded. "Yes, sir. That was my word for it. He liked to be up here better than anywhere."

"Good. That's as I understood it from your husband. Come over here, will you?"

Anthony beckoned Mrs. Toplady to the writing-table. He pointed to the blue blotter in front of her. "Have a look at these rough drawings, Mrs. Toplady. On the blotting-pad here. Like little sketches they are. See them? Here in this corner—and again over there on the other side of the pad. Would they be Mr. Lovelace's drawings? Can you tell me, please?"

There was no hesitation about Mrs. Toplady's reply. It almost smacked of something like enthusiasm.

"Oh yes, sir. That's an old habit of the master's. They're his all right. He was always at it, as you might say. Couldn't resist doin' 'em. Whenever I cleared an old pad away and put him clean paper in the folder—there was always funny little old drawings on the dirty pad. Fair made me laugh—some of 'em did."

Mrs. Toplady nodded again towards the drawing of the spoon and said "that's Mr. Lovelace's work all right. You needn't have any doubt about it."

"Thank you, Mrs. Toplady," returned Anthony. "I imagined that *was* the case, but I just wanted to make sure. You can get back to the trivial round."

Mrs. Toplady sniffed and took her departure. Anthony sat down again in Lovelace's arm-chair, leant his arms on the Lovelace desk and looked at the Lovelace drawings. A tea-spoon, the "Laughing Cavalier", and the ring of a circus complete with ring-master and clown. Hippodrome—possibly! Tea-spoon, cavalier and circus. Cavalier Circus! Good lord—how simple, after all. He had arrived somewhere at last. Of course he knew where Cavalier Circus was. Cavalier Circus was that small *cul-de-sac* which turned out of New Bond Street on the eastern side. Cavalier Circus!

Anthony remembered clearly having noticed the name one afternoon in a recent January when the snow was falling thick and fast. He pushed back the arm-chair from the writing-desk and stood up. His next step was obvious to him. Cavalier Circus and the vicinity of Cavalier Circus might well repay a visit. Concerning the making of which there was certainly no time to be lost.

4

The heavy spots of rain had stopped. The thunderstorm that had promised had rolled away to another place of visitation and the sky was clear again. The wind that had sprung into a fierce strength had changed its mind and died away, but the earth was cooler when it had gone. The engine of Anthony's car was cold. Anthony made adjustments and suddenly without warning the engine decided to burst into life again. The car shot away towards London. For some miles Anthony drove almost on the crown of the comparatively clear road.

5

Anthony garaged the car and came into Oxford Street at ten minutes past three in the afternoon. The sun was reigning again. Twenty minutes later he had turned into New Bond Street and twenty-three minutes later he found himself in the little cul-de-sac of Cavalier Circus. As he had remembered it, it was on the eastern side of the main street. There were nine shops on its left-hand side and eight on its right.

Anthony was somewhat surprised to discover that the general quality of the seventeen shops was unusually high—even allowing for the excellent standards of the contiguous area. A costumier's, a milliner's, a most unusually artistic picture and portrait establishment, and a shoe-shop, all displayed within their windows goods and wares of general excellence. The eighth shop on the left-hand side of Cavalier Circus—that is to say the last shop but one—belonged to that category usually referred to as "antique". As with the neighbouring shops, the quality and value of the many and varied articles shown in the window and in the body of the shop itself were both arresting and unmistakable.

In the forefront of the window was a tapestry which depicted the myths of Dietrich of Bern, an ancient Venetian drug-pot, a Galehault flagon, two ancient swords with flamboyant edges, a picador's gilt spear, a fourteenth-century hooped drinking-pot, one of the dogs of Fo K'ans Hsi and a really magnificent ivory peacock.

Anthony walked between the main windows and looked at the objects within the focus of his vision with the greatest possible interest. From what he had already seen he was inclined to rate this shop as the finest of its type which had ever come his way. He wondered if he would come across any form of tea-spoon in any part of the window! Taking into consideration, however, the general character and the wide range of objects at which he was now looking, it seemed rather heavy odds against such a contingency.

And yet—he had come to Cavalier Circus with a purpose. With a definite end in view. There must have been *some* reason for Lovelace to have made the drawings he had made. And there could be no possible doubt with regard to the implication of the tea-spoon. The word that had been on Lovelace's lips when he looked on death. And yet, when one came to grips with the problem what possible connexion could a tea-spoon . . . Anthony looked up suddenly in an effort to see the name of the shop's proprietor.

The name was there all right.

It was in small letters—gilt on a black ground—over the middle of the doorway. That seemed to be the reigning fashion in this particular row of shops. And as Anthony looked up at the name the blood raced through his veins and his pulses beat a little more rapidly. For the name at which he looked was "A. Temple Spooner".

"Well—I'm blessed," muttered Anthony. "A. T. Spooner. So that's what Lovelace really meant. The name of the man in Cavalier Circus. Well, well, well."

Mr. Bathurst rubbed his hands with satisfaction. The hunt was up at last!

6

Anthony walked to the main door at the front entrance of the shop and pressed down the handle. A man with a long, lugubrious and somewhat equine cast of face greeted him immediately his foot crossed the threshold.

"I've been expecting you, sir," said the horse-faced man. "I knew it was only a matter of time before you came in to see me." Anthony was taken aback, rather, at this somewhat surprising form of greeting and was also a trifle puzzled.

"You say you were expecting me," he said. "I had no idea I was so honoured. How come?"

The man spread out deprecating hands. The moment he began to speak again, Anthony saw his mistake. The man offered the simple explanation.

"I saw you contemplating some of the articles in the window, and I knew from the look on your face that you'd never be able to resist the temptation of comin' in the shop. I know that look only too well. Believe me, mister, when you've been in the trade the years I have you can always tell. I said to myself, as I watched you from inside here, this gent'll be inside in a brace of shakes and I must be prepared to help him—both as a customer and as a fellow human being. That's how I look on life, mister. It's been my way for years. For some reason that we 'umans can't perhaps fathom. we're all in it together. We all make contributions to a kind of general scheme and we all make mistakes—and there's not one of us that can't do with a helping hand sometimes. At least that's what I think and what I've nearly always found. Now what is it I can do for you, sir? If I can be allowed to make a sort of prophecy, it'll be the little hound of Fo K'ans Hsi. Very handsome antique that, and of a type very much sought after. Am I right, sir? Shall I get it from the window, mister?"

Anthony smiled at his questioner and shook his head. "You've got me wrong. I'm afraid I'm here under a sort of false pretences. I don't know that I can really be regarded as a prospective customer. But tell me first of all—have I the pleasure of addressing Mr. A. T. Spooner—the proprietor of this establishment?"

The equine-faced man shook his head sadly—almost pityingly so, Anthony thought.

"No, mister—you've got me wrong . . . like I got you. So that makes us all square. I'm not the Guv'nor. Merely an hireling in the vineyard, as you might say. There's room for all kinds in the vineyard. The Good Book tells us that. Did you want to see Mr. Spooner on a particular matter of business?"

Anthony nodded. "Yes. You can call it that. What time could I catch him in?"

The head at which Anthony looked was shaken again. On this second occasion there was no doubt whatever that it was shaken in pity. The head continued to shake in this fashion.

"I don't fancy you know Mr. Spooner, do you, mister? You're not by way of being a friend of his?"

"To my knowledge I've never actually met him in the flesh. But that fact doesn't prevent—"

The shopman cut in. "Look here, I'd better explain. Then you'll get a better idea of things. The Guv'nor's got places like this all over the British Isles. With an expert manager in charge of each. He's the king-pin of this sort of business. Manchester, Liverpool, Bournemouth, Brighton, Penzance, Cheltenham, Bristol, Harrogate, Edinburgh, Leamington, Buxton, Newcastle—mister, I could go on for ever stringin' the names together, you'd think I was a human time-table. He's got his finger in hundreds of pies. We don't see 'im up here not once in a lunar blue. In fact I can't remember when I did see the old gent last."

Anthony was disappointed at what he had just heard, but he smiled when he replied "I see. That does explain things, I agree. I assure you I had no idea of the manifold nature of Mr. Spooner's interests. All the same, I particularly want to see him and I presume he's 'seeable' somewhere? Can you give me *any* address where I could make contact with him?"

The horse-faced man stroked his long chin. "That means you're wantin' his private address, I suppose? That's about the size of it. Well, now let me see . . . I can't give you the details—I haven't got 'em here—but I can give you the name of the place where he lives. And I'm told it's quite a small turn-out, so you'd have no difficulty in runnin' him to earth, as it were, when you get there. It's a village in Hertfordshire—somewhere near St. Albans. Now let me see . . . Splash—no—that's not it, but it's something like it—I know, Plashet. That's the name of Mr. Spooner's place—Plashet, near St. Albans, Herts. Shall I jot it down on a piece of paper for you so's you won't forget it?"

Anthony declined the generous suggestion. "No. That's all right, thanks . . . I'll remember it."

The shopman seemed doubtful and expressed the doubt by looking regretfully at the window and its contents.

"You're sure I can't interest you in anything, mister? That little dog, now, that I mentioned? One of the authentic hounds of Fo K'ans Hsi. You won't find another like that—well—anywhere on the face of the earth! And you wouldn't have to pay a licence for the little fellow, either. Not to mention the matter of canine cleanliness. Would you care to handle it, sir . . . it's a smashing piece of work—it is really."

Anthony shook his head. "No, thanks, old chap. I don't doubt its worth for a moment, but actually it's not in my line."

The shopman, nothing daunted, came again. "Well, then, what about the peacock, sir? The ivory piece. Did you ever clap eyes on a better bit of work than that? Let me get it and show it to you, mister. In the words of the poet, a thing of beauty and a joy for ever. Once you've held it in your hands you'll never let go of it! Anybody can see you've a taste for beautiful things. Directly I clapped eyes on you I knew it—sticks out a mile."

Anthony smiled and shook his head again. "No, thanks, old chap. Not just now. Please forget me as a prospective customer. And I'm sorry to have taken up so much of your valuable time. You must forgive me. Cheer-o."

Anthony turned quickly and made for the door. When he reached the pavement he wiped his forehead with his handkerchief and looked at his wrist-watch. There was still time for the Hertfordshire village of Plashet—and Mr. A. Temple Spooner himself. Anthony walked rapidly to the place where he had parked his car. He must run the man to earth as soon as possible.

CHAPTER 6

1

Anthony drove fast and came to the "Green Dragon", that stands between Chipping Barnet and South Mimms. The inn is built by the side of what to-day would be called a "by-pass" and was constructed some time about the year 1820. Even now this road is called the "new road", although for a hundred years and more it has formed part of the main highway to Holyhead and the northwest. When this new road was opened, the inevitable happened—the posting and coaching traffic deserted the "old road", the once-thriving inns on the latter wilted, sickened and died, and the "Green Dragon" began to flourish, and eventually reigned in their stead.

Anthony drove on past the inn and within a few yards came to a right-hand turning which led to the Great North Road. A signpost here told him what he most desired to know—"Plashet—11 miles". From what he had been able to gather the village he sought seemed to lie about midway between Hatfield and Hertlngfordbury. Anthony wasted no time—he drove the car hard towards the Hertfordshire village of Plashet and the dwelling-place of Mr. A. Temple Spooner. The road was not too good, but the car behaved well so that he made his destination without mishap and in good time.

As he entered Plashet he encountered another old inn, but charming in the extreme. So charming, indeed, that he slowed down the pace of the car in order to appreciate more fully the inn's compelling and breathtaking beauty. The sign was unusual—it showed the inn of the 'Golden Gloves'. Anthony determined there and then that if by any chance Fate detained him that evening in Plashet, he would make the best of such detention with the hospitality that would be offered by the "Gloves".

A minute or so later he spotted the local Post-office. True to type, it combined the activities of a general shop, which was exactly what he had expected. Anthony stopped the car and alighted. A bell I rang loudly as he entered the shop. A wizened old woman with slanting eyes, two warts and a nutcracker chin peered at him sharply from the official side of the counter.

"Please help me," said Anthony smilingly, "with the address of a Mr. Spooner, who I have reason to believe lives near here. Full name A. Temple Spooner. Know the gentleman by any chance?"

"That I do," replied the old woman with bright pertness, "very well indeed. We get 'eaps of 'is letters through our 'ands 'ere. More for 'im than for the rest of the village put together. You want Wilton Lodge—that's the name of Mr. Spooner's 'ouse. Straight on from 'ere through the village, up the 'ill and it's the big 'ouse on the left—right at the top. You can't miss it—it's a big 'ouse, and when I say a big 'ouse, I mean a big 'ouse—d'ye get me?"

Anthony made for the door. "I think it may be said, madam, that I approximate understanding. Many thanks for your kindness."

2

Anthony drove straight in the direction of Wilton Lodge. Straight on through the village and up the hill. When the car reached the summit of the hill he saw a trail of chimney-smoke coming from a house some little distance away to the left. The house, he felt certain, from the old woman's description, must be Wilton Lodge.

He turned the car down the lane which presented itself and soon saw the end and edges of a lawn. The lawn was far from trim and obviously needed the quick ministration of a well-conditioned mower. Anthony stopped the car under the hedge and made the edges of the lawn without difficulty. As he stepped on to it the house came into better view immediately.

It was large and old-fashioned, but Anthony noticed, as he crossed towards it, that a modern, rather pretentiously imposing whitewashed wing had been recently added to it. Attached to this modern wing was a verandah, and as Anthony approached he could see the figure of a man standing on this verandah shading his eyes with his left hand. In Anthony's opinion this man was watching him. Watching him closely as he crossed the ill-kept lawn and advanced towards the house.

In due course Anthony came to the entrance to the verandah, and as he did so the man who had been watching him dropped his hand and took a couple of uncertain steps towards him. The room that was now revealed behind the verandah was both pleasant and inviting. On one side was a profusion of books, on the other glass.

Anthony looked expectantly at the man who now stood at the door, almost confronting him. He was of medium height, there was darkish hair on his head in places, his eyes were dark, his nose broad and flattish, his complexion rather florid and he had an unusually long line of jaw. The first impression to which Anthony came upon seeing him was that his restless eyes held a strangely peculiar light. When he spoke, the words he used came to Anthony almost as a shock—certainly very much as a surprise.

"Are you from the Police?" he asked simply and directly. The question took Anthony off his guard. It was almost the last question he would have anticipated. He had to make a quick decision. He made it—with the thought uppermost that one can always come back to things.

"No," he replied. "I merely wanted a few words with Mr. Temple Spooner. I may say that I have come rather a long way for that privilege. Have I the pleasure of—"

The man cut into the question with a decisive shake of the head. "I am not Mr. Spooner, if that's what you mean. This is Mr. Spooner's house—which you can say is in my charge, more or less. Certainly so just at the present moment. Can I do anything for you?"

There was something competent and efficient about this man which Anthony recognised immediately. Something keen . . . sharp-edged . . . almost knowledgeable. And his voice had a rather peremptory note in it. Anthony was acutely conscious that something inside himself was sounding a warning to him . . . advising him hotly and ardently to go slow . . . to have a care . . . to watch his step.

"I'm afraid," he said, feeling for his words, "that my business is of such a nature that it must be with Mr. Temple Spooner himself."

"In that case, then," came the instant rejoinder, "I'm afraid you won't be doing any business."

The man who spoke set his jaw. Anthony was struck by a most peculiar tone that was now in the man's voice. It had become more than peremptory. There had come a grating, gurgling, guttural sort of sound—something like the suction of soapsuds by a greedy sink. And he realised, of course, the full import of what had been said.

"You mean," he said, "that Mr. Spooner is not available?"

The man nodded briskly. "You can call it that if you like."

Anthony reflected. There were hidden meanings here. "Am I to take it," he said again, "that Mr. Spooner is not in residence? Is that what you mean?"

The man who faced him nodded again. "You couldn't put it better. That's just what I do mean."

"I see," replied, Anthony, "in that case, then, can you give me an address where I can find him?"

Before the man could reply, Anthony heard a light step behind him. He half turned so that he would be able to see the newcomer and received his second surprise since his arrival at Wilton Lodge. A second man was standing a few yards away from him. Save for the fact that the hair on his head in places was white in colour instead of dark, he was the exact replica of the man with whom Anthony had been in conversation. Brothers? Or father and son? Either condition was likely, so Anthony thought.

"What's this all about?" asked the elder man, "is it the Police?"

Curious! Each man evidently had formed the same first impression.

"No, father," came the reply, "I understand not. I thought the same thing as you myself, and said as much almost at once—but it's not so."

The elder man gestured with impatience. "What's this man's business, then. Have you asked him?"

"That's O.K., father. Don't worry about it. I've asked him. He says he's come here on some sort of business—to see Mr. Spooner."

"And you've told him Mr. Spooner's not here? That he can't see him?"

"Naturally I was just—"

Anthony judged it prudent to intervene. He addressed himself mainly to the man who had interrupted.

"Your son has told me that Mr. Spooner is not here. I thereupon enquired of him as to whether he could furnish me with Mr. Spooner's present address as I am extremely anxious to get in touch with him. That was the point at which we had arrived when you entered."

The elder man looked Anthony up and down—with evident suspicion. Then he turned to the dark and younger edition of himself.

"That's just about what we can't do, isn't it, Jim?"

"You've said it, James," came the somewhat surprising answer.

"I'm afraid I don't understand," said Anthony.

"And I'm afraid," said James, a little provocatively, perhaps, "that that's your funeral and we can't do anything about it."

Anthony began to make assessments. Speedy, searching assessments which he now knew that, had he been wiser, he should have made before. There was something abnormal here—that was becoming increasingly evident. Although he wasn't at all sure what it was. Each of these two men, between whom he stood, had thought at the point of original encounter with him that he was from the Police. Each, without the slightest beating about the bush, had actually asked a question to that effect. Why? Why should each of these men have anticipated a visit from the Police? What was wrong with the Temple Spooner *ménage*? And where was Temple Spooner himself? These thoughts and questions raced through Anthony's brain like the tumblers that enter the circus arena before the beginning of the performance proper. He determined to grasp the nettle.

"Look here, gentlemen," he said, "I have no wish to waste your time. I have still less wish to waste my own. You can understand that. You're men of the world and you know what business is. Why did you ask me when you first met me if I were the Police? Each one of you—independent of the other? You must have had a strong reason for so doing. Please be frank with me. Because, whatever happens, I can assure you that I intend to get in touch with Mr. Temple Spooner just as soon as I possibly can. It's vital that I should . . . please understand that."

The elder man looked rather apprehensively at his son. Each had listened to Anthony patiently and without comment. "What do you think, Jim?" said the senior man. "You've heard what this gentleman says. Shall we take a chance? Or shall we—"

The younger man shrugged his shoulders. "I think we might, James. Taking everything into consideration."

"I guess we will, then," said James. He turned to Anthony again and gestured. "Step inside, will you?"

3

Anthony accepted the invitation and stepped into the room behind the verandah. He saw the rows of books which evidently belonged to Temple Spooner and appraised them. A collection far beyond the average in number, in quality and in taste. But then he remembered. Spooner, no doubt, had unique opportunities to indulge in the collector's art. Books would be one of his first lines of attack. The elder of Anthony's hosts waved him to a chair.

"Sit down, will you? And before we proceed any further, may I ask your name? It isn't by any chance Berners, is it?"

"No. My name is Lotherington," replied Anthony, shaking his head, "and as I've already told you I have important business with Mr. Temple Spooner. Was he expecting a Mr. Berners, then?"

"Not necessarily," said James, somewhat uneasily; "it was a shot in the dark on my part. Forget it."

There ensued a period of silence. James broke it, as Anthony had intended him to.

"Well, Mr. Lotherington, I said I'd take a chance. And my son here more or less agreed with me. All I hope now is that I've done the right thing. Because if I haven't—the consequences may well be disastrous. To me, I mean. I'm too old to look for work—and I'm too old for a good many jobs . . . if I was lucky enough to land one of 'em. But that, I suppose, is neither here nor there as you might say. Especially from your point of view. I'd best put the cards on the table."

He paused. The pause had come, Anthony full well knew, at something very much like the critical moment. James of the grey hair was silent. Jim of the dark hair breathed hard, and his eyes were restless. Anthony waited quietly. He knew in his heart that anything in the nature of a prompting or an incitement would, in all probability, throttle the truth before birth. *Père et fils* were at the breaking-point of sensibility. James took a long breath. He looked across at Jim, his son, and then back to Anthony. "It's coming," thought Anthony, "whatever it is." His confidence was not misplaced. It came!

"The fact is, Mr. Lotherington," said James, in a husky sort of voice, "Mr. Spooner—the Guv'nor—has, as you might say, disappeared. We've heard nothing of him since a week last Tuesday. Not a blind word!"

Anthony tingled at the news. Once again in this extraordinary case something had come to him which he hadn't in the least anticipated. The two men in front of him, moreover, seemed to have shed something. They had become much more natural.

4

James continued. "That's the reason why both my son and me thought as how you must 'ave come from the Police. We thought you'd come with bad news for us. For days now we've feared the worst."

The last four words achieved headline importance from the emphasis which James gave them. Anthony began to question his two companions.

"What have you done about it? What steps have you taken? Have you actually informed the Police?"

"No," replied James, with a dubious shake of the head, "up to now we've done nothing about it. We've taken *no* steps. And as to going to the Police . . . " he broke off abruptly and shrugged his shoulders.

Anthony looked at him sharply. "Why is that?" he asked.

James shrugged his shoulders very much as he had before. "The Guv'nor's the Guv'nor and he's the wrong kind of man to upset. I don't suppose you know 'im as well as we do. I wouldn't cross him for all the gold in the Indies. Mind you, I've no complaints against him—don't think that he's fair and he's just and he's generous. But when it comes to a business deal where there's a spot of competition, I shouldn't like to do anything against his wishes. And it's possible that's what he's on now. That's what's took 'im away for so long. At least, that's pretty much the conclusion Jim and me have come to after thinkin' things over. That's so, isn't it, Jim?"

"That's so, James. That's it. I agree with every word you've said."

The filial support came immediately.

"Are these absences, then, a fairly regular occurrence? Does he often stay away like this? You say you've heard nothing of him since last Tuesday week?"

There was no ready reply to Anthony's questions. James looked across at Jim.

"What would you say to that, Jim?" he asked.

"Well . . . he *has* been away before—admitted . . . as we're both well aware of, but for not more than a couple of days or so. At the most. Certainly never as long as this time. It was when it came to the full week that father and me got a bit rattled. And when it went over the week we both fair got the wind up."

Anthony decided that the best results would be forthcoming from the boldest measures.

"Gentlemen," he said curtly, "you and I are equally in an unusual position. You don't know me—and I don't know you. In other words we're complete strangers to each other. But you've asked me to come in here this evening to discuss something with you which I can readily see is an anxiety and a worry to you. Now please understand that if it's at all in my power, I'm ready to help you. In that case, then—if you're ready and willing to accept that help which I've offered—please do what you said just now that you would do. Put all the cards on the table in the frankest way possible. Unless you do that. . . well, gentlemen, you can see for yourselves, you're handicapping me to such an extent that I just *can't* help you."

James approximated indignation and his aspirates became less frequent. "But we 'ave! We 'ave put the cards on the table! What is it you're suggestin' we've 'eld back?"

Anthony smiled. "Nothing. How can I? Suggestions are not for me. I'm in the dark."

"Listen 'ere, Mr. Lotherington," said James, "we don't know more about the matter than what we've told you. We don't enter into any of the Guv'nor's business deals. Never 'ave since we entered 'is service. We just look after this place for 'im—Wilton Lodge and serve 'im and look after 'im when he's 'ere. A week ago last Tuesday Mr. Spooner went out. 'E 'ad 'is suit-case with 'im—I can tell you that for certain. My son drove 'im to Plashet railway station in the car, as 'e always did when 'e went from there. 'E used to go from Plashet to the main line at Hatfield. When Jim left 'im at Plashet station last Tuesday week all 'e said to 'im was that 'e mightn't be back that same night, but if 'e wasn't 'e might be away for two or three days. That's all we know, and now you know it as well."

James had spoken quickly, and he paused for breath.

"I see," said Anthony, "and, of course, I accept what you say as true. But you see what it means, don't you? It means that if I'm going to help you I must question you with regard to Mr. Spooner and also with regard to the nature of some of his activities. And it will be up to you, of course, whether you answer my questions-or not. Whether you choose to go all the way with me. In other words, are you prepared to trust me?"

James looked cautiously at Jim. The latter's face was dark and brooding. Then it seemed to brighten suddenly.

"Maybe, father, with this gentleman we can take a chance and answer 'is questions. Don't you think so yourself?"

The elder man's caution was a long time leaving him. He considered carefully what his son had just said. Anthony watched the two faces in front of him. The likeness was certainly extraordinary. There was a silence lasting some seconds. Then the face of James brightened in the manner of the face of Jim.

"Maybe we can, Jim," said James. "Take a chance, as you say." He turned slowly towards Anthony. "What would be the questions, sir, that you'd be wantin' to ask us?"

"First of all," demanded Anthony, "I should like to ask you this. Who is this Mr. Berners?"

"Berners?" echoed James questioningly. "Berners?" repeated a second or so later.

"Yes," replied Anthony, "Berners. You asked me if my name were Berners when you first saw me here. Surely you remember?" "Of course I did," said James, his face clearing, "you're quite right. I should have remembered the name at once."

He looked towards Jim. Anthony thought that he was looking for a lead of some kind.

"I'll repeat my question, then," said Anthony. "Who is Mr. Berners? You must have had the man on your mind to ask me if I were he."

"I couldn't tell you," murmured James, with a slow shake of the head. "I don't know the man from Adam and that's Gospel truth if ever it were spoken." He saw the doubt in Anthony's face, and at once proceeded to justify his apparently contradictory statements. "When I asked you, Mr. Lotherington, if your name was Berners, the name came to me in this way. Some few days before the Guv'nor disappeared I happened to overhear 'im speaking on the telephone in 'is room. I wasn't eavesdroppin'—I wouldn't like you to think that for a minute. I'd taken something into the room that he'd asked for—that's why I was in there. And as I came out I was just closin' the door behind me—I distinctly 'eard 'im say 'well, in that case, then, you must get in touch with Berners at once. He's the man who can supply the information.' That was why, when I first clapped eyes on you, my mind jumped to the idea that you might be this fellow Berners I'd 'eard Mr. Spooner speakin' about."

James paused and took a pipe and pouch from his pocket. "And that's the honest truth," he concluded, as he slowly started to fill the pipe.

Anthony, when he had heard him out, realised that he must accept the statement for what it was worth. He had no means of checking its authenticity and there seemed no strong reason, as far as he could see, why James shouldn't be speaking the truth. So he tucked away the name "Berners" in one of his mind-pockets and tried another approach.

"You say that Mr. Spooner has been away since last Tuesday week? You did say that, didn't you?" James and Jim both nodded.

"What about his correspondence, then? Has anything come during that time that might possibly give you a lead anywhere?"

James looked at Jim and Jim looked at James. "Well, it's a peculiar thing," said the latter slowly, "now you've mentioned it, but since the Guv'nor's been away there's been little or no post come for 'im. As a rule 'is mail's pretty thick and 'eavy—and you've 'it on one of the main reasons why Jim and me's been on the worry-guts since 'e's been gone. It's given us a sort of feelin' at the back of our minds that in some way the old fellow's been put out of circulation, as it were. See the way I'm thinkin'?"

"I'm afraid I do," replied Anthony, "only too well—there's a significance about it which can't be ignored . . . I agree with you."

"Well, then, Mr. Lotherington," said Jim, "seems to me it comes to this. And it's no good our shuttin' our eyes to it. What do we do about it?"

"I don't know," answered Anthony, "that's a question that requires a good deal of thinking about. I'm too much in the dark to give an opinion. Are you sure—absolutely sure—that you can't help me any further? Try to think now."

Each man shook his head. Anthony didn't give up, however. He came at them with admirable persistence.

"Are you absolutely positive that neither of you can think of anything which might help to explain Mr. Spooner's absence? Or, looking at it in another way, which might suggest a reason for somebody doing him an injury?"

The dual head-shaking was again in evidence. Anthony tried yet again.

"Don't confine yourselves to thinking entirely of important things. It might conceivably be something absurdly trivial. Something that Mr. Spooner said. Something that he did."

More shakes of the two heads. Anthony still maintained the attack. "Somebody who called here?"

Jim spoke first. "No. Nothing. There isn't anything. We're just Mr. Spooner's servants—no more. We've never been anything more than that. His life—his business life—didn't concern us—it didn't touch us at all. We shouldn't know anything about it."

"That's right," confirmed James. "Jim's dead right. Servants! 'Ewers of wood and drawers of water. No more than that."

"Yes," said Anthony, with a final effort. "I can understand all that perfectly well, you've made it clear to me, but what about Mr. Spooner's private life? The life that he led here, away from his business and the cares which the business inevitably must have brought? What about that? You touched on that side of him, didn't you? You must have, if only for the fact that you lived here with him?"

"So we did," said Jim sturdily; "but that was all. We lived 'ere with 'im. You've said it, Mr. Lotherington. That's where it began and where it ended. Because the Guv'nor 'ad no private life. His business life was the lot. The 'ole bundle. He never thought of nothing else—nothing. And if you don't believe me, you ask father."

James puffed tobacco-smoke and looked deadly serious. "Jim's right, Mr. Lotherington," he said. "Jim's dead right. Do what you like, you can't get away from it. The Guv'nor was business first, last and always. 'Im and 'is private life were strangers to each other. And now you see 'ow things are with us, and why we can't 'elp you—much as we should like to. If we could, believe me nothin' would give us greater pleasure; but we can't—it's not in our power."

Anthony submitted with reluctance to the inevitable. "In the circumstances, then," he said judicially, "I think you should lose no time whatever in going to the Police and informing them of Mr. Spooner's disappearance. I think you owe it to him—and to yourselves."

James took his pipe from his mouth. "You honestly think that?"

"I honestly think that."

"You wouldn't give 'im a day or two longer? Wait and see if 'e turns up? Just in case like?"

"Not five minutes or even five seconds. And I'll tell you why. I have strong reason to think that about the time you say Mr. Spooner disappeared he was in some kind of communication with a certain Mr. Lovelace of Loveridge in Essex. That, for your information, happens to be the same Mr. Lovelace who a few days ago was murdered in his own house. Or as good as. You may have seen references to the affair in the daily Press."

Anthony paused to see the effect of this statement. Jim turned red. James went white. Then the latter nodded.

"I certainly 'ave seen about it, Mr. Lotherington, and no doubt Jim 'ere 'as, too. Just through readin' the papers in the ordinary way. But I'll take my oath I 'ad no reason to connect it in any way with the Guv'nor. Neither the name of the murdered man nor the place where 'e was killed conveyed nothing special to me. And if that's not the truth may I never speak another word in this life."

The normal colour slowly ebbed back to his face. Jim contributed support.

"That's true enough," he declared stoutly, "that murder in Essex meant nothing to us. I'll swear it didn't—same as father. All we did was read about it."

Anthony cut in before Jim could go any further. "That's as may be. All the same, you can see why the Spooner disappearance is a case for the Police, can't you? The issue's clear cut. One murder, you know, very often leads to another."

James nodded his head slowly. "That's very true, Mr. Lotherington—very true indeed. And the more I see of things in this business—and the more I 'ear of 'em—the more I'm forced to the conclusion that my poor old Guv'nor's 'ad it. What do you say, Jim?"

"I don't like the look of things at all, father." Jim shook his head with grave foreboding. "And that's a fact. And I reckon this gentleman's right. We ought to report the Guv'nor's absence without any further delay. If not to-night—then certainly first thing in the morning."

"Well spoken," said Anthony. He looked at the time by his wrist-watch. "Very well, then," he continued, "no good purpose can be served by my remaining here. I'm glad you've come to that decision, and I'll wish you gentlemen a very good evening."

As he rose to take his leave he gestured significantly towards the telephone. "Don't forget the old adage, gentlemen. Delays are dangerous. This evening would be even better than to-morrow morning."

CHAPTER 7

1

Anthony kicked off a shoe in his bedroom at the 'Golden Gloves'. The problem of Lovelace's death grew more complicated and more intricate at every turn. The steps he had already taken he retraced in his mind, as he brushed his hair before retiring for the night.

Scudamore, Lovelace (or his house, to be precise), Forbes and company, Mrs. Forbes (the delightful Evelyn), Temple Spooner, the man in the shop in Cavalier Circus, James and his son Jim, and now he was faced with a man by the name of Berners. Berners! Who the heck was Berners? And how much of what James had said had been true? Was Berners a clue worth following up? Or was it altogether too faint, too shadowy, too nebulous?

Anthony slid into his pyjamas and took his problem into bed. There was so much conflict in his mind that he was afraid sleep would tarry in its coming. The sequence of names danced through his brain again. This time with additions. Helen Repton, Scudamore, Dixon, Forbes and his crowd, Toplady and his better-half, Spooner, the God-fearing counterman in Cavalier Circus, Jim and James, his father, and now this XYZ Berners fellow. Berners! Berners! The name was by way of being familiar to him. Peculiar thing that. Now he came to think of it, he'd seen it somewhere—very recently, too. Now where the blazes was it? That name Berners! He'd read it somewhere. Not so very long ago. Something he'd been reading indoors. Not in the street—or out-of-doors anywhere. Certainly not a poster or on an advertisement hoarding. Something he'd read in his own arm-chair in his flat. Was it a name often met with? On the whole, Anthony thought, no. There was Berners Street, of course, in London. All the same he wouldn't say that it was a common name by any means. Yes, he'd read it. No doubt about that. Now what was the connexion?

Anthony racked his brain for the appropriate association. First of all methodically, systematically. Then, by a change of tactics, carelessly, lightly and even nonchalantly with just mere ripples of thought. But the threads at which he grasped would not come to him. Twice he thought that he was within an ace of achievement, but success eluded him. And in time, as was inevitable, perhaps, Anthony Bathurst fell asleep.

2

And then, as luck would have it, Anthony caught up with his elusive Pimpernel when he was shaving on the following morning in the bathroom at the 'Golden Gloves'.

Just as the razor-blade took the first line of hair from his cheek, leaving the line of drying soap, and when his mind was mainly concerned with the prospective possibilities of the breakfast which the 'Golden Gloves' was about to produce, the association for which he had fought so fiercely the night before slid quietly and smoothly into his brain and said "Good morning! Nice day! I believe you wanted me, didn't you?"

Anthony removed the razor from his face and stood there with it poised in the region of the tip of his ear. The *Sunday Times* issue of about two Sabbaths back! Might be three, perhaps. But certainly not more. On the literary page—where the new books are advertised and some of them criticised. Yes, that was the place all right. There had been an advertisement of a book by a fellow with the surname of Berners. At the foot of the second column on the left. Yes, he could see the full set-up now in his mind's eye—right bang in front of him. The publisher had been Walloon and Co., of Nightshade Street. The name of the particular book had been *Lincolnshire Laziness*. By a man named Berners.

And then Anthony gasped, for his memory, now working at full stretch, had brought something else back to him. This visual memory that had so suddenly drifted to him was keen and accurate. "Ready next Thursday. 9s. 6d. net. *Lincolnshire Laziness*, by C. L. D. Berners. Author of *The House of Berners, Charcoal Berners and Others* (6th impression), and *Girls in Lincoln Green*, Messrs. Walloon and Co., London, New York, Bombay, Calcutta, Montreal, Melbourne, Sydney, and Cape Town." And the piercing point of it all which had brought him, as has already been said, to the gasping point, was the author's full name. C. L. D. Berners! Or rather, to be more precise, the author's initials. C. L. D.! Those confounded initials which Anthony had conjured with on innumerable occasions during recent days. Indeed, since he had first encountered them down the avenue of Martin Scudamore's story, they had rarely been out of his thoughts or absent from his calculations. Charles Linklater Delevigne! And there had been no surname Delevigne with those other Christian names in the telephone directory when he had looked, or had the P.M.G. reported one. Could it be that this unknown fellow Berners with whom Spooner had sought contact just before his disappearance was the writer of books with initials to his surname—C. L. D.?

And following up the same line of argument, did those letters C. L. D. stand for Charles Linklater Delevigne? Anthony thought that it certainly looked like it. He brought the razor along the line of his jaw with his customary certainty and firmness. He was feeling distinctly pleased with himself. Things were moving at last.

Directly after breakfast he'd get away from the 'Golden Gloves' and establish contact with Andrew MacMorran. The Inspector could then deal with the new Temple Spooner entanglement, apart from the promised activities of James and Jim with the Police authorities which might or might not materialise. This would leave Anthony free to go after the mysterious Berners—and go after him he certainly must!

3

Fortified by an unusually good breakfast in this country of fair shares for some, Anthony drove away from the 'Golden Gloves', determined to make touch with MacMorran at the earliest possible moment.

The main question in his mind as he drove concerned the Inspector's present whereabouts. He might be at the 'Yard'—on the other hand he might have started off again for Loveridge. The thing for Anthony to do was to make sure on that particular point as soon as he could. He would look out for a telephone kiosk and get through to the 'Yard' from there. About a quarter of a mile along the road the kiosk he was looking for presented itself, and Anthony lost no time in 'phoning through to the 'Yard'. His luck, for once, broke the right way. MacMorran was there. After a few moments of waiting, Anthony heard the well-known tones.

"Look, Andrew," he said, "I rang now because I wanted a word with you. As soon as possible. Tell me, did you intend going to Loveridge to-day?"

"I did and I do," replied MacMorran, "but what are you on to? Something important?"

"Yes. I rather fancy it is. Although, of course, it's early days. Look here! Hang up on Loveridge until I've had that word with you. I shan't be too long. I'll come straight to the 'Yard'. Be with you at half past ten or as near to that as I can make it. Can you do that?"

"Yes. That can be managed. I'll wait here for you."

4

The room of Andrew MacMorran at the 'Yard' was, for once, silent. Every now and then MacMorran looked up and glanced at the clock. When he wasn't doing this his pen was scratching a petulant path across paper. At thirty-three minutes past ten he frowned.

Just as the frown gathered power and dimension the telephone bell rang and MacMorran, nourishing the frown gallantly, leant over and picked up the receiver. Then he said curtly after a moment or so, "O.K. Send him in at once."

The door of his room opened and Anthony entered—grey-suited, grey-eyed and debonair. He went to his favourite seat on the corner of the Inspector's table and smiled on his host.

"Sicklied o'er—eh—with the pale cast of thought? And I come with enterprises of great pith and moment. Well, well, well! And no cordial greeting for this silver-footed messenger. Beyond the great-grandfather of all MacMorran frowns."

"You seem in good spirits. Afraid I'm not." MacMorran sounded grim.

"Why? What Ate has come hot from hell to plague you, Andrew?"

"Look in the ruddy glass for that answer. But for you, and listening to you, I should have been in Loveridge by now." MacMorran's smile had no cordiality about it.

"Tush," replied Anthony. "Likewise tosh. Loveridge and its like may wait. Behold I come with news of Loveridge. The affair marches. Unpin your ears and listen to me, my unmerry Andrew and you'll see what I mean."

MacMorran laid his pen by the side of his blotting-pad and picked up a pencil.

"Tell me," he said. As he spoke he began to draw letters of the alphabet-ornate and decoratively shaded as to their uprights and cross-pieces.

Anthony grinned at what he saw. "Have a care, Andrew. That's more or less what Lovelace did. And I deplore the mention to you of his sorry and untimely end. I should hate to think—"

MacMorran pushed back his chair. "What on earth," he said, "are you talking about? Do you mind telling me?"

Anthony told him—with a plenitude of detail. MacMorran shed his irritability and listened attentively.

5

From time to time during the telling of the story MacMorran and Anthony exchanged significant glances. Then MacMorran filled his pipe and there soon came a heavy haze of tobacco smoke. When Anthony had finished his recital of the facts relative to Temple Spooner plus all relevant Spoonerisms, MacMorran spoke.

"I don't want to quench your enthusiasm. Far from it. But the absence of Spooner for the time being may mean just nothing. Coincidence—no more! Still, you've done well. I won't deny that. To get on to him in the way you did. The point that occurs to me now is this—have those two fellows at this Plashet place come across yet as they agreed to? I can find out, of course. What do you think? Shall I?"

"Please yourself. Whether they have or not isn't so frightfully important. As I see things, the case must break before long. What *is* of importance is Spooner's disappearance. I suggest you go to Plashet, see the local police, and then have a look round Spooner's place yourself."

Anthony rose. "Andrew, this case grows more absorbingly interesting each turn it takes. And I still can't hazard a guess as to *why* Lovelace was killed. From Loveridge we've got to Plashet. Who knows where we shall line up next?"

"Will you come to Plashet with me?"

Anthony considered the Inspector's question. "I'd rather not, if you don't mind, Andrew." He paused and the Inspector was quick to notice the pause.

"Why not?" he asked sharply.

Anthony grinned at him cheerfully. "Don't want to go to Plashet. Been to Plashet. Want to go somewhere else."

MacMorran pursed his lips. Then he sat well back in his chair and began to scratch his head. Anthony stood there and looked at him.

He seemed as though he were about to speak again and the Inspector glanced up at him. Anthony suddenly changed his mind, however, and MacMorran said,

"I see. Mustn't ask questions, I suppose. Not good for me. Is that it?"

"Not exactly, Andrew. I don't know that I'd put it like that. Anyhow, I won't make any secret about it. There *is* something I want to follow up. It may turn out to be less than useless. On the other hand it may be a real winner. At the moment it's no more than a mere name. All the same, I have hopes. Let's leave it at that."

MacMorran grunted. "H'm. Like that, is it? Right-o then." There came a silence. MacMorran looked at Anthony. Anthony looked at MacMorran. As Anthony smiled, the Inspector began to speak, slowly and deliberately.

"I put up with you as I do," he said, "because I suppose I've got used to you. You have a knack of doin' things—when other people can't—of bein' right when by all the Gods of Logic and Plain Fact you ought to be wrong—it's funny—but there it is. It wouldn't surprise me if one day they put a statue up of you—just at the entrance down below. Short of deifyin' you, that's about—"

MacMorran ducked just in time. When he reassembled himself, the door was shut and Anthony Bathurst had gone. The Inspector chuckled as he picked up the copy of *Stone's* from where it nestled on the carpet.

"I was quicker than he was," he muttered. The chuckle took on fresh life. MacMorran felt decidedly better.

CHAPTER 8

1

Anthony sat on the arm of his favourite arm-chair and dialled a number. The reply came as anticipated. "Walloon and Co."

"Good morning. My name's Bathurst. Anthony Bathurst. Will you put me through, please, to your Mr. Ainsworth if he's about?"

"Please wait and I will."

Within a few moments a new voice came to Anthony's ears. With tones that were soft and deep and rounded.

"This is Ainsworth speaking. Is that you, Bathurst? Good! Rogers rang up a little while ago and told me you wanted a word with me. So I've been more or less expecting you to come on. What can I do for you?"

"My dear Ainsworth, something excessively simple. I want the address of one of your people."

"Staff do you mean?"

"No—one of the people writing for you. One of your authors. As a matter of fact you've published a book of his very recently. Within the last month I should say from memory. C. L. D. Berners. *Lincolnshire Laziness*. That's the name, isn't it?"

"Quite right, my dear fellow. Selling very well, too. Which is something these days, I can tell you. You want Berners's address? Wait half a jiffy and you shall have it. I can tell you one thing about it, it's not in London, I do know that, or even near London. Hang on a minute."

Anthony could hear the rustling of files and the crisp crackling of paper. Then Ainsworth's voice came again.

"Are you there? Here's the gen you're wanting. 'Neville House, Burgoyne, near Old Leake, Lincolnshire'."

Anthony noted the details. "Now can you oblige me with the gentleman's Christian names?"

Ainsworth chuckled. "I can. Only too well. Rather a mouthful. Charles Linklater Delevigne."

"My best thanks, Ainsworth—good for you." Anthony replacedthe receiver. Then he straddled the arm of his chair and began furiously to think. Lincolnshire! Interesting—definitely! There was a link with Lincolnshire. Lovelace, the murdered man, had possessed Lincolnshire connexions. He had actually lived in Lincolnshire before moving into Essex. Anthony distinctly recalled Scudamore's statement to that effect when he had brought Helen Repton to his flat and first set the ball rolling.

Anthony attempted to fit the various links in the chain. Lovelace from Lincoln. Lovelace pulls in Spooner of Cavalier Circus. Spooner, before his disappearance, conjures up Berners, and lo and behold Berners takes the case back to Lincolnshire, the very place from which Lovelace had come in the beginning. And most telling point of all perhaps, Berners's Christian names turn out to be the very names featured by Scudamore in his original story.

Anthony slid off the arm of his chair and walked to the window. He began to rub his hands. An early visit to Mr. Berners, the author, of Neville House, Burgoyne, near Old Leake, was most certainly indicated.

2

Anthony travelled by train from King's Cross by way of Peterborough, Spalding and Boston. The carriage of his choice was appallingly hot and the air was stifling. It was a relief for him to alight at Boston and feel on his face the keen east wind blowing from the sea. A taxi outside the railway station was a welcome sight. Anthony commissioned it immediately and the driver seemed quite conversant with the directions Anthony gave him.

"It's not over-far," he said in a confidential sort of voice, "and almost a straight road."

Just over a quarter of an hour's driving brought them to the village boundary and Anthony spotted the directional sign from the window of the taxi. When Burgoyne actually came into sight as a real place distinct from a mere name it was huddled round the village church. To Anthony's eyes there were three prongs as of a fork. There was the road to Old Leake, the road from Boston down which they were travelling, and a sort of country lane that ran in a southerly direction. The driver nodded towards this lane.

"Mr. Berners's 'ouse be down at the end o' this 'ere."

The lane turned out to be a good quarter of a mile in length. On one side of it were pastureland and woods. On the other, all that Anthony could see suggested the remnants of a forest. On the left, the hedge screened the sight after the first hundred yards or so and the taxi began to pass a small and rather ancient cluster of half-timbered cottages.

Soon after passing these, the taxi began to slow up and Anthony saw a house away to the right of the lane. It was a biggish, red brick affair and the first impressions it gave the onlooker were of solidity and comfort. It had a double front with a large bay window on each side. The garden at which Anthony looked was well-kept and flaunted a wealth and surprising variety of colour from as fine a collection of gladioli as Anthony had ever seen.

"'Ere you are, sir," said the taxi-driver, 'Neville 'Ouse', as asked for."

He peered forward from the driving-seat to look at the clock. Anthony handed him a ten-shilling note.

"That's all right, driver."

"Thank you very much, sir," said the driver; "you wouldn't like me to wait, I suppose?"

"Might be too long, old chap. Probably will be. So I don't think I'll trouble you."

"If you should want me to come for you, sir, you can always 'phone through to the railway station. They'll deliver a message to the rank. Say it's for Stump Motor Services and ask for Bob Cherry. That O.K.?"

Anthony smiled. "Thanks for the gen. I'll certainly remember what you say. But I may not need your valuable services. Who knows? It's possible that my host may take pity on me and drive me back."

"Some 'opes," said the driver, as he let in the clutch. "Still, 'ave it your way."

"Like that, is it?" thought Anthony, as he made his way up the gravelled path to the house of red brick.

3

A prim, white-aproned maid with fair hair and rosy cheeks answered the door. Anthony used one of his best smiles as an opening gambit and handed her his card.

"Would you be good enough?" he asked—"to Mr. Berners? Thank you so much."

The maid looked at Anthony and then at the card with equal diffidence.

"Do you happen to have an appointment with Mr. Berners?" she asked, "does he expect you?"

"Not exactly," said Anthony hopefully, "but I'm sure Mr. Berners will see me. If you'll just be good enough to give him that card I have no doubt that he'll—"

"In that case, please wait here then," returned the maid.

Anthony waited as he had been bidden. The maid returned. "Come this way, if you please," she said rather mincingly—and Anthony went.

There seemed to be two halls to the house separated by an unusual-looking staircase of wood. They were floored in a kind of black and white marble. Anthony could hear a voice beyond the halls, which were full of sunlight. The maid led him to a room on the right. It had lime-green panelling with deep windows on two sides. The sun was reaching and flooding this room as it had reached the halls. It was a cheerful room, sunny and benignant. In the middle stood a table covered with green baize. In a chair at the table sat a man. There were shelves against the walls of new white wood and on them were piles of papers and stacks of blue books. On the table, in front of the seated man, were a typewriter and three filing-baskets. As Anthony followed the maid into the room the man at the table stood up. Anthony confessed inwardly to some surprise at his appearance. Berners was evidently a man in early middle age. His body was lumpish and heavy and he was dressed in a suit of loose country tweed. It would seem, too, thought Anthony as he took in more of the picture, that he wasn't too sartorially scrupulous. The collar of his beige-tinted shirt was distinctly dirty and crumpled, the suit was ill-fitting, and his latest shave must have been at least forty-eight hours old. His hairy face was florid and red-veined in places, but for all its colour it conveyed no strict impression of definitely good health. It was friendly, however, which, from Anthony's standpoint meant a good deal, but at the same time it left him with a most clear impression that from some cause Berners's nerves were all to hell, that Berners himself was fully aware of this, and because of it, Berners was almost at all times fully on his guard and inordinately wary.

Anthony opened the ball at once. "Sorry to disturb you like this, Mr. Berners. I know how busy you must be, but if you could spare me say half an hour I'd be eternally obliged to you."

Berners frowned a little—made a sign to the girl and she at once withdrew from the room. As she closed the door behind her he went across to one of the shelves and moved a heap of papers from a chair. He carried the chair to a place near the table and gestured to Anthony rather jerkily.

"Here you are, my dear chap. Sit yourself down there. More comfortable than standing."

Anthony smiled at the courtesy, thanked Berners and sat down. As he sat, Berners cackled into a rather extraordinary sort of laugh. It was high-pitched and non-masculine.

"Now what's it all about?" he inquired. His strange restless eyes darted round and about the room and Anthony became even more aware of the oddness and extreme nerviness of the man. "I won't say," said Berners, "that I'm absolutely bursting to talk to you, because I'm not. Far from it in fact. I'm too damned busy. So please get it over as soon as you possibly can."

"I'll do my best. I'll cut everything in the nature of preliminaries. First of all, are you acquainted with a man by the name of A. Temple Spooner?"

"Never heard of him," replied Berners blandly. Inwardly Anthony was both surprised and disappointed. The blank wall had appeared in front of him all too quickly for his peace of mind.

"Who is he?" followed up Berners, "when he's at home? Should I know him?"

"Not sure," returned Anthony, "but I had hoped your answer would be different. Still, I'll be frank—franker perhaps than I've been hitherto. But there's a murder on the menu—hence my journey up here, my call on you and the bother I'm causing you at this moment."

Berners looked at him in astonishment. "Tell me," he said simply. "Murders aren't exactly daily occurrences." Anthony told him the bare story of the Lovelace killing. Berners listened to him with rapt attention. Anthony concluded his narrative by saying,

"I have reason to believe that Lovelace, the murdered man, had been in recent contact with this man Spooner, who is himself missing at this moment, and I also believe that Spooner himself was desirous—I won't go beyond that yet awhile—of meeting you. Hence these tears."

Berners looked genuinely surprised at Anthony's statement. "Desirous of meeting me? What on earth could he have wanted me for?" His florid face grew florider.

"That," replied Anthony, "is just the information I hoped to obtain from you, Mr. Berners. But it seems that my confidence was misplaced."

Berners shook his head decisively. "I'm afraid you're barking up the wrong tree. I tell you candidly, I've never even heard of the man—let alone seen him."

"I accept your word, of course. But now, would you be good enough to tell me this? Some time ago a statement was received by the police authorities to the effect that a certain person had called on you with regard to a matter that concerned, shall we say, this very Lovelace who was subsequently murdered. It may well have been with regard to something that was in Lovelace's possession. In fact the odds are very heavily in favour of this. Can you recall the incident? Because this person may very well have been Spooner."

"Lovelace? To do with Lovelace—who you tell me lived in Essex? No, sir, I regret to disappoint you yet again, but very definitely no, sir! The name in this connexion, like the other, is entirely unfamiliar to me."

Berners blew out his cheeks and his collar seemed to become dirtier and more disreputable every minute. He rose from his chair with the obvious intention of terminating the interview.

"Well, there it is. I'm afraid I can't help you. Is there anything else that I can do for you? Otherwise—"

He gestured towards the papers on the table in front of him with a significance that Anthony could not possibly misunderstand. Anthony rose as Berners had.

"No," he said. "I don't think there is in the circumstances that you've outlined. You see, you've knocked away my supports. My case, or rather the beginnings of my case, were almost entirely built on the supposition that you and Temple Spooner were not unacquainted. Directly you denied that condition, my supports, as I said, were knocked away and my case fell to the ground. As it was inevitable it should. I won't detain you a second longer, Mr. Berners. Thank you for your courtesy, and my sincere apologies for having taken up so much of your time."

Berners made some sort of a bow in acknowledgment and pressed the bell. Anthony wasted no time in making for the door—he knew that the moment had come to get out.

4

On his way down the gravelled drive Anthony stopped to admire one of the beds of amazingly lovely gladioli. There were in colours, lavender, coral salmon, pink, yellow, wine-red, magenta, deep purple, flame, orange and white. Anthony lifted his horticultural cap to them. One particular specimen which he identified as "Paradise", would, he felt positive, have been a prizewinner almost anywhere.

The question at once rose in his mind with regard to transport for the return journey to the railway station. Decision was quick. Anthony resolved to walk back. He would trouble neither Bob Cherry nor the Stump Motor Services. He was not aware of the fact at the time he made the decision, but it was by way of being momentous. Had he telephoned for the taxi as advised by his driver on the recent journey, and ridden back to the railway station, he might never have solved the Lovelace problem. At any rate, it is certain that he would not have solved it as quickly as he did. Thus is History made.

CHAPTER 9

1

As Anthony came into Boston and reached the main lines of shops his attention was attracted by a rather high-class stationers, bookshop and circulating library. The three services mentioned were combined in the one establishment. This fact was well advertised to the public in the windows.

Something caused Anthony to stop and to glance into them. Many recently published novels were displayed on a glass stand, including almost all that had achieved anything like success. As Anthony looked in the windows at them he knew what it was precisely that had caught his eye. Standing on one of the hanging glass supports were six books—or rather six volumes of the same title. Anthony's curiosity was at once aroused by the card which was displayed above the books. In large black letters on a white ground he read "Your Local Author. Read *The House of Berners*, by C. L. D. Berners. Price 9s. 6d."

Anthony felt in his pocket for a stray currency note. "If I'm any judge," he said to himself, "old Andrew MacMorran would charge this on his expenses account. When I've finished with it, I'll make him a present of it."

Anthony entered the shop and made the purchase. If it did nothing else, the book would beguile the journey, or at least part of it, between Boston and King's Cross.

As he entered the door of his compartment the thought struck him— all he had obtained from his journey to Lincolnshire was a new book. For which he had expended the sum of 9s. 6d. Plus, of course, the railway fare from town. Anthony grinned at his thoughts. He was thinking once again of MacMorran. If MacMorran had been with him on this journey, the

Inspector, by this time, would have been enveloped in a deep depression. A depression which would have lasted all the way back to King's Cross. If not farther!

About a quarter of an hour out of Boston Anthony picked up the Berners book from the seat beside him and began to browse through its pages. To his surprise somewhat, the book was not a work of fiction, as he had imagined it to be when he made the purchase. It was no more and no less than an account of a famous house situated at Orme in Lincolnshire which, according to the author, had once been in the Berners family for a period of nearly six hundred years.

The title now explained itself. According to Berners, the author, the house had been built by an ancestor of his in the twelfth century and had remained in the Berners family until the year 1733, when it had been sold as it stood to an Army officer named Colonel Sir Clive Braund. Many extravagant claims were made for the house in the book, but there was no doubt whatever in Anthony's mind after he had read the opening chapters that it was a building of supreme historical interest. The author made it abundantly clear that in his opinion it had been a crying and lasting shame on his family that the Berners house had ever been allowed to go out of their hands. Even though the separating had been dictated by increasing poverty.

The first De Berners in England had been a close companion of the Norman William from whom had come the first grant of land for services rendered. And the De Berners influence had evidently reached its zenith nearly one hundred and fifty years after in the reign of King John. Lackland. So much so in fact that the Roger de Berners of that time had been an unusually close and intimate friend of that ill-starred monarch. Anthony read the following extract with more than normal interest.

It must be partly admitted that King John had never possessed the happy touch. Either as a ruler or as a man. Under his rule, the country went progressively from one trouble to another. One of the worst blunders he ever made in an astonishing series of false steps was to incur the anger and displeasure of Pope Innocent III. The immediate result was that the Pope placed England under an interdict. The King had refused to sanction the Pope's nomination to the Archbishopric of Canterbury, and, much to the King's annoyance, the ecclesiastics at Canterbury had supported his Holiness. John, therefore, proceeded to treat the unfortunate clerics with the utmost brutality. This conduct of his persisted so long that a reproval from Rome was inevitable. It came! In the form of a threatened interdict, if immediate and adequate reparation were not forthcoming. John, true to form, treated the Pope's threat with royal contempt. Roger de Wendover, the contemporary historian, has recorded these interesting facts.

"The King became nearly mad with rage when he received the Papal threat and realised its full import. He broke forth in words of furious blasphemy against the Pope and all his cardinals, swearing by God's Teeth that if they or any other priests soever presumptuously dared to lay his dominions under an interdict, he would retaliate to the hilt by the banishing of all the English clergy and by the confiscation of all the property of the Church; adding that in the event of his finding any of the Pope's clerks in England he would pack them off back to Rome with their eyes gouged out and their noses split so that they should be at once recognised and distinguished there from all other people."

This oath of John's, however, as may well be imagined, had no effect upon his Holiness's determination. For, on the Easter Monday of the year 1208, Innocent III carried out his threat. His own legates, the three Bishops, London, Ely and Winchester, proclaimed a general interdict on the whole of England. The consequences of this were many and far-reaching. All religious services were discontinued almost immediately. The two exceptions to this ban were auricular confession and the last ministrations of Holy Church to those in extremis. The plight and discomfort of his subjects, however, did not disturb the obstinate and stubborn King. He was oblivious to them and he immediately devised a form of retaliation.

Much of the Church property was confiscated and the clergy reduced to a most miserable standard of existence as regards both food and clothing allowances. To quote again from the historian Roger de Wendover,

"The corn of the clergy was everywhere locked up and distrained for the benefit of the royal revenue. The concubines of the priests and clerks were taken and held by the servants of the King and forced to ransom themselves at great expense. Monks and other ordained persons, if they were found travelling on the roads, were dragged from their horses, robbed of all they had and basely ill-treated by the King's satellites and there was nowhere where Justice could be obtained for them."

"At John's side at this time and perhaps most prominent of all in these activities were Roger de Berners and William de Courcy Hillisleigh, who each pillaged, purloined and pilfered to such an extent as to amass considerable riches for themselves in a comparatively short time. The papal interdict lasted into the year 1214 and the English peasantry, whose piety was such a conspicuous feature of the Middle Ages, suffered greatly. It is clear to all close students of this period of history that Roger de Berners remained a close favourite of the monarch until John's death in 1216 and in addition to the wealth that he had amassed, was the recipient of many costly gifts and royal favours."

"Hillisleigh, on the other hand, fell from grace as far as the royal intimacy was concerned and it is believed that John had him put to death in circumstances of extreme cruelty just prior to the signing of Magna Carta in 1215. In this connexion, it is held by some historians that Hillisleigh was betrayed by de Berners."

Anthony stopped reading for a time and let the book rest on his lap. Where was he getting to? Although he had gone back over seven hundred years he asked himself this question for the reason that he had a strong idea that he was getting somewhere!

Spooner was after Berners. He knew that! Why? Had Spooner been after Lovelace also? If so, why? Anthony racked his brains for reasons that would satisfy.

Roger de Berners, this gentleman of the early thirteenth century, had evidently been somebody in his time. A close favourite of the King, near the King, and with the ear of the King! He had been a man of great wealth and the recipient of—what had been the exact words? Anthony referred to what he had just read. "Many costly gifts and royal favours."

Anthony closed the book again and unwrapped some more thoughts. When had John died? 1216—the year after the historic act at Runnymede. After the notorious disaster that overtook him in the Wash. The Wash! Lincolnshire again. The territory which Anthony had left but a short time ago. The territory where Lovelace, the murdered man, had himself lived and resided prior to moving to Loveridge. Lincolnshire yet again! The territory of the Berners family and the territory of Lovelace.

It would be interesting to find out where exactly Lovelace had resided. Had Martin Scudamore mentioned it? Anthony ransacked his mind in an effort of remembrance. To no avail. He could find no recollection of Scudamore referring to any particular place. And yet . . . !

Anthony set to work again on a course of mental gymnastics. How had Dick Lovelace come to reside in Lincolnshire in the first place? He fancied that Scudamore had supplied that information. Now what had it been? The reason for Lovelace going there after he had left the Army? The answer came very soon. The property had been left to him. That was the reason. It had come to him from an aunt. The details of the affair gradually came back to Anthony. After Lovelace had left the Army he had come into money and property. Yes, the legacies had come from an aunt. But he had found the east coast propinquity too bleak for him and he had moved into Essex for reasons of health. To Loveridge—which was much more inland than where he had resided in Lincolnshire.

At that precise second Anthony had a brain-wave. Was it at all likely that the house which had belonged to Roger de Berners back in the thirteenth century had come to Lovelace from his aunt? The house had been sold out of the Berners family in 1733—the book on his lap had made that clear. The book had actually given the name of the purchaser, the man who had taken the house out of the Berners family. What had been the name of this purchaser?—so Anthony mused.

He referred to the book again for the information he desired. He knew precisely the place where he would find it. Anthony turned up and read the reference. The Berners house had remained in the Berners family until the year 1733, when it had been sold to an Army officer named Colonel Sir Clive Braund.

Anthony closed the book again, and as he did so something jolted in his mind and caused him furiously to think. Braund! Braund! That name had been under his eyes within the last forty-eight hours! In connexion with the Lovelace problem, too! Braund! Anthony castigated his brain, and in a flash the association winged its way home. He had seen the name amongst Lovelace's papers. When he had sat at Lovelace's desk, looked through the contents of the drawers and seen the drawings on the blotting-pad. "Sincil Hall—Arabella Braund."

2

They were the words. Anthony tossed the Berners book on to the cushioned seat again and began to rub his hands. Was Sincil Hall the original Berners house? He began to think that there was a strong probability in this direction. Anthony grabbed at the book again— to test the likelihood of the question. He was disappointed to find no reference to the name "Sincil Hall" in the index at the end. But this was not conclusive, he argued to himself. To Berners, the present-day author, it would always be the house of Berners. If Lovelace, or one of the Braund family before him, had renamed it, it was quite feasible that Berners would always reject the new name for any purposes of reference. To him, the only name which would ever count would be the old name and the old name would be the name which he would always use. This would be entirely natural from the Berners point of view.

Anthony looked at his watch. Not more than a quarter of an hour or so to King's Cross. There were several things that he must do now, with as little delay as possible. *Inter alia* he must again examine the file in Lovelace's drawer marked "Sincil Hall— Arabella Braund, Deceased", and, also, he must get in immediate touch again with MacMorran.

3

Anthony went straight from the terminus to MacMorran's room at the 'Yard'. MacMorran was quick to talk and eventually sat back in his chair and looked at the lean, lithe figure sitting in its customary position on the corner of his table.

"So you think I'm on to something," said Anthony, "you found out that James and Jim were not figments of my overworked and sometimes overheated imagination?"

The Inspector nodded. "Yes, we're on to something. No doubt about that."

Anthony smiled at the spoken subtlety. "Had they been in touch with the police? Before you saw them?"

MacMorran smiled back. "I'm not altogether sure on that point."

Anthony knitted his brows. "How do you mean—how did you manage to explain your arrival then?"

The Inspector's smile broadened. "I rather fancy," he said, "that James and Jim each thought that the other had 'phoned to us and that I was the answer therefore to the maiden's prayer. Anyhow, no questions of any kind being asked, I was spared the task of answering. For which, in a way, I was devoutly thankful."

Anthony nodded his understanding. "What do you think of things, then—generally? Let me enlarge on that. What do you think of my particular hunch with regard to Temple Spooner and Lovelace?"

"As I said just now, I think we're on to something. But what, exactly, I'm very far from knowing."

The Inspector paused and started to fill his pipe. Anthony waited for him. MacMorran got the pipe burning and spoke through the smoke. He spoke, Anthony thought, with unusual quietness.

"While I was down at Plashet I ran into something strange. In connexion with the Bullocks."

"With the Bullocks?"

"Ay. James and Jim. Surname Bullock. That's something you don't appear to have found out. But listen—never mind about that. I couldn't get a reasonable description of Spooner from either of them. Should have been able to, don't you think?"

MacMorran sat back in his chair as he put the question. "Of course." Anthony stared interestedly. "Tell me more of this, Andrew. Exactly what you mean."

"Well, this sort of thing. This is what I had from them. Couldn't exactly say the age Spooner is. That was the start-off. Average height. Ordinary coloured hair. Couldn't definitely say the colour of his eyes. Neither of them had ever actually noticed. No distinctive features they knew of. No mannerisms. All vague. No earthly use at all." MacMorran waved his hand contemptuously and continued. "When they'd finished describing the man to me after their fashion, I knew no more of what he looked like than I did when they started. Bit hooey-isn't it? How does it strike you?"

Before Anthony replied, MacMorran had gone on. "Then I ran into something else. Also peculiar."

Anthony still stared at the Inspector. "What was that, Andrew?"

"Well, when the description hung fire, I did what any reasonably intelligent person would have done. I asked the Bullocks for a recent photograph of Spooner, so that I could form my own impressions. What do you think happened then?"

"No idea. What? Tell me."

MacMorran took his time. Removing his pipe from his mouth, he placed it carefully on the table in front of him.

"Well, nothing happened. Nothing whatever. Like the rich, I was sent empty away." "

"Just what do you mean by that? That they point-blank refused to give you a photograph of Spooner?"

"No. I could have dealt with an authentic refusal. No, they stymied me by saying that they hadn't one. There wasn't such a thing in the house. Which left me with no grounds for argument."

Anthony grinned at the disconsolate expression on MacMorran's face.

"Might be true, you know, Andrew. It's just on the cards Spooner was allergic to the studio from early infancy. What was your reaction when they handed you that one?"

MacMorran spread out his hands. "Well, my dear chap, what could it be? As I said, I was stymied. According to further information which the two Bullocks were good enough to pass on to me, it was very much as you just playfully hinted. Spooner just did not have his photograph taken! Never, never, never. And that's all there was to it. So what could I damn well say? All the same I think it's funny. Funny-peculiar. Don't you?"

Anthony rubbed the ridge of his jaw. "Can't say, Andrew. You see, I've never known the man. Never met him in my life. Spooner, I mean." Anthony paused before continuing. "When you've never met a person, it's absolutely impossible to assess, anything like accurately, anything you hear about him, or her."

MacMorran nodded agreement and started on his pipe again. "I suppose that's right enough as far as it goes. All the same, it's got me wondering. I don't mind admitting as much."

"Re Spooner himself? Or are you harbouring doubts with regard to the Bullock twain?"

"Well, the latter chiefly, I think. To tell the truth, I hadn't thought so much concerning the other line. Shall have to now, though."

Anthony jerked himself from the corner of the table and stood upright. "Bit awkward, I admit, chasing a chap when you haven't the foggiest idea what he's like. We'll have to do some digging, Andrew. That's what it comes to. Mr. A. Temple Spooner, when he's at home, may be an even more interesting person than we've hitherto supposed."

As he finished speaking, the internal telephone on MacMorran's table rang. The Inspector picked up the receiver with a glance at Anthony of supreme resignation.

"Yes? Chief Detective-Inspector MacMorran speaking. Who? Right-o. Yes."

There ensued a silence as MacMorran listened. "Yes," he said again, "I know all that. I moved in the matter myself. I left the file and all the details with Evershed this morning. Yes? To-day! Early to-day. What about it? What?"

There came the second period of silence. "I see," said MacMorran eventually, "if I need you, I'll ring through. So it's like that, is it?"

He replaced the receiver quietly and thoughtfully before turning to Anthony.

"Your words have more or less come true. A man's body has been found on the edge of Lapping Wood. From certain articles and personal properties in his possession, it would seem to be the body of the man we've been discussing, Mr. Temple Spooner. He's been bashed on the head and, according to what I've just been told, there was probably a fractured skull. Been dead a day or two. At least, so the doctor thinks."

"Most interesting," said Anthony quietly, "the plot certainly thickens as I feared it must. And Lapping Wood, unless I'm very much mistaken, is not so very far from the village of Loveridge. What's it all about, Andrew?"

MacMorran shook his head. "Don't know. Wish I did. What do you think yourself?"

Anthony took some little time in replying. "Well, sometimes I think there may be something fantastic about the affair, at others I'm tempted to think that the explanation may eventually turn out to be comparatively simple. But I'm quite decided on one thing. And that's this. I'm going back to Loveridge at once for another look round. I rather fancy the key to the problem is down there and nowhere else."

"I'll join you there later," said the Inspector, "after I've looked at this second corpse."

CHAPTER 10

1

A grim-looking MacMorran alighted from the police car and shut the car door. He walked across the yard of the police-station at Chelmersley and entered the building. An Inspector of Police met him almost as he crossed the threshold.

"Good morning, sir," said Inspector Hurst, "you haven't been long."

"Good morning, Inspector Hurst. I didn't intend to be long. I've got the two chaps in the car. They're father and son. Name of Bullock. Or did I tell you that?"

"You didn't tell me their names. But I knew they were father and son."

"Are you ready?"

"Quite."

"All right, then. I'll fetch them over."

"Don't bother, sir. I'll send a man over to the car to bring them."

"Thank you, Inspector." Inspector Hurst turned to give his orders.

2

James and Jim Bullock followed MacMorran and Inspector Hurst to the mortuary. A uniformed constable seemed to appear from nowhere carrying a large bunch of keys. At the appropriate moment he slipped unobtrusively to the head of the miniature procession and opened the mortuary door. Then he pushed the keys into his pocket, walked to a kind of large locker and pulled something towards him which slid forward smoothly and easily. Inspector Hurst took a step forward and turned back the white covering that lay on the top. Then he turned to the two men who had come from Plashet on their grim errand.

"Now, gentlemen," he said quietly, "come here, will you, please?"

MacMorran looked curiously at James and Jim as they stepped towards the body now revealed in front of them. What he had already seen of them made him wonder. Each of these two men appeared now to be more concerned with his companion than with the corpse they had been called upon to identify. There were sidelong glances at each other and the impression they gave MacMorran suggested to him that they were strangers who had just met for the first time. Whereas MacMorran knew, and could indeed see, that they were close blood relations. With a surreptitious glance at Jim and a stifled cough, the senior Bullock stepped up close to the corpse. He stared at it silently, almost uncomprehendingly.

"Well," said Inspector Hurst sharply after an interval of some seconds, "can you identify it? Or can't you?"

"Yes," replied James, his voice just a little unsteady and wavering. "This is Mr. Spooner. Isn't it, Jim? What do you say?"

Again the sidelong glance from father to son, accompanied this time by a nervous movement of the head and a twitch of trembling hands. The younger Bullock ranged himself at his father's side and peered down at the body.

"Yes," he said, "this is our poor old Guv'nor all right. No doubt about that. Poor old fellow. What an end to come to." Jim shook his head sorrowfully.

"Ow was he killed?" inquired James, "I can't exactly see any—"

"Bashed on the head," said Hurst curtly, "and a hefty bash at that. Fractured the poor fellow's skull. Not a lot of chance when that happens. Right-o, then, that finishes it. You're sure—both of you? That it's Spooner?"

James and Jim nodded in unison. "Oh yes. That's the Guv'nor. No mistakin' 'im," said Jim. James added his contribution to that of his son. "Wish we could say different. But we can't. Bad day for us. My son and me. Very bad indeed. Makes the future pretty black for both of us. Almost as black, I suppose, as it very well could be. I'm too long in the tooth to start on a new kind of job."

James turned away. His worry and sorrow were plain to see. MacMorran questioningly said, "you must have known Spooner very well?"

James said "yes, very well, I suppose you might say. Been in his service a long time."

"Well then, what do you make of this business? Any ideas on it?"

James shook his head tragically. "Nothin' at all, Chief. It's fair got me guessin'. If you'd 'a known him as I did, you wouldn't 'a thought nobody would 'ave 'armed a 'air of 'is 'ead. And that's a fact. But if you ask me—"

James paused.

"That's just what I am doing," said MacMorran, "I am asking you. I thought you knew that."

"Well then, I'd say as 'ow a gang must have laid for 'im."

"Why? What makes you think that? What are you basing that opinion on?"

"Because we read about such things, don't we? Why, the papers are plastered with 'em. Pick up any paper you like. Any day you like. What do you find? Battle, murder and sudden death, Chief, and you can't deny it. It's all been brought about by education. Still . . . " James made a sudden gesture that might have meant anything, "you don't want me to tell you things like that, a man in your position, you know too much about 'em yourself."

"Just a minute, Mr. Bullock." MacMorran's tone was certainly on the cold side and rather peremptory. "As far as I can see, what you say means nothing, or very little. Can you give me anything definite in support of your suggestion? Anything that you've actually seen or heard about? Any facts? Can you describe anything that has ever happened to your employer which would give credence to your opinion?"

James Bullock shifted his feet uneasily under MacMorran's sharp scrutiny.

"Can't say that I 'ave, Chief. That is to say—nothing definite. If you put it like that. But I wasn't alongside the Guv'nor always, was I now? Ask yourself! Still, that isn't to say—"

MacMorran cut him summarily by addressing the younger Bullock. "Well, you've heard what your father's had to say. What have you got to say about it?"

Jim looked just about as uneasy as his father had. "I agree with father," he said slowly, "'e's usually right, is father—I reckon as 'ow a gang got the Guv'nor. Laid for 'im, bided their time and bob's your uncle. I can't see nothing else for it."

"Any special reasons for thinking like that? Or are you just the same as your father?"

"Reckon I'm the same as father. Mother liked it like that. We've got the same ideas."

MacMorran turned away impatiently. "I don't know that I'd put it quite like that," he said to nobody in particular.

He gestured to Inspector Hurst. "They're all yours, Inspector. These two gentlemen. I don't know whether you'd like to question them at all."

Hurst looked doubtful for a few seconds before shaking his head. "I don't think so, sir. They've identified the body as that of Spooner. Which is as we thought and what they really came to do for us. I think that's about all as far as I'm concerned."

MacMorran nodded his acquiescence. "O.K. That suits me, then. I'm through. Arrange transport to take them back to Plashet, will you? I shan't be going back yet. I shall want my car. I'm going on to Loveridge again."

3

While MacMorran was overlooking the identification of the body found in Lapping Wood as that of Temple Spooner by Bullock *père et fils*, Anthony had returned to 'Cherry Fair'. Sergeant Dixon was still knocking about the house when Anthony arrived—much to the annoyance, and perhaps trepidation, of the Topladys. So much so, evidently, that Toplady himself seemed decidedly pleased at Anthony's arrival. The butler bowed ceremoniously when he saw Anthony come in, and, approaching him rather diffidently, said deferentially, "I'm pleased indeed to see you, sir. I am that! In fact, I'll go as far as to say that there's no person I'd rather see."

Anthony smiled at this greeting. "Oh, why's that, Toplady? Why am I thus flattered?"

"Well, it's like this, sir. I feel I need your advice, sir. In that feeling I'm joined by my wife. Mrs. Toplady and I, sir, see eye to eye in this matter—we both feel that we need your advice."

"In what particular direction, Toplady? Please tell me."

"With regard to our position 'ere in this 'ouse, sir. Are we doing the right and proper thing, sir, by staying on 'ere? After the death of poor Mr. Lovelace? It's plain that we can't still be in 'is employ, sir, and that raises the question of finance, sir. Unpalatable though that may be. What's the position, if I may be allowed to ask sir, with regard to our wages? Mrs. Toplady's and my own? Are we to assume that—"

Anthony judged it discreet to closure him. "You don't want my advice, Toplady. It's not exactly my province. The man you want to see is Mr.

Ilsley. The late Mr. Lovelace's solicitor. He's the man to settle all those questions. You have a word with him and he'll put you right, I've no doubt, with regard to all those points that you mentioned."

Toplady looked at Anthony doubtfully. "He wouldn't take it amiss, I suppose, sir, if I approached 'im. I shouldn't like to—"

"Good lord, no. Not a bit of it. Don't you worry about that. That's his job. That's what he's here for. You see him, Toplady, as soon as you can make it."

"Thank you very much, sir. I'll convey your advice to Mrs. Toplady. If I may say so, sir, you 'ave taken a great weight off my mind. It's very kind of you."

"Good. Glad to have been of service. Now I'll tell you what I want from you. Take me up again to Mr. Lovelace's room, will you, Toplady? You know, the room your missus called 'the den'."

"Very good, sir," replied the butler, "that is a simple matter. Come this way, sir."

4

Anthony went straight across the room to Lovelace's writing-table. From memory, he pulled a drawer open and took out a file of papers. When he saw that the file was the one he required he gave it a glance of satisfaction. The tab on the front of it showed in neatly printed letters, "Sincil Hall—Arabella Braund deceased."

Anthony removed the contents of the file and began to study them one by one. Everything was clear and in good order. Chronological and otherwise. The house had come to Richard Lovelace through the will of his Aunt Arabella. Within a period of but a few minutes Anthony was able to satisfy himself on the main point of his curiosity. "Sincil Hall" of the Braund family and the "House of Berners" were one and the same property.

This fact gave Anthony a thrill of satisfaction. For if it meant nothing else, it meant this. Some of the theories with which he had begun to coquet had a solid foundation, to say the least of it. And, while he was where he was, he might as well go through the Braund file systematically.

Anthony sorted out the various papers and documents which the file contained carefully and methodically. After about half an hour's intensive concentration on much correspondence between different solicitors, he was compelled to admit that the various letters had yielded him nothing. Each of the documents he examined was to do with the owning of the house by the late Arabella Braund and the acquisition (by legacy) by Richard Lovelace, nephew of the deceased. Try as he would, Anthony could find nothing in any of the letters or deeds to excite his slightest suspicion. It seemed to him, as he sat there examining the Braund papers, that if the Lovelace-Spooner crimes had their genesis in any shape or form in this house of his interest, it must be to do with the ancient "House of Berners" rather than with the more modern Sincil Hall. That is to say from the angle of Time. But even if this were so, what on earth could the genesis be? What was the connexion, firstly between Lovelace and Spooner, and secondly between Spooner and Berners? If he knew that he'd probably know a heck of a lot!

Anthony replaced the papers in the Braund file and the file in the drawer. That he faced a somewhat complicated problem he had no doubt. Had Lovelace and Spooner died for the same reason? Or putting it slightly differently, for the same cause? Another interpretation of the same question would be—had the same person killed both Lovelace and Spooner?

Anthony shut the drawer of the writing-table and rose from his seat. As he made his way downstairs, he was still undecided as to his next step.

CHAPTER 11

1

As he came to the last stair he heard the sound of a familiar voice. Then he heard Toplady say "very good, madam, I fancy I 'eard Mr. Bathurst coming downstairs. If you will allow me, I'll make sure."

Toplady came to meet him. "Mrs. Forbes is 'ere in the 'ouse, sir, and is inquiring after you. I rather think from what she 'as told me that she would like a few words with you. Shall I tell 'er that it's convenient?"

"Oh, yes—certainly. I shall be only too delighted. We'll go in the library, Toplady."

"Very good, sir. I'll escort Mrs. Forbes to you, sir."

Anthony went into the library and waited. When Evelyn Forbes came in she acknowledged his bow with a slight movement of the head.

"Good morning, Mr. Bathurst. I'm so glad to be able to see you. I hope I'm not inconveniencing you."

"Good morning, Mrs. Forbes. On the contrary, I assure you."

Anthony eyed her steadily. She coloured a little under his scrutiny and then laughed. But the laugh had a quality of coldness. "That's as well to know. What I wanted to ask you you can probably guess. Is there any news?"

"News?"

"Yes. News. Are you any nearer to discovering Dick Lovelace's murderer?"

Anthony saw the light in the eyes and the small hands clenched as she asked the question. For the moment he was in doubt as to the best manner in which to answer her.

"If I said 'yes', Mrs. Forbes, I might be considered guilty of an exaggerated optimism. So I will refrain from saying it."

Evelyn Forbes tapped the carpet with an impatient foot. "The Police," she said contemptuously, "never seem able to do anything. It's almost always the same. Why is it?"

Anthony smiled and shook his head. The uppermost thought in his mind at that moment was that the lady was looking very beautiful.

"I can't let you catch me that way," he replied.

"Oh dear, I'm not trying to catch you, as you put it. Please don't be so trivial." Her lips were parted and her expression held a keen intentness. Her foot began to tap again. "But *you*. You yourself! Have you nothing to tell me? Surely you must have made some progress?"

Anthony thought that she looked disdainfully lovely. "Tell me, please," she insisted.

He smiled at her encouragingly. "Perhaps I can claim a little progress. To use your own word, Mrs. Forbes. Nothing like as much, however, as I should have desired."

He leant his back against the table and waved Evelyn Forbes to a chair. She took it and looked up at him in the evident expectation of his going on. Anthony accepted the position without demur.

"To discover Lovelace's murderer, Mrs. Forbes, is a problem which falls, directly you begin to examine it, into two distinct parts. Let me explain just what I mean. Many aspects of it appear to be comparatively simple. On the other hand, it has issues which are very definitely complicated, involved and even obscure. For instance, I don't know yet, with anything like certainty, why Lovelace was killed."

He paused—to see the effect of his statement. Evelyn Forbes gave a rather impatient shrug of the shoulder.

"Does that matter so much—I shouldn't have thought that it did. Isn't it the fact that he's dead that counts?"

"I take your point, Mrs. Forbes. And it's a good one. But don't you see, in a case of this kind, where you haven't a murderer caught *in flagrante delicto*, the police are compelled to build up their case against the criminal step by step? That takes time. If, however, you know *why* the crime was committed, that time for the building-up process is necessarily lessened." Anthony stopped, to proceed almost immediately. "In that particular connexion, Mrs. Forbes, I've found myself wondering more than once if you would be able to help us. Do think that you could?"

A spot of bright colour burned in each of her cheeks. "I? How is it possible for me to help you?"

"Well, for one thing, you were a close friend of the dead man."

"Yes."

"Because of that you may have been to some extent in his confidence."

"How do you mean, Mr. Bathurst?"

"Quite simple. All I mean is that at times he may have confided in you."

Evelyn Forbes sat upright in her chair. "Mr. Bathurst. Let us both be frank. Please! I hate all this fencing with one another and beating about the bush. If you have any questions to ask me, please ask them." The colour spots burned even more brightly.

"Very well, Mrs. Forbes. I will. Did Lovelace ever mention the name of Spooner to you? Recently? It may have been Temple Spooner. Can you recall the name at all?"

The reply was as prompt and as decisive as the questions had been. Anthony was just a little surprised.

"Oh, yes," replied Evelyn Forbes, "only a few days prior to his death. The actual name he mentioned to me was T. Spooner. Which I presume would be the Temple Spooner you mentioned just now. But why do you ask me that? It had nothing to do with Dick's death, surely?" There was a new anxiety in her voice.

"I'm not sure," replied Anthony with a grim earnestness. "For the moment, I'm more or less feeling my way. Not a lot removed from groping in the dark. But tell me more, if you can, about this Temple Spooner gentleman. In what particular connexion did Lovelace mention him to you?"

"I will if I can. Let me think now." Evelyn Forbes pursed her lips at Anthony's questions. There came silence for some seconds. Then she began to speak—very slowly. "It was in connexion with a letter that Dick had received—about a month ago, I should think. Perhaps not quite as long as that. I'm not sure."

"Was the letter from Temple Spooner himself?"

"Yes, it was. The letter came from the man himself. I rather fancy from an address in London somewhere. I can distinctly remember Dick telling me that. Dick was puzzled by the letter. Completely puzzled. I think that's why he spoke to me about it, because he wasn't able to understand it and felt that he'd like to discuss it with somebody."

"How do you mean—puzzled? Do you mean that it wasn't plain?"

Evelyn Forbes wrinkled her forehead. "No. Not exactly that. It's hard to explain, because Dick Lovelace couldn't tell me much about it. Because he was puzzled! He hadn't a clue. That's what he said. It was a sort of, how can I put it so that you'll understand, a sort of proposed business deal. Or business *offer*, perhaps, would be a better description."

Anthony waited for her to go on. But he waited in vain. "Try to tell me more," he said quietly, "because it's all pretty nebulous at the moment. Try to think of everything that Lovelace told you at the time. Everything! No matter how trivial it may have been. It may be tremendously important."

Evelyn Forbes nodded. "Yes. I suppose it may be. Well, let me put it like this. To the best of my memory this letter which this man Temple Spooner sent to Dick Lovelace offered to do certain business with him. There was to be a big profit for Dick in it if he were prepared to play ball, but the point was that Dick just didn't know what it was all about. That's what he told me. I know it sounds silly, Mr. Bathurst, and all that, but that's just how I remember it."

Anthony thought that he saw a glimmer of light in the darkness.

"It might be said, then, to come to this. Lovelace received an offer from Temple Spooner by letter. As an offer it would have been an attractive proposition if only Lovelace had properly understood what Spooner was driving at? Would that be a fair description of it?"

Evelyn Forbes nodded rather eagerly. "That's it. That's just what I intended to convey to you. It's how I understood it."

"Good. We progress then. Now tell me this, Mrs. Forbes. What sort of a did reply Lovelace eventually make to the Spooner offer?"

The lady frowned. "As far as I know, he made no reply."

"No reply whatever?"

"No. After a time Dick Lovelace began to think that Spooner was trying to hoax him. In other words, that the letter was all boloney and that the best thing he could do would be to ignore it. So he deliberately refrained from replying."

"Are you quite sure of that?"

"Almost. Why do you doubt me?"

She turned towards Anthony with an impulsive gesture. Anthony smiled at her reassuringly.

"My dear lady," he said, "I don't doubt you for a moment. I was merely tightening up your story, as it were. If Lovelace acted as you think he did, it may explain one or two matters which have been puzzling me for some little time. You can't think of anything else, I suppose, which Lovelace did in connexion with this Spooner letter offer? Or of anything which he spoke to you about? Please think hard. See if you can rake anything up."

Evelyn sat with her head slightly on one side, thinking hard. "Yes," she said, "there was one thing he said at the time which I thought rather strange. Now—what was it?"

Anthony waited patiently for inspiration to come to her. Suddenly she shook her head rather petulantly.

"No, it's no earthly good. I can't remember. It's gone from me completely and I can't get it to come back to me. It's just one of those things. I'm frightfully sorry."

Anthony encouraged her. "You may think of it later, Mrs. Forbes. Or it may come to you spontaneously. If you do, please let me have it. It may be important, as I said just now."

She nodded. "I'll tell you, though, what I have thought of. Which might be more important still. I'm not sure." Anthony eyed her with keen interest. "What's that, Mrs. Forbes?"

"Why, I've been thinking it over and I don't believe that Dick Lovelace ever destroyed the letter. Spooner's letter."

Anthony felt a twinge of suspicion. "What makes you say that?" he asked her.

"Because I have a distinct recollection," she answered clearly, "that Dick Lovelace told me some time after he received it that he had kept the letter by him. I firmly believe that he had a purpose in so doing. I mean a purpose out of the ordinary."

"Did he tell you that?"

"No. I wouldn't go as far as to say that. But I'd say that he hinted as much."

Anthony left his place by the table and began to walk about. He came back to her—seated in the chair.

"If what you think is correct, Mrs. Forbes, there may be yet another side to it."

"What do you mean?" He thought that her eyes looked startled.

"Why, this. If Lovelace kept the letter up to the time he was killed, it may still be in existence. It may never have been destroyed. That's so, isn't it?"

"It would appear so," she replied rather listlessly. Anthony kept it up.

"Any suggestions as to where it might reasonably be?" he questioned.

She looked up at him, before shrugging her shoulders. Then she shook her head.

"It might be in one of a thousand places. I wasn't in Dick Lovelace's confidence to the extent that you're suggesting."

As she finished speaking, Anthony thought that her face had cleared and that she brightened perceptibly. "Perhaps," she said slowly, almost conversationally underlining the word, "I *could* make a suggestion with regard to that, after all. Your words may have borne fruit."

"Where?" said Anthony quickly.

"Possibly," she continued demurely, "but only possibly, the letter *might* be in the pocket of Dick Lovelace's dressing-gown."

"Why?" asked Anthony even more quickly than before.

"It was a habit of his," she said readily, "to put letters in there. I remember him telling me once why he did it. He said that people on the look-out for such things would never dream of looking for important papers in the pocket of a man's dressing-gown, which he usually slung at the back of the bedroom door. There might be something in it," she concluded both hopefully and whimsically.

"Which do you mean," asked Anthony, "something in the idea or something in the dressing-gown pocket?"

"The answer's both," replied Evelyn Forbes with the ghost of a smile, "but it can soon be put to the test. Why shouldn't we go upstairs and have a look."

Anthony shook his head. Evelyn Forbes sensed his disappointment.

"Don't you agree with me?" she asked.

"It's not that, Mrs. Forbes. But it's not going to be so easy." "What isn't?"

"Looking in the dressing-gown pocket?"

"Why not?" She was startled now.

"For the reason that Lovelace was wearing the dressing-gown when he was struck down."

"Well, how does that—"

"Think, Mrs. Forbes. If there had been any letter or any papers in Lovelace's dressing-gown pocket when he was killed, that letter, assuming that it were a letter, would now be in the hands of the Police. And I can assure you that it isn't."

There's no doubt about that, is there?" She sat staring in front of her, wide-eyed and wondering.

"Unless," continued Anthony slowly, "the letter had been taken from the dressing-gown pocket by the murderer."

"How would the murderer know it was there?"

"He wouldn't, but he might search for it. It might well be that the letter would incriminate him seriously. So seriously, in fact, that he dared not leave the house, *after* the murder, without having the letter in his possession. You see that, don't you?" Before Evelyn Forbes could comment Anthony went on again. "There's also another possibility. Can you see what I mean? Or what I'm getting at?"

She shook her head at him vaguely. "I'm afraid I'm not used to thinking about affairs of this kind. It's not my ordinary line of country. I'm slow. Tell me."

"Why, it's on the cards that the letter was taken from Lovelace's pocket by a third party. Neither by the murderer nor by the Police. There, I've told you. It's on a plate for you. I won't mention the parsley butter."

"Yes," she said nodding her head, "yes, I get you now. You mean by the person that found Dick's body. Am I right?"

She spoke the words as though they frightened her. Anthony looked at her meaningly. "You know who that was?"

"Naturally. It was the Topladys. At least, so I've been given to understand. First the woman. Then she called her husband. That was the story, wasn't it?"

"Quite right. Both the Topladys qualify."

"You've made me think," said Evelyn Forbes, "you've made me think quite a lot." She paused abruptly.

"What are you thinking?" demanded Anthony, "I could bear to know."

"Why," she said, "putting the Topladys on one side for a moment, it seems to me that we must get in touch with this man Temple Spooner at once. This man who wrote the letter to Dick Lovelace in the first place. He *may* hold the clue to all the—"

"My dear lady," returned Anthony, "I couldn't agree with you more. Unhappily, though, it's now impossible. At least I'm afraid so."

"Impossible?" she reiterated contemptuously. "With all your resources it should be comparatively easy. I've always been led to believe that Scotland Yard—"

Anthony shook his head. "Not even the 'Yard' can reach him now, Mrs. Forbes."

"Why not?" she demanded imperiously, "he can't be so very far away."

"Alas! He can—and is. The undiscover'd country, Mrs. Forbes, from whose bourn . . . doubtless you know the rest. And Temple Spooner's no different from all the other travellers."

Her eyes were fear haunted. "You mean . . . " she faltered.

"The body of Temple Spooner was found yesterday on the outskirts of Lapping Wood. I haven't heard that it's been identified yet, but the Police don't appear to harbour any doubts about it."

"Dead?" Her voice faltered.

"Murdered," said Anthony gravely.

2

"Murdered? The colour drained from the face of Evelyn Forbes. "Is that really true, Mr. Bathurst?"

"To the best of my information. Oh, yes, I'm afraid there's no doubt about it."

"How was he killed?"

"Much in the same manner as Lovelace. A heavy blow on the back of the head. Fractured skull."

She placed a hand on his arm. "What does it mean, Mr. Bathurst? What's it all about?"

He shook his head at the questions. "Ah, there's the rub. I wish I knew. It may be that Spooner's proposals to Lovelace in the letter you've just told me about are the clue to the problem. They may even be the flames which started the whole pot boiling. That's what we've got to find out."

"Who do you think *did* take the letter, Mr. Bathurst?"

"Who? Out of our three runners? Murderer, Police or discoverer of body? I'm afraid that there's little doubt, Mrs. Forbes. The murderer took that letter after Lovelace was struck down. The balance of probability is very much that way. Now, can you do something for me?"

"If it's in my power, of course."

"Tell me where I can find Martin Scudamore. He lives near here, I fancy."

"Quite near—as distances go. I'll tell you. When you turn out of Oriel Lane, turn left. Then go straight on down the hill until you come to the fork of the road. Take the left-hand fork, go past the farm on the left-hand side and it's the first big house to which you come. Just past the little row of cottages with long front gardens. You can't mistake it." She paused and then continued. "I'm sorry you're going to the Scudamores. You don't know how sorry."

There was something in her voice which caused him to look at her sharply. "I'm afraid that I don't understand."

"Oh, it's nothing, really. I was going to ask you to have dinner with us. There'll be some people there whom you already know. But, of course, if you're—"

"That's very charming of you, Mrs. Forbes. I shall be back in time for that and I shall be delighted to accept the invitation. If you'll be gracious and waive the formalities sartorial."

"That's all right. You needn't worry about that. We shan't change. Shall we say a quarter to seven this evening? Will that be convenient?"

"Command me," returned Anthony.

"You can't miss the house—it's next to the surgery."

When Anthony walked up to the front door of the Scudamore house he harboured certain misgivings as to whether he'd have the luck to find Martin Scudamore at home. But at the back of his mind, somewhere, there was an idea tucked away to the effect that Scudamore was on a few days' holiday. Anthony felt moderately certain that he'd heard Martin Scudamore tell that to somebody in his hearing since he and Scudamore had made each other's acquaintance. Anyhow, he'd chance his arm and put the matter to the test. He was soon to know that his memory hadn't failed him.

He was shown into a spacious lounge by an apple-cheeked maid with blue eyes and tumbling fair hair and was soon joined by Martin Scudamore himself. Martin Scudamore came in from the garden, shirt-sleeved, open-necked and pipe in mouth. From the expression round his mouth as he entered, Anthony wondered whether the visit was ill-timed.

"Why, Bathurst!" he said, removing the pipe from his mouth, "of all the unexpected! Why didn't you 'phone us, old chap, and let us know you were coming? I should have hated to be out when you rolled up. And it's not a five minutes' journey by any means. I'll say it's not! Sit down, my dear fellow, and make yourself comfortable."

"Thank you. But don't get me wrong, Scudamore. I haven't exactly come straight here from town. As a matter of fact, I was over at 'Cherry Fair' on a checking inquiry, and while I was there I decided to come along here and have a word with you. You know—the birds and the stone. I'm not intruding, am I?"

"My dear fellow," Scudamore gestured vaguely with the pipe stem, "don't suggest such a thing for a moment. You've caught me on the wrong foot, though. I was doing a spot of graft in the rose garden. My father and mother are up in town. They do go up occasionally. About once a month."

"That's all right, Scudamore. Don't worry about that. You needn't count this as a social call exactly."

Scudamore evinced surprise. "No? Oh, I see. Professional stuff, eh? The old sleuth still? Sorry if I was slow on the uptake. Yes, I begin to see. What can I do for you?"

Anthony smiled at him. "So glad you're willing. That's a good beginning, at least."

"How are things going? Anything to report?"

"Well, there's one thing I can say. There are complications about Lovelace's death that were not entirely foreseen at the beginning. Despite the fact that the Police were on the spot almost immediately, as it were. Thanks entirely to your own good offices. Which, in time, I feel sure, will prove to be of inestimable help to us. And that's really what I've called in to see you about. Shall we talk? Is it convenient?"

Scudamore glanced at his wrist-watch rather significantly. "Yes, I think so. More or less. The only thing is I'm dining in town this evening. And I haven't exactly a lot of time." He paused and then said pointedly, "you know the lady. I'm sure you'd positively hate me to keep her waiting."

Anthony ignored the bait. "I shan't keep you more than half an hour. If that."

Scudamore shrugged his shoulders. "O.K., then. But please don't make it any more than that. Go ahead."

"What I wanted you to do was to verify my memory of the story you brought me which more or less started this business off. Do you feel that you're able to do that?"

Scudamore seemed a little taken aback. "I'll try, of course."

"Thank you. I want to revert, if I may, to the conversation you overheard in the cinema that evening. Between the boss and the henchman. To use, more or less, your own descriptions. Now this is, roughly, my own memory of what you said you overheard. The first point made was that four rings were essential. Essential and vital. Right?"

Scudamore nodded. "Quite right. They were the exact words that were used."

"Good. The second point was that a man named Charles Linklater Delevigne had confirmed 'the colours'. Which were in the order of green-blue-red-yellow. Right again?"

Another nod of corroboration from Scudamore. "Absolutely."

"Excellent. The boss then made a remark concerning 'proving innocence'. To which the henchman replied with a question. This question was 'what will you do?' The boss said in reply 'go and get it' and the other fellow said 'when?' Do you still agree, Scudamore?"

"Oh, yes. I agree entirely with everything you've so far said."

Scudamore answered Anthony's question without the slightest demur or hesitation.

"Good again," said Anthony. "I'll go on from there, then. The boss chap replied to the 'when' question something in this fashion. 'As soon as I can. Perhaps by to-morrow or even before that.' Am I still doing all right?"

"Yes. Go on."

Anthony now began to speak somewhat more slowly. "This is the stage where my memory isn't quite so clear. But I rather think that the henchman asked yet another question. Something about 'supposing nothing comes of it? What will you do then?' And the reply that the big shot gave him was to the effect that he didn't propose to let anything stand in his way whatever. That he meant seeing the project through, no matter what opposition was encountered. If it were a person, and a person who looked like being obstinate or awkward, then that person would be eliminated without the slightest compunction. Now what would you say to all that, Scudamore? Am I so very much off the mark?"

"No-o," admitted Martin Scudamore after a momentary pause, "that's a fair *précis*, I suppose, of the stuff I overheard. There's not much wrong with it. If anything."

"Well, that's satisfactory, then. My memory hasn't exactly let me down. Now the point I brought the story to was the point more or less where they got up and went out. Yes?"

"Yes. I should say that 'ud be about correct. That is to say as far as I can remember after the lapse of time."

"Good. Would you say that I'd omitted anything? Think it over carefully. Don't answer too quickly."

Scudamore, who had been standing by the mantelpiece, came to the middle of the room, straddled a chair and leant his arms on the back of it. After a few moments' contemplation he said "I wouldn't say that you'd left anything out that was of any importance. As I look back on things."

"You don't think so?"

"No, really I don't. If I did, I'd be the first to tell you so."

"I've a hazy sort of idea," said Anthony, "that I have omitted something. Whether it's important or not I haven't the slightest idea. That's where I'm just a trifle worried. Perhaps it may come to me later on. We'll hope so. What a tremendous pity it was you didn't catch sight of the two men."

"You're telling me," said Scudamore warmly. "Don't I know it." He got off the chair and pushed his pipe into his pocket. Anthony thought that he looked nervous. "I'll tell you what, though, Bathurst. Since you've come along to see me to-day, I won't keep it from you any longer. Damn' silly though it may be. More than once I've been on the point of telling you, but honestly I couldn't summon up the guts. It sounds so frightfully ridiculous. Still, here goes. I believe that I've heard one of the two voices again. The voices I heard in the cinema. And that's a solemn fact."

Anthony regarded him intently. "You believe you have? How strong's the belief?"

"Oh, quite strong, come to that. I won't assert that I'm absolutely certain, but almost."

"You interest me," said Anthony, "where was this?"

"Here in Loveridge somewhere. That's funny, isn't it? But I'm hanged if I can put my finger on the actual place. And that's the annoying part of it which worries me."

"When did this happen, Scudamore?"

"On the day Dick Lovelace was buried. On that very day. Makes you think, doesn't it?"

"Tell me everything, Scudamore, if you don't mind. And when I say everything, I mean everything. This is just about the last word in importance."

"Well," Scudamore patted his trouser-pockets for cigarettes, "as I said at the outset, I funked telling you of the incident, because it all seems so blitheringly absurd. And that's the part of it that I can't get out of my mind."

He found a cigarette and lit it. "You say tell everything. I should be hard put to it to do that I assure you. Because it's all so hazy, so uncertain, so bewilderingly puzzling. I'll tell you what happened, though. I can do that. And just *as* it happened, too. Then you can judge for yourself. You remember the day Lovelace was buried?"

"Very well indeed."

"Well, it all goes back to that day. To the end of that day. When I'd finished with everything over at Lovelace's place and had come home here to sit down quietly. You remember the crowd that was there, Evelyn Forbes and her husband, those two Service chaps, Mapperley and I forget the other fellow's name—Philip Sheridan, yourself, Robin Ilsley and the two Topladys floating in and out. Well, as I say, I got home here and began to think things over. The sort of day it had been, one of its kind in a thousand years would be more than enough for me, and of how the funeral itself had gone off. I suppose in a way I began to reconstruct the various incidents of the day, as you might say."

Martin Scudamore straddled the chair again and leant over the back towards Anthony. "Well, this is where the really curious part comes. As I said, I was more or less reconstructing the events of the day. In a sort of rough, chronological order. The drive to the church with the *cortège*, the actual service in the church, the scene at the grave, and then the return to 'Cherry Fair' and what took place subsequently. And I thought of the different people and their conversations, of Ilsley's announcement of Evelyn's legacy and so on, and of the various reactions, and of the ebb and flow of remarks as you might describe them, that I'd heard in all the different places I'd been, uttered from time to time, and then I suddenly began to dwell on one particular remark that had somehow drifted to my ears and sort of lodged itself in my brain. It's an extraordinary sort of remark, too, and where actually I heard it, the good God alone knows."

Scudamore paused in his narrative. "What was it?" asked Anthony quietly.

Scudamore answered very deliberately. " 'Well, he knew what it meant, but he went.' That was the expression. The actual and complete expression."

Anthony stared at him uncomprehendingly. "Say that again," he said.

Scudamore repeated the phrase. Then Anthony repeated it after him.

" 'Well, he knew what it meant, but he went.' Right-o. I've got it. Go on please, Scudamore."

"Well, that's how it was. When I began to concentrate on this remark and to wonder what exactly it might mean and who it was that had said it, I suddenly seemed to catch my breath. I could *hear* it being said. If you can see things with your mind's eye, you can surely hear them with your mind's ear. And that's just what happened to me. I could *hear* it! As I sat here in my arm-chair. And the voice was familiar. One that I'd heard before . . . somewhere! Where? That was my problem. I worried at it for a heck of a time. Then I got it. The voice was one of the two voices I'd overheard in the cinema that evening."

Scudamore looked across at Anthony and smiled. "Sounds sheer tomfoolery, doesn't it?"

"Which one of the voices?"

"Now, that's another funny thing! I can't be certain as to that. Yes, I can see you're looking surprised, but there it is. And it's no good whatever asking me to explain myself. Because I can't. You see I can't remember now what the voice I heard say that phrase was really like. That's gone from me now. All I can recall is, that *when* it was spoken, my brain took in the association and held it for a time, but only *partly*. It sort of registered, but the bell it *did* ring didn't ring loudly enough until some hours afterwards, and then *part* of the sensibility, as it were, had been lost. I say, do you think you understand what I'm trying to say?"

Anthony nodded. "Yes. I think I do. But it's a queer business, all the same. You're certain, you say, that you heard this remark on the day that Lovelace was buried?"

"Positive."

"Any idea when? What time in the day?"

"No. Not really. If I chanced my arm and said I had, I shouldn't be truthful."

"Try separating the day into different parts. It may help. Say before the funeral service, during the funeral service, and after the funeral service. Does division of things get you anywhere?"

"No. I've tried it myself that way, more or less. But it's no good at all."

"Did you go anywhere else on the day of the funeral?"

"Nowhere. That's what makes it so damned funny."

"Well," said Anthony, "you see what it boils down to, then, don't you?"

"How do you mean?" inquired Scudamore.

"Why, it means this. That the voice you can't identify exactly is almost certain to have been the voice of one of the people who were there in Lovelace's house. The same people went to the funeral as came back here. You listed the names just now."

Scudamore gave Anthony a peculiar look. "My dear chap, but that's absurd, isn't it?"

"Why?" demanded Anthony calmly.

"Well, it must be. Look at it for yourself. It's next door to an impossibility, isn't it?"

"Is there such a thing?"

"Well," Scudamore spread out his hands, "I ask you!"

Anthony tried reasoning with him. "Look here, Scudamore, however much you may want to, you can't have the best of both worlds. And that's, almost, what it seems to me you're trying to get. Look at things for yourself. You say that you heard the voice again that you'd previously heard in the cinema. You're quite certain of that. And as it happens, you're the only one whose opinion has any value. You heard the voice at some time on the day of Lovelace's funeral. And the funeral service was the one event in your life that day. You went to the church, you came back from the church to Lovelace's house, and then you returned home here. You say that you went nowhere else. Did you speak to anybody that day outside your own circle or the group that attended the funeral? Because the crux of the whole affair lies in that question. Think hard and think carefully."

Anthony watched Scudamore's face intently as he pondered the question. The reply was not long in coming.

"As far as I know, Bathurst, and as far as I can remember, I spoke to nobody. Outside those two sets of people that you named. But don't forget this. I did my best to make this point clear before. I don't say that the remark in question was made to me! Not for a moment would I assert that. I may have happened to overhear it, and that's what I think actually did happen. Doesn't it make a difference?"

Anthony thought it over. "Yes. I suppose it does—to an extent. But even then, this house and 'Cherry Fair' were the only two houses you were in that day. Two houses and a graveside and a church."

Scudamore shook his head. "It's no use. I've tried no end of times to bring it back to me. But I just can't do it. It eludes me always. In a way I'm sorry I told you."

Anthony tried another approach. "Tell me, Scudamore. I'm testing another angle. You've no idea, you say, what the two men in the cinema looked like?"

"None at all. I told you that at our initial encounter. Don't you remember asking me the question?"

"Yes. But let's look at it in a different way. It won't do any harm. Have you noticed anybody in Loveridge recently or in the vicinity of Loveridge that you couldn't place? In other words that was a stranger to you? A new face, let us say?"

"No. I can't say that I have. But that mightn't mean a terrible lot. I don't know all the people in Loveridge. Far from it, in fact. I don't work in Loveridge, for one thing. Or even in the vicinity. I'm out of the place for many hours most days of the week."

"H'm. Not much help there for me, then." Anthony rose from his chair. "Well, I won't detain you any longer, Scudamore. Many thanks for listening to me, and many thanks also for the information. Good of you. By the way, one last question before I make myself scarce. Did you ever hear Lovelace refer to the name of Spooner? Or possibly Temple Spooner?"

There was no hint of hesitation about Scudamore's reply. "Never. Never heard the name at all."

"Thank you. Good-bye, then. And as I said—many thanks."

"Good-bye. Any message for Miss Repton?"

"My dear Scudamore! You've got me all wrong. I never communicate with a lady through a third party. Whatever gave you the impression that I should?"

Anthony waved to Scudamore as he turned away. Scudamore's face was a study as he walked to the window and watched Anthony make his way down the path.

CHAPTER 12

1

When Anthony arrived back at 'Cherry Fair' he found MacMorran there. It appeared that the Inspector was waiting for him. "I'm glad you're back," said MacMorran with a hint of impatience, "because I wanted to have a word with you."

"Good," said Anthony, "my ears are all yours. What is it, Andrew?"

"I've just got back from Chelmersley. Well, about half an hour ago. The body I went to look at has been definitely identified as that of your friend Temple Spooner. What do you make of it now? Satisfied?"

"I don't know about being satisfied, Andrew. I'm not surprised. I wasn't when you first heard the news. Who identified him?"

"The two Bullocks. Father and son. James and Jim. I took them down in the car."

"I see. Anything unusual about the body?"

"No. According to the M.O., blow on the head with the time- honoured blunt instrument. Savage sort of blow. Nothing else noticeable."

"I suppose you had a nice long talk with Jim and James."

"Naturally. One of the main reasons I went down there."

"Get anything?"

"A large ball of nothing. James, however, views the future with great trepidation. Too old to start a new job. That was the principal burden of his song. Otherwise I might just as well have saved my breath and not asked them anything. Do you know what I think about them?"

Anthony grinned. "I'll buy it."

"I think they're either a couple of dumb clucks or a brace of cunning rogues. I can't make up my mind which. But I shall—in God's good time."

Anthony chided him gently. "Andrew! That's a serious admission. And I thought you always prided yourself on being a judge of character."

"All right. Come out into the open yourself. What's your opinion of them?"

Anthony shook his head at the challenge. "Don't rush me, Andrew. I refuse to be rushed. Hang it all, I've only once seen the beggars."

His mood changed suddenly from gay to grave. "So Temple Spooner has definitely joined Lovelace, eh? Trodden the same road. Now I wonder why. Unless, of course, it's a case of . . . "

He broke off and stood there with the far-away look in his eyes which MacMorran knew so well. The latter, however, became severely practical.

"By the way," he said, "Sergeant Dixon was here when I came in. In the house here. I had a fairly lengthy conversation with him. Did you see him when you first arrived? Was he here then?"

"I saw him—yes. Frankly, I was rather surprised to find him here."

"Did you discuss the case with him?"

"No. Not at all. Beyond the conventional greeting, I don't think we spoke."

"Dixon's got a bee in his bonnet. Did you know that?"

Anthony smiled. "Go on! One solitary bee? Or a hive?"

"One—and it's a big fellow, I can tell you. Never off the buzz."

"What's the colour of it?"

"It concerns the disposition of Lovelace's will. The unusual nature of it. With regard to the legacy. You can guess what I mean."

"Mrs. Forbes?"

"Ah-ha! That *was* the idea."

Anthony made no further reply. MacMorran showed his persistence. "What do you think of it yourself?"

"The Mrs. Forbes business? Nothing different from what I told you before. *At the moment.* Nothing's happened so far to cause me any qualms. That isn't to say, of course, that it *won't* happen. All the same, though, Andrew, if I were in your place I'd tell Dixon to confine himself entirely to the routine enquiries you give to him and to forget all about his bees. Certainly at this stage of the case."

The Inspector nodded his acquiescence. "Yes. I think I will. But I thought I'd tell you about it. Let you know."

"O.K., Andrew. Thanks. I understand."

MacMorran went on. "I'm trying to get a line on Temple Spooner's past. Got two men working on it. Up to the moment they've turned out precious little. Nothing, really, of any significance. He seems to have had the establishment in Cavalier Circus for a good many years, and there's nothing against the place's reputation. Or against his, either. Rather the reverse as a matter of fact. All fair and aboveboard."

"No relatives at all, are there? No family? No anything?"

"That's the story according to the Bullock brothers. They seem to know more about him than anybody. Certainly nobody's turned up in connexion with his death."

"H'm. I wonder. Bit early days yet. Now that we know what we do know, and now that we've picked up what we have picked up, how do you value the story that Scudamore brought us? What we'll call the cinema story?"

"Looks like there was something in it."

"How big's the something?"

"Well, looks like there was a lot in it. If that's what you want me to say. But what chance have we of identifying the men Scudamore overheard talking? Two men whom he never even saw, mind you! All he can pass on to us are his impressions. And they're pretty vague."

"Now I'll tell you something, Andrew. I went over to Scudamore's house just now to have a word with him. Mainly with regard to his original story of the cinema business. That's where I'd been when I came in. In the course of our talk he told me something that made me sit up and take notice. What do you think it was?"

"No idea. Tell me."

"Well, it takes a bit of believing, but Scudamore told me not more than an hour ago that he'd heard the voice of one of his two cinema men here in Loveridge since Lovelace was killed. And, which makes the story even more interesting still, the day he heard this voice was the day of Lovelace's funeral. He's absolutely positive with regard to that."

MacMorran stared at Anthony. The stare was full of incredulity. "Pretty difficult to believe that, isn't it? What do you think? Who was the man?"

"Scudamore doesn't know. That's the main snag. All he knows is that the voice came to his ears. He doesn't know where. He doesn't know who. He hardly knows when—except that he heard it the day that Lovelace was buried."

"That's pretty thin, I must say." MacMorran bordered on indignation as he continued. "It sounds to me a ridiculous sort of thing to say. What do you think of it yourself?"

"To tell you the truth, Andrew, I don't quite know what to think about it. I must think it over very carefully. Don't forget, I haven't had it very long."

"But—but . . . " MacMorran almost spluttered, as he found words, "why did he keep it to himself all that time? Why has he only just told you about it? Why didn't he out with it at once? Of all the—"

"He explains the delay," replied Anthony, "by saying that he knew the story sounded rather feeble and that quite frankly he jibbed telling us about it. Says he thought you'd pour scorn on it."

"Pour scorn!" MacMorran's indignation knew no bounds. "If you ask me, that's no more than a lot of utter 'bull'—pour scorn, indeed! I like his style! If that's the case, what made him unload it on you just now? The two things won't wash."

Anthony shrugged his shoulders. "Don't know. Unless, seeing me rather unexpectedly shocked him a trifle and shook it out of him. That's just a possibility, I think."

MacMorran shook his head hopelessly. "I just don't get it. As I said, I think it's plain 'bull'. In fact I'm rather surprised that it's got by you as it has."

"It hasn't got by me. I told you, I hadn't had time to consider it properly. You see, Andrew, there's perhaps a little more in Scudamore's story than I have made clear in the bare telling."

MacMorran was adamant. "I still don't get it . . . "

"Well, don't forget that the only identifying factor that remains to Scudamore of his experience that evening in the cinema *is* the voice factor. He heard two voices. He never saw, well enough to recognise, that is, either of the owners of the two voices. So that there is no visual memory for him to hang on to. Now a voice memory is of an elusive quality. Nothing, perhaps, could be more so. And his story amounts to this. What I told you just now I'll amplify a little. This is how I understand it. Because Scudamore tried hard to get me to understand. On the day of the Lovelace funeral he went to the church in one of the cars that followed the hearse. He listened to the funeral service in the church. From the church he went to the graveside for the last offices. He returned here for the subsequent formalities and, when the day was over, he went back to his own home. All this would be in the natural order of things. When he was thinking over the various events of the day something floated out of the ether, as it were, and titillated his memory. A spoken phrase that he'd heard *at some time or other during the day*, and he realised with a sort of shock that the voice which had uttered the phrase was one of the two voices he had heard that evening in the cinema. Now, do you get it better?"

MacMorran frowned at the question. He made no direct answer. "Well, and what was this wonderful phrase that brought about the great Scudamore voice-resurrection? Anything which touched on the killing of Lovelace?"

Anthony met the MacMorran frown with a smile. "Well, you can sort that out for yourself when you hear it. The phrase was 'Well, he knew what it meant, but he went.' "

Anthony waited for it to sink in. "Who knew?" demanded MacMorran suspiciously.

"Search me," replied Anthony. "I don't know who said it, or where it was said, or when it was said. But presumably—only presumably mind you—the 'he' might conceivably apply to Lovelace. It might equally conceivably apply to the tom-cat which the Lovelace house may or may not hold."

The Inspector turned and looked at Anthony with even more suspicion. He made no comment, however, on Anthony's statement.

"The strange thing, Andrew," Anthony continued, "is that this wretched sentence which Scudamore says he heard seems familiar to me in some way or the other, but I'm hanged if I can place it."

"Don't know about it being familiar, it all sounds pretty daft to me," declared MacMorran. "It reminds me of a line in one of those weekly paper competitions that used to be so popular some few years ago. You know the kind of thing I mean." MacMorran rumbled into laughter as clearer reminiscence came to him. "I can recall one now," he announced, "went like this."

> There once was a tenor named Fred
> Who was singing one morning in bed.
> When he took a top note
> It stuck in his throat,
> So he boraxed his thorax instead.

"Ha-ha-ha-jolly good that. I remember that the missus showed it to me. I've never forgotten it. 'He knew what it meant, but he went.' Yes—that's the idea."

The laughter of the Inspector gradually subsided. Anthony shrugged his shoulders and waited for him to quieten down. in "Well, there you are, that's the Scudamore story as I had it."

"So it may be. And I'll say again I don't think much of it. And in your heart of hearts no more do you."

MacMorran looked at his watch. "I think I'll 'phone the 'Yard'. I arranged to when I left—somewhere about this time. They may have something more for me in connexion with Temple Spooner deceased."

Anthony nodded. "Let me know if you do get anything."

"I will," replied the Inspector, "although I'm not really too hopeful."

"Why not?"

"Don't quite know. Just a hunch. We all get 'em at times." The Inspector walked away towards the telephone.

2

The windows of the Forbes house looked out across the drive and commanded the road from Loveridge to Chelmersley. It was a long room, the dining-room, low-ceilinged, cool and eminently comfortable. Anthony and his fellow-guests were gathered round their host and hostess—Robert and Evelyn Forbes.

Dinner was over, and on all counts it had been excellent. Anthony, on the immediate left of his hostess, was ready to concede as much, with no limitations. There could be no cavilling at its high standard. The food had been unostentatious, the cooking really first class, and the service beyond reproach. Both the sherry and the claret had been wines of clear, unmistakable quality. The guests were those people who had been present at Lovelace's funeral with the exception of the two Army officers, Mapperley and Hargreaves. Conversation had flowed easily throughout the entire meal and there had been no undercurrents of discomfort to produce any lack of ease. The quietest member of the company during dinner had been the Vicar of Loveridge—Philip Sheridan. His conversation had been confined almost to monosyllables, and Anthony had little doubt from the uniform nature of his replies that Sheridan was deliberately playing a part.

Ilsley, on the other hand, had been most talkative. By deft handling and easy control the solicitor had manipulated the wires of the conversation so that it travelled lightly and easily from the O.P. riots at the Covent Garden Theatre at the beginning of the nineteenth century to perfumery, the Ignorantines, the gap-toothed Wife of Bath of Chaucer, the prophetic utterances of Mother Shipton, Boule marquetry, and ultimately to a certain delectable type of kedgeree which Robert Forbes had tasted when he had been in India, and which, it seemed, he had never been able to forget.

Anthony lit a cigarette from a case which his hostess proffered to him and waited for something to happen. He felt that something was almost certain to happen, if only for the fact that Evelyn Forbes had so deliberately invited him to dinner with these other guests. By the time the decanter of port came in and started its circular progression Anthony was still waiting for his anticipated climax. For Evelyn Forbes had not yet left the table. When she did, some few minutes later, her husband rose and opened the door for her departure.

With Evelyn's going the conversation amongst the men became desultory. Anthony had a feeling come to him that all natural incentive for good talk had passed. The decanter of port went from hand to hand with something like regularity, but despite this, good talk still seemed to lag and almost dried up completely. When Forbes offered the wine to Anthony for the third time in rather rapid succession, Anthony declined the courtesy with a smile. Soon afterwards the host rose and pushed back his chair.

"Shall we join Mrs. Forbes? I think we might as well, don't you?"

There was a chorus of almost eager assent from the men, and Anthony and the others followed Robert Forbes out of the dining-room, across the corridor and into the lounge. It was altogether a delightfully charming room of several windows. The furniture was just right, the pictures elegantly excellent, the general colour scheme beautifully attractive, and the lighting in the wall embrasures soft and shaded.

"It's surprisingly dark for the time of the year," said Evelyn, "the sky has clouded over. I do hope we aren't going to have a storm. I loathe thunderstorms."

"Shouldn't be surprised," said Sheridan, rather surprisingly for him. "I didn't like the look of my glass when I came out this evening. And the radio report wasn't any too good, either." Evelyn came to them with a tray that contained coffee-pot with cups and accessories. She came to Anthony first.

"Coffee for you, Mr. Bathurst?"

"Thank you, Mrs. Forbes."

"Black, or would you rather—"

"Black, please."

Anthony took the little cup that she indicated on the tray and watched her interestedly as she floated off to serve her coffee to the others. He moved away and found a seat on a low settee. Gradually, when all had been served with coffee, Evelyn worked gracefully back to the middle of the lounge. She sank languidly on a large pouffe. The men appeared to be gathered round her almost in a circle. Anthony felt positive that she had engineered both the scene and the circumstances of its setting. Ilsley raised his coffee-cup and drank to her.

"The general position," he said, with a rather flamboyant air of gallantry, "has been reversed. Instead of being at the feet of beauty we have beauty at our feet. We are flattered. My felicitations."

Evelyn coloured a little as the company accepted Ilsley's mood.

"Beauty," she repeated, with a touch of weary cynicism, " 'all that Beauty e'er gave'. I needn't go on, I feel sure."

A silence ensued. Even Ilsley seemed a little taken aback by the lady's reply. Suddenly she looked directly and deliberately at Anthony. She fanned away cigarette smoke so that she could see him better. Anthony knew that something was coming—he wondered what. Was the curtain about to rise on something interesting?

3

Evelyn exhaled smoke with the utmost coolness, and reached for an ash-tray. Her husband assisted her. She acknowledged the courtesy with a graceful little movement of the head. Sheridan sat in a low chair near the end of Anthony's settee. Ilsley was slumped forward in an arm-chair with Evelyn's back and shoulders close to his knees. Forbes himself sat by the hearth in a chair of cunning shape and style. Away in the distance could be heard the rumble of thunder. Thunder which seemed to be coming nearer.

Anthony thought, as he watched, that Evelyn Forbes shivered a little at the sound. But he saw that the curtains had been drawn at all the windows so that the sudden, sharp shock of lightning would not beset her. And he still wondered what was coming next because the other curtain by now was most definitely up.

"I wonder," said Evelyn Forbes, in silky tones, "if any of you have seen in the newspapers about a man's body having been found a day or two ago on the outskirts of Lapping Wood?"

As she finished, the voice was less silky—more incisive. Anthony watched intently, to see the various reactions to Evelyn Forbes's question. She herself lifted her head somewhat, and at the movement Ilsley shifted his position slightly in the arm-chair. Forbes looked surprised and wondering. Ilsley seemed puzzled. Sheridan answered the question.

"Yes," he said, "as a matter of fact I noticed a paragraph to that effect in this morning's local paper. *The Chelmersley Weekly News*. But why do you ask? Is there any particular point about it? Is it particularly interesting in any way?"

"Did you notice the name of the dead man? Or wasn't it given in the local paper?"

Sheridan gave a sort of half-smile. Evelyn looked across at him as she spoke.

"I believe the name *was* given," said the Vicar of Loveridge, "but I'm afraid that my memory is unequal to the task of reproducing it. But you didn't tell us, Evelyn. You didn't answer me. What's your point in mentioning it?"

She turned and addressed Anthony. "What was the name of the dead man, Mr. Bathurst? You can tell us, I feel sure."

"It is believed by the Police," answered Anthony, "that the dead man's name was Temple Spooner. He has been identified as such."

Forbes laughed. But the laughter held but little humour. On the other hand it sounded cynical and contemptuous.

"Well, I'm blest if I know," he said, "but what's this all about? Where are we getting to? Come on, Lyn, let's have the gen. What's on your mind? This kind of cat-and-mouse game—"

His wife checked his speech before he could finish. "You've heard what our guest Mr. Bathurst said. That the dead man's name was Temple Spooner. That's the name I saw in the paper which I read. Is the name by chance familiar to any of you?"

Forbes came back at her at once. "Why? Do you think it is?"

"I have an idea that it may be," answered Evelyn evenly.

"Well, you can strike me off the list," said Forbes. "Never heard it before in my life."

The Vicar shook his head. "Same with me, Evelyn. Same as Robert. It's entirely unknown as far as I'm concerned."

"What about you, Robin?"

Ilsley pursed his lips in consideration. "Well," he replied at length, "I may have met the name at some time or the other. But I just can't say with anything like certainty. You see, my job as a solicitor brings me into contact with a great many people. It's certainly possible, even likely, that I've run across the name at some time or the other. I shouldn't remember the names of all the people that cross my professional path. Or that have crossed it in times past. So you see, that's how it is with me. But perhaps if Evelyn were to explain to us a little more fully what she has in mind we should all be in a position to answer her queries with much more certainty and understanding."

Ilsley looked at his hostess invitingly. Forbes added argument to Ilsley's. He spoke with emphasis.

"I agree with you entirely, Robin. Come on, Lyn, let's have it."

Evelyn Forbes, thus challenged, answered with a definite hint of impatience.

"I should have thought," she said, "that you would either have known or recognised the name, or the contrary. That, in other words, it was a clear-cut issue. Anyhow, here's another question that I'll put to you in the same relationship. Did any of you ever hear Dick Lovelace mention the name? Recently?"

Again Anthony watched with interest. But the faces of the people to whom the appeal had been made were blank. There was no response from anybody beyond head-shaking. The first spoken reply came from Ilsley.

"I don't think that I quite understand. I'm still where I was. What connexion had Lovelace with this dead man?"

"That, my dear Robin, is precisely what I'm endeavouring to find out. In the hope that one of you may be able to help me."

"So you may be, but all the same you must have a reason for asking us what is, after all, a rather surprising question."

"I have an excellent reason. I'll tell you what it is. Dick mentioned the name Temple Spooner to *me*. Only a short time before he was killed. Which has caused me to wonder since if he had mentioned the same name to any of you."

"In what connexion," riposted Ilsley immediately, "did he mention it to you?"

"I can't remember," replied Evelyn Forbes coolly and unblushingly.

"I'm afraid, then," countered Ilsley swiftly, "that you're not going to get any help from any of us here. Looks like it to me."

"Pity," said Evelyn; "still, it was worth trying. There was always the chance."

"You've told Bathurst, of course? That Dick had mentioned it?"

She replied evenly and steadily. "Yes. Mr. Bathurst knows."

Forbes broke in impetuously. "Well then, that's all right. That settles the matter. Why should you worry, Lyn? The authorities will link the thing up, and if there's anything in it they'll thoroughly investigate it and sort it all out. There's certainly no point or purpose in your meddling."

To Anthony's surprise, rather, the lady accepted the rebuke with complete composure.

"Very well, then," she said, rising from her sitting position, "we'll leave it at that; none of you can help me. Perhaps you'd like me to sing something."

There was a chorus of assent. Evelyn went to a small grand piano, chose some music with deliberate care and accompanied herself. The song which she sang, "Were It In My Power", was unknown to Anthony. The lady at the piano sang well, with feeling and understanding. And her contralto voice was musical—she hit her notes with ease and clarity. Her voice didn't spread itself over the notes, which in Anthony's experience is the habit of most modern singers. More songs followed. There was no disputing the singer's supreme art.

When the time came for Anthony to leave there had been no other incident.

CHAPTER 13

1

A nthony had walked from 'Cherry Fair' to the Forbes house earlier in the evening inasmuch as the distance was comparatively insignificant. For the same reason he declined upon leaving the offer made by Robert Forbes to drive him back.

"It's very good of you, my dear Forbes," Anthony had said, in reply to the gesture, "but I won't trouble you. Really I won't. I can stroll back as easily as I came."

Anthony was sincere in this, especially as the storm had rolled away to the coast and the rain had ceased. The storm, too, had cleared the air. The humidity of the early evening had gone, giving place to much pleasanter conditions.

"Well, my dear chap, it's up to you," Forbes had said. "I'm at your disposal—only too pleased."

But Anthony had smiled and persisted in his refusal and shortly after ten o'clock he shook hands all round and started on his return journey. As he walked down the gravelled drive a rather sickly moon was beginning to show through the clouds and at odd times the path he travelled was silvered beyond his feet. The grass still glistened under the rain which it had so recently received, and the shrubs and bushes held great drops of dangling water which lightened under the new conditions so that they looked altogether artificial and unreal.

Anthony made no haste over his journey—his car was parked at the Lovelace house—and he walked slowly but firmly from the drive to the road. As he made it he could still hear the voices of his host and hostess, speeding, probably, others of their guests. A few yards along the road he decided that he would smoke. He took a cigarette from his case and stopped in his tracks to light it. There was no wind whatever, the air was cool, quiet and still. The task, therefore, was easy.

Anthony drew the first puff of smoke into his lungs and slowly exhaled. On the whole, he thought, and taking everything into consideration, a decidedly interesting evening. Especially with regard to the way Evelyn Forbes had played her hand. He had not been prepared for that. Which quality had been uppermost in the playing? Anthony began to wonder. Subtlety or insouciance? Another thing—had she got anywhere? Anthony doubted it. Had she made a mistake to come out into the open, as she had? Had she given away anything of value? Possibly! But difficult to say yet awhile. Time alone would tell. There was the definite possibility, however, that Evelyn's gambit would produce sequels of some kind. They must be watched for and prepared for.

Musing thus Anthony walked steadily on and came to the fork-roads, one of which would take him into Oriel Lane. He crossed at the appropriate spot, and as he did so the sound of his own footsteps was challenged by another sound. The sound of different footsteps, and footsteps, too, if he were any judge, that belonged to more than one person. Anthony tried to locate the sound with some exactitude. The people of the footsteps were certainly not behind him. Indeed, he felt pretty certain that they were coming towards him. Approaching him from one of the roads of the junction away to his right.

For some reason which would have been difficult for him to explain had he been asked, he halted at the beginning of Oriel Lane and inserted himself adroitly into the shadow of a high hedge. In this sanctuary he waited quietly for some few seconds. Until the figures of two men came in sight. From the direction they were taking, Anthony guessed that they were making for the centre of the village. If he were correct in this surmise they would not come past him, but would swing away sharply to their left. He prepared, therefore, to leave the haven of his high hedge and to proceed down Oriel Lane to 'Cherry Fair'. And then, at the precise moment that he came out of the hedge and twisted round to resume his walking, something in the walk of one of the men caught both his eye and his imagination. It was familiar to him—most certainly familiar. Now where the . . .

Anthony stopped again, turned and watched the two figures as they receded into the distance. To his surprise, somewhat, he saw that they walked in complete unison. Each walked in exactly the same manner as the other. There was the same swing of the arm right from the shoulder, the same stiff holding of the head and body, and the same outward fling of the feet. Now where the heck had he seen that walk before—and recently at that? It was as familiar to him as the morning. Revelation was sudden and surprising. Anthony caught his breath.

The two men whom he had just seen on their way into the village of Loveridge were none other than James and Jim Bullock. They looked, Anthony thought, more like twin brothers than father and son. What had brought them to the scene of the first murder?

Anthony resumed his walk to 'Cherry Fair' at a slower pace, giving full and serious consideration to the question. This was a new complication, to be sure. The time, too, presented a problem to him. Between ten and eleven o'clock at night. And not only why were the Bullocks in Loveridge, but also where exactly were they going? What house in Loveridge would give them hospitality for the night?

Anthony had much on his mind as he came to 'Cherry Fair'.

2

MacMorran was waiting by the car when Anthony arrived. The Inspector looked at his watch. There was criticism on his face.

"I was beginning to think you'd made a night of it," he said.

"No, Andrew," replied Anthony, smiling, "nothing like that. I never let a man down."

There was a silence. Anthony broke it. "I'm not over late, am I? Didn't I say I'd be back about this time? I think I did. I left the Forbes place about ten o'clock. Which was more or less about the time I expected to."

MacMorran grinned back at him. "O.K. Not a lot in it, perhaps. Well, what do you say; shall we buzz off? Nothing else to wait for, is there?"

Instead of taking the driving-seat, however, as the Inspector had anticipated, Anthony put his back against the car door and leant against it. MacMorran turned and looked at him with some suspicion. Very soon the suspicion which had showed on his face changed to a frown.

"What's going on here?" he asked, "what have you picked up at that dinner-party of yours? Tell me, what's on your mind?"

Anthony shook his head. "Nothing, Andrew. Nothing like that. Not a sausage. The dinner-party, as you were pleased to call it, to which I was invited, was prim, proper and decorous in the extreme. No tigers passed my way while I was there, I assure you. No, it's what's happened on my way here to you since that's tickling the old grey matter. So much so, in fact, Andrew, that I'm seriously wondering whether it's our best policy to return to town tonight. Suppose we motor over to Chelmersley and stay at the 'Infidel's Head'? Won't take us much more than half an hour. Not a bad show, you know. What do you say to the suggestion?"

MacMorran became direct.

"Will you kindly tell me the story of what happened after your party so that I can pass judgement, or won't you?"

Anthony grinned as he took a cigarette. "Come and sit inside the car, Andrew, for a little while. There's no reason why we shouldn't be comfortable. Then I'll tell you."

3

MacMorran, saying nothing, accepted Anthony's invitation. Anthony took the seat at the driving-wheel and the Inspector inserted himself into the car at Anthony's side.

"Now," declared MacMorran, "let's have it. Quit stalling. What's all this tarradiddle about tigers? To hear you talk anybody 'ud think we were on the track of a ruddy circus. What tigers did you expect to pass you, anyway?"

Anthony began to speak gravely and quietly. "Well, as I just told you, nothing much happened at the Forbes dinner, Andrew. You can take it from me that I came away with just about as much as I took in. That was on the disappointing side, I admit, because, frankly, I had hoped for better things. Other guests were Sheridan, the Vicar, and Ilsley, the solicitor. I expected them to be present when I accepted Mrs. Forbes's invitation. They're all as thick as thieves in Vallambrosa. Scudamore, no doubt, would have been there also but for the fact that he'd fixed up another engagement. But that's another story which needn't be gone into at this juncture."

"Go on," said MacMorran.

Anthony ignored the interruption and proceeded on an even keel.

"When I came away from the Forbes house, Andrew, I refused the offer of a lift in the doctor's car, as I felt I'd like to walk back here to you. I'd walked there, and I wanted to return in the same way. For one thing the distance is inconsiderable, and for another the night was fragrant and cool after the storm, as you yourself know. I left there, as I said just now, round about ten. Well, nothing happened until I came to the place where the roads fork— you know where I mean."

MacMorran nodded confirmation.

"Well, as I reached the fork of the roads and began to cross in the Oriel Lane direction, I heard the sound of footsteps, and as soon as I heard it I felt almost as certain as I could be that they were being made by more than one person."

Anthony paused. "Go on," said MacMorran again, but rather differently, this time.

"I'm going on," replied Anthony. "For some reason which I couldn't adequately explain—it was a sort of spontaneous impulse —I got under cover of a rather high hedge at the beginning of the turning there. I think that I thought it strange that people should be walking into Loveridge so late in the evening, and that's the direction which I fancied the footsteps were taking. I was moderately certain, as I stood there, that they were *approaching* me. You know how it is in these 'ere parts—you scarcely ever see a soul in the streets after ten o'clock. I know that I never have."

MacMorran nodded corroboration. "I agree. Same here."

"Well, Andrew, I waited there under the high hedge, and sure enough, making for Loveridge, two figures appeared. They reminded me of a couple of soldiers—walking in step. They were men, naturally. And then something hit me, and hit me so forcibly that I took a good look at them. The moon was up, so it wasn't difficult. Andrew, you old ruffian, they were buddies of yours. Two of your recent discoveries. What have you got to say about that, eh?"

Anthony half turned in the driving-seat and regarded MacMorran whimsically.

"Pals of mine?" declared MacMorran incredulously.

"That's the idea." MacMorran shook his head. "I don't get it."

"Think of those tigers of mine."

"Tigers? Here, what's all this about?"

"Keep on with the Noah's Ark. Try another animal."

"Animal? Another animal? What the—"

"Think of Yorkshire pud. and horseradish sauce."

"Tell me," said MacMorran.

"Bullocks, Andrew! In other words, our friends James and Jim. All the way from Plashet in the county of Herts."

MacMorran whistled under his breath. "The last I saw of them they were *en route* there from the mortuary at Chelmersley. I'd just arranged for their transport home."

"They've come back, then. All the way from Plashet. May have given your bloke the slip. I'm positive it was they. Not a shadow of a doubt."

MacMorran's face was set as he heard what Anthony had said. "H'm," he remarked. "The ruddy, cunning baskets—makes you wonder, doesn't it?"

"It does and all," replied Anthony facetiously, "makes you wonder all sorts of things. One, why are they so suddenly transported to Loveridge? Two, if they were sent for, who sent for them? Three, what has Loveridge, small village that it is, to do with two employees of a man who is now dead? If you like, for 'dead' read murdered. There are other questions which might be added to the list, many of which, doubtless, you can think of for yourself. But time is short and we can't stay here all night."

MacMorran, at Anthony's side, grunted non-committally.

"Now you know the reason, Andrew," continued Anthony, "why I thought we might with advantage remain a little nearer at hand than town. What do you say—Chelmersley? Can I persuade you? Or can I tempt you? The beer at the 'Infidel's Head' is, so I am informed by experts, of an unusually high standard of excellence. It's delightfully cool, it has a beautiful amber colour, and its flavour—"

"Make it Chelmersley," said the Inspector, "and tread on it."

"Very good, sir."

"The reason I decided on Chelmersley had nothing whatever to do with—"

"I'm sure it hadn't, Andrew," replied Anthony.

CHAPTER 14

1

Being the Saturday prior to the August Bank Holiday, the streets of Chelmersley were unusually thronged, as Anthony and the Inspector drove back to Loveridge on the following morning. "What's the programme?" asked MacMorran, as the car turned into the Wagbury road.

Anthony shook his head. "Don't know, Andrew. Been wondering myself. Haven't made up my mind yet. But it certainly won't do us any harm if we're on the spot early. We shall be in a position then to watch points. It's possible, I think, that if we move about in the right places, we may perchance run into our two friends. Whatever their activities may be, they should be of some interest to us."

MacMorran nodded his agreement. "It'll be worth trying. But they may have gone to earth somewhere. That's what I fancy will happen in all probability. At any rate we must be prepared for something like that. Can't see James and Jim showing their faces in Loveridge to all and sundry. I told you before what I thought of that pair. Cunning rogues, if I'm any judge. And what you told me last night only strengthens the opinion. It actually kept me awake thinking of it. Incidentally, I called in at the station this morning and had a word with the Inspector at Chelmersley. After breakfast, while you were getting the car ready. For one thing, I wanted all the information he'd got in relation to Temple Spooner."

The Inspector paused. Anthony favoured him with a sidelong glance. "Oh, what did you get out of him?"

"Well, it's yet another strange thing. According to what I heard this morning they haven't got anywhere. They haven't the foggiest idea yet how he came to be in Lapping Wood. Or even near it! The whole business really amounts to this. That since Temple Spooner left his home at Plashet (as per the Bullock story), and his body turned up on the edge of Lapping Wood, there hasn't been a trace of him or a whisper about him to appear from anywhere or anybody. Blank wall—all the time. And that's the latest from Chelmersley!"

Anthony turned the statement over in his mind. As he directed the wheel of the car to negotiate a corner, he said "darned peculiar, that, Andrew. I'm absolutely with you. And, of course, if we become severely analytical, there's also this to it. For the story that Temple Spooner *did* actually disappear from his home at Plashet we have only the word of the Bullocks. Seems to me, Andrew, that we must walk warily. The possibilities that have opened up are tremendous. We mustn't take *anything* for granted." As he spoke, the car moved into Oriel Lane.

2

Immediately upon arrival at 'Cherry Fair' a surprise awaited Anthony. Mrs. Toplady met him and the Inspector almost as they crossed the threshold. With a face as heavy and impassive as ever, the lady allowed MacMorran to pass her before she made an advance towards Anthony.

Anthony, sensing that she needed him for some purpose or the other, stopped short and waited for her to come up to him.

"Good morning, Mr. Bathurst," she said, almost with an air of apology, "but I wanted to see you. There's a letter come for you this morning. Sergeant Dixon said I was to give it to you directly you showed your face here."

"Oh, and what's Sergeant Dixon writing to me about?" asked Anthony.

The butler's wife shook her head. "No, Mr. Bathurst," she said, "that isn't what I mean. You've got me all wrong. A letter 'as come here for you by the post this morning. I didn't mean that Sergeant Dixon had written you the letter. Perhaps I misled you the way I put it to you. As I said just now, a letter has come for you in the post. this morning. When the Sergeant came along—and I can tell you I wasn't altogether expectin' 'im—I showed it to 'im and I asked 'im what I should do with it, and 'e said wait till the gentleman comes along, Mrs. Toplady, and then deliver it into 'is 'hands—personal. That's what I meant I'm sorry."

"That's all right, Mrs. Toplady," said Anthony, "no harm done. Where is this letter you're talking about?"

"I'll get it for you," replied Mrs. Toplady, "it's on the mantelpiece in the kitchen. I put it up there for safety. If you'll be good enough to wait just a moment, I'll fetch it for you."

"Thank you, lady," said Anthony smilingly, "you're the tops. Or at least one of 'em."

Mrs. Toplady bustled off in the direction of the kitchen. Before she had time to reappear, MacMorran had turned back.

"What did I hear her say? Letter for you—addressed here? That's rather remarkable, don't you think? Who knows that you're here who can't communicate with you in person? Who has to write a letter about it?"

Anthony signified his acquiescence. "I entirely agree, Andrew. I've been thinking on exactly similar lines. But we shall soon know all about it. Here comes La Toplady."

Mrs. Toplady put the letter into Anthony's hand. "There you are, Mr. Bathurst. That's the letter. I've done as the Police told me—delivered it into your hands."

Anthony thanked her. "Let's see what it's all about, Andrew." Anthony examined the envelope. "The writing is unfamiliar. Also unscholarly. And the postmark is Chelmersley. Chelmersley, you observe. Neither London nor Loveridge."

Anthony opened the envelope. The message which the letter contained caused him to raise his eyebrows. The letter had neither date nor address of source. This is what he read.

Sir. If you would discover some of the truth at least with regard to the strange problem which is now engaging the attention of Scotland Yard please note that the sun will be shining to welcome the day! That is to say in this particular case come to the fair in the evening. And when you're there let your watchword be—"A horse, a horse, my kingdom for a horse." Ha—ha—not so bad, that! Yours, and leagued against crime and criminals

—Anxious Observer.

Anthony frowned, rubbed the ridge of his jaw and re-read the letter. Then he handed it to MacMorran. "There you are, Andrew. Read it for yourself. Pick the bones out of that."

He watched the Inspector's face as the latter read the lines of writing. When MacMorran had finished reading he shook his head. He handed the letter back to Anthony.

"Your guess," he said, "is as good as mine. It may even be better. Please understand, you're very welcome. But this case is certainly one out of the bag."

Anthony said nothing for a moment or so. Eventually MacMorran prodded him.

"Come on! What do you make of it, chum?"

Anthony replied with a counter question. "To-day," he remarked slowly, "is the beginning of the annual August Bank Holiday period. To-day is also Lammas. And Monday next, according to some people, is known as St. Lubbock's Day. Is there a fair in the vicinity, do you know?"

"Search me," said the professional. "Ask old Toplady. He ought to know. He's been here a year or two. It may be an annual event in the district at this time of the year. As a matter of fact, fairs at holiday times are quite the thing in rural districts. You must have noticed that yourself."

"Like *crime passionel*, eh? Maybe the two go together."

"Send for the old buzzard and ask him. Let him put you out of your misery. Then I shall feel better myself."

Anthony nodded, walked towards the kitchen and called out to the butler. Toplady heard the summons and came at once. Anthony thought that his arms looked longer even than ever.

"You wanted me, gentlemen?"

"Yes, Toplady. We do want you. A question for you that I'd like you to answer. Fairs, Toplady! Hoop-la, swings, roundabouts, shooting galleries, fat women and lovely bunches of cokernuts."

Toplady almost winced at Anthony's words, and a pained expression came over his face.

"Yes, sir," he replied frigidly, and with a most decided suggestion of distance.

"Can you tell me, Toplady," Anthony continued, "if there's a fair in this district at the present time?"

Toplady shrank into himself. Distance grew and lent less enchantment to the view.

"I'm not in the 'abit, sir," answered Toplady, "of frequenting such places myself. I never 'ave been—I dislike the general air of vulgarity and ribaldry that pervades them—I dislike it very much, but I believe that there *is* such an exhibition in Loveridge at the present time. I understand, too, from certain gossip that 'as reached my ears, that it will remain in the vicinity over the Bank 'Oliday. It caters for the entertainment of the masses, sir, or at least so I'm led to believe."

"I see," replied Anthony, "thank you for the information. That's just what I wanted to know. Could you tell me the exact site of this hive of iniquity?"

"Yes, sir." Toplady coughed behind his hand. "The affair is usually 'eld in Holloway's Meadow. That's where the discordant noise 'as come from in previous years, and I 'ave no reason to suppose that this year will be any exception."

"And where exactly is Holloway's Meadow?"

"You would walk from 'ere as far as the forked roads, sir, take the right-'and fork—that is to say the Chelmersley road—and the place is about two 'undred yards down on the right-'and side. You will realise, sir, when you are approaching the . . . er . . . affair . . . by the . . . er. . . rather unseemly noise which seems, if I may say so, quite inseparable from its normal h'activities."

Anthony thanked the butler for his information with a show of gravity.

"Is there any further information, sir, that you require?"

"No, thank you, Toplady. You've given me what I wanted. I'm glad I approached the right man. Many thanks."

Toplady bowed gravely and withdrew. Anthony turned to the Inspector.

"You heard, Andrew! We seem to have run to earth the appropriate association. Holloway's Meadow is the place we want. On the Chelmersley road. Strange we didn't spot it as we came along. Any comments thereon?"

MacMorran shook his head. "No. Fair's evidently fair in this case in more directions than one. What will you do? Turn up at the fair this evening?"

"I think so, Andrew. Turn up there and wait and see what happens. Just in case our theory's the right one. What about you? Don't you think that you might have a run, too? To strengthen the ranks?"

MacMorran rubbed the tip of his nose. "You think I might lurk a bit? In the background?"

"That was the idea, rather? Any snags about it that you can see?"

MacMorran rubbed his nose for the second time. "Depends. Depends, it seems to me, on who sent the letter."

Anthony smiled. "Not much doubt about that, is there?"

MacMorran looked at Anthony. "You mean—the Bullocks? Or may be one of them?"

"Looks very much like it to me. One—or both—as you say. Knowing what we know of their recent movements. Why—did you have any other nominations?"

"No. I can't say that I had. All the same, you never know. You've contacted a fair number of people since you've been on the case and you don't know how many different interests you may have aroused. I admit that it looks like the Bullocks. Because there's no doubt that they know a great deal more than they've led us to believe. As I said yesterday, a pair of cunning baskets. One of these days they may feel my hand on their shoulders."

MacMorran scowled. Then he changed his tone rather. "So you'll keep the appointment this evening? That's agreed, eh? And I'll do a spot of lurking. Then maybe it won't be two against one. Even things up a bit."

"I think so, Andrew. It's an opportunity, perhaps, to learn something. When you're on a problem of this kind it doesn't do to slam a door that's on the point of opening."

MacMorran remained practical. "What time?"

"What time? Oh, I don't know. Let's see now. Our friends of the letter have used the phrase 'in the evening'. They probably prefer a touch of darkness. Just here and there, say. What would you say to eight o'clock, Andrew? Or is that a shade on the late side? What do you think?"

"No," replied MacMorran. "I think that would be about right. At this time of the year. We'll decide on that, then. Eight pip emma."

"O.K.," returned Anthony.

3

That evening Anthony and MacMorran made their ways to Holloway's Meadow separately. The Inspector went first and by eight o'clock was mingling with the crowd of men, women and children, and hoping that he was a comparatively inconspicuous figure.

The number of people present in the meadow amazed him. Whereas he had expected an attendance of hundreds, he now assessed the figure upon arrival at a good three thousand. It was soon clear to him that the people had come from many towns and villages beyond Loveridge. Indeed, MacMorran formed the early opinion that there was a considerable contribution from Chelmersley itself.

He jostled and rubbed shoulders with the crowd generally, and looked on casually at the hoop-la, "wheel 'em in", shooting-gallery, some sort of game that looked to him as much like bagatelle as anything, and eventually found himself standing in front of a large booth which advertised "many and valuable prizes" for "throwing on the square" or "ringing the top". From somewhere about the middle of the arena came the strident strains of the roundabout which was going about its work to the ancient tune of "I'm ninety-five, I'm ninety-five and ain't I glad that I'm alive". Near to the roundabout were the swings, chair-o-planes, and the cokernut shies.

The Inspector moved with the crowds quietly and unostentatiously. Many faces were scanned by him without the person of the scrutiny knowing anything whatever about it.

After completing the full circuit of the fair twice, MacMorran drifted over to the cokernut-shies and hung round there on the fringe of the participants. As the evening wore on the noise increased. But he had no stroke of fortune. Nobody accosted him or excited in any way the Inspector's suspicions. Since he entered the fair he had seen nobody whom he recognised. He looked at his watch. The time was past nine. He had been there over an hour. The time had certainly passed quickly.

MacMorran decided on a third tour of the fair in Holloway's Meadow. He began, therefore, to retrace his steps, still scrutinizing carefully many of the faces of the company round him. MacMorran walked slowly, but such was his art that he didn't appear to be doing so. At a quarter past nine he found himself back at the shooting-gallery. And the evening was still without incident.

4

Unlike MacMorran, on his roving expedition, Anthony felt that he had a definite objective. Crookback's cry, so unmistakably featured in the letter he had received that morning, indicated, Anthony felt positive, the roundabout. Anthony therefore made for the roundabout in the middle of the fair, and when he got there looked about him generally.

According to his calculation there were forty mechanical horses on the move, an outside ring of twenty and an inside ring which contained a similar number. The noise was prodigious. Anthony took careful stock of the riders as the horses careered round in front of him. But to no avail—from the particular point of view of his presence there. Not a rider was known to him. Not a face was familiar. As far as he could tell, every rider was a complete stranger, as far as he was concerned. He waited where he was for the horses to come round again. It made no difference, however—the position remained the same.

Anthony began to think again. Had he jumped to certain conclusions too quickly? Had the writer of the letter, "Anxious Observer", been a *stranger*? Had he himself made a mistake in attributing the authorship to a Bullock or Bullocks? On second thoughts it might conceivably be an unknown who had communicated with him that morning. Still, it was comparatively early yet—no good jumping to further conclusions yet awhile.

The roundabout began to slow down gradually, and the raucous din of its musical accompaniment followed suit. Anthony watched the various riders descend from their horses to the platform and from the platform to the grass. Almost all of them were flushed and excited. He turned and looked at the queues lining up for the next revolving ride. Again there was nobody in the line whom, as far as he knew, he had ever seen before.

He decided, therefore, when the roundabout re-started, to walk round the fair generally, and keep his eyes open as he went. He could and would return to the roundabout later. If, by any chance, he ran into MacMorran, he wouldn't know him! It would be better that way. From what he knew of the Inspector, the latter would take the cue and lie low. Anthony turned away from the merry-go-round and began to walk in the direction of the shooting-gallery where the crowd seemed at its thickest. The time now was 8.32.

5

MacMorran, it may be recorded, had reached the roundabout just about a couple of minutes after Anthony had left it. The result was that there was no encounter between them. And, actually, for the next half-hour or so, they toured the fair, one at a reasonable distance behind the other. By 9.15, when the Inspector had arrived back at the shooting-gallery, Anthony found himself looking again at the roundabout and listening to the strains of its old song.

The current tour of the horses was just on the finish. Anthony searched the faces of the various riders as they descended. But again all were unknown to him and not one of them seemed to show the slightest desire to make his acquaintance. Girls and young men, teen-age children with an occasional middle-aged woman, made up the motley crew of riders. Elderly men were conspicuous by their absence.

He turned to look at the queue for the next ride, and as he did so an idea came to him. It might well be, he thought, that the writer of the letter meant him to *ride* the horse and not merely stand and look at it!

Anthony came to a quick decision, turned on his heel and took his place within the queue. There were a good many people in front of him, as may well be imagined, but he was just in time to make the next ride. He found himself on a horse within the inside ring and an attendant with a rattling cash-bag quickly collected his fare. The strident blare of the music started up and the wooden horse on which he sat began to move . . . forward . . . up . . . down . . . but always forward. The roundabout gathered speed and Anthony's hands went to the wooden neck for balance. He saw that the name of the horse he rode was "Fair Judgement".

Rather extraordinary that, he thought. Was it an omen or merely an aid to delusion?

6

As things turned out, it proved to be the latter. Anthony completed his hilarious ride without untoward incident of any kind whatsoever. He saw nobody whom he knew. Nobody took the slightest interest in him beyond the commonplace glance or ordinary contact. Nobody actually spoke directly to him. Nobody even jostled him. Many smiles, a few screams and some laughs came his way as he took his part in the musical ride, but that was all. The music ceased yet once again, the roundabout came to yet another standstill and Anthony slid from his wooden steed, walked to the edge of the revolving platform and slipped down to the grass of Holloway's Meadow.

Back in the crowd again, he looked at his wrist-watch. The time was just on a quarter to ten. Not so terribly late, perhaps. On the other hand, though, so he considered, it was probable that had there really been an appointment for him it would have been kept prior to this time. He decided, however, to walk round the fair again. Just in case . . . !

As he made his way from the neighbourhood of the roundabout, MacMorran came towards it from the opposite direction. Once again encounter was avoided. A triumph of unplanned planning!

7

About an hour later MacMorran glanced at the time by his watch, left the dining-room at 'Cherry Fair' and walked out to the waiting car. Just as he reached the car he heard the sound of approaching footsteps. He listened for a few seconds and then walked away from the car towards the sound. As he had anticipated, it was Anthony. MacMorran grinned at him when he came up. "Much cry?" he inquired.

Anthony nodded. "As you say, Andrew—and little wool. No— worse than that even. Neither a skein nor a semi-skein. No wool at all."

MacMorran grinned again. "Come to the fair," he said cynically, "I'll say! And we both went. Smoked pair! Well, well, well! Don't tell the boys."

Anthony grinned back at him. "My kingdom for a horse. And a wooden one at that. Did you spot me in the saddle?"

"No."

"I was there, Andrew. I did the thing properly. Rode the merry-go-round. Surrounded by much of the world and quite a number of its wives. Incidentally, you might care to know that the name of my horse was 'Fair Judgement'.

MacMorran rumbled into laughter. "Go on! That's a ripe one, I must say! Well, what do we do now?"

"We drive back, my dear Andrew, to the rest and comfort of the 'Infidel's Head' at Chelmersley."

"Do you refer, by any chance, to that place where the beer is so good?"

"I do."

"And what do we do after that?"

Anthony took the wheel. "I've remarked to you more than once in the past, my dear Andrew, that to-morrow is also a day. The philosophy applies, I suggest, with equal force, to the day after to-morrow."

"That," replied MacMorran brilliantly, "will be August Bank Holiday."

"Exactly," returned Anthony, "and there will be a fair again in Holloway's Meadow. And within that fair will be a merry-go-round."

The Inspector eyed him shrewdly. "I see. That's the game, is it?"

"As you say, Andrew. That *is* the game. Are you?"

MacMorran took the point adroitly. "I am."

"Good. We'll hunt again, then. I'll ride, and you can lurk. Maybe the luck will turn."

CHAPTER 15

1

If the Saturday attendance at the Loveridge fair had been surprisingly good, that of the Bank-holiday Monday which followed exceeded it considerably.

Anthony and MacMorran, following a short, preliminary discussion, agreed to adopt exactly the same tactics as they had employed on the preceding Saturday. They decided, as well, to arrive at Holloway's Meadow at approximately the same respective times.

Upon arrival, MacMorran at once mingled unobtrusively with much larger crowds that seemed to be here, there, and everywhere. Anthony, as before, made for the middle of the arena where the roundabout, alas, was rotating almost intemperately to the accompaniment of the same hurdy-gurdy tune.

When he reached a spot fairly close to the roundabout queue he looked round carefully. Once again, however, no contact was made with him. As before, all the people in the vicinity were entirely unknown to him and not one of them denoted in any way any desire to approach him.

Anthony's thinking-cap went into a huddle with itself and began to work overtime. Questions he had asked himself before came back to torment him. Had he misinterpreted the terms of Saturday morning's letter? Or, looking at it from a different angle, had it been a gigantic leg-pull? Was "Anxious Observer" laughing up his sleeve somewhere at the way Anthony had gulped down the bait? Or, possibly, up *her* sleeve? The thinking-cap buzzed again. Anthony glanced at his watch. The time was now 8.22. And, as things were, he looked very much like having another fruitless evening.

2

Anthony strolled round the fair in Holloway's Meadow until approximately 9.30. At intervals he had stayed by the various side-shows just long enough to escape comment. At half past nine precisely he turned back towards the roundabout and joined the waiting queue for the next tour. Like Destry, he would ride again.

When he made the platform, he eventually found himself on a horse in the outer circle. Whimsically, he looked down at the wooden neck to ascertain the horse's name. It was "Now or Never". Anthony smiled to himself to see it. Perhaps it would turn out to be more appropriate than the "Fair Judgement" of Saturday. The music started and the mechanism began to revolve as the peals of laughter began to come. Anthony wondered if anything would happen this time. At the back of his mind, ransack it how he would, he felt that by using the merry-go-round he was doing the right thing. Making the proper gesture—playing, if you like, the correct card.

And then something did happen! As the horses, going well, passed the queueing line for the third time Anthony saw with something of a shock a face that was familiar to him. It was the face of the man who had tried to sell him a little hound of Fo K'ans Hsi. In the shop in Cavalier Circus!

3

With rioting thoughts, Anthony waited impatiently for the wretched roundabout to stop. Such was his anxiety to descend that it seemed to him that this tour of the merry-go-round lasted considerably longer than usual. Thus are we fretted by impatience!

When at last the contrivance did reach a standstill Anthony slid like an expert from the back of "Now or Never" and jumped quickly to the grass. He made at once for the spot where he had seen the man from Temple Spooner's shop, fully expectant that the fellow had seen him on the merry-go-round and had waited for him in the same place. To Anthony's profound disappointment, however, the man was not there. He had disappeared.

The crowd was thicker than ever round the queueing line, but there was no sign of the horse-faced man from Cavalier Circus. Anthony circled the immediate area of the roundabout. Dash it all, the man couldn't be so very far away! There hadn't been time. Anthony came back, however, to the place from which be had started, smarting under a keen disappointment. There was still no sign of his quarry. Well, he'd try another method before he gave up. He wouldn't perambulate again—and stay put. In the exact spot, as far as his memory could judge, where the man had been standing. As he waited, dodging the people all round him, seeming to move with them and away from them, and yet not really moving at all, he wondered if by any chance the man had spotted Andrew MacMorran, known him for what he was, and scrammed!

After a time of consideration, Anthony rejected this theory. After all, why write to Authority, off your own bat, and then sheer off at Authority's intelligent response? No rhyme or reason in such tactics. Just pure waste of time. If he waited only long enough . . . Anthony put his plan to the test and waited in more or less the same place until 10.30. At that time he looked at his watch, called it a night and turned away reluctantly, to rejoin forces with Andrew MacMorran, in accordance with their arrangement.

4

As on the Saturday evening, Anthony found MacMorran waiting near the car. And as before, MacMorran greeted him facetiously. "Good evening, dear teacher, good evening to you. 'Appy Bank 'Oliday and many of 'em. Do you know what you can do with all your fairs and all your horses? You can—"

Anthony replied with mock solemnity. "Desist, Andrew. I need neither advice nor prompting. Also, I know exactly how you feel. Because I feel much the same myself. Get into the car and I'll talk to you."

MacMorran, realizing that Anthony had become serious under the layer of levity, did as he had been directed. Anthony followed him into the driving-seat and the car started off.

"Now, Andrew," said Anthony, "you just sit there quietly and listen to what I'm going to tell you. Because I think you'll find it interesting. Remember my telling you of my call at Spooner's place in Cavalier Circus? Where I managed to get his home address—Wilton Lodge, Plashet?"

MacMorran nodded assent. "Ay. Well enough. What about it?"

Anthony turned the car out of Oriel Lane. "Do you remember the horse-faced chap I told you about? The salesman there? Who did his best to sell me a pup? A special pup of Fo K'ans Hsi?"

"Ay. I remember. But I misremember about the animal. What about him?"

"Well, he was at the fair this evening. In Holloway's Meadow. And now that I've seen him I'm beginning to wonder whether he isn't trying to sell me another pup—of the ordinary breed this time." Anthony paused.

"Go on," prompted Andrew MacMorran, "spill it."

"There isn't a lot to spill, Andrew. After wandering about this evening, with both eyes open for what seemed a heck of a time, with nary a bite of any kind, I repaired once again to that instrument of torture known as the merry-go-round. The time, then, I should say, would be just after half past nine. Once again I queued up in due course and in time rode a horse."

"'Fair Judgement' again?" queried the Inspector with a quizzical glance at his companion.

"No. Not this time. A stayer this evening. 'Now or Never.' I do pick 'em, don't I?"

"Granted. Carry on with the report."

"Well, as I said before, there isn't a lot. Just as we were circling round for the third time I spotted the merchant I'd previously seen in Temple Spooner's shop in Cavalier Circus. He was standing about a dozen yards from the merry-go-round, looking up at it. I'm certain that he must have seen me. I was on the outer ring. Naturally, I thought he was our man. Who writes letters to us under a sobriquet. Wouldn't you have thought the same?"

"I should. Nothing else for it. But tell me the rest."

"I'm going to. Well, when the blessed thing came to a full stop I jumped off pronto and simply hared for the spot where I'd just seen the fellow. I anticipated he'd been on the look-out for me, had spotted me on the horse and would be waiting for me to contact him as soon as I reasonably could."

Anthony paused. "Well," prompted MacMorran, "what actually did happen?"

"Nothing doing, Andrew. Nothing whatever! Not a sign or a whisper. He'd scrammed. Later on I looked everywhere for him. But I did no good."

MacMorran made no reply. His brow was furrowed and his lips pursed as he thought over what Anthony had told him.

"What do you make of it?" said Anthony eventually.

"Don't know. And that's a fact. Unless, of course, the chap saw a red light shine somewhere and decided on the quick that discretion was his best suit. That's the obvious explanation."

"Yes. I see the way you're thinking. Do you think he could have spotted you? Recognised you? Out of the pages of the past? *His* past? All dark and murky?"

"Maybe. It's an idea. I've had a few clients through my hands in my time. All kinds! Some from Eton and some from Eton Mission. They're all fish in a 'busy's' net."

"Well, that's the story, Andrew. That's what happened to me to-night in Holloway's Meadow. I'm beginning to wonder where we're getting to. Whether we're really getting anywhere. Or just running round in circles with our tongues out. In other words, Andrew, I'm profoundly disturbed."

Anthony trod on the juice and the needle hovered round the fifty. They came to the 'Infidel's Head' at Chelmersley in quicker time than ever before. When the journey finished in safety, MacMorran heaved a sigh of relief. Anthony listened carefully for the heave.

5

Anthony garaged the car and within a few minutes rejoined MacMorran in the smoking-lounge of the hotel. The Inspector rallied him.

"Well, any afterthoughts? Or do we call it a day?" As he spoke, MacMorran busied himself with tobacco for his pipe.

"I think we'll call it a day," replied Anthony, "or night, come to that."

"I think we should. I'll have a pipe before I hit the hay, though. What do you say?"

"Good idea. And a beer, I think." Anthony went across to the appropriate corner and pressed the bell for the porter. "I'm thirsty, Andrew. I could drink the Thames dry. I don't know about you, but I've a thirst many a man would trade rubies for. It's the result of chasing Horse-face."

The porter came to the summons and Anthony ordered the drinks. When the porter had taken his departure Anthony felt in his pocket for his cigarettes. MacMorran, who was watching him through a haze of tobacco-smoke, saw his face suddenly change.

"What's the trouble? Been dipped?"

Anthony shook his head. "No. Rather funny. On the contrary, Andrew. As far as I can tell, I appear to have collected something." He took from his pocket a piece of folded paper which he examined curiously and carefully before opening it. MacMorran began to chuckle. "The biter bit, eh? Well, well, well! If you didn't find anybody, somebody evidently found you and made you a present. Scotland Yard for ever!"

Anthony grinned at the thrust. "I hang my head in shame, Andrew."

As the porter brought in the beers Anthony looked up from reading the paper.

"This is rather interesting, Andrew, and at the same time rather absurd. You listen to it and see what you make of it. I'll read it to you. It's that old doggerel which features anagrams. You've seen it yourself, no doubt, more than once. Most magazines have published it in their time. But you listen to it. This is how it starts. Seven of them. Don't forget that. Because it's doubly important. 'A sutler sat in his ulster grey, Watching the lustre of moonbeams play, On a keg that low in the water lay. Thou rulest the weak, thou lurest the strong, The result of thy ways is woe and wrong. And the rustle of leaves took up the song. "Anxious Observer." ' "

MacMorran embraced contempt. "Fairs, horses and now sutlers! What the hell's a sutler? When he's at home? One who sutles?"

"Precisely, Andrew. One who followed an army and sold provisions and liquor to the troops. Chiefly the latter, I believe. Its popularity is eternal."

"Is that so," MacMorran seemed somewhat impressed. "A decent sort of bloke, eh? Ah well, we live and learn."

He held out his hand for the piece of paper. "Let me have a dekko—do you mind?"

Anthony handed it over. MacMorran furrowed his brows and read it studiously.

"What's this seven joke?" he demanded eventually, with a touch of impatience. "Any idea?"

"Why, there are seven anagrams there, Andrew. In that piece of doggerel. The seven words—sutler, ulster, lustre, rulest, lurest, result and rustle—are all variations of the same six letters. And that's what our friend the writer means to convey, I take it. He stresses the number seven. But what the blazes it all means or what it's about—well, ask me another! There's no doubt that he means something, though, otherwise he wouldn't have taken the trouble that he has. He's already bunged two communications at me. I shall have to get down to it. See if I can make anything of it."

MacMorran shook his head. "Fairs, wooden horses and now ruddy sutlers," he growled "why can't the man say plainly and outright what he wants to say and have done with it? That's what beats me."

Anthony shook his head gravely. "Fear, Andrew! Fear! Our friend 'Anxious Observer' has no wish to share the fate of Lovelace and Spooner. That's the answer for a certainty—depend on it." Anthony paused and then went on again. "For one thing, look at the manner in which he kept out of my way at the fair to-night. After he had showed himself to me. Doesn't want to come too far out into the open or show his hand too much. Sort of 'thus far, and no farther'. Pretty obvious, isn't it? Don't you think so?"

"Looks like it, I suppose," conceded the Inspector lugubriously. "What do we do, do you think?"

"Sleep on it, Andrew. I may find inspiration that way, who knows? I may endure 'through watches of the dark, The abashless inquisition of each star'. Francis Thompson, Andrew."

"Never heard of him," replied MacMorran, "and if I had, man, I tell you he'd not be fit to black the boots of Bobbie Burns. Ah, there's a poet for you! Why, I can recall one night in Abairdeen when I was a braw laddie aboot so high—"

"I'm going to bed," said Anthony. " 'Night, Andrew. I'm sure the reminiscence will be atrocious."

MacMorran stared at Anthony's retreating figure with a look of amazement mingled with incredulity. Then, as the door closed, he shook his head in speechless indignation. Francis Thompson indeed! When there was Burns!

CHAPTER 16

1

It was some time, however, before Anthony got to sleep that night. Apart from the problem of the sutler in his ulster grey and what exactly the message about him meant, Anthony's main mental concentration was on the rather startling fact that the small village of Loveridge, or its near vicinity, now held, in addition to James and Jim Bullock, the shopman from the establishment of Temple Spooner in Cavalier Circus. The man who had dealt in antiques.

What did it all add up to? If Lovelace had died as he had, why on earth had Spooner died as well? What had been the reason behind the second murder? Had Spooner robbed Lovelace in the first place and then had the murderer in turn robbed Spooner?

Anthony shook his head more than once as the various questions presented themselves to him. The best policy that he could pursue would be for him to assemble without further delay all the clues and half-clues which he had so far managed to pick up. He attempted to arrange them mentally, in some sort of list. The following is the list at which he eventually arrived and which he visualised with his mind's eye.

A. The two words that had been on the lips of the dying Lovelace 'tea-spoon' and 'innocence' (or 'innocent'). The first of these had been already explained—not so, however, the second.

B. The fragments of conversation which Martin Scudamore had overheard in the cinema which had been the beginning of the whole business. These had included 'four rings' and 'innocence'. The word 'innocence' appeared, therefore, for the second time in the series.

C. The 'Berners' thread in the tangle. Berners had written a book about the house in Lincolnshire which had come to Lovelace as part of a legacy from his aunt. And Berners's initials had been mentioned in the cinema conversation. Yet Berners disclaimed all knowledge of Temple Spooner.

D. The pictures in the library of Lovelace's house had been tampered with presumably and most probably, also—on the night of the murder, and in view of what Toplady, the butler, had stated later, a similar attempt might well have been made subsequently on the pictures in the dining-room, during the night following the murder. Vide—the cigarette stub that had been found in the wrong place and which the butler was unable to account for.

E. The sensational disclosure of Robin Ilsley of the Lovelace will, with Evelyn Forbes the sole legatee—or as good as! With that, Anthony listed Evelyn's story of the letter which Lovelace had received from Temple Spooner just prior to his death.

F. The strange behaviour of James and Jim Bullock—the dead Spooner's servants. What could be the real cause of their appearance in Loveridge last Friday night? Who had sent for them? Or, alternatively, whom had they come to see?

As he considered the various points of the problem, Anthony realised how much depended on the statements of the different people. Particularly with regard to those statements which it was not possible to verify. In order to assess better the relative values of the various statements made to him and to others, Anthony went over the clues and the semi-clues again.

A. Lovelace's spoken words had *both* been verified. Sergeant Dixon and Doctor Forbes had agreed thereon and it would be difficult indeed to believe that any degree of collusion could exist between them.

B. On the other side of the picture, Martin Scudamore's account of the conversation he had heard in the cinema was almost entirely uncorroborated as regards the details. But the trend of events since he had first reported it had certainly gone far to confirm its main points.

C. Berners. Berners came into the affair first of all *via* Martin Scudamore's story. According to Scudamore, initials which corresponded with his had been used by one of the two men in the cinema. Again, what had taken place since strongly tended towards confirmation of this. For the reason that Berners, through his family antecedents, was definitely connected with the house in Lincolnshire where Lovelace had previously resided. But—and here Anthony came to the point to which he had arrived before—Berners denied all knowledge of Spooner. Important point was, of course, *was Berners telling the truth*?

At this stage of his mental review Anthony decided to leave points D and E for the time being and go straight on to point F. Point F—because James and Jim Bullock had also linked up with Berners. *Was their tale true* that Temple Spooner, just prior to his death, had endeavoured or had intended to get in touch, with Berners? If the Bullocks *had* lied with regard to Berners's story it would put an entirely different complexion on Anthony's general problem. But again, so Anthony thought, the probabilities were that they had told the truth. If only for the fact that their account of the disappearance of Temple Spooner from the house at Plashet in which he resided had been most thoroughly substantiated by the discovery of his dead body which they had been called upon to identify by the Chelmersley police.

Anthony retraced his mental steps to the points he had listed under D and E, but which he had temporarily passed over. He reviewed the latter point first. Mainly in relation to Evelyn Forbes. The fact of the legacy, of course, and its conditions, was unassailable. He himself had heard Robin Ilsley read the clauses of Lovelace's will. But what about the story of the letter which Lovelace had received from Spooner? There was only Evelyn's word for it. And she had been somewhat tardy in disclosure.

And yet, Anthony pondered, the general circumstances of Lovelace's murder, together with the Spooner sequel, seemed to suggest that Evelyn Forbes's story had the weight of truth behind it.

Anthony then took point D—the only one that remained for the second inquisition in which he was indulging. Toplady's story, that the dining-room at 'Cherry Fair' had been entered during the night that followed Lovelace's death. Toplady had pointed to the cigarette-stub lying on the floor near the wall. And conceivably, below certain pictures. The butler had been positive in his assertion that the stub had not been there when he had retired to bed on the previous evening. He had hinted gravely and unmistakably at a person or persons unknown. Once again, there was only Toplady's word for all of these statements. They were entirely uncorroborated and unconfirmed. He might easily have dropped the stub himself.

Anthony began to calculate values and possibilities. Into what skein could he thrust his hand and feel that his fingers had clutched round the right strand? It seemed to him, as he lay there meditating, that first of all he must attack the message which had been placed in his pocket that evening as he had strolled round the fair in Holloway's Meadow. For it had certainly not arrived there by accident.

Thus musing, Anthony fell asleep. In his dreams he rode a wooden horse that was swathed in an ulster grey. Other horses ran at his side. There were seven of them.

2

After breakfast at the 'Infidel's Head', on the following morning, Anthony retired to the smoking-lounge with the lines of doggerel concerning the sutler who sat in his ulster grey and who moralised on the temptations of alcohol. What had been the opening words of the communication that had accompanied them?

Anthony referred to them again, to refresh his memory. "Seven of 'em. Don't forget that. It's important." The operative word, thought Anthony, must be "seven". No subtlety about it—stuck out like a sore thumb. In what particular manner, though, was this "seven" intended to operate? First of all, there were seven lines of doggerel. Secondly the words of the respective anagrams also numbered seven.

Anthony checked these with care to make certain that his premises were right and tight without loophole. Yes, seven it was—sutler, ulster, lustre, lurest, rulest, result and rustle. Seven lines, therefore, and seven anagram words within them. Taking the seven anagram words, however, as an example for a connected or even semi-coherent sentence, Anthony arrived nowhere. How many words were there in the doggerel altogether? Anthony counted them. He had a kind of excited idea when he started the count that there were going to be 49. That is to say seven squared. But when he had completed the tally he discovered with a certain amount of absurd and almost childish disappointment that it came to only 48. One short of the square of seven. He'd still arrived nowhere. Back where he started.

Why the heck, then, was seven so important and such insistence placed upon it? Because the sender had certainly insisted on its importance! There must be something in it. Seven must play a part in some way. And it was up to him to find that way. Supposing he extracted every seventh word? Would that get him anywhere? An idea worth trying possibly! Anthony tried it. He found himself with grey, on, water, lurest, ways, rustle. Anthony considered the six words he had thus distilled from the angle of all possible arrangements. And once again he arrived nowhere.

He took the first letters of each of the words with similar result. And then, quite idly, as it were, he noticed something. He noticed that, reading from the beginning, the seventh word was "grey" and that reading from the end, the seventh word was "rustle". "Grey and rustle." "Grey and rustle." And then, suddenly as the words tinkled round his brain, Anthony stood up from his chair and smiled. Well, well, well! There might be nothing in it, of course. It might be just one of those coincidences with which Life abounds. But, on the other hand, it might not. Anthony's smile broadened. It was akin to the smile on the face of the tiger!

3

On his way out from the smoking-lounge Anthony ran almost straight into MacMorran. As he did so, he got an impression that the Inspector was in an unusual hurry. The impression was immediately confirmed.

"I've just had a 'phone message from the station," said Mac- Morran. "Inspector Hurst wants a word with me with regard to something that's been turned out concerning the late Temple Spooner. The 'Yard' have been in touch. Wants me to go along as soon as convenient. So I thought about going now. Is that O.K. by you? Or had you anything particular in mind for us?"

Anthony shook his head at the question. "No, Andrew. That's all right as far as I'm concerned. You pop along there at once and pick up whatever gen that's going. I think I'll take another stroll round Loveridge. For a change."

MacMorran looked a little mystified at Anthony's remark. His head jerked up.

"How do you mean? It can't be change of air, very well, and it can't be change of scenery. What is it?"

Anthony shook his head. "Hard to say, Andrew. Now that you've put me on the spot. The nearest answer, I suppose, would be 'change and decay'. Or in other words, the old firm, Andrew. Business everywhere. Families waited on daily. Brass handles an extra."

MacMorran frowned at Anthony's reply. "Why can't you—"

Anthony smiled and closured him before he could finish. "I'm sorry, Andrew. When I used the word 'change', I spoke carelessly in the first place. I'm going into Loveridge—leave it at that for the time being. If I'm lucky I'll tell you more later on. Perhaps at dinner this evening. Now you run along to Inspector Hurst and the antecedents of Temple Spooner and leave me to the devices and desires of my own heart."

MacMorran nodded. "Ay. I'll be content to do that. Especially as you said it yourself. And I hope you'll be turnin' away from your wickedness to do that which is lawful and right."

4

Anthony left the car in its customary sanctuary at 'Cherry Fair' and proceeded at a comfortable walking pace in the direction of the main street of Loveridge. It might even have been written truthfully, the only street in Loveridge. For certainly this street was unique in its possession of a collection of shops and business establishments. Anthony's mind was in conflict as he walked.

He knew that within a comparatively short time he was destined to embrace either elation or disappointment. He knew, at the same time, all about the two impostors and the treatment which should be accorded to them by all good men and true.

It was in this semi-critical, semi-wondering mood that he came to the 'Ring o' Bells' at the corner of the High Street. Next to the quaint-looking inn was the forge, then came a row of thatched and whitewashed cottages, and after them the establishment which did duty as the Post-office, general stores and handy shop. After the Post-office, Anthony passed the butcher's, the fruiterer's and the fishmonger's. Hard on the last-named was the clothier's—which exhibited a typical store of clothes, caps, coats and the like, to dress the male inhabitants of Loveridge—*cap-à-pie*.

Anthony knew now, although relying on memory, that he was close to his objective. He was right. After passing a tiny dairy with creeper-covered front and publicly named 'The Churn', he came to the establishment which had, an hour or so ago, aroused his keener interests. Yes, the shop-front told him what he wanted to know. Once again his memory had been accurate. The name on the front and tricked out on the glass of the windows showed plainly. 'Gray and Russell, Funeral Undertakers'. Grey and rustle! Described too, thought Anthony whimsically, as 'Undertakers' and not 'Directors of Obsequies and Professional Morticians'. Out of step, evidently, with the march of Time.

Anthony went to the front door of the establishment and tried the handle. Somewhat to his surprise, he found that the door wouldn't open. He tried a second time, but again the door refused to yield—either it was locked or fastened. Anthony peered through the glass. He could see nobody inside the shop, but many of the more familiar signs of the undertaker's trade were there to be plainly seen. He looked for the bell or a knocker, but neither was visible to him. Another shake of the door brought him nothing but a jarred thumb, so Anthony repaired to the small dairy next door, with the creeper-covered front.

The girl behind the counter, who looked up at his entrance, afforded him yet another surprise. Her make-up generally would have befitted the front row of the chorus. But it was definitely a good show and by almost all standards quite a tasty piece of home-raised crackling.

"Good morning," said Anthony, at his brightest and best. "I'm sorry to trouble you, but I'm wondering whether you could help me. I wanted the people next door—Gray and Russell—but the place doesn't seem to be open this morning. At any rate, I can't get into the shop. Could you advise me at all?"

The girl seemed to understand the position at once. "I know," she said promptly; "the place seems to have been shut up like that for several days. There doesn't seem to be anyone there. We can't make it out at all. All I can think is, it must be a case of holidays. But it's funny, isn't it? You'd have thought they'd have put a notice up for the public to see. Either on the door or in the window. We've had several inquiries for them during the last few days."

Anthony nodded. "I've no doubt you have. And there certainly should be a notice put up somewhere. Who is it that's away—can you tell me—the Gray part or the Russell portion? Or both?"

The dairy girl shook her head decisively. "Oh, no. Neither. Those names don't mean anything. There isn't any Gray or Russell there now. It's been like that for some months. Gray and Russell sold the business early in the year, but the new people who bought the business chose to carry on the business under the old name. Something to do with the goodwill, I believe."

"Really," returned Anthony, "that's decidedly interesting. Who were the people that bought the business from Gray and Russell— any idea? The new people?"

To Anthony's dismay the dairy girl shook her head for the second time.

"No, I haven't," she said; "the man who's been carrying on there has seemed to me to be some sort of a manager. I don't think he's the actual proprietor. His name was Da Costa. When the business changed hands, the ordinary everyday staff, as you might call it, were kept on. Like the coffin-maker and those other dismal Jeremiahs who turn up for duty whenever there's a funeral."

"I see," said Anthony slowly, as the information began to sink in, "so it's Mr. Da Costa that's really absent from the outfit? Is that the idea?"

The girl nodded briskly. "Yes, I suppose it would be—looking at it like that."

Anthony threw out a line. "Let me see now," he said contemplatively, "Da Costa's the tall, thin, dark fellow, isn't he? With dark hair and dark eyes? Or am I mixing him up with somebody else?"

"Oh, no," said the girl, "you're quite wrong—that can't be Mr. Da Costa—the man that you've described. It's you who's mistaking somebody else for him. Da Costa's an elderly man. Sixtyish, I should say. Not very big. Plump, not to say fat, and not much hair left on his head. Looks something like a prosperous publican. Quick-moving and rather penetrating dark eyes. If you're familiar with Loveridge, you must have seen him about here from time to time. He gets about quite a lot."

By this time Anthony's thinking apparatus was working hard and beginning to tick over.

"Oh, I think I know the man you mean," he said, speaking slowly "yes, I think I recognise Da Costa now from the description you've just given me of him. I *have* seen him in the village. And I'll tell you where it was that I think I saw him last. At the funeral of the late Mr. Lovelace. I rather fancy that Da Costa was the man who had charge of the funeral on that occasion."

The dairy girl nodded vigorously. "That's quite true and you're quite right. I remember that day well. Seeing the dreadful business it was with the poor man murdered like that. But as I said—you're quite right. I saw them go off from here that morning. I mean on the morning of the funeral. On the way to the house. I saw the hearse *and* the corteedge—and Mr. Da Costa was in charge. I should think they've closed down for a holiday week or something like that. It *is* August, after all. Lots of firms do give their staff the Bank Holiday week off—I know that for a fact. The laundry does for one."

Anthony remonstrated. "But didn't I understand you to say that the place next door had been closed for some days? I certainly thought you said that when I first came in. If it had been closed for a few days only you might be right when you suggest there's a vacation on, but—"

The girl intervened promptly. "Yes. You're right—of course. I was forgetting. It can't be the August holiday."

"And they're undertakers, you know," continued Anthony; "not exactly a luxury trade. They undertake! After all, people do die—every day, and when they're dead there's the body, you know. Got a knack of being left behind. Got to be put away somewhere. Can't very well leave it lying about. In the way, for one thing. The M.O.H. wouldn't approve. Take rather a dim view."

"Still," said the girl, from behind her large white milk-basin, "there's always Chelmersley, isn't there? Not exactly a frightful distance, is it? And there are three funeral directors in Chelmersley. I know that for a fact." She paused and then added brightly "one of 'em was the Mayor the year before last. His name was Downham. Funny, it was at all the big local functions that year the Mayoress was always dressed in black. People used to talk. One woman who was supposed to be a dressmaker said her dresses were made out of the palls they used for the funerals. Creepy, isn't it?"

"Appalling," returned Anthony "but there you are—the combination of business with pleasure is frequently misunderstood and misinterpreted, even by the nicest people with the nicest qualities and the nicest minds. I'm afraid it's a habit that will refuse to die out."

The dairy girl regarded him rather doubtfully and then deserted the lightly conversational for the severely practical.

"What will you do then?" she asked, "go to Chelmersley? You'll have to, won't you? There isn't much option."

Anthony shrugged his shoulders. "Do you mean," he asked, "in search of the vanished Da Costa?"

"Why, no," replied the handmaid of 'The Churn', round-eyed. "I thought it was a case of death. In your family or something. Don't you want them to—"

Anthony shook his head. "No. Not exactly. It's a death all right, but not quite in the way you imagined."

"You mean you don't want a coffin?"

"Not at the moment," replied Anthony "even if it means disappointing you, and I also have no wish to anticipate events. Who would have?" He paused and smiled. The dairy girl seemed somewhat taken aback that the offing contained no coffin. Then he said "thank you very much for your information."

The dairymaid recovered her poise and smiled back at him. "It's a pleasure," she said. "I'm sorry I misunderstood you about what you wanted."

"I echo the first sentiment," said Anthony, "but on the other I have an open mind."

A second later he closed the door of 'The Churn' behind him. "Funny," said the maid of 'The Churn' "if he didn't want a coffin—what did he want? Oh, I know—must have wanted a tombstone."

CHAPTER 17

1

S o that it had come to neither elation nor disappointment! He had missed his man. The bird, of whatever type it had been, had flown. Nevertheless, it was something to know that there was a definite bird which had taken cover not so very far in front of him. Who was Da Costa? This undertaker's manager? And why was he missing from his chisels, coffins, corner-stones and constructed cherubim? Was Da Costa a corpse as well? Number three in the series?

As he walked back to the car at 'Cherry Fair', Anthony deliberated as to his next step. For the life of him he couldn't be sure of any immediate procedure that looked at all likely to pay dividends. Had the Bullocks come to Loveridge to meet Da Costa? No! Da Costa, according to Patience, the milkmaid, had almost certainly removed or been removed from Loveridge *before* last Friday evening. It was doubtful if the Bullocks had been there before that. But there was no doubt whatever about one thing. The horse-faced salesman from the shop in Cavalier Circus had directed Anthony's steps towards the undertakers in Loveridge High Street. He had wrapped the message up, through fear of discovery and its sequel, no doubt, but his intentions were now clear and obvious.

Anthony came back to 'Cherry Fair', stood by the bonnet of the car and scratched his cheek. So many clues—and comparatively simple clues at that—but none that shewed what he himself would call a clear ribbon of road. Should he return to Chelmersley to see MacMorran or should he cast a line elsewhere? For one thing, the day was young yet and the car was there in front of him.

Anthony took a cigarette and lit it. Before the flame of the match had died away his thoughts went again to the Scudamore cinema incident.

There was something tucked away somewhere in that conversation, as Scudamore had reported it that first afternoon in Anthony's flat which Anthony desired to drag again into the light of day. Gradually, by strong and concentrated mental process, Anthony revived the words which he wanted. They had concerned a business of some kind. Buying a business. One of the men, the man Scudamore had described as "the boss", had made use of the expression—"why do you think I bought that business when I did? Because I loved you?" That was the gist of what had been said (according to Scudamore), at any rate!

Anthony stood by the car, thought of those words again, and began to rub his hands. That business! Could it have been the undertakers at Loveridge which had belonged originally to Messrs. Gray and Russell? If it *had* been that way, it would explain what Patience the milkmaid had said with regard to the way the business had been run since the sale by Gray and Russell early in the year. She and her people, no doubt—had had good reason to look on this man Da Costa who had taken over as a manager and not as the actual proprietor.

But what was it all about? What was behind it all? Anthony reviewed the human links in the chain. Lovelace, Spooner, Berners, the Bullocks, and now Da Costa. Two dead men and one missing from his familiar place. If Da Costa had been one of the men whom Scudamore had heard talking in the cinema, who had been the other? The man who had seemed to be the other's boss? If only Scudamore had seen them better and been able to describe them. That would have put a different complexion on the affair altogether. There was another point also. If Martin Scudamore had merely . . . and at that precise second an idea was born in the Bathurst brain. It was so fantastic, and yet at the same time so appealing, that Anthony whistled softly under his breath. On the day of the funeral . . .

His thoughts stopped and hung on the idea. He opened the door of the car and sat down at the wheel. Slowly and methodically, he began to trace the various steps of his theory. It was odds against perhaps, but it could be! At long last Anthony thought that he could see the pattern of the crimes.

2

Anthony looked at the watch on his wrist. What he saw pleased him. The day had by no means shed its course. He would have ample time to accomplish at least one of his intentions. He started the car and drove quickly down Oriel Lane. When he reached the High Street a few minutes later he ran into a surprise. As he reached 'The Churn' he was forced to slow down almost to a dead stop because a lumbering haycart with a driver half asleep was hogging the road. As he slowed down, he was surprised to see Patience, the milkmaid, on the pavement in front of 'The Churn' and waving to him. She had evidently recognised him as the car slowed down. Anthony pulled into the kerb and waited to see what would happen. Patience came to the car door and spoke to him.

"I'm so glad I saw you," she said, "because I've some news for you about what you asked me this morning."

Anthony gestured his appreciative acknowledgment and got out. He joined Patience on the pavement."

"It isn't very much, perhaps," she went on, "but I think it's something you might like to know. When I saw you in the car just now it occurred to me that I could tell you, so I came out and waved. You didn't mind, did you?"

The glance she gave him was arch—almost coquettish. Anthony smiled and gave the lady his most sincere assurances to the contrary.

"I'm so glad you don't mind. I should have hated you to think that I was interfering, as you might say. But you see it was like this. After you'd gone this morning, I told my dad about your coming in and inquiring about the place next door and about that Mr. Da Costa. Well, he told me something that I didn't know myself. At least not until he told me."

Patience paused for breath. Anthony wondered what revelation was due to appear. But the girl was soon in her verbal stride again.

"It's this. According to my dad there were two men next door last week-end. Two strange men whom he'd never seen before. He says he saw them inside the shop. They weren't working there—or anything like that. And he says that they weren't there for very long. Seemed to be sort of looking round the premises, sizing the place up, so Dad said. But they were there all right—because, as I said, he actually saw them. He thought, perhaps, that the business was changing hands again and that these two men might be the new purchasers. He also told me that he thought they were brothers, because they looked to him so very much alike."

Patience paused again. Anthony was thinking hard. "Did your father speak to them?"

The girl shook her head. "No. I think he would have spoken to them had they stayed there for long, but you see, they didn't. They cleared off, and he says he didn't get the chance."

"When exactly was this—could you tell me that?"

"It was sometime last Saturday morning. Between half past nine and eleven, say. And they'd gone again before mid-day." Anthony was silent as he digested Patience's information. But Patience was still a little perturbed at the action she had just taken. "I do hope I've done the right thing in stopping you and telling you. I should hate to—"

Anthony hastened to reassure her. "My dear young lady," he said, "I'm very pleased that you *have* taken the trouble to tell me. The information may be valuable to me. So you may harbour no regrets."

The doubt on the girl's face disappeared. It melted like a cloud in the silent summer heaven.

"Well," she said, "that's that—and I'm so glad that I've been able to help you. I must get back now—into the dairy."

Anthony smiled and raised his hat. "The dairy's gain," he said, "will be my loss. Perhaps in a day or so I may see you again. Mr. Da Costa may return to the place that knew him. Who knows?"

He got back into the car and drove away. Patience the milkmaid watched him go with regret in her eyes and despondency in her soul. She was by no means the first of her kind to succumb to the Bathurst magnetism.

Anthony drove straight down the High Street and turned into the London road. At the corner he ran into his second surprise that morning. He saw a man hail him. It was Martin Scudamore. Anthony stopped the car. Scudamore came up.

"I knew it was you," he said. "I recognised the car. I wonder if you'd do me a favour. Are you going to Town?"

"I am," said Anthony.

"Oh, good," returned Scudamore, "could you run me up? I loathe bothering you, but my car's in dock. Trouble with the carburettor—take a day or two to put right. So the mechanic's just informed me."

"Jump in," said Anthony.

3

Martin Scudamore needed no second bidding. "Don't get in the back," said Anthony, "otherwise I may be taken for your chauffeur—and I'm positive that such a suggestion would be distasteful to you."

Scudamore shot a shrewdly critical glance at Anthony as he took his seat.

"By the way," he said, "something I've not told you. Miss Repton sent her kind regards to you the other night. That night you dined with Bob and Evelyn Forbes. I couldn't deliver the message before because I don't think I've actually seen you since then—until just now."

"No, I don't think you have. As you say, better late than never. Thank you for the courtesy."

Scudamore favoured Anthony with another penetrating glance. "Charming girl," he continued, "rather refreshing to find beauty combined with intelligence. These days especially. Don't you agree?"

"Not altogether."

"Why not?" Scudamore's eyebrows went up.

"Possibly because I don't need refreshment. In the sense that you meant."

"It may be," went on Martin Scudamore, "that I shall soon be in a position to receive your congratulations."

"Oh," said Anthony, with two eyes on the road, "and in what particular direction will that be?"

Scudamore smiled at the question. "I fancied that you would have guessed. From the trend of the conversation. Last Friday evening I asked Helen to marry me."

Anthony's face was expressionless. The car was travelling at a fast pace and he was driving it.

"I thought that you might be more than ordinarily interested," continued Scudamore. "I've always understood that Miss Repton was an old and rather special friend of yours."

"Quite," said Anthony. "Miss Repton is a lady for whom I have the highest regard. Am I to understand, then, that your proposal was accepted?"

"Not definitely, but I think as good as. Miss Repton is giving me her answer at the end of the week. I understand that there are one or two matters . . . family matters . . . that she would like settled—before she gives me a definite answer. But I have the highest hopes, as you may well guess."

"Why?"

"Why—what?"

"Why may I well guess with regard to your hopes and the volume thereof? Who am I to gauge the extent of Miss Repton's interest, regard, or affection as far as you're concerned, my dear Scudamore?"

He caught sight of Scudamore's self-satisfied smile in his mirror.

"I made up my mind to marry her," continued Scudamore pompously, "the first time I met her. At a dance a pal of mine dragged me to. For a time £ s. d. was a bit of a problem to me, but that's adjusted now, I'm delighted to say, and the way has become clear. I've had a slice of luck ... in the business ... that's made all the difference. I want to give Helen the life she deserves and now I feel that I can."

"Good of you," remarked Anthony drily, "definitely altruistic."

"Yes," went on Scudamore, "it happens like that sometimes. You get the break you want at the psychological moment. I suppose in reality, it's the ... er ... operation of Destiny. That's what happened with me. When I saw the chance you bet I grasped it with both hands. She's a smashing girl! I've fooled around a bit in my time—no more, though, than most men—and I flatter myself I know the real thing when it comes along."

Anthony took a corner with expert adroitness and made no reply. He had an idea that Scudamore was talking at him. Suddenly Scudamore changed the subject.

"That reminds me. How's the Lovelace affair going? You were full of that the last time I saw you. You came to the house, if you remember. Thirsting for information. Gave me a grilling on the cinema conversation with which I set the ball rolling. Wanted all the minor details. Made any progress? Or just where you were in the matter?"

For a second or so. Anthony was silent. Scudamore tried again. "Or shouldn't I ask damned inconvenient questions?" queried Scudamore.

"No, it's not that. I was thinking. I was wondering which was the best way in which I could reply. We have made certain progress, but it's a case of definitely deep waters. That isn't to say, however, that we shan't make even more progress. Let me see—what's to-day—I'm hoping that we may make an arrest ... say ... about the end of the week. With a streak of luck, of course, you must have that."

"Is that a fact?" returned Scudamore. "Well—that's the best news I've heard since the affair started and poor Dick Lovelace got his packet. I'm a bit surprised, though, I must say, to hear you express that opinion. Had I been asked, I should have said that you were miles off an arrest. I had the idea that you and your people were stone cold."

"You never can tell," said Anthony; "the vital clue, you see, may turn up from nowhere—and then entirely unexpectedly. As a matter of fact, as recently as yesterday I was groping in the dark. But this morning has made a tremendous difference. In a flash, as it were, quite a number of mystifying matters were illumined, and became reasonably clear to me.

I got the break just as you said a few minutes ago—at the psychological moment. You did say that, didn't you, Scudamore? I should hate to misunderstand you."

Scudamore's look was full of distrust and suspicion. When he replied, there was a hint of resentment in his voice.

"Yes. I said that. *And* I meant it."

Anthony, ignoring the resentful tone, resumed the attack. "Why did you feel so sure that the Police were off the target? What caused you to think like that? Perhaps you're allergic to them are you?"

"Well, no arrest and no hint of an impending arrest in the Press. None of the normal ballyhoo. What else could a mere layman think? And I reside in Loveridge, don't I? I'm near the centre of things. Don't forget that. If there were rumours or whispers that the Police had clicked, or were on the point of clicking, my ear would be pretty close to the ground, wouldn't it? Surely I should be among the first of the rank and file to know the time of day?"

"We're up against a particularly cunning criminal, Scudamore. I'll make you a present of that piece of information. I fancy that he's completely confident that he's thrown dust in the official eyes. I'm hoping, however, that his overweening confidence will eventually bring about his downfall."

Anthony slowed down the pace of the car—they were approaching the area of traffic congestion. Scudamore was silent. He seemed to be mentally digesting what Anthony had just told him. Some minutes passed.

Then Scudamore said "from the way you speak, I presume that you're certain you know the identity of the criminal? Or am I putting two and two together—and making it twenty-two?" Anthony smiled. " 'Certain', you say? That's not allowing me much margin, you know. The word certain is so final—so conclusive. 'One thing is certain that Life flies; One thing is certain, and the Rest is Lies; The Flower, that once hath blown, for ever dies.' "

Scudamore wrinkled his brows. "Shakespeare?" he said questioningly.

Anthony shook his head. "Old Khayyām. Otherwise old Omar. Or at least, what Fitzgerald made of him. By the way, Scudamore, I don't remember your telling me—where do you want me to drop you?"

Scudamore affected to consider Anthony's question. "If you could drop me by the Abercorn Rooms, by Liverpool Street station, that would suit me down to the ground. Or would it be too—?"

"No. I can manage that for you. Without any trouble at all."

"You, I take it," went on Scudamore, "are en route for the 'Yard'. The emissary of the arrest to come?"

Anthony smiled again. "No. Not yet. You're indulging in anticipation. Can I recall your Juvenal to you? '*Duas tantum res anxius optat, Panem et circenses*'. Remember, Scudamore? And how we used to construe it? Remember? Limits the Roman people's anxious longing to but two things—bread and the games of the circus.' Well, it's the latter in which I'm interested on this occasion. The circus! In this case, Cavalier Circus. But here we are, I fancy, at your rendezvous. The Abercorn Rooms. Delighted to have been of service to you."

Anthony turned and looked round as Scudamore opened the door of the car and alighted.

"Thank you, Bathurst," said Scudamore rather stiffly.

"Don't mention it. Oh—and give my love to Helen, will you?"

The car shot away. Scudamore's reply was lost in the noise of the traffic.

CHAPTER 18

1

A nthony made the necessary arrangements for his car and turned into New Bond Street. The sun was as brilliant as it had been on the occasion of his previous visit. He walked down the eastern side of the street and three minutes later he found himself in the *cul-de-sac*, Cavalier Circus. When he came to the antique shop which was his immediate objective he stopped and looked in the window. Most of the articles which had caught his eye on the previous occasion were still on show. He noticed, however, that the ivory peacock was not on view. Some person unknown had evidently fallen a victim to the salesman's persuasive tongue. The name A. Temple Spooner was still on the front of the shop. Anthony noticed this with particular interest.

Anthony pressed down the door-handle and entered. There was no salesman to be seen as he went in. After a few moments of expectant waiting Anthony tapped on the counter. His summons met with an almost immediate response. An elderly man shuffled towards him from the back of the shop.

"Good afternoon. What can I do for you, sir?"

Anthony looked him over quickly and formed the opinion that, on second thoughts, he wasn't as old as at first glance he had appeared to be. He stooped, it is true, but his shoulders were good and well shaped and his hands steady. His face was sallow, but constitutionally so, probably, and not from advanced age or indifferent health. His eyes were bright and questioning under heavy, dark brows. His clothes, however, were his most arresting feature. To say the least, they were somewhat unusual. An old-fashioned frock-coat was buttoned loosely round him and to Anthony's eye looked as though it had been tailored for a considerably bigger man. On his head he wore a black, closely-fitting skull-cap. On his feet he wore a pair of camel-coloured slippers. These, like the coat, seemed too big for him.

Anthony opened the interview as he had intended to open. "Good afternoon," he said. "If possible, I'd like a word with Mr. Temple Spooner."

The old man shook his head slowly. "That, I'm afraid, is impossible. Perhaps you haven't heard? Mr. Spooner, alas, is no more. He died about a week ago in somewhat tragic circumstances. By an accident, shall we say?"

Anthony had heard all right, and knew all about the accident, but the opening, from his point of view, had been sound and reasonable. It formed no part of his plan to appear to know too much. He expressed his regret, therefore, at the sad news.

"Really—I had no idea. That's bad news. I must have missed hearing about it, I suppose."

"Can I get you anything?" went on the old man, "anything that you have admired in the window, perhaps, or something that you particularly want?"

Anthony affected to have become reminiscent and side-tracked the direct questions.

"Wasn't there another salesman here? Who's attended me in the past? I seem to recall somebody."

Anthony's eye wandered meditatively to a really exquisite Chinese carpet. The man in the frock-coat coughed behind his hand.

"Yes. There was another salesman here when Mr. Spooner was alive. That is true. I believe that he gave up the employment on the death of Mr. Spooner. The precise reason is not known to me. Things may have become . . . just a little . . . how shall I put it now . . . *comme çi, comme ça* . . . and I rather think that he decided to take another job. A better one, let us hope. There is no reason why any one of us should ever wish a man any harm."

Anthony spoke deliberately. "I presume, then, that he knew what it meant, and he went."

But there was no response of the kind that Anthony would have liked to see. The man in the frock-coat was completely unruffled. His face was calm and there was no flicker in his eyes. His reply was eminently commonplace.

"Something like that, I suppose." As he spoke, he threw his head up in a strange, jerky fashion. "But let us get to business. I am taking up too much of your time, sir. What is it that you wish to purchase or to inquire about? I shall be pleased to help you and, if necessary, give you the benefit of my advice."

Anthony smiled. To gain time, if for nothing else. "Tell me," he said, "now that Mr. Spooner has passed away, in whose hands is the business? Believe me, I am not asking idly. I have a special reason for putting the question."

The elderly man shook his head and then patted his skull-cap. "That, sir, is a question which I am not qualified to answer. I am, naturally, no more than an employee. Just a servant of my employers. I took this position when it was offered to me—that is to say when your friend that you mentioned left—because I needed the money. I am not ashamed to say that for many years I have known the sting of poverty. It was not always so, however."

The man who spoke squared his shoulders and found a certain dignity.

"Well," said Anthony, "the point is that, not having been aware of Mr. Spooner's death, I don't quite know now where I stand. From the business angle. It's like this, you see. I had a proposition to make to the late Mr. Spooner. But the trouble is, my own position in the matter is not entirely secure. I am not acting on my own behalf. I represent a third party."

"I see. May I inquire the name?"

"Berners," replied Anthony. "C. L. D. Berners. My client is some distance from London, though. Lincolnshire, actually." The elderly man's face was impassive but Anthony's close watch gave him the impression that there had been just a faint quivering of the left eyelid.

"I realise, though," continued Anthony, "that the proposition, such as it is, could be conducted only by principals, so I'm afraid my visit this afternoon must, of necessity, be futile."

"Yes, I'm afraid that is so," came the reply, "in the circumstances."

"So you see," went on Anthony, "I don't quite know what to do—or what steps to take. I think I'll report to my principal, Mr. Berners, that Mr. Spooner is dead and let him act as he pleases. Leave the matter to his personal judgement. In fact, I think that's about all I can do."

The elderly man nodded sagaciously at Anthony's suggestion. "Yes, I agree. That would be the best step for you to take, in the circumstances."

He patted the skull-cap again. "Perhaps, if the matter's at all urgent," he continued, "you might care to telephone to your principal . . . Mr . . . let me see now . . . what was the name you mentioned . . . Burns . . . and let him know of Mr. Spooner's death and the position generally? You could use the telephone here, if you so wished."

Anthony shook his head. "Not Burns . . . Berners."

The other man's face retained its impassivity. There was no suggestion of a quivering eyelid this time.

"Ah—yes! Berners. I remember now. Would you care to telephone to your principal from here?"

He indicated the back of the establishment with a wave of his hand. Anthony finessed. He attempted to give the impression that he was considering the offer.

"You are very welcome," urged the elderly man.

"No. It's extremely good of you to put your telephone at my disposal," said Anthony, "but I think I'll write. I can probably explain the position more satisfactorily by a letter than by telephoning."

"As you wish," replied the man in the skull-cap; "you must please yourself in the matter, naturally."

He turned and with a comprehensive gesture towards the stocks which the shop held, said gravely "in the meantime, can I interest you in anything that I have here? I have some really valuable articles in stock to satisfy even the most expert connoisseur. This jade salamander, for example? Exquisite, don't you think? Just examine the superb craft and workmanship. And an absolute bargain at the price."

Anthony expressed his admiration. "As you say—exquisite. But, as I previously stated, my business here wasn't of that kind. I'm sorry, but there it is."

The man in the skull-cap bowed with some dignity. "In that case then . . . "

He left the rest unsaid. The implication was glaringly obvious. Anthony accepted it without demur.

"In that case then," he repeated "I won't detain you any longer. Let me thank you for the information you have given me."

The elderly man bowed again. "Good afternoon to you."

"Good afternoon," answered Anthony. He turned and closed the door of the antique shop behind him.

2

Anthony drove the car hard towards Plashet and Wilton Lodge. Past the "Green Dragon" and down the right-hand turning which he knew would take him to Plashet itself. He looked at the signpost as he flashed by—11 miles. His memory had been accurate. Within a quarter of an hour he shot past the 'Golden Gloves', past the Post-office at which he had inquired the way when he had come before, through the village of Plashet, up the hill and finally down the lane which he remembered as the route to Wilton Lodge.

Leaving the car pretty much where he had left it before, he walked quickly towards the house and, as he approached, looked up at the verandah. There was no figure of a man to be seen on the portico, however, on the present occasion. The verandah at which Anthony looked was empty. Anthony crossed the lawn which still needed the gardener's care and made his way towards the house. As he came nearer a voice hailed him from one of the shrubberies, so Anthony turned and walked towards the area from which he thought the voice had come. A man stepped out into a path in front of him and Anthony saw that it was the elder Bullock—James.

"Good afternoon, Mr. Bullock. I hope that you remember me. I told you we might meet again. This is it. Although," he continued immediately, "I was by no means certain when I set out that I should find you here."

"We're 'ere," replied James Bullock sullenly, "you wouldn't find us anywhere else." He pushed a hand nervously through his white hair.

"So it seems," said Anthony, "but may I go into the house with you? I want a few words with you, if it's not too inconvenient."

James looked somewhat troubled at Anthony's request. "Well," he replied doubtfully, "I suppose you can. But I'm not clear what I can be doing for you. Our ways 'ere and yours lie in different directions."

"Ah—that's the point," returned Anthony, "but let it rest until we get inside the house."

James shrugged his shoulders and led the way into the room behind the verandah—the room with the books. Anthony heard him call out as they entered.

"Jim! Come along in 'ere, will you—you're wanted."

An answering shout followed and then there came the sound of feet descending a staircase not far away. A moment or so later the door opened and Jim Bullock entered. His face fell obviously when he saw Anthony standing in the room. James gestured apprehensively.

"This gentleman's back, Jim. He says 'e wants to talk to us. But I don't know yet what it's all about and I wish 'e'd keep away from 'ere."

He turned to Anthony and indicated a chair. "Sit down, sir." Anthony sat down. Jim Bullock stared at him, looked at James, shook his dark head and said nothing.

"Well," said Anthony, "I won't waste time. There's no sense in doing that. So I'll tell you why I've come here again."

He paused. Jim Bullock was breathing heavily. Anthony went on again.

"What I want to know from you chaps is this. Who's running the Temple Spooner business now that Spooner himself is dead? Who's behind the show? A perfectly simple and straightforward question that requires only the same kind of answer."

He looked keenly from one to the other of them. What he saw plainly telegraphed from eyes to eyes served to aggravate his suspicions. Neither of the Bullocks, however, spoke for some little time. The silence was heavy and oppressive. Eventually James found a reply, spoken slowly.

"I think, sir," he said, feeling for his words, "that you've come to the wrong place for an answer to that question. Information of the sort you're asking for isn't in our line at all. You see, as we explained to you before, we were only the late Mr. Spooner's servants, as you might say. We are nothing whatever to do with the business. Never 'ave been. So you see, in a manner of speakin' you're as wise as we are."

Anthony shook his head. Jim Bullock's hands were restless and nervous. Anthony determined to strike harder.

"Now look here, Mr. Bullock," he said, "that's all very well, but I'm afraid that it won't do."

Bullock's eyes hardened. Anthony saw the ugly look and went on.

"You're still here in Spooner's house, for one thing. I take it you aren't natural philanthropists—you don't work for nothing? Which immediately raises the question in an ordinary man's mind—who pays you?"

"That's nothing to do with you," said James Bullock with sturdy antagonism, "but if you must know, we've 'eard nothing from the solicitors yet. Mr. Spooner 'asn't been cold for so very long, after all. When we do 'ear from the solicitors, we shall know what our position is—'ow we stand. I expect it'll mean we shall 'ave to clear out."

"I see. Very well. Tell me this, then. Who are the solicitors from whom you expect to hear. And what is their address?" There ensued another period of silence. Jim Bullock still fidgeted with his hands. His father, however, stuck to his guns.

"That I can't do because I don't know myself. I say again, we're naught to do with Mr. Spooner's business—we're no more than 'is servants, who looked after this 'ouse for 'im when 'e was alive."

Anthony's tone became sharper. "When you identified the body of Mr. Spooner—I know you did this because I've been to Scotland Yard and made inquiries—you made the statement to the Police authorities that this death would mean your seeking fresh employment. Have you done so?"

"I 'aven't. Not yet. My son 'as. And I shall 'ave to, directly I 'ear 'ow I stand from the solicitors."

"Of whose name and address you're entirely ignorant?"

"That's what I said," returned James Bullock.

Anthony realised that he wasn't getting anywhere. He would be compelled to bring up heavier artillery.

"Very well, then, Mr. Bullock. Your refusal to co-operate with me leaves me no alternative. I shall be forced to put certain facts which are in my possession before the Police authorities at Scotland Yard."

He rose from his seat as though on the point of imminent departure.

"You've no cause to threaten." James Bullock stuck out an obstinate-looking jaw. "And you can't threaten us," he persisted, "not with truth *or* justice. You've got nothin' on me or my son 'ere."

Anthony played his last card. "Not so very long ago," he said crisply, "a man named Lovelace was murdered at a little village in Essex called Loveridge. Do you happen to know the place, by any chance?"

The question took James Bullock by surprise. He changed colour. "I've 'eard of it," he replied guardedly.

"Ever been there?" Anthony struck at him again.

"I may 'ave been. In my time. I can't rightly say."

"I see. Well, I've been there," continued Anthony, "and not very long ago at that. In fact I was there over the recent August Bank Holiday."

He paused. Jim Bullock's hands were trembling and uncontrolled and a small vein in his father's temple was working at full pressure.

"While I was there," went on Anthony, "I became extremely interested and believe me there was a definite reason for this interest—in an undertaker's business. In the High Street at Loveridge. It trades, I understand, under the name of Messrs. Gray and Russell."

Anthony paused for the second time. James had an ashen pallor. Jim was flushed and scarlet. Each looked miserably unhappy.

"Until but a short time ago," Anthony was in his stride again, "this business seems to have been managed—I use the word 'managed' advisedly—by a gentleman who called himself Da Costa. But Da Costa, whoever he may or may not be, has disappeared in the most extraordinary circumstances. Vanished. With the result that until Gray and Russell find a successor, any Loveridge dead must obtain their last ministrations from the neighbouring town of Chelmersley."

"What's all this got to do with us?" demanded James Bullock in hoarse tones.

"That's exactly what I'm endeavouring to find out," replied Anthony. "Because I continually find myself wondering if the vanished Da Costa has joined Richard Lovelace and your late employer, Temple Spooner, in Hades, Valhalla, or what you will? What do you think about it yourself, Mr. Bullock?"

Anthony paused abruptly as he shot the question at the elder man. But James Bullock's hard and inflexible obstinacy was not to be routed by shock methods.

"It's no good you asking me questions like that. You talk of this murder and that murder. Murder may be *your* trade, for all I know. I don't know anything about these murders. Why should I? How should I? I'm just a plain everyday sort of man. Who takes most things as they come. And my son is like me. I brought 'im up like that. Ever since 'e was a little feller. So there's no call for you, Mister, to talk to us as you've been doin'."

James took a handkerchief from his pocket and wiped the beads of perspiration from his face. His agitation was plain to behold. Anthony cut in quickly.

"You take most things as they come, eh? You most certainly do! Even to the murder of your employer. I might even have said your benefactor. You saw Spooner's dead body in front of you when you were taken to Chelmersley by the Police to identify it. Did it make no impression on you? Did it arouse no feelings of resentment in you? No desire to see his killer brought to justice? By Heaven, it doesn't seem to have done! Come, come, why not tell the truth? And when I say the truth, I mean the whole truth."

Neither of the Bullocks made any reply. Anthony struck again. "What took you to Loveridge—after you'd been to Chelmersley? Who sent for you? Tell me that."

There was a quick shuffling movement from the place where Jim Bullock was standing. His father said doggedly "who says we went to Loveridge? Who can prove it? Just talk—'earsay!"

"Oh, no. I do! I can prove it. Since you throw out the challenge. And in the best of all ways and for the best of all reasons. *Because I saw you there.* Now, Mr. Bullock, play that one back—if you can."

By now, Anthony was embracing annoyance. For sheer unadulterated obstinacy and pigheadedness, these two Bullocks were in the championship class. Must have come from the King's herd.

"You must 'ave made a mistake, Mister," answered James, "you must 'ave *thought* you saw us. You wouldn't be the first man in the world to make a mistake of that kind." He turned to his bucolic son. " 'Ave we been in Loveridge, Jim? You tell this smart Alec feller 'e don't seem to believe me. Set 'is mind at rest."

"No, father," replied Jim in a flat-toned voice, "of course we 'aven't been to Loveridge. I say the same as what you say. People *do* think they see other people when they don't. Their eyes deceive 'em. Look when a man's missin'! And it's in the papers. All sorts of clever people see 'im. All over the place. Sometimes 'e's seen in 'alf a dozen different places at the same time. It's just wishful thinkin', as they say."

"Very well, then," countered Anthony, "you have it your way and I'll have it mine. All I need to do to convince a Court of Law is to bring other witnesses to confirm what I've just said. Concerning your most unexpected visit to Loveridge." Anthony paused for a second, and then decided to chance his arm. There are occasions in Life when something of this nature becomes absolutely necessary, and the present time, he considered, was most certainly one of them.

"I shall produce witnesses," he declared, "who will assert that they saw you on the premises of Gray and Russell, the undertakers in Loveridge High Street. This visit of yours to which I refer took place on the Saturday morning prior to the recent August Bank Holiday. And when my witnesses have had their say, Messrs. Bullock *père et fils*, I shall request the Police authorities to apply to you for news of the missing man, Da Costa. For by that time your connexion with him will have been made obvious." Anthony waited for a few seconds before adding, "does the prospect appear pleasing, gentlemen?"

Jim Bullock twisted his fingers and looked rather helplessly at his father. James made more play with his handkerchief. Eventually, the latter shrugged his shoulders.

"That's your story," he said with the same dogged air that he had assumed previously; "my story would be different. What I've said I stick to. My son 'ere will do the same. And it might be as good a story as yours. That's for others to decide."

"That's right," croaked Jim from his corner.

Anthony smiled. He had to, because their attitude had defeated his principal aim. Which had been to get them to talk.

"Very well, gentlemen," he said. "I have no more to say. I've given you every chance. But I warn you that you will shortly find yourselves in serious trouble. Murder is a crime which the English law machine does not overlook and certainly does not condone. And sometimes it waits years to get its man—or men. I'll wish you a very good day."

Anthony turned on his heel and made for the lawn at the back of Wilton Lodge. Jim Bullock walked to the verandah and watched his retreating figure.

"I wonder," he said "'ow much of the truth that bastard really does know? And 'ow much of what 'e put over was bluff?"

" 'E knows too much," replied his father with gloomy pessimism, "whichever way we look at it."

"What are we goin' to do?" asked Jim.

"Search me," responded James.

"Wait, I suppose," went on Jim, "until we 'ear again from—you know who. Can't do much else that I can see. Considerin' 'ow we're placed."

"You've just about 'it the nail on the 'ead," remarked James.

"Don't put it like that," said Jim, "gives me the creeps. I can still see that blood-stained—"

"Shut your trap," said James; "one o' these days that tongue o' yours might 'ang you."

"It might 'ang both of us," assented Jim lugubriously. James Bullock turned somewhat savagely on his son and (it is regretted) invited him to perform an impossible procedure.

"And you," retorted Jim dutifully.

CHAPTER 19

1

The sun was hot and fierce on this August afternoon. Anthony lounged in a deck-chair in the garden of the house of Doctor Robert Forbes. The grass showed the effect of the summer's fierce sun, and many patches of the tennis-court at which Anthony looked were far more brown than the traditional emerald green of grass-court perfection.

Anthony sat with Ilsley, Philip Sheridan and Robert Forbes himself. On the court at which they looked, a singles was in progress. Evelyn Forbes was matched against Martin Scudamore. Each, Anthony soon saw, was a good player. Much better, in fact, than average club form. But Scudamore, with the stronger backhand, was slightly the better. Evelyn, however, had many tactical qualities. Many times she deliberately lured Scudamore from the net to his undoing. She made him run about, too, more than he made her. Each, so far, had taken a set off the other and the third set was now being played. The two players ran, jumped, lobbed and volleyed. Scudamore had taken the lead in this third and deciding set by three games to two. He was now serving, after having broken through Evelyn's service in the previous game and thereby taken the lead.

As Anthony watched the rallies, Evelyn raised herself for a smashing drive down Scudamore's forehand, but he got to it and returned it magnificently.

"Oh—shot!" cried Sheridan from the line of deck-chairs. "I'm afraid Evelyn's almost had it." He smiled back at Anthony, "if I may be permitted to use the vernacular."

"I wouldn't agree with you," said Forbes—"yet. She wants a rare lot of beating on this court. Knows every blade of grass on it." As he spoke Evelyn took a point with a beautifully executed drop shot, which fell just over the net with Martin Scudamore yards away from it and still in the position almost to which Evelyn had lured him. Anthony watched the lady with the keenest interest. She was well made, with the litheness, symmetry, superb body balance and physical poise of the born ball-games player. Scudamore drove, lobbed, volleyed, smashed, turned and twisted at a pace surprising for so hot an afternoon.

"They're good, you know—these two," commented Robin Ilsley. "I've seen worse stuff at Wimbledon before now. In the preliminary stages."

"I agree," said Anthony. "Lawn tennis doesn't happen to be one of my games, but I know a class player when I see one. I fancy, though, that Scudamore will just about pull it off."

The trees at the back of the garden were beginning to throw their shadows and such a handicap as these shadows presented was against Evelyn rather than against her opponent. The game was so close and each point so fiercely contested that conversation in the deck-chair colony ceased almost entirely. Scudamore at length drew ahead to reach match point. Anthony saw Evelyn smile as Scudamore prepared to serve. The service was a gem of purest ray serene, and with cannon-ball velocity scorched past Evelyn's forehand to give Martin Scudamore game, set and match. Anthony, keenly interested, saw her run to the net to shake hands with her conqueror.

"What an absolute snorter! No playing that brand," remarked Robert Forbes. "That's where the man usually has the edge—in the service—no matter how good the woman may be."

"I couldn't agree with you more," said Ilsley.

Sheridan laughed it was a sombre laugh with but little hilarity in it. Anthony waited for what he was about to say, but nothing came after the mirthless laugh. Scudamore and Evelyn Forbes, racquets under arms, came walking towards the ring of deck-chairs. Evelyn was still gay and smiling—defeat, before a company which included her husband, appeared to hold no sting for her. You're a good loser, thought Anthony, whatever else you may be, and I mark you high for it. Scudamore, a few paces behind her, seemed grave and somewhat preoccupied. He wore his honours rather heavily upon him.

"He tore me to bits," cried Evelyn, as they reached the deck-chairs, "made me look like a Blue Beveren with a ribbon round its neck. I feel about so big." She gestured towards the ground with her palm downward.

"On the contrary, Mrs. Forbes," said Martin Scudamore, "you extended me fully. Made me work like a dog to win."

For the first time a look of annoyance swept over Evelyn's face. "Go on," she said, "you're just being over-generous. Magnanimous in triumph. Big-hearted Martin. You know, Martin, you are rather marvellous."

The tone of her voice was evident and everybody who heard it knew what it meant. Scudamore flushed.

"You asked for it, my lad," thought Anthony, "you stuck your neck out. You mustn't scream if you collect."

"I'm going to have a shower, Bob," said Evelyn to Forbes. "Martin can please himself. Perhaps he'd like to play somebody else." She looked down at Anthony. "What about you, Mr. Bathurst? Can't you give him a hiding? You look to me as though you might be pretty useful."

Anthony smiled and shook his head. "I'm afraid I can't at lawn-tennis, Mrs. Forbes. I might, perhaps, at one or two other games."

"What are they?" demanded Scudamore rather frigidly; "lawn-tennis isn't my—"

Anthony shook his head as he intervened. "Forget it, my dear chap. I was about to shoot a line—unpardonable of me. Write me off as a 'never wasser'. Now your *amour-propre* can re-establish itself and harbour no uneasy doubts."

Scudamore shot a shrewdly suspicious glance at Anthony, just as the Vicar of Loveridge inserted himself in the conversation.

"But surely, Bathurst, you played at Lord's against Cambridge? I saw the game, man. What year was it now? 1927? Onslow-Lamb skippered. He was a Charterhouse man. Charterhouse and Oriel. Or was it '28? Oxford won. I'm pretty confident about that. Let me see, now, what did they win by? Six wickets, was it?"

Anthony grinned at Philip Sheridan. "Full marks, padre! Your facts are accurate. A tribute to the quality of your memory. But you mustn't rake over the ashes of the past in order to defend my sporting reputation. Another thing—Scudamore, in all probability, has Tab sympathies. He looks to me as though he has. Don't ruffle his complacency with the histories of Oxford triumphs of the long ago."

Scudamore shrugged his shoulders and pulled an unoccupied deck-chair towards him.

"I'm tired," he announced, "those three sets with Evelyn were warm work. They've flopped me out. What a wonderful thing sunshine is."

Ilsley turned to the Vicar. "What about a game, Philip? Feel like it? Or shall we leave it till after tea?"

"Think that's a more attractive proposition, Robin. The temperature will be several degrees cooler by then."

"That's a bet, then," returned Ilsley.

2

Looking extremely attractive in her comparative coolness, Evelyn Forbes halted by the line of deck-chairs. Robin Ilsley beckoned to her to come nearer. She shook her head in response.

"No, Robin, I can't come and talk to you—yet. You'll have to wait a while. For two reasons, my dear. First of all there's tea, which will be coming along in a matter of minutes from now. And then—secondly—I've got to have a chat with our special guest, Mr. Bathurst. He's not here, you know, just to see Martin Scudamore take me down at lawn-tennis. Or to admire Bob's roses. He's here because he wants to have a special talk with me. That's true, isn't it, Mr. Bathurst?" She beamed on Anthony as she waited for his reply.

"Something like that, Mrs. Forbes."

"There you are, Robin. You heard what Mr. Bathurst said. So you see, you'll have to wait for me until after tea, at least."

Ilsley smiled back at her. "That's all right, Evelyn. I'll wait. Patience is one of my strongest suits and all good things are worth waiting for."

"Good. I'm glad you look at it like that." She shaded her eyes with her hand and looked back towards the house. "You may not have to wait so *very* long. Here's Mary—blessed amongst girls—on the way with the tea-waggon. I know you're all sitting there with your tongues hanging out."

The trim-aproned maid came nearer.

"This way, Mary," called Evelyn, "bring the waggon here to me, will you?"

Mary pushed the tea-waggon across to her mistress.

"Thank you, Mary. Now then, you men. Tell me what you'd like. I've tried to cater for all tastes. Tomato and cucumber sandwiches. Lobster patties. White and brown bread and butter. And ice-cream to follow. No strawberries. I'm sorry, everybody, about that, but Bob reports that they're finished. Now wade in, all of you, and help yourselves."

Evelyn knelt gracefully on the scorched grass and began to pour out the tea and all began to go as merry as a marriage-bell. "Anybody who doesn't take sugar, please call out."

Anthony, after calling out, watched Martin Scudamore. Ilsley watched Evelyn. Evelyn watched Anthony. Philip Sheridan watched Ilsley. Robert Forbes watched Evelyn watching Anthony. Scudamore watched the lobster patties and their somewhat alarming tempo of disappearance. He was overfond of shellfish . . . and Evelyn's lobster patties were certainly things of beauty—if not joys for ever.

3

When tea was over and Mary had gathered up the fragments that remained, Ilsley and the Vicar of Loveridge took their racquets to the court in accordance with their ante-tea arrangement. Evelyn Forbes moved over to Anthony.

"Shall I sit here, Mr. Bathurst, next to you?" she asked, indicating the empty deck-chair at his side, "or shall I take you for a stroll through the rose-walks?"

Anthony thought of the proximity of other ears and assessed chances. He lifted himself from his chair.

"The rose-walks have it, Mrs. Forbes," he said smilingly, "the stroll it shall be."

They crossed the grass and turned towards the long lanes and lines of roses—in flower and in bud. Evelyn stopped by an exquisite specimen.

"Isn't that a beauty?" she demanded, "my favourite—'Shot Silk'."

Anthony inspected and added his contribution of admiration. She turned to him impulsively.

"Well, ask me what it is you want to ask me. Otherwise my anxiety will increase. It's about Dick Lovelace, isn't it?"

4

Anthony nodded. "Yes. It's about Lovelace. And it also concerns the person who killed him."

She shook her head slowly and sadly . . . "That's the person I'm afraid you'll never find. The days have passed—and they're still passing. Soon it will be September. There's been no arrest and if the newspapers are anything to go by there doesn't seem much likelihood of one. It doesn't seem to me that the Police have made any progress at all. I may be wide of the mark, of course, but"—she shrugged her shoulders—"that's how it seems to me."

Anthony heard her out. When he replied he spoke in quiet tones. "That's how it may seem, Mrs. Forbes, but very definitely that's how it's not."

She looked up at him eagerly. "Do you really mean that, Mr. Bathurst?"

"I really mean that, Mrs. Forbes."

Her eyes met his. She used all her charm on him. "Can't you tell me more? Or must I be content with the bare statement?"

"No. I can amplify what I told you." Anthony paused, and then continued. "I sincerely believe that the identity of the person who killed Lovelace is known to me. I assure you that that is no idle boast on my part. Why, exactly, he was killed, I am not entirely sure about—yet. I have certain ideas on the subject, naturally, but they are by no means as clear as I should like them to be." He paused again. When he went on he said, "what I mean is this. I am minus certain details. I lack certain knowledge. If I were in possession of that knowledge, I should be in a position to particularize. As it is, I can merely generalise."

She regarded him doubtfully—and Anthony knew it. "Is that all you wanted me for?" returned Evelyn, "to tell me what you have?"

Anthony shook his head. "No, Mrs. Forbes. You side-tracked me with your question. Your surmise is accurate. There is something else. Now I should like *you* to answer a question or two, if you will be so kind."

"Do these questions concern Dick Lovelace, too?"

"Yes, Mrs. Forbes. May I proceed?"

She bowed her head. "As you know," continued Anthony, "I was present at the house on the day of Lovelace's funeral when Ilsley read Lovelace's will."

Two points of scarlet coloured her cheeks. "Yes. I am fully aware of that. That was, by the way, the first time I had the pleasure of meeting you."

"It was. And that brings me to my first question. I beg of you not to misunderstand it. I assure you in all sincerity that it contains no implication of any kind whatever."

Evelyn smiled. "And I accept that, Mr. Bathurst, in equal sincerity."

Anthony returned the smile. "Here comes the question, then. And it's a personal one. Did Dick Lovelace ever make you presents? Personal gifts?"

"Never." Her response was prompt and emphatic.

"You are perfectly certain of that?"

"Well, nothing of any value. Certainly nothing like that. A box of chocolates last Christmas. Some rather thrilling soap once on a birthday. You don't refer to that sort of present, do you? He'd give Bob a box of cigars for his birthday, for example. And of course, both Bob and I were in the habit of returning the courtesy. On special occasions. I'm afraid as a family we're rather hot on birthday recognition." She spoke calmly, but her cheeks still flaunted the scarlet.

"No, I didn't mean conventional presents of the birthday and Christmas vintage. They're the 'ping-pong' presents. I regard them in an almost exactly similar light to you. For example, I have an ancient aunt who habitually 'pings' me an utterly unwearable tie and I 'pong' her something which causes me an infinitely protracted time of selection and which, when she gets it, probably sends cold shudders down her withered back. By the way, I suppose backs do wither?"

"No. Not backs, Mr. Bathurst. Breasts."

"I regret to hear that, but I shall beg to differ. Just to maintain my position. Now, to recapture our serious mood. And to come to my second question. I know that it should be covered by my first, but I do want to make absolutely certain of everything, so you must forgive me. Did Lovelace ever make you a present of a picture? Any picture? Which might appear at first sight to be almost valueless? Please give this question your strictest consideration before you answer it,"

"There's no need to." The reply was immediate. "Dick Lovelace has never given me a picture of any kind, Mr. Bathurst. Valuable or otherwise."

"I see. That's absolutely certain, then. Anything at all resembling a picture? A miniature, say?"

"No. Nothing of that kind whatever. You can take that reply as absolute, definite and certain. Satisfied?"

"Thank you, Mrs. Forbes. I'm disappointed, but that can't be helped."

"Any more questions to ask me?"

"No. But three requests to make."

"What are they?"

"Here's the first. Essentially simple. Please regard this conversation as entirely between you and me."

She nodded brightly, "of course—need you ask. What are the others?"

"If, in the course of a day or two, you should see a reference to yourself in the Press . . . shall we say . . . just a trifle overheated . . . please ignore it and sit tight, using at the same time a judicious and restraining influence on your husband. O.K.?"

"Certainly, if you ask me. And now, the third?"

"A photograph of yourself, Mrs. Forbes."

"Whatever for?"

"Well, it *might* accompany that Press reference. Afterwards, of course, there's no knowing what might become of it."

"I see," she said slowly.

But Anthony could not fail to see the frown that came to her brows.

"You shall have it, Mr. Bathurst—when you leave here this evening."

"I am trebly your debtor," replied Anthony; "and now show me the roses."

CHAPTER 20

1

Anthony sat with Andrew MacMorran in the writing-room of the 'Infidel's Head' at Chelmersley. MacMorran had told him of the interview he had recently had with the local Inspector Hurst. The main topic of conversation at this interview had been the general antecedents of the late Temple Spooner. Or perhaps a better description would be the somewhat surprising lack of precise knowledge concerning those antecedents.

"According to what Hurst told me," said MacMorran, as he crammed tobacco into his pipe, "the one thing that's known for certain about the man is that he's a Greek by nationality. His parents had a small fruit business near the dockyard at Salamis. Although it was small, it flourished, and they prospered. He didn't spend many years, though, under the parental roof and nobody knows when or where he first turned up as Temple Spooner. As turn up he did. The other point that's a near certainty is that he was a man of considerable wealth. The money's been amassed by a medley of ventures—almost all of them highly successful—not the least of which by any means has been the antiques business. If there do happen to be any kith or kin still breathing—which I'm told is highly doubtful—they're somewhere near the Ægean. Certainly not in this country."

Anthony nodded. "That's pretty much in accordance with what I thought, Andrew. Now I'll tell you a string of interesting facts. You listen for five minutes, smoke that pipe of yours and don't interrupt."

Anthony talked and the Inspector listened. When Anthony had finished, MacMorran looked up at him.

"All very interesting," he declared, "but all the same, I'm extremely doubtful as to what we can do about it."

"Listen to me again, Andrew," replied Anthony, "and I'll tell you what I think we *might* do. In fact it's my proposal here and now, that we *do* it." He produced something from his breast-pocket. "How do you like that, Andrew? I'll bet you've seen worse during your chequered career."

MacMorran picked up the photograph of Evelyn Forbes. "I have and all. A bonnie lassie and no error. Pretty enough to be Scots. How did you cajole this out of her? What was the tale that you told?"

"No kidstakes, Andrew. No knavish tricks. All fair and aboveboard. I put all the cards on the table. We're after a big fish—too much cunning often outwits itself. Do you see the way I'm thinking?"

Macmorran nodded. "Ay. I take your meaning. But tell me these proposals of yours. What's the lassie's photograph for? The bait? The sprat to catch the mackerel?"

"Just fancy likening that lovely photograph to a sprat! Well, well, well! I'd thought better of you, Andrew—I had indeed."

Anthony grinned as he chaffed the Inspector. "This is the idea," he continued, "after I've outlined it to you, tell me what you think of it. I purpose using the Press, Andrew, and you can pull the strings to see that the idea's executed properly. What I suggest, actually, is something on these lines. Suppose we say . . . "

Anthony talked on and MacMorran paid heed. Eventually, Anthony reached his conclusion.

"Well," he asked, "what's the verdict? What do you think of the idea? Don't rush at it. Think it over well before you start tearing it to pieces."

Macmorran slowly shook his head. "No," he said, "it's an idea and it may well pay dividends. There's no r-risk about it—we can't lose over it, even though it should come unstuck. I've known you make far riskier suggestions."

Anthony smiled at the professional. "I thought that the absence of risk would be a source of comfort to your Aberdonian soul."

"Comfort?" retaliated MacMorran. "I like that, I must say. Where would the comfort be?"

"I quite agree, Andrew," returned Anthony, "no matter where. Of comfort no man speak."

2

On the afternoon and evening of the following day, in the social columns of the three main London evening newspapers, the *Evening*

Record, the *Evening Banner*, and the *Astral*, there appeared under an excellent reproduction of Evelyn Forbes's photograph the following paragraphs (it may be stated that Wat Tyler, "Londiniensis" and "The Diarist", the three columnists concerned, commented thereon in almost identical terms).

Evelyn Forbes, whose photograph appears within this column, is the wife of Doctor Robert Forbes, M.D., M.R.C.S., of Loveridge, in the County of Essex. Mrs. Forbes, who is as charming as she is beautiful, and who, with her husband, leaves this country at the end of the week for a holiday in Greece, has recently been the recipient of a legacy of considerable value which came to her under rather sensational circumstances. We refer to the bequests which were made to her under the will of the late Richard Lovelace, also of Loveridge, whose recent tragic death will be fresh in the minds of many of our readers. We are informed—and the information is undoubtedly authentic—that among the bequests are many valuable heirlooms and objects of historical interest previously in the possession of the Lovelace and Braund families. In this connexion it may be stated that the late Richard Lovelace, reference to whom was made above, was the nephew and heir of the late Miss Arabella Braund, who herself was a direct descendant of Sir Clive Braund who fought with John Churchill, Duke of Marlborough, at Blenheim in the year 1704.

As Anthony had suggested, MacMorran had pulled the necessary strings and the London Press had risen, as always, to the occasion.

When the telephone-bell rang in Anthony's flat, late in the afternoon of the day on which the paragraph referred to in the previous section appeared for the delectation of the reading public, he moved towards it with mixed feelings of curiosity and expectancy. For he had no certain ideas as to either the precise form which the more immediate reactions to the paragraph were likely to take or the precise direction from which they were likely to come. And it was to his surprise, somewhat, that a woman's voice spoke to him when he answered the ring.

"Bathurst this end," he said.

The woman's voice that had greeted him said "Good afternoon, Mr. Bathurst. I'm Evelyn Forbes. I'm so glad to find you at home. I was more than half afraid that you wouldn't be. But I rang you, because I particularly want to talk to you."

"I can't think of a better reason," replied Anthony, "so talk on, Mrs. Forbes."

He heard the laugh at the other end of the line. "I've seen this afternoon's paper," she announced. "Whom have I to thank for the flattery? You? Are you the inspirer?"

"Not inspirer. Joint author . . . shall we call it? And I boggle, too, at your word 'flattery'. 'Compliment', Mrs. Forbes—that's the true word. A genuine tribute and a sincere recognition of merit and true worth. Whereas flattery is always counterfeit."

There came a second laugh-tinkle. "That's very sweet of you. You don't know how I value what you've just said."

"Who's the flatterer now?" demanded Anthony.

"I guessed you'd say that. By the way, my cases aren't packed yet. For that holiday I'm supposed to be having. What do you know about that? What's the actual destination?"

"Salamis."

"Salamis? You don't say! I guessed wrong then. I guessed Athens."

"That doesn't matter," replied Anthony, catching her spirit; "we'll accept the fact that the Greeks had another word for it, and that there's plenty of time to pack the cases. You should see me do a quick pack when it's necessary. I'm a thrower and bang-'em-downer."

"Those methods wouldn't suit me. I'm the reverse. I'm a 'tick-tack-toer' and a 'spick-and-spanner'. If I ever went mad, I should go mad methodically."

"That's as it should be. All the best people have a method in their madness. For instance, Gertrude's royal son. What else have you to tell me?"

"Oh—this and that. Robert's a little stuffy. Which is only what I expected, knowing him as I do."

"Do you mean with regard to the paragraph?"

"Of course. What else?"

"What doesn't he like about it?"

"Cheap publicity! That's what he calls it. Doesn't like the features of his missus sold for a penny to the proletariat."

"An utterly inexcusable position to assume. Why should he have a monopoly of the good things of this world?"

"Isn't that a rather dangerous thing to say? Just think of the implications."

"I suppose it could be construed as such. Tell me, though. What else did he say?"

"Oh, grumbled and grunted, moaned and misery'ed. You know why, don't you?"

"Reference to the Lovelace legacy, I suppose. Am I right?"

"You're always right. Believe me, when it comes to sheer jealousy, Robert's not so very far behind the God of Israel."

"Pity."

"Why?"

"So destructive—jealousy. So comprehensively destructive. You never know what it's going to destroy next."

"He's only seen one of the papers so far. The Record. I've stuffed the others under one of the cushions on the settee. The balloon'll go up properly, though, when he does find them."

"Perhaps he won't."

"Not a hope. You don't know him. He'll have the later editions for the racing returns and the cricket scores. And if Yorkshire go down it'll be a case of Heaven help little Evelyn. I may contrive, though, to be missing at the psychological moment. It's a technique that I'm perfecting these days. I loathe 'words'. Especially when they're rounded off with a North British accent."

"What else did you have to tell me? Something insists within me that my real moment on the telephone is yet to come."

"You know—you're really wizard. I *have* something else to say to you. And I've kept it to the last—on purpose. You know—as a *bonne bouche*. For one reason, I'm not altogether too sure about it."

"In what way do you mean? I don't think I quite understand. That last statement of yours is a trifle perplexing."

He heard Evelyn's laugh again. "Well, you know what you asked me the other day about Dick Lovelace giving me things. When he was alive. Personal gifts, you said."

Anthony's nerves came to tingling point. Was the goal in sight? Was the curtain about to be raised at long last?

"Yes. Very well, Mrs. Forbes. And I still regard the point as most important. Your answer was most emphatically in the negative. To my intense disappointment."

"Well," came the voice of Evelyn Forbes, "I owe you a profound apology. But I assure you that I didn't lead you astray intentionally. It was just something that took place some time ago and which had passed almost entirely out of my mind. To-day, though, I thought of it. I can't tell you why, or even what made me think of it. It suddenly flashed into my mind. But Dick Lovelace *did* give me something once. A long time ago, soon after he came to Loveridge and we had just begun to know him. What do you think it was? I'll give you three guesses?"

Anthony suppressed his mounting excitement. "I should say, Mrs. Forbes, without the slightest hesitation, a picture of some kind."

"Wrong, at last. And never mind about the other two guesses I was going to give you. It was an old chair. Weather-beaten and as black as ebony, nearly."

Anthony probed. "What made him do that? What prompted the gift?"

"Oh, just because I admired it one evening when we were over there. And it was beautifully comfy to sit in. That was all. But Dick was like that. Give you the earth if he thought you wanted it. Definitely not—er—North British. See what I mean?"

"Yes. I think I do. What's the chair like? Tell me more about it."

"Only medium size. Curved wooden arms at the sides. You know—goes back to the year dot. When Adam delved and Eve span. You can imagine William the Conqueror having sat in it to eat muffins at Mountfield—that's near Senlac, in case you don't know."

"I did know. Actually, I have connections at Robertsbridge. That's near Mountfield—in case you don't know."

"Oh, but I did, I assure you. Actually I have—"

"Stop it," said Anthony, "life's brief. Its brevity is here our portion. It's art that is long. Tell me more about this chair that came to you from Lovelace. Where does it live?"

"Here, in the lounge-hall. It's enshrined by two pairs of ancient bellows. Can you remember it? You may be able to."

"No. I can't recall it—though I suppose I must have seen it. What's the back of it like?"

"The back? Solid wood. No bars, or anything of that kind. Black. With age and stain and all the other black producers. I'll tell you what it reminds me of. Always. Irish bog-oak. I've a little cauldron that's made of it."

"I get you. I've seen specimens. Is it particularly heavy? The chair, I mean?"

"No-o. I wouldn't say that it was. Just about what you'd expect by looking at it. But why all these questions? What's so mysterious about it?"

"I wish I could answer that, Mrs. Forbes. If I could, my mind would be considerably easier, believe me."

"I see. By the way, I got your message. Well, what time are you and Scotland Yard moving in? You said tennish, didn't you?"

"Yes. Round about then. Have you made all the other arrangements your end? Re Doctor Forbes and so on?"

"Yes. It's all fixed."

"Nobody else knows anything about it?"

"Nobody."

"What about the doctor? How did you work the oracle?"

"Oh—*comme çi, comme ça*," she replied airily. "You need have no anxiety. I think I've seen to everything."

"Excellent. I'll be seeing you, then."

Au 'voir," she replied. "Oh, before I ring off, tell me something—how long?"

"How long—what?"

"How long before. *You* know."

"If I answered, the answer would be based on sheer conjecture. I really couldn't say, Mrs. Forbes. If I did, I should only be guessing."

"Well then—how long do you *think*? You must have *some* idea."

"In my opinion, for what it's worth, Saturday should see us through. If my idea works, of course. It may not. You never know. I may have gravely miscalculated. It wouldn't be the first time."

"I don't suppose you have. And in case you'd like to know, I think you're pretty marvellous. Cheer-o."

Evelyn Forbes rang off. Anthony replaced the receiver and said aloud "You do—do you? I wonder if you'll be thinking that by this time next week."

He pushed a chair beneath a table. Then he looked at the time. "Five minutes to five. Let me see now—I'll have an hour and a half with my friend Mr. Berners. A closer walk with him this time. I've something to work on at last."

Thus thought Anthony, as, book under arm, he strolled towards his favourite chair.

CHAPTER 21

1

Anthony opened his copy of *The House of Berners*, by C. L. D. Berners, price 9s. 6d. First of all he turned to the index at the end of the book. The operative word as far as he was concerned was "chair". If the theory with which he had been toying for some time had any solid foundation, there was a link between Berners and Lovelace which might well travel back to this "house of Berners"—this house which had gone from the Berners family to the Braund family and then to Richard Lovelace himself.

What this link actually was, it was up to him to find out, and the conversation on the telephone with Evelyn Forbes which he had just concluded had given him his first real clue and definite lead. Disappointment, however, came quickly to him. The index of the Berners book contained no reference to a chair of any kind. Anthony felt despondent—he had fallen, as it were, at the first fence. He sat back on his chair with the book on his lap and concentrated on careful thought. He decided that he would try another word, "picture". There were, after all, the stories of the Topladys. Assuming, that is, that they were true and authentic. Mrs. Toplady had declared that the pictures in Lovelace's library had been turned round on the night of Lovelace's murder and her husband had projected a subsequent suggestion concerning the dining-room which had given colour to her declaration. There was, however, no reference in the Berners index to any special pictures.

Anthony looked at the time again. If it came to the pass that he must read the Berners book from cover to cover, time was getting acutely short, and he began to blame himself that he had not essayed the task before this.

As he considered these things, and idly turned the pages of the Berners index, his eyes caught a reference which suddenly quickened his pulse and made his senses dance. The reference in question was to "four rings". Four rings! The words which Martin Scudamore had overheard in the cinema! Anthony recalled them and their immediate text. "Four rings" had been stated to be "essential".

There *must* be four rings. So the principal had stated—according to Martin Scudamore.

Anthony, with his finger between the leaves of the Berners book, sat quietly in his chair and made his calculations. Before he tested the value of the reference, he chastened himself. To think that he owed the mere knowledge of this reference to an idle, almost accidental glance. A glance which had certainly not been parented by intelligence. If the testing which was so soon to take place bore fruit, he'd never complain of the gods of chance again.

Anthony turned quickly to the appropriate part of the text proper. He tried valiantly to stifle his excitement. What he eventually read, however, thrilled him. C. L. D. Berners wrote as follows,

Four rings. These four rings which eventually came into the possession of Roger de Berners were more often known as "Innocent's ring" or the "ring of Innocent". And the true story about them is this. On May the 29th, 1205, the Pope Innocent III, that same Pope who had adopted the title of "little Vicar of Christ", or "Vicar of God", twelve years previously, sent John, King of England, four gold rings set with precious stones—emerald, sapphire, garnet and topaz. He explained to the King at the same time that the "rotundity" signified eternity—that we pass through time into eternity. The number four, he pointed out, signified the four virtues which make up constancy of mind—namely justice, fortitude, prudence and temperance. The material signified wisdom from on high which is as gold, purified in the fire. The green of the emerald, so said his Holiness, was emblem of "faith", the blue of the sapphire of "hope", the red of the garnet of "charity" and the deep bright yellow of the topaz of "good works".

John was inordinately proud of this gift from His Holiness and it is by no means clear how it eventually came into the possession of Roger de Berners. Whether it was a gift from John at a critical stage of his monarchy or whether it was recovered in some manner from the disaster which occurred to him in the Wash and subsequently passed into de Berners hands is open to a wealth of conjecture. My own opinion as a direct descendant of Roger de Berners, and for what it is worth, is this. From certain evidences which were in the possession of the Berners family for several generations, there is strong reason to believe that

John stayed with Roger de Berners at his house in Lincolnshire immediately prior to the catastrophe which overtook him in the Wash, and my idea is that the ring changed hands on this historic occasion. It may well be, I consider, that Roger de Berners, the loyal and generous host of his King, was made the recipient of this most valuable gift, as a reward for his loyal service, for John, by this time, it must be remembered, had become a soured man, with but little interest in many worldly matters which had previously captivated him. The full story of the ring, however, has not yet been told.

It is believed that many attempts were made to steal the rings during the centuries which followed until it eventually disappeared. This occurred about the beginning of the seventeenth century and many versions have since been put forward in explanation. Certain it is, though, that the rings disappeared during the lifetime of William de Berners, that is to say, between the years of 1616 and 1653, but from a number of admittedly obscure references to be found in various historic documents of the de Berners family still extant, there is good reason to think that this William de Berners cunningly concealed the royal rings in the four corners at the back of a certain picture. But no authentic information has ever been discovered which would serve to identify this picture. This unfortunate deficiency is due, in all probability, to the fact that William de Berners himself died instantaneously as the result of an accident whilst hunting.

As has been stated elsewhere in this book, the house of de Berners, together with its furniture, passed into the hands of the famous militarist Sir Clive Braund in the earlier years of the eighteenth century.

Anthony closed the book and placed it on the table at his side. He surveyed himself through a haze of supreme disgust. The vital clues had been in his hands all the time—almost right from the beginning, in fact. "Four rings" and the word "Innocent". Both expressions had been heard by Scudamore in the cinema. In his stupidity and blindness, Anthony had imagined the former to have the commonplace association of the telephone, and the latter its conventional reference as the opposite condition and natural antithesis to the adjective "guilty". Shades of Holmes and the gallery of the masters! With all his years of experience, he was still no more than a bungling amateur—such was his personal castigation.

He rose from his chair and paced the room. A new problem had arisen. Why the chair—and not the picture? Strange that—if his theory were the correct one. Surely it should have been a picture?

He endeavoured to trace in some detail the major pattern of the crimes. It hinged mainly, he thought, on the letter which Lovelace had received from Temple Spooner just prior to his death. The letter which had meant a great deal to the sender and less than nothing to the recipient. To some extent, that would explain the chair. There was something else, too. The characters of the crime-cast placed themselves into two simply defined categories. Those with knowledge and those without, and there were, it seemed, many more in the latter category than in the former. Stay a moment, though! That condition applied only as far as he *knew*. His knowledge was strictly limited. How did *he* know—how on earth *could* he know—the real knowledge possessed, possibly, by any of the people whom he had so carelessly listed in the second of his categories?

A scrap of knowledge picked up fortuitously might well have started an alert and cunning brain on a quest to which had come the ultimate success of complete knowledge! This was a condition and a possibility which he must never ignore until the case was completed and for which he would have to be constantly prepared. The trap which he had already baited was a trap which depended for its effectiveness on the soundness of the theory he had already formed. But there was this to be said. If the bait failed to attract, he would be no worse off. As MacMorran had pointed out, he would still be able to retrace his steps and to cast another line. And yet, as Anthony turned over the different possibilities in his mind, he became more and more confident that his solution of the problem, surprising and shocking as it was, would be found to be the right solution. It was, indeed, the only one which satisfied the facts of the case as he knew them, his own intelligence, and the science of deduction.

He looked at the time again. Not so long now before the start of the final move. His pulses quickened. His eye caught the telephone. He'd ring the 'Yard' at once and ask for Andrew MacMorran. There were a few things he wanted to talk over with him.

3

MacMorran came on the line almost immediately. Anthony wasted no time.

"All fixed, Andrew?"

"Ay. What do you think? But what are you 'phoning for now? Not altered your mind, have you?"

"No. Not exactly. What time shall I expect you?"

"Just about when we said. As near eight o'clock as I can make it. Seen the papers?"

"Yes. Good show. Had a response already, as a matter of fact."

MacMorran asked warily "oh, who was that? The lady?"

"Full marks, Andrew. The lady it was."

"Was that why you've rung me?"

"In a way. The point is that she's suddenly remembered something. I'll pass it on to you going down this evening—take too long to tell you now. Anyhow, I want you to do something. I hesitated to ask you before, but I feel more sure of my ground now."

"What is it?"

"Bring a warrant with you, Andrew. For both murders."

"Confident, aren't you?"

"Very. As near as dammit—certain."

"Tell me," said MacMorran simply.

Anthony told him. He heard the Inspector's gasp of astonishment. "I say," rejoined MacMorran, "but this is fantastic. You've knocked me flat. Both of them? Are you sure, laddie?"

"I told you, Andrew. You heard! As near as dammit—certain. Made you whistle a bit, didn't it?" Anthony paused, and then went on again. "The one snag is that the trap we've set may be avoided. Side-stepped. That depends on one or two factors that are right away from our control and which we can't possibly plan to counter. But even if it does work out that way, it doesn't matter too much—the bait can be dangled again. Sooner or later the jaws of the trap are bound to close, for if I'm any judge the bait will prove irresistible. Then, my dear Andrew, will come the moment of your triumph. If not this week, then the next—or the week after that."

"H'm. Sounds all right. Hope you haven't slipped up, that's all. Still, leave it to me."

"Andrew," said Anthony solemnly, "they made a grave mistake when they took you to the font. You should never have been christened Andrew. The name given you should have been Thomas. Likewise Didymus."

"I'll be seeing you," said MacMorran, "and you leave my godfathers and godmothers out of it."

"Nothing," replied Anthony, "could give me greater pleasure. I'll expect you at eight o'clock."

CHAPTER 22

1

Anthony and MacMorran came to Loveridge again in the darkness of a late August day. This time they made for the house of Doctor Forbes—not for the house named 'Cherry Fair' which had been Dick Lovelace's.

Evelyn Forbes, eager and anxious, greeted them in the hall. "Congratulations on your excellent timekeeping," she said.

"We have to be punctual in my business," answered MacMorran, "otherwise we might always be too late. And if I kept on being too late to catch people, it'd be a bowler hat for me and slippered ease."

Anthony turned to Evelyn Forbes. "All arrangements O.K., Mrs. Forbes? As agreed on?"

"I think so."

Anthony ran through a series of questions. "Scudamore?" "Yes." "Ilsley?"

"Yes."

"The Vicar?"

"Yes."

"And Doctor Forbes?"

"He told me he was going to Frinton. I accepted that without demur. Seemed to me that it would be as good a place as any. Do you agree, Mr. Bathurst?"

"I think so. Oh, I'd almost forgotten. The Topladys? O.K., too?"

Evelyn Forbes nodded. "The same goes for them. Or it should do. And Mary—she's a local girl—has gone to her people. I assure you, I left no stone unturned. Carried out your instructions to the letter."

"Good." Anthony looked round the hall in which they were standing. "Now show it to us, Mrs. Forbes. The Lovelace chair. I'll call it that temporarily, though I could give it a better name."

She led them to a corner. "There you are—there it is—beneath the bellows, as I told you."

Anthony and MacMorran looked at the chair in front of them. As Evelyn had stated to Anthony on the telephone, it was as black as any blackness very well could be. The arms were curved, the back was solid, the legs substantial. Anthony hoisted it from the floor by its legs and examined it. He showed it to MacMorran.

"How old, Andrew, would you say?"

"No idea. Hundreds of years, I should imagine from the look of it."

"So should I." Anthony tapped the back with his knuckles. "Solid enough. But I'm not a carpenter, joiner, cabinet or chair maker. So my opinion's worth nothing." He smiled at Evelyn. "We shall have to ask your permission, Mrs. Forbes, to dismember it. Sometime between now and then."

"What on earth for?"

"You'd be surprised."

Evelyn Forbes frowned. "Must you? Really? Seems a pity rather, doesn't it?"

"Afraid so. Though dismember may well be too strong a word. The necessary process may eventually prove to be much less drastic. We'll take an expert's opinion. An expert who works in wood and who'll understand exactly what's best to be done."

Evelyn's frown wrinkled again. "What do you expect to find after the chopping up?"

Anthony shook his head. "Don't rush my fences for me. Be patient."

"Very well, then," she replied huffily, "you said sometime between now and then. I know when 'now' is, but when's 'then'?"

Anthony smiled. "Depends. On one or two things. Finding the expert, for example. Is your car ready?"

"Turning me out?"

"Extremely unwillingly—but needs must. Even though *I'm* the driver, and not the usual gentleman."

"All right then. You're the skipper. When shall I see or hear from you again?" As she spoke, she turned her face up to his. She looked very beautiful. Anthony's eyes met hers.

"Yet another question, Mrs. Forbes, that I find myself unable to answer."

Evelyn Forbes shrugged her shoulders. "Good-bye, Inspector MacMorran," she said as she turned, "I must go now—for me a fond heart waits."

"Good-bye, ma'am," replied Andrew MacMorran.

"Good-bye, Mr. Bathurst."

"*Au 'voir*, Mrs. Forbes," returned Anthony quietly.

2

As the noise of the car wheels died away, MacMorran looked significantly at Anthony.

"Before we settle down," he said, "how about short-circuiting the expert and having a bash at that ancient sit-me-down? While the coast's clear?"

Anthony shook his head. "No, Andrew. I'm every bit as eager as you are, but the operation's too delicate for amateur carpenters. Needs a man on it who thoroughly knows his job. I don't know what we might damage, and if there were damage, it might be too far-reaching. Might involve more than the chair itself. Now to business. I suggest four-hour shifts. For this evening, at any rate. What do you say? Commencing, say"—he looked at his wrist-watch—"at half past ten? Yes?"

MacMorran nodded. "That'll do for me. And before we begin we'll spin the coin. Heads I start—tails you do."

The Inspector took a handful of coins from his pocket, sorted them carefully on the palm of his hand and selected a halfpenny. "I've known 'em roll before now," he said, "and this is an unfamiliar house. I'm taking no risks."

He spun the coin, which landed on a rug. "Woman," said Anthony, as he bent to look, "that's means me."

"That's good," remarked the Inspector, "that just suits me. There was a bit of divine justice about it. A little shut-eye will be very welcome to a tired man."

"Right-o, Andrew—I'll expect you then at half-past two. And if you don't come down, may Heaven help you."

"The lassie told you the room I'm to go to was marked, didn't she?"

"She did. You'll be O.K., Andrew. You're an old campaigner."

"Ay," returned MacMorran, "don't you be worryin' your head over me. I'll soon be as snug as a bug in a rug." He walked to the door and stopped. "I'll tell you what," he said, "there's just one thing I could do with—a wee glass o' beer. Not two. Just one. I was always an abstemious man. I suppose there wouldn't be—"

"Andrew," said Anthony, "you do me less than justice. The merciful man is merciful to his beast. You come along in here with me."

MacMorran's face took on a radiance. He came along.

3

When MacMorran had quenched his mighty thirst and had departed temporarily for his ration of well-earned shut-eye, Anthony picked up the Lovelace chair from its position in the hall under the bellows and carried it into the Forbes's dining-room. A quick glance round the room showed him the place where he'd choose to sit. He placed it, therefore, in an angle of the wall by the French windows. From this coign of vantage he could see the garden, the lawn and the tennis-court beyond and should also hear at once any sound which might come to the front of the house.

It was twenty-two minutes to eleven when Anthony switched off the electric light. Then he almost closed the *portières*—but not quite. He left a small chink on his side of the windows. The electric torch which he took from his pocket he put on the window-ledge. He patted his pocket for his revolver. Best to be on the safe side. Then he lit a cigarette, keeping the glowing end well covered by his hand. Anthony settled down to his four-hour vigil. The time was now exactly 10.45.

Punctually at 2.30 ack emma, MacMorran appeared at the door of the dining-room.

"I've had it," he said, "and man, I'm the better for it. You'd be surprised! What's been doin'?"

"Nothing, Andrew. Same as on the western front. I've seen nothing I've heard nothing. For two very good reasons—there's been nothing to see or hear."

"Ah, well, we must cultivate patience. How many times must I be telling you that? There are times when I think you'll never learn."

Anthony grinned. "I'll work that one out, Andrew."

MacMorran's eyes suddenly caught sight of the Lovelace chair. "Well, well, well! Been sittin' in that?"

"Yes. That's the idea, Andrew. And I can thoroughly recommend it. Mrs. Forbes's judgment is altogether admirable. I've been very comfortable indeed. The only trouble with you—assuming that *you* sit in it—is that you're likely to go to sleep again. Knowing your unsurpassed capabilities in that direction."

"Half past six to you," replied the Inspector as he seated himself in the chair, "and when I say half past six, I mean half past six."

Anthony made his way upstairs to the bedroom that had been allocated to him. As he lay down he thought things over. "I don't anticipate," he thought, "that anything will happen until the weekend. I never have. Until Mr. and Mrs. Forbes set out for—where was it now? Oh yes, Salamis. I'm afraid that Andrew will be called upon to draw further on his reserves of patience."

CHAPTER 23

1

Anthony's anticipations were realised. All remained quiet in the house of Forbes until the coming of the week-end. During the period of their official occupation the house was never left unoccupied. If Anthony went into the village, MacMorran stayed behind. If MacMorran strolled into Loveridge for a pipe-opener, Anthony remained in the house. And neither of them ever used the front of the house for either exit or entrance. All the normal supplies to the house from local tradesmen ceased. Everybody in Loveridge knew that the doctor and Mrs. Forbes had left Loveridge for their annual holiday.

On the morning of the Saturday which followed their arrival Anthony walked from the gate at the bottom of the Forbes garden into the village. It was a comparatively simple matter to stroll unobtrusively along the trim-cut laurel hedge which marked the boundary of the Forbes garden and then slip unobserved from the wooden gate at the hedge's end. He walked casually into the main street of Loveridge, and as he crossed over, he suddenly resolved to say good morning to the girl who should be on duty at 'The Churn'.

When he came to the window of the dairy, he saw, to his satisfaction, that she was in her customary place behind the great white milk-bowl on the counter. After a casual glance at the shop-front of Messrs. Gray and Russell, he pushed down the handle of the door of 'The Churn' and went into the dairy. After waiting for a moment while the girl served a customer, Anthony smiled and said,

"I felt I had to come in. I'd like to wish you the top of the morning."

The girl smiled back at him and the smile had the quality of recognition.

"Oh, good morning! Fancy you coming back. Don't tell me you've had another death in the family."

"No. Have no fears. Nothing like that. No more deaths. No change. I just happened to be passing, that's all." He inclined his head in the direction of the closed shop. "How does it go next door? Any change there?"

The dairymaid, he thought, looked a little startled. "That's funny," she replied, "your asking me that."

"Why?"

The girl slipped from behind the counter and came closer to him.

"I'm almost certain," she said quietly, "that there's somebody there. If there is, they came sometime last night."

"Tell me. What makes you think that?"

She came right up to him. "Because I'm positive that I heard noises in there during the night. I told Mum so at breakfast this morning and got ticked off for my pains. She told me if I had—it was no business of mine."

As she spoke, a new light seemed to dawn in the dairymaid's eye and she drew away from Anthony a little.

"Oh, I've just thought," she said, "is that why you're here this morning? Because there's somebody there?"

Anthony shook his head at the question. "I don't know," he answered her, "it might be—and yet it might not. Still, thanks for the information. I'm glad I called in to see you. For more reasons than one. One day I may come and see you again—if you'd like me to. Would you?"

"You know I would," returned the slave of 'The Churn'.

Anthony raised his hat and turned towards the door. His hand hesitated on the handle. It would be just as well, he thought, if the visitor next door didn't see him. He must do his best to negative that possibility. If he were seen here—and recognised, as he undoubtedly would be . . .

2

Anthony made a rapid and stealthy exit from 'The Churn' and cut away equally quickly from the danger area. As he walked back to the house a multitude of thoughts, ideas and fancies danced in his brain. The entire pattern of the crime had now become almost clear to him. How long would it be before Da Costa's body was brought to light and the last portion of fat in the fire? And what an amazing *dénouement* it was going to be when it came!

He entered the Forbes house from the gate at the end of the garden and found MacMorran laboriously sweeping the kitchen.

"Hallo," said Anthony, "Inspector's broom? A broom is the sign for me? Good man. It warms my heart to see you. Do the work that's nearest, though it's dull at whiles, Helping—"

MacMorran projected verbal rudeness. With singularly pungent and effective adroitness. Then he handed the broom to Anthony with a polite bow.

"It's all yours."

Anthony shook his head and propped the broom against the kitchen wall.

"Andrew," he said, "to serious business. I've news for you. It will be to-night. Almost for a certainty."

"Oh—and what makes you so positive? Or is it just another hunch?"

Anthony shook his head. "No, Andrew. Not a hunch. There's an obvious indication. Which the science of deduction tells me is a sign and a portent."

"Oh—and what is it? This sign?"

"There's somebody back at Gray and Russell's. Our undertaking friends. Spent the night there. And I've no doubt in my mind as to what this means. This sudden return to the shop. Or rather, this fresh occupation and use of the shop. The plan becomes clear. The shop will be used as H.Q. for the last stages of the campaign." Anthony rubbed his hands. "But this time, Andrew, old scout, the visit won't be a surprise one—the red carpet will be down with 'Welcome' on it—in large letters." He paused, and then continued. He nodded to himself as he went on. "Of course. I should have known. It all fits. Gray and Russell's place is the natural venue for headquarters when you come to work everything out. The only place, really."

The Inspector looked at him searchingly. "Where has all this come from? Have you actually seen the—"

Anthony cut into him. "No, Andrew. I've seen nobody, actually. But I picked up that vital piece of information, which I just passed on to you, in Loveridge this morning. The lady certainly—"

This time it was MacMorran who cut Anthony. "I suppose *you* weren't seen, were you? That wouldn't help, would it?"

Anthony shook his head. "No, I don't *think* I was seen, Andrew. Pretty sure I wasn't, in fact. I took darned good care not to be. But I *almost* walked into it! It was culpable negligence on my part not to realise the significance of Gray and Russell's. Makes me shudder to think how close I may have been to disaster."

Again MacMorran scrutinised him steadily. "If you're as certain of this as you seem to be, it would be as well if we cut out the element of risk entirely. From now on."

"I couldn't agree with you more, Andrew. That's absolutely sound."

"It would be as well," continued the Inspector, "if we both stayed put for the rest of the day. Let there be no life about the house. What do you think?"

"Again I agree, Andrew."

MacMorran nodded. "That's O.K. then. It's nice to know when the balloon's going up. Shall we stick to the shifts? Will it be wise, do you think?"

Anthony thought over the Inspector's question. "Perhaps not, Andrew," he replied eventually, "leaving out the proverbial matter of heads, four arms are certainly better than two."

"They are. We'll cut the shifts out, then. That's settled. Make a double watch of it."

MacMorran suddenly walked towards the kitchen window. Flattened against the side wall he stopped and said quietly, "Keep still. I'm either seeing things or there's somebody in the garden. Don't move."

Anthony saw the Inspector's eyes harden as they looked out into the garden. For some seconds there was complete silence. Anthony whispered. "What is it, Andrew? What can you see?"

"Nothing—now," replied MacMorran, "but I swear I saw something move down there just then. Keep back for a little longer, in case. This is serious, you know. If we're spotted before to-night our little game's up. We'll have had it. They'll call our bluff. No flies'll come into this parlour."

All the time he was speaking, MacMorran's eyes never left the garden. "I can't see a thing now," he said again, "and we dare not go out and look. All we can do will be to wonder."

"Where was it, Andrew? That you saw it?"

"Right by the hedge down at the bottom. Near the gate. You know, anybody can get in that way, quite easily—*and* out."

"I know. One of the delights of country residence. Fewer bolts and bars needed. I had that in mind when the cheese went into the trap. But tell me—what did it look like?"

"It was human," replied MacMorran drily, "I'd go as far as to say that, but as to the sex of it, my lips are sealed. Seemed to me to duck down quickly by that hedge there and then dart away. Certainly far enough for me not to see it any more."

MacMorran's tones were glum. He shook his head pessimistically. "The more I think about it, the less I like it. Looks very much to me as though you *were* spotted this morning. In other words, the enemy's been along and had a dekko."

Anthony made no answer. He was attempting to assess the chances of MacMorran's last statement. Before he could reply, he heard MacMorran say, "another thing. Looked to me, from what I saw, like a person that knew the lie of the land. You know what I mean surefooted like."

Anthony shook his head. "I told you, Andrew, I don't think that I was seen. There was no sign of life about Gray and Russell's when I was in the vicinity, whatever. Not a glimmer."

"That's all very well. You don't know. You might have been spotted in the village. Anywhere! Not necessarily from the shop itself. It might have happened before you got near the shop. Surely you can see that."

"There's the possibility, I admit. But the odds are well against it."

"All right. You should know, but I'll stake my oath there was somebody in that garden a few minutes ago. How do you explain that?"

"How do I explain it? Just as you did. That the enemy's having a look round. As a preliminary to further action. To-night! It doesn't necessarily follow that the action was taken because I was seen in Loveridge."

"I'm not so sure," grumbled the Inspector.

"We'll wait and see," said Anthony.

"I'm going to," returned MacMorran, as he came away from his place by the wall.

3

Anthony looked at the clock on the mantelpiece of the Forbes dining-room. As he looked, MacMorran nodded. His despondency had not left him.

"Ay," he said, "I know exactly what you're thinking."

"Oh, Andrew, and what's that, may I ask?"

"That it'll soon be the Sabbath. A matter of mere minutes now—and we're still in here waiting."

"We've waited before, Andrew—you and I—and I've no doubt that we shall wait again."

"It 'ud be more cheerful if we had a glimmer of light."

"Might be worse, Andrew—might be in a drear-nighted December. Besides the present discomfort we might then have cold as an additional attraction."

"Don't be so ruddy cheerful about it. I'm in no mood for little rays of sunshine."

Anthony realised that he must play the Inspector with extreme care. It wouldn't be a bad idea to entice him into the territory of argument.

"I'll ask you a question, Andrew," he said. "You've already heard my solution of our present little problem. What odds would you have laid against it being the correct one? A fortnight ago, say?"

"I never lay odds, laddie. It's my habit to take 'em. When they're generous."

Anthony grinned. "Well then, I'll word the question differently. "What odds would you have wanted—given to you?"

"Since you're so persistent then, I'd be puttin' it at about a thousand to one. But I'm tellin' you this at the same time, I'm by no means convinced yet that you *are* entirely on the right track. I'm reservin' my judgement. Maybe you're right—maybe you're not."

Anthony shook his head. "Any doubts I might have had were dispelled this morning when I heard the news about the visitor or visitors to Gray and Russell. When I heard that, all the pieces of the Lovelace jigsaw clicked into place."

"You're an optimist if ever there was one. When you've been at this game the years I have, you won't feel certain about anything. Many's the time I've thought I was home and dry, and I found I had another think coming. I remember a case—just after the First World War it was—I was stationed at Islington at the time."

The clock on the mantelpiece began to chime the hour. Twelve silvery-sounding chimes. MacMorran checked the time by his own watch.

"There you are. Twelve of 'em. Sunday morning. Now what was I saying? Oh, I remember—when I was stationed at Islington. It was a dirty, sordid murder. The body of a young girl was found early one morning—"

Anthony cut in suddenly. He spoke almost in a whisper. "Quiet, Andrew. I'm almost certain I heard something. Listen, man."

Each of them strained his ears. Suddenly, MacMorran nodded. "Yes, you're right. Somebody in the garden. I heard the steps on the gravel. Coming in this direction, too."

"This is *it*," whispered Anthony. "Quick—position's as arranged. They're almost bound to come by way of the French doors. You know what to do—and when to do it."

Anthony slipped behind the extreme left-hand *portière*. MacMorran left the dining-room noiselessly and crept into the curtain-drawn kitchen. He knew that the back door was bolted and locked. And he also knew what to do about that—at the critical moment. He crouched on the mat at the kitchen door. No doubt about it now. The steps outside, although by no means loud, could be heard plainly and distinctly. The midnight visitor, whoever it might be, was very close now to the house and to the French doors of the dining-room.

MacMorran smiled a grim, wintry smile. The next few moments would be the moments that counted. MacMorran looked at the bolts on the door. He had oiled them himself—they would slip back smoothly and silently . . . when the time came.

CHAPTER 24

1

The sound of the footsteps outside ceased. Anthony waited. MacMorran waited. All was silent until the clock of Chelmersley cathedral chimed the first quarter. The figure that had approached the Forbes house stood on the grass—a mere dozen yards or so from the members of the reception committee who had assembled on its behalf. Then it tiptoed silently to the wall of the garden and stood there for some moments in the shadows.

In these shadows it busied itself for some little time. . . until it straightened itself again and crept forward towards the house carrying a long-bladed knife in the right hand. With quick, short strides it came to the French doors and began to work on them with the long blade of the knife.

Anthony, concealed behind the *portière*, heard the insistent gnawing of the knife on wood . . . and then the metallic snap which meant the ultimate forcing of the catch. After that, all was quiet for a matter of some seconds until Anthony's ear caught the sounds which meant that the middle *portière* had been pulled aside, that one of the doors had opened, and that the way of entrance was clear.

A shadowy figure leant forward and then stepped into the darkness of the room. So close indeed was it to Anthony behind his *portière* that he could almost hear the breathing.

2

The figure fumbled in pockets as it stood just inside the room. Then it advanced slowly towards the mantelpiece. Anthony could still see nothing. He wondered what was actually happening. A moment or so later he knew. From the side of his heavy curtain he saw the soft glow of candlelight. Then, with but the slightest adjustment of the *portière*, he saw the figure at the mantelpiece—its face plainly lit by the light of the candles—and his heart leapt with exultation. For the figure was familiar to him—it was the figure that for some days now he had expected to see.

There were two lighted candles on the mantelpiece, one at each end, and as he saw them Anthony realised that the centre *portière* had been carefully redrawn, so that no light shewed through the glass to the garden. The intruder turned away from the mantelpiece and the candles and walked to the table. Here he stood for some time looking up at the four pictures that hung on the walls. He looked at them appraisingly and then slowly shook his head. Anthony had wondered whether he would take them down as Lovelace's had been taken down, but the shake of the head that he now saw was an eloquent answer to his wonderment.

Then Anthony had somewhat of a surprise—if only for the quickness of the action that was taken. The intruder picked up the two candles from the mantelpiece and hurried from the room. Anthony moved from behind the *portière*. The man with the candles had gone into the lounge. Anthony slipped soundlessly from the dining-room and joined MacMorran at the back of the house.

"Well?" whispered the Inspector, "is it as you said?"

"It is," said Anthony softly.

"Where now?"

"Upstairs, I fancy. Been in the lounge and come out. I heard the footsteps on the stairs."

"What do we do?"

"Wait for our friend to come down again. But it'll be some time, Andrew."

"Sure of that?"

"Almost. What's being looked for will take a deuce of a time to find up there. It's in the dining-room, Andrew. We've both sat in it. So it won't be discovered upstairs." Anthony beckoned to the Inspector. "Come here. Hark! Can you hear the search warming to work? Hard at it now, Andrew."

MacMorran and Anthony walked quietly into the hall and stood in the shadow of the staircase.

"This'll do," whispered MacMorran, "just right for us—the reception will be with open arms."

"Hark!" whispered Anthony in reply. There was no mistaking now the noise from the floor above. MacMorran smiled a grim smile.

"And all for nothing," he said quietly. "A sad waste of energy, whichever way you look at it."

He glanced at Anthony, who was listening hard. The Inspector began to speak again, but Anthony held up a warning finger.

3

Very suddenly the noise upstairs ceased. MacMorran looked at Anthony, who shook his head in return. Anthony's finger was still up.

"What is it?" whispered the Inspector.

"Not quite sure, Andrew. But I think it's a case of tempers being a little tried. I fancy I heard spoken words a moment or so ago. Self-castigation in all probability. You'll hear the search start up again in a few moments. I wonder what the pictures look like." There came a sudden clanging noise which suggested the impact of something fairly heavy on a waterpipe, close at hand.

"What was that?" said MacMorran. Anthony, looking puzzled, shook his head again and said nothing. The noise was repeated, followed by a series of shuffling sounds. MacMorran's eyes still held questions. Anthony's held uncertainty.

"Listen, Andrew," he said, "what can you hear now from upstairs? Anything?"

MacMorran listened hard before shaking his head. "No. Nothing. Not a sound. Quiet as a church!"

Anthony looked grave. MacMorran was quick to see it. "What's the trouble?" he demanded.

"I don't know, Andrew. But I don't like it. Something's happened that I didn't bargain for."

"What do you mean, man? What can have happened?"

"If I knew, Andrew, I'd tell you. But I don't. We must go up there at once. Something's all wrong."

Anthony took his revolver from his pocket. MacMorran saw the action and nodded.

"Yes. Same here—I think. Never know. We may be sticking our necks out."

"I don't think so," returned Anthony, "but we can't take the risk of it. Come along, Andrew. With me."

MacMorran switched on his torch and the two men began slowly to ascend the stairs.

4

No sound whatever came from the upper part of the house. When they came to the turn of the banister, MacMorran said "where?"

"I should imagine front bedroom. That's where I thought the noises were coming from."

Anthony and MacMorran made the main landing and moved slowly towards the front bedroom. The door was closed.

"Use the door as cover," whispered the Inspector, "in case."

Anthony shook his head—almost absentmindedly. He was engaged in a last, almost desperate attempt to picture what had happened. And he was beginning to think that he knew. MacMorran—in front of Anthony—pushed open the door. As he entered, he gave a sharp exclamation. Then he moved rapidly towards the middle of the room. Anthony, now in the room too, saw at once why MacMorran had so acted. Two candles were burning on the mantelpiece. There was a body lying at the side of the dressing-table. It lay on its back, with its knees up and bent. The tongue was out and the general effect far from pleasing. Every now and then the candles flickered. MacMorran knelt by the body.

"Dead," he said to Anthony after a short wait, "dead as mutton. And strangled, too. Strangled, by a pair of powerful hands." Anthony looked down at the body as MacMorran got to his feet again. "Yes, Andrew," he said, "he's dead all right. We've been cheated after all."

"Who is it?" demanded the Inspector.

"Who is it?" repeated Anthony. "It's Temple Spooner, of course, as I told you it would be. Temple Spooner—the murderer of Richard Lovelace and of his own employee, Da Costa. When I last saw him he was wearing a skull-cap and trying to sell me antiques in his shop in Cavalier Circus. Justice has caught up with him at last."

MacMorran stared down at the strangled man and slowly shook his head.

"I don't understand it—even now. Who killed him? That's what I'd like to know."

"The man that killed him, Andrew, was the man whom you saw in the garden this morning. That's where I went wrong. I didn't consider such a possibility. I've learnt another lesson. I *think* I can tell you—within a little—what took place. This man, whom you spotted in the garden this morning, came here to get Spooner. He saw the three Press paragraphs, just as Spooner himself saw them, and knew that they contained a bait which it was a thousand to one Spooner wouldn't refuse. Some time to-day he entered the house. This evening, in all probability. I'll tell you how I think he got in. Because we heard him escaping in the same way—he used the big outside waterpipe on the wall, that leads to the bathroom. Don't you remember that clanging noise we heard? That was the impact of his boots on the pipe. When he got in the house, he crept upstairs and hid. He was waiting for the same man as we were. But he was luckier than we—he got him. Directly Temple Spooner went upstairs he was doomed. My fault, Andrew! I left this other fellow out of my calculations altogether."

MacMorran shook his head in bewilderment. "But I still don't understand. Who is the man? What's his name? Why has he strangled Spooner?"

"Three questions, Andrew. All in a row. I don't know that I can answer them immediately. The man was in charge—up to comparatively recently—of Spooner's shop in Cavalier Circus. An employee, like the Da Costa I mentioned just now. His name? I'm not *sure* of this. But I fancy if you called him he'd answer to the name of Da Costa as well. And that last statement, Andrew, supplies the data, I fancy, which will enable you to answer your third question yourself."

Anthony thrust his hands into his pockets and looked down at the body of Temple Spooner. Many thoughts tormented his brain. Then he heard MacMorran say, "well, this won't do, whoever the man may be! He can't be far away—he hasn't had the time. I'll spread the net for him."

The Inspector turned to Anthony. "I'll 'phone Chelmersley at once. As I said, he can't have got far. Come on."

MacMorran hastened downstairs and picked up the telephone receiver. "Give me Chelmersley police-station at once, please. If possible, I want to speak to Inspector Hurst. He may be there. Yes, Hurst—that's it."

He placed his hand over the receiver and beckoned to Anthony to come closer.

"If you can give me his description. Yes?"

Anthony nodded and MacMorran nodded back. Then he began to speak again on the telephone.

"Inspector Hurst? Yes? Good. Though it might be too late for you. MacMorran here. You know where I mean. Now listen carefully. Perhaps you'd better take it down. I want a man picked up as soon as possible. He left here less than twenty minutes ago. Act on that—cover all the usual lines, and you can't go far wrong. Now here's the gen. Name probably Da Costa. Christian or forename not known."

MacMorran paused and looked across at Anthony. Anthony began the details. The Inspector repeated each detail over the telephone.

"Age about 53."

"Age about 53."

"On the tall side."

"On the tall side."

"Dark hair and dark eyes."

"Dark hair and dark eyes."

"Long face, rather pointed chin, melancholy cast of feature."

"Long face, rather pointed chin, melancholy cast of feature."

"Might with justice be called horse-faced."

"Might be said to have a face like a horse."

Anthony paused at MacMorran's altered phrase. He stopped.

"Any more?" snapped back the Inspector.

"Wait while I think. Yes . . . clean-shaven . . . very long neck . . . and possibly a broken tooth top jaw right-hand side. I think that's about all."

"Why only possibly the broken tooth?"

"May have been attended to since I last saw him. National Health Service. Can't say these days."

MacMorran gave Hurst the additional details which Anthony had just supplied. Then Anthony heard him say,

"Thank you very much, Inspector. Now for the second point. When you've seen to that first little matter, send an ambulance out here at once, will you? Yes, that's right. At Doctor Forbes's. Good. That's O.K., then. Glad you stayed on. Be seeing you."

The Inspector replaced the receiver and looked at Anthony, "only a question of time, he says. All the likely places will be covered and the messages are already being sent out. Meantime we wait for the ambulance."

"Amongst a number of other things," replied Anthony.

CHAPTER 25

1

"I't's cold for the end of September," said Anthony to his guests, "that's why I told Emily to light the fire. I always prefer to be too hot than too cold."

"How thoroughly I agree with you," said Evelyn Forbes, "and this chair's almost absurdly comfortable."

"Is that a challenge?" asked Anthony, "remembering that other chair that came into your possession?"

Evelyn laughed, "you would say that." She turned to Helen Repton. "What a treasure Mr. Bathurst's Emily must be. I don't know when I've eaten a more delicious dinner. Her *soufflé* was exquisite. Even my husband wouldn't argue with me over that—would you, Bob?"

"Not for a moment, Lyn. I endorse every word you say."

"That's another triumph for Emily," said Helen. "Her conquests are legion. She adds to them almost daily. Whenever I hear Emily's name mentioned, it's in terms of praise. Mr. Bathurst's a lucky man—not only to have her, but to hold her."

"To have and to hold, eh?" said Forbes, "there's a familiar ring about that. If ever you marry, Bathurst, your wife will have to pull her socks up to achieve the Emily class."

Anthony laughed as he turned to fill MacMorran's glass. "Depends on whom I choose. I might out-Emily Emily. You never know."

Evelyn Forbes looked pointedly at Helen, but Miss Repton's gaze was directed to the heart of the fire.

"Surely," declared MacMorran, "you're not puttin' forward, Doctor Forbes, that a man's wife must be a guid cook, and a guid cook only? Because I'm not havin' that. And I'll tell you for why. The first time Mrs. MacMorran cooked a haggis—well—words fail me."

There was a chorus of laughter. "The first time I tasted one," said Evelyn, "words failed me."

Anthony looked round at the glasses of his four guests. "You all have a drink, haven't you? Good. I'll come and sit down." He took the third chair, so that the order of seating ran, Forbes, Evelyn, Anthony, Helen, Andrew MacMorran.

"That's right," said Evelyn, "and do please start telling us the whole story, because that's what I'm sure we're all dying to hear."

"You speak for yourself, my girl," said Forbes.

"I did. I am dying to hear it, and I don't mind in the least admitting the weakness. Not that I'm sure that it is a weakness." Anthony passed the cigarettes round and lit those of the ladies. When he had lit his own he smiled and said,

"Well, it was a remarkable case right from the kick-off, and I constantly wonder how it might have ended if Martin Scudamore hadn't gone to the cinema that evening in July. Because, as Andrew MacMorran here will tell you, there's all the difference in the world between coming to a scent that's warm and coming to another that's stone cold. In this instance our luck was in—thanks to Scudamore—and I'm bound to confess that Andrew and I had the luck all the way through. Sometimes that's the way it goes. Although we were just too late to save Lovelace, poor chap, we stumbled on the first clue almost immediately. Mrs. Toplady put us on to the matter of the pictures having been moved in Lovelace's room. A little later Toplady himself shewed us something which rather corroborated his wife's story. I'll come back to that later. But anyhow, both the Inspector here and I became convinced eventually that the motive behind the murder was the acquisition of something which Lovelace either had, or had had, which the murderer so fiercely coveted."

Anthony put a cigarette-stub in the ash-tray and took another cigarette "By the way," he remarked, "if anybody wishes to ask a question at any time, please do so and I'll try my best to answer it. All right, so far?"

Forbes and his wife nodded. "O.K. Please go on," said the former.

"Right. Well, then—there we were. What had Lovelace possessed? Had the murderer or murderers taken it? You, Forbes, had given me the words the dead man had used a short time before he died. 'Tea-spoon' and 'innocent'. Which meant, of course, at the time—apart from the fact that Scudamore had heard something like the latter word in the cinema— little or nothing to me. Until, mind you, I had my second stroke of luck."

"What was that?" asked Forbes.

"Why—this. Lovelace had received a letter from Temple Spooner, addressed probably from the shop in Cavalier Circus a week or two before the tragedy. The contents of that letter I can do no more than conjecture. Because the actual letter has never been found—either Lovelace destroyed it himself or Spooner destroyed it. But it almost certainly embodied an offer from Spooner to purchase. And this is the rather amazing feature of it—it's almost certain that Lovelace hadn't the foggiest idea what it was that Spooner desired to purchase! Whether he actually replied to it, I don't know. I'm almost certain that he didn't. But I regard it as a sure thing that Spooner realised that he would be forced to go and get the object that he wanted."

"Just a minute," intervened Evelyn, "you said you had your second stroke of luck. In what way? I don't think I quite understand that."

"In this way, Mrs. Forbes. Lovelace was a 'doodler'. And on his blotting-pad, when the thought of Spooner's letter—which he couldn't fathom—was uppermost in his mind, he doodled a teaspoon, the allusion of which is obvious, and two other objects which were easily distinguished as a 'cavalier' and a 'circus'. They naturally suggested to me the only place of that name of which I know. The little *cul-de-sac* off New Bond Street. If Lovelace hadn't 'doodled', I doubt whether we should have ever solved our problem. That's a sorry confession, isn't it?"

MacMorran raised and emptied his glass. Anthony gestured to him to refill it. The Inspector was in like a flash.

"Well," continued Anthony, "my next step, of course, was to visit Cavalier Circus and I immediately got 'warmer' still, as the kids used to say. For the good reason that, tucked away there, was an 'antique' shop of really exceptional quality, the owner of which was publicly proclaimed as 'A. Temple Spooner'. I went in, and met for the first time Joseph Da Costa. You all know what ultimately happened to him. After strangling Spooner in your bedroom, Mrs. Forbes, he threw himself under a train between Chelmersley and Coakley. For the moment, leave him there. You'll hear more of him later. Well, he gave me Spooner's home address. I went straight there and found the two Bullocks—employees of Spooner's. They were housekeepers of a kind—Spooner was a bachelor. And it was when I interviewed them, ladies and gentlemen, that my feet were placed firmly on the main road to the solution of the whole intricate entanglement."

"Why," interrupted Evelyn, "what happened there to make all that difference?"

Anthony smiled at her evident eagerness. "Three things. The first of these three were just impressions. Mine. That the two Bullocks feared the coming of the police and were as jumpy as a couple of Chinese crackers. That was the first thing. The second and third were facts. Vital, pregnant facts. Supplied to me by the two men. That Spooner had disappeared, that they hadn't any idea where he was, and that before his disappearance his chief concern had been to make contact with a person by the name of Berners."

There was an interested stir from the circle of listeners. Anthony was sensible to it and he could see from the look in her eyes that the name was not unfamiliar to Evelyn Forbes. For he had lent her his copy of *The House of Berners*.

2

"Now you must understand," continued Anthony, "that when the Bullocks mentioned the name of Berners to me, it was the first time that the name had cropped up. Beyond the mere name, they could tell me nothing. Who he was, where he hung out—I hadn't the slightest idea. All the same, the name continued to tickle a chord in my memory. I knew that I'd actually *seen* it somewhere and recently, at that. I let the tickling process go on—until the bell rang. When this happened, I remembered that the man was an author, and that I'd seen a book of his advertised in the *Sunday Times* and—and this, ladies and gentlemen, is the important point—that his initials were 'C. L. D.'. Significant? I should say so. Because Scudamore, in the cinema, had overheard the names 'Charles Linklater Delevigne', and when Andrew MacMorran and I endeavoured to trace 'Delevigne' as a surname in the telephone directory or by contact with the P.M.G., we drew a complete blank. Was it a coincidence or wasn't it? Anyhow, I 'phoned a pal of mine named Ainsworth, who's on the staff of Walloon and Co., Berners's publishers, and asked for the address of this Berners bloke. It was at Burgoyne in Lincolnshire—near Boston—which you will observe was the district from which Dick Lovelace had come."

Forbes grinned from his seat at the end. "The plot thickened, eh?"

"Looked like it, didn't it? I went up there, of course, had a few minutes with Berners—quaint sort of merchant—and came away, I confess, distinctly disappointed. Disappointed because I was unable to establish any link or connexion between Berners and Spooner. The former denied all knowledge of the latter. I realise now why this was. Spooner sent Francis Da Costa to Berners to obtain certain corroborative information for him—and Berners had no idea that Da Costa was Spooner's agent. The name Spooner never came out at all. Thank you, Helen."

Anthony took a cigarette which Helen Repton offered him, lit hers and his own.

"But don't think that my Lincolnshire visit was altogether barren. On the way to Boston station for the homeward train I ran into my third stroke of luck. In the shape of a bookseller's specially featuring one of Berners's previous books in the window. The book was entitled *The House of Berners*. I bought a copy, gave it a quick run-through in the train, and by the time I reached King's Cross I strongly suspected that this famous house in Lincolnshire, which had been in the Berners family for generations, was the identical house which had also been Dick Lovelace's. That suspicion I subsequently confirmed."

Evelyn Forbes leant forward. "Please tell me how you were able to do that."

Anthony smiled. "By remembering the name 'Braund'. Lovelace's aunt, from whom had come his inheritance, had been Arabella Braund. In 1733, so the book said, the house had been sold 'as it stood' to an Army officer by the name of Colonel Sir Clive Braund." The Forbes eyes shone and the other lady present murmured softly "good show."

"You were moving then, eh?" said Robert Forbes.

"Yes. I was moving, but don't forget two things. 'Spooner', the man whom I had begun to suspect, had been found dead down in Essex, and I hadn't any fixed idea yet what the object was that he had been after. But I kept certain ideas in my mind. Oh—several. I'll attempt to remember some of them. It will help you to follow me later on. Here they are. According to the Berners book, the founder of the Berners line, Roger de Berners, had been a close friend and favourite of King John—the John who once had a disastrous affair in Lincolnshire—that's one. Here's another."

"That when I called on the Bullocks again—the men, mind you, who had identified the second dead man as Temple Spooner—they were evasive, frightened, uneasy, and obviously waiting for something, *but they were still at Wilton Lodge, Spooner's house*, and until I mentioned the matter, entertained no definite idea of vacating it. That's two."

"Thirdly, I was convinced by now that Spooner had been the 'boss' of the Scudamore cinema conversation, and that I must discover as soon as I possibly could who had been the second man. As I said, that's three."

"May I ask a question?" said Evelyn.

"Of course."

"That second man, I take it, was Francis Da Costa? Am I right?"

"You are. Until Spooner quarrelled with him and killed him, Francis Da Costa had been his—well—first lieutenant, right-hand man—take your choice. But more of him later. As in the case of his elder brother, Joseph."

Anthony turned and saw MacMorran raise his hand.

"Yes, Andrew? A question from you?"

"Ay. Why do you think the Bullocks identified the body of Francis Da Costa as that of Temple Spooner? To me, too, of all people! The cunning—"

"Yes, Andrew, I know. They did so under strict instructions from Spooner himself, who had by then communicated with them. They feared him. He had been their boss for years, and they invariably obeyed his orders."

"I see. Well—well—I'd thought much the same myself."

Anthony looked round the company. "How are we doing? All right? I'll carry on then. I think I'll travel straight to my fourth stroke of good fortune. Because in all sincerity, I can't justifiably call it anything else. Once again, it came from Martin Scudamore. What I owe that man!"

Anthony looked directly at Helen, but as on a previous occasion, the lady was serenely studying the flicker of the flames. Anthony went straight on.

"Scudamore passed on to me a most remarkable piece of information. I can call it nothing else. He told me that in Loveridge, on the day of Dick Lovelace's funeral, he had heard the voice of one of the men whose conversation he had overheard in the cinema. Those gentlemen who had set the ball rolling! When I tackled Scudamore and probed him, I elicited the fact, that inasmuch as he had been nowhere else on that particular day, he must have heard the voice either at the funeral service in the church or at your house, Doctor Forbes. I proved that unmistakably and entirely to my satisfaction. I thereupon asked Scudamore if he could recall the exact words which he stated that he had heard spoken. He said he could. He told me what they were. I was surprised. I think that you will be too. These are the words Scudamore said he heard. 'He knew what it meant, but he went!'"

"In a vague sort of way, they seemed familiar to me, but it wasn't till a few days ago that I succeeded in placing them. They're from Langford Reid's *Limerick Book*, and the entire limerick runs like this. "There was a young lady of Kent, Who said that she knew what it meant, When men asked her to dine, Gave her cocktails and wine, She knew what it meant, but she went!'

There was a laugh as Forbes said "and not only of Kent." Anthony laughed too, and continued.

"Well, no matter where it had come from, if anywhere, implication of the remark was fairly plain. It had been said at Lovelace's funeral. It applied, therefore, almost certainly, to him. That he had stuck his neck out and got what he asked for. But who had been the speaker? That was my problem. It must have been somebody at the funeral. Which meant one of the mourners—or one of the undertakers. That was a strange idea, wasn't it? But I remembered, then, another rather interesting incident. According to Toplady, somebody had been in Lovelace's house on the night of the day Lovelace died. There were evidences of this underneath certain pictures. That was the night the undertakers brought his body home from the hospital! Please note the coincidence, at least. At any rate I felt that I might be getting somewhere. When Joseph Da Costa took a hand, I *knew* that I was."

Anthony paused. "Joseph," he went on, "unable to understand the prolonged absence of his brother, nursed his own ideas on the subject, left the shop in Cavalier Circus, and ran Spooner to earth. Probably, I think, in the undertaker's establishment in Loveridge High Street— Messrs. Gray and Russell's. Certainly the Bullocks visited him there. I fancy Spooner lay doggo at the shop after he'd dealt with Francis Da Costa. Joseph vowed revenge, but fearful of Spooner—who he knew was a 'stick at nothing' gentleman—did his work under cover. He'd seen me in the antique shop, guessed I was on the case, saw me again doubtless in Loveridge and decided to put me on the track of Spooner. He sent me to the Bank Holiday Fair, proved my identity to his own satisfaction and in order to make sure that his message to me didn't fall into wrong hands, slipped it into my pocket. In a crowd, no doubt. The message was ambiguous—Joseph was taking no chances—but moderately simple to unravel, and I soon solved it. In a word, it told me to go to Gray and Russell's, the undertaker's. That's when I knew that MacMorran and I were in the straight."

"But tell me," intervened Forbes, "who were these people—really?"

"Well, I did intend to leave that explanation till later, but now will do just as well. As you already know, I think, Spooner's real name was Stefanopoulos. He was a Greek by birth and upbringing. Everything he touched turned to money and he had a burning passion for antiques—especially those with famous historical associations. He picked up with the two Da Costas and the elder Bullock during the First World War—probably, I think, in Gallipoli. They all came to England in Spooner's—I'll call him Spooner still—employ. Francis had been an undertaker's assistant at some time in his career and when Spooner got on the track of King John's rings, and came to the accurate conclusion that Lovelace had them, he purchased Gray and Russell's business in Loveridge and put Francis Da Costa in charge. He'd be conveniently near to Lovelace."

"May I interrupt?"

"Certainly, Helen. What is it?"

"How did Spooner get on the track of the ring?"

"By reading Berners's book. The same way that I did, eventually. But he had several months' start of me. Incidentally, while we're on this point, I've learned from experts since the case closed that 'the ring of Innocent', as it's usually called, has been a coveted piece by the very wealthy class of collector since it was known to have disappeared. Spooner, I fancy, had been well after it for many years."

Anthony turned to Evelyn. "You've brought the rings, of course? Let Miss Repton see them, will you, please?" Evelyn took four objects from her handbag and handed them to Anthony.

"These four circles of discoloured metal," he said to Helen, "are the rings which Pope Innocent III gave to John of England, and which afterwards came into the possession of Roger de Berners. You can just see the sparkle and the intrinsic brilliance of the stones. I'm assured that when they've passed through the hands of the polishers they'll present a very different appearance."

Helen balanced them on the palm of her hand. "You'd never take them to be frightfully valuable, would you?"

"You should have seen how they were hidden," said Evelyn.

"Tell Miss Repton," said Anthony.

"Well," replied Evelyn, "the de Berners, who concealed them first of all, put the four rings in the four corners at the back of an old picture and fastened them to the frame—it's the picture of an old English church—Norman—and then the picture itself was fitted into the back of a chair, between two solid pieces of wood. It took some finding, I can tell you."

"William de Berners did that sometime about the year 1650 and died before he could pass on the secret to his heirs." Anthony smiled as he made the statement and then went on to say, "like Spooner, MacMorran and I were thinking in terms of a picture and when I searched the present Berners's book for any further details I found nothing to alter that view. But I had this point to consider. Spooner, who had presumably tested all the Lovelace pictures, had had no success in his search for the rings. For these reasons. No picture had been stolen and none had been damaged. They'd merely been looked at. *Ergo*—he was still minus his desired object. So I began to think! Had Lovelace given away to Mrs. Forbes, before he died, any object which might conceal the picture and the picture's rings? I asked her. She told me about the chair. But not at once. It came to her after a time. It was something he'd given her some time ago."

Anthony looked round. "I think that sums it up, doesn't it? You know how the Inspector and I baited the trap and how Spooner fell for it. Only to meet his fate at the hands of Joseph Da Costa."

"As far as I'm concerned," said Forbes, "you've covered everything."

"Good," said Anthony, "in that case I feel that the occasion calls for another round of drinks. Mrs. Forbes—what shall it be? And what about you, Helen?"

A few seconds later, Anthony moved towards the cocktail cabinet.

3

Anthony looked across at Helen. "They'll be home in next to no time—all of them. Andrew's had to go back to the 'Yard'. What about you? May I drive you home?"

"You may. I was hoping that you'd ask me. What an absolutely shameful confession!" She laughed.

"By the way, how's Scudamore?" said Anthony. "I asked him here this evening, but he cried off. Another engagement, so he said."

"I've really no idea," said Miss Repton coldly.

"H'm. Pity."

"Why? Why a pity?"

"Oh—I gathered that you and he were such close friends. I know that he cherished a great admiration for you."

Miss Repton's reply was colder still. "Is that so surprising?"

Anthony smiled. "Good lord, no! My dear girl—"

Helen cut in before he could finish. "I'm sorry. But the point is this. I shall not be seeing Mr. Scudamore in the future. That's all."

Anthony spoke quietly. "I see."

"It all started in the Summer—near Midsummer. I think it must have been Midsummer madness."

For once Mr. Bathurst was at a loss for words. "I see," he said again.

"Are you pleased?" asked Helen, with lowered lids.

"I'm delighted—not pleased."

"Why?"

"One day," said Anthony, "I'll tell you, but there's more than one reason." He linked his arm in hers.

"I'm not on duty," she said.

"I know you're not. But you will be to-morrow. And the day after. One day—later on—perhaps you won't be. Come along. I'll get the car for you."

Helen Repton looked up at him. She spoke almost in a whisper. "I'm glad you were pleased . . . Mr. Bathurst . . . I mean delighted."

THE END

Printed in Dunstable, United Kingdom